"WONDERFUL!"
Dallas Morning News

"SPELLBINDING!"
Florida Times-Union

"STUNNING!"
Providence Journal-Bulletin

"AN ENJOYABLE READ!"
Columbia State

Praise for
Elizabeth Lowell
and
RUNNING SCARED

"Romantic suspense is her true forte."
Minneapolis Star-Tribune

"Wonderful . . . Romance melded with
mystery . . . [and] colorful settings."
Dallas Morning News

"Fun to read . . . Lowell manages to balance
the right amount of intrigue, romance, and
research. . . . The dialogue . . . is snappy
and witty . . . [The] characters come alive."
Columbia State (SC)

"Lowell's keen ear for dialogue and intuitive
characterizations consistently set her
a cut above most writers in this genre."
Charlotte News & Observer

"One can only hope she will bring back
Rareties Unlimited for the inevitable sequel."
Publishers Weekly

"I'll buy any book with
Elizabeth Lowell's name on it."
Jayne Ann Krentz

Also by Elizabeth Lowell

EDEN BURNING • MOVING TARGET
AMBER BEACH • JADE ISLAND
PEARL COVE • MIDNIGHT IN RUBY BAYOU
BEAUTIFUL DREAMER • FORGET ME NOT
LOVER IN THE ROUGH • A WOMAN WITHOUT LIES
DESERT RAIN • WHERE THE HEART IS
TO THE ENDS OF THE EARTH • REMEMBER SUMMER
ONLY HIS • ONLY MINE
ONLY YOU • ONLY LOVE
AUTUMN LOVER • WINTER FIRE
ENCHANTED • FORBIDDEN
UNTAMED

And in Hardcover

THIS TIME LOVE

Coming Soon

DIE IN PLAIN SIGHT

ELIZABETH
LOWELL

RUNNING SCARED

AVON BOOKS
An Imprint of HarperCollinsPublishers

AVON BOOKS
An Imprint of HarperCollins*Publishers*
10 East 53rd Street
New York, New York 10022-5299

Copyright © 2002 by Two of a Kind, Inc.
ISBN: 0-06-103108-9
www.avonbooks.com

First Avon Books paperback printing: June 2003
First William Morrow hardcover printing: June 2002

Avon Trademark Reg. U.S. Pat. Off. and in Other Countries, Marca Registrada, Hecho en U.S.A.
HarperCollins® is a registered trademark of HarperCollins Publishers Inc.

Printed in the U.S.A.

10 9 8 7 6 5 4 3 2 1

Prologue

The silvery disc of a nearly full moon kept Virgil O'Conner awake. He liked it that way. At eighty-one, he had long since decided that watching shades of darkness twist across the Arizona night was better than being in their grip and screaming himself awake.

"I'm sorry I took it," he whispered to the night. "Sorry, sorry, sorry, sorry . . ."

The darkness didn't answer. It never had.

His heart faltered, skipped, and settled down. He let out a long breath that wasn't quite relief. He wanted to die, but not yet. Not until the dead forgave him for touching their sacred gold.

Neckrings of braided gold chains, as smooth and heavy and supple as he once had been.

Armbands as wide as his spread fingers, heavy gold covered with symbols so eerie and beautiful they raised the hair on his scalp.

Cloak pins as big as his hand, pins carrying the likeness of an animal, yet frighteningly human.

A mask that was more than human.

Shapes of gods or demons or dreams long dead.
Twenty-seven pieces of gold. Beautiful gold.
Deadly gold.

A chill condensed on his skin. Automatically he reached for the lap robe, but its soft warmth couldn't heat the freezing in the marrow of his bones.

He was a dead man screaming.

"No," he said hoarsely. "I didn't mean it! I never sold any of it, even when I needed money. I worked two jobs. Worked hard. I could have melted it all down or . . . or . . ."

His voice died into a whispery rasp. He knew the spirits that hounded him couldn't hear his words. He wasn't a channel. He couldn't reach his tormentors to explain his innocence.

Unless, just maybe, he held some of their gold in both hands. No gloves this time. Nothing to protect his flesh. Just his skin and potent gold.

The thought made him shudder. He had touched the gold once, long ago, with his naked fingers. He had never touched it that way again. He didn't even want to think about touching it. But he kept thinking about it just the same, reliving every black instant of the night so long ago when he had followed his dead great-uncle's instructions, borrowed a metal detector from military stores, and gone digging in Britain while the death throes of World War II echoed around.

The sacred oaks where neither Romans nor Anglos dared to go. Nine hills. Six groves. Three man-rocks facing in. One spring. Three times three times three of gold.

He jerked his head sharply. He didn't want to remember. It made his heart twist as it had that night, pain lancing through every cell in his body, in his soul.

"Hold tight," he whispered to himself. "Just till to-

morrow. Midnight. That's when they'll finally understand why I did it."

Or he would die.

He wasn't sure if he really cared which happened, life
or death. He only cared that the gold stop killing him by
inches.

"Hold tight. Tomorrow. Midnight."

One

Even though Risa Sheridan was only an occasional consultant to the international firm of Rarities Unlimited, she didn't resent flying from Las Vegas to Los Angeles for a few hours of work. She never knew what treasures a client might have brought to the company's headquarters so that Rarities could "Buy, Sell, Appraise, Protect." All she could be certain of was that whatever she would be inspecting was at least four hundred years old—and usually much older—because ancient jewelry was her specialty.

Risa's feeling of anticipation flattened when she looked through the double glass doors that led to Rarities' offices; Shane Tannahill was already on the other side of the bulletproof glass. Despite the fact that she had left Las Vegas before he did, her boss had beaten her to Los Angeles.

Shane had one of his hands tucked into a pocket of his black slacks. The other hand anchored the soft leather jacket he had slung over one shoulder. A visitor's badge hung on a chain around his neck. Angular face impassive, jade green eyes narrowed, dark hair neatly trimmed, he lounged against the guard desk. Waiting for her.

He wasn't a patient man.

Bloody L.A. traffic, she said silently.

It wasn't her fault that her plane had been held on the ground in Vegas for a security check. Then in L.A. a semi truck hauling gasoline had turned over on Sepulveda, blocking the easiest exit from the airport and thoroughly screwing up the city's already overburdened surface streets.

And making her late.

Risa's pulse might have kicked with more than irritation when she spotted Shane, but her steps didn't hesitate or quicken. Nor did she check that her short black hair was smoothly in place and her unstructured blue jacket was hanging straight. Other women might have licked their lips for that extra shine or sucked in their belly or stuck out their chest to look their best for Shane Tannahill.

Not Risa.

She had fought to get where she was. She loved her job as curator of gold objects for the Golden Fleece, Shane's Las Vegas entertainment complex. She wasn't going to lose everything she had worked for simply because of his handsome face and killer grin. Better that she rub her boss the wrong way than the right.

Shane's work ethic was simple and inflexible: no lying, no cheating, no stealing, and no sex. He didn't touch the female employees. End of subject. But if a woman didn't want to accept that, and he was interested in an affair, he would find her another job. Only then would a good time be had by all.

No matter how intelligent, appealing, rich, and maddening Shane might be, Risa wanted her job more than she wanted to do laps around the sex track with any man. Even one of the few who had ever really interested her.

It's the forbidden fruit thing, Risa told herself briskly. *No man is that sexy after you wake up with him. Or without him, more likely.*

The guard released the automatic locks for Risa. The door swung open.

She gave the uniformed man a bright smile. "Good morning, Jersey. How's the thumb?"

Jersey, who was about seven feet of muscle and bone, blushed. "Who told you?"

"Mmmm" was all she said. She didn't want Shane to know how often she and S. K. Niall chatted. Shane was friendly with the two heads of Rarities, but that friendship didn't slop over into business. Shane wouldn't be pleased knowing that his curator talked several times a week with Niall—*Rhymes with kneel, boyo. I'm not a bloody river.* At the moment the Golden Fleece didn't have enough business with Rarities to justify such frequent communications. But Risa was lonely, and Niall was safely involved with Dana Gaynor, the other head of Rarities.

"I can't believe I slammed my thumb in the desk drawer," Jersey muttered.

"Yeah, Dana really ought to wear a warning bell when she walks around," Risa sympathized, fighting a smile.

Shane didn't bother to fight it. He flashed the kind of grin that made men and women alike blink and draw closer, as though to a fire.

Jersey's blush deepened.

"You'll get used to Dana's walk," Risa said. She

tossed her purse on a moving belt like those at an airport checkpoint and strolled through the metal detector's field without setting off a single buzz. "All the men do. Eventually."

"Uh, yes'm." But Jersey was shaking his head while he watched the screen that displayed the contents of Risa's purse. Nothing but the usual. The metal alarm didn't quiver. The nitrate alarm didn't go off. Neither did any of the other chemical alarms. Not that he expected anything like that to happen—not with a consultant. But he wasn't paid to make personal judgments. He was paid to put everyone who walked in those doors through the scanners, and that included Dana Gaynor and S.K. Niall.

Shane took Risa's purse as it popped out the other end of the scanner. He tossed it to her with a quickness that had caught more than one person off guard.

She snagged her purse with a deceptively lazy movement of her arm. He wasn't the only one with good reflexes. "Thanks." She turned to Jersey. "Anything else?"

"Just this." He handed her a staff pass dangling on a long neck chain. "New rules."

She put on the chain and the colorful bit of plastic that stated she was a consultant. "Since when?"

Shane answered before Jersey could. "Since someone threatened half of Rarities Unlimited."

"Dana was threatened?" Risa asked, startled.

"No. Niall."

"Whew," Risa said, blowing out a breath. Besides being a friend, Niall was half owner and head of security for Rarities Unlimited. Dana owned the other half and ran the "Fuzzy" or Fine Arts side of Rarities. "Remarkably stupid of whoever made the threat." She gave her boss a speculative glance out of eyes that were a clear, dark blue. "When?"

"Three days ago." Shane started toward the elevator at the end of a wide, short hallway. "They're waiting in the number-two clean room."

Without missing a beat, Risa matched her boss's long-legged stride. If it strained the hem of her knee-length fitted skirt, too bad. No way a man was going to have her at a disadvantage. "What was the guy mad about?"

"He had a tray of Roman cameos he wanted appraised," Shane said. "Turned out most were pretty good forgeries. He didn't like it, so he started yelling and cursing. Niall showed up real fast and escorted the client out. The client didn't like that either. Said he was going to send someone to teach Niall some manners."

"Dumb, dumber, dumbest." She shook her head at the client's lack of insight. Not to mention simple smarts. "Niall isn't as big as Jersey, but he's a lot tougher."

The corner of Shane's mouth kicked up, and his eyes gleamed with sardonic humor. "Meaner, too. And I'll bet on mean every time."

"No argument here." Risa knew better than most people just how far mean could go. Growing up cockroach poor taught you all about the difference between mean, tough, and merely big. You learned to size up men and situations fast—and accurately—or you paid in pain.

Shane slanted a speculative glance at his curator. She was very businesslike in her dark tailored skirt and loose, jewel blue jacket, her hair a sleek black cap, her makeup understated, her curvy figure all but hidden, and the kind of mouth that could make a man forget all the reasons he shouldn't bite it. He almost hadn't hired Risa because of her body and those sin-with-me lips. Then he had measured the unflinching intelligence in her eyes and remembered the ambition that had fairly radiated from her résumé.

Risa was everything he had wanted and more than he had bargained on getting when he asked Niall to help him find a trustworthy gold curator who would agree to live in Las Vegas. Niall had sent Risa.

Knowing that he would probably regret it, Shane had hired her. Then he had kept as much distance as possible from his new curator.

Given the nature of her work, it wasn't enough space for comfort. Getting ready for his upcoming "Druid Gold" show had had them stepping on each other's shadows for months. More than once he had thought about finding another curator so he could have sex with this one. But he needed Risa's expertise and her fierce intelligence more than he needed an affair, so they just kept circling each other like strange dogs that didn't know whether to bite or lick.

Most of the time Shane was thankful that Risa put up as many GO AWAY signs as he did. The rest of the time it irritated him that she was every bit as wary of him as he was of her. He couldn't help wondering why she kept backing up. Certainly not out of fear of losing the only good job around. In the past year a well-known private museum and two wealthy collectors had offered Risa employment. He knew because he had bettered their offers in order to keep her.

And his common sense told him that he should have let her go. She was the kind of trouble he really didn't need.

Risa tapped on the door of the number-two clean room, so called because it was a safe, neutral territory where buyer could meet seller and not fear fraud or outright robbery. In this case Shane was the designated buyer. At least that was what Rarities' client hoped.

"Sorry I'm late," Risa said to Dana and Niall, who were going over some papers on the long metal table that ran down the center of the room. "Security hold in Vegas, and then a gas tanker truck flipped on Sepulveda."

"You two should be honored," Shane said.

"Why?" Dana asked, looking up.

"I'm her boss, and she didn't apologize to me."

Risa's eyes narrowed. She didn't say a word.

Niall cleared his throat. Shane and Risa had been at sixes and sevens from the first day they met, but lately the air was beginning to smoke whenever they were in the same room. With a mental sigh he decided to start looking for a new opening for Risa; if she didn't quit pretty soon, Shane would fire her. On the plus side, Shane was noted for his generous severance packages. Maybe she was holding out for that.

"Why should she apologize to you?" Dana asked, stacking the papers with brisk motions. "Rarities is paying for her time at the moment, not you."

"Ouch," Shane said.

"One day you'll learn, boyo," Niall said, grinning. "The lady could teach cutting to a sword."

Shane cocked a dark brown eyebrow at Niall, who was kicked back in his chair as though he didn't have a worry in the world. "Voice of experience, I presume."

"Bloody right." His low-voiced growl was at odds with his amused blue-green eyes and clipped brown hair. He shifted his broad shoulders and reached for his shirt buttons. "Want to see my scars?"

"I don't think his heart could stand it," Dana said. "And Risa is far too young for such a manly display."

"Hey, y'all, I'm thirty-one," Risa drawled, letting her

Arkansas upbringing pour through her smoky voice. "That's old enough to know better than to let some male show me his, um, scars."

Dana's laugh made her look much younger than Risa suspected she was.

"Right," Niall said. "If you're not interested in a manly striptease, how about a look at some old gold jewelry?"

Without waiting for an answer, he pushed back and walked to a long, spun-aluminum case at the far end of the table. The box was about the size that a professional pool player might use to protect his favorite cue. There was a similar, smaller box on the opposite end of the table.

"Recorders on," Dana said to no one in particular.

"Running," answered a disembodied voice from a ceiling grille.

"Is that Factoid?" Shane asked, gesturing toward the grille.

"No," Niall said. "Our research guru is off today."

"With Gretchen?" Shane asked, smiling. Joe-Bob McCoy, aka Factoid, had a permanent lech for his boss, the head of research. Gretchen Miller was twice his age and half again his weight. A real Valkyrie.

"At the moment she's working with Ian Lapstrake and Lawe Donovan," Dana said. "The Rutherby inheritance."

"Too bad," Shane said. "I've got a great menu for Factoid to try out on his next date with Gretchen, assuming he ever talks her into another one. Food guaranteed to make the woman of his dreams lust for him."

Niall snickered. "What is it—oysters twelve ways?"

Dana rolled her dark eyes. When it came to matters biological, men were such simple creatures.

"A bit more elaborate," Shane said. "First, a bunch of candles surrounded by agates."

"Why?" Niall asked.

"Guaranteed, time-tested aphrodisiac."

Dana snorted softly.

Shane kept talking. "Shrimp cocktail, celery soup, endive salad, halibut with paprika and juniper. Wine, of course. Benedictine and chocolate for dessert. Then the night of your dreams awaits."

"For that I'd even eat endive," Niall said.

Dana cut him a glance that said she would remember his words and use them against him. He hated endive.

Without realizing it, Risa let out a soft moan at the thought of Benedictine and chocolate. "You're killing me. All I get for lunch is carrots and celery."

"Why?" Shane asked, startled.

"The usual reason. I can't afford new clothes if I eat my way out of these."

"Are you hinting for another raise after the one that I was forced to give you to—"

"Argue on your own time," Dana cut in. Then she said to Risa, "The client's request is that you do a 'cold' appraisal. Visual inspection only."

"Cold appraisal for hot goods?" Shane suggested.

Dana gave him a look that could have frozen fire. "The provenance on these goods is above reproach. The collector is merely reluctant to invest in a full appraisal if, after a quick look, the goods seem to be less than they were advertised to him."

Shane smiled and tugged on his forelock like a peasant standing before his lord.

Dana ignored him, though her lips twitched around what might have been an answering smile. She had a weakness for men who were smart, easy on the eyes, and hard on the opposition.

Niall opened the first aluminum box and lifted the lid. Inside, each within its own individually cut nest, pieces of gold jewelry gleamed.

Instantly Risa forgot everything else in the room. She went to the open case and simply stared at the contents. After a long, silent minute, she began talking.

"First impression. Celtic, of course. Styles and techniques range from La Tène to Mediterranean. Age could be anywhere from fifth century B.C. to fifth century A.D. If you need dates on individual pieces, it will take several days for detailed stylistic comparisons with artifacts in museums, published papers, auction catalogs, online collections, that sort of thing. Most of my references are in Las Vegas, because you said you only needed a fast look."

"If a more detailed appraisal is required, would you need the actual artifacts, or would the virtual ones do?" Dana asked.

With intent, narrowed eyes, Risa looked through the collection again. "Did you search for modern machining marks when you had these under the 'scope?"

"The client assured me there were none," Dana said. "We checked, of course. Nothing caught our expert's eye."

"Right." Risa let out a breath. "Then I'd start with the virtual and go to the real only if I ran into problems."

Dana nodded. "So noted."

"For now," Risa said, "of the nine real objects in this case, one shows obvious signs of recent repair—the gold alloys simply don't match. Two of the pieces have repairs that appear much older, but that's only a preliminary visual examination. Some of the rest certainly could use repair, but that's to be expected. In all probability they're two thousand years old."

"You think they're genuine?" Dana asked. "Again, this is a nonbinding verbal opinion based solely on a limited visual examination."

Risa waited while the legal niceties were recorded before she said, "I haven't seen anything to put me off. Yet."

Nor had she seen anything that made her heart kick with excitement at being in the presence of a truly fine artifact. A showstopper, as her boss would say.

That was what Shane needed to launch his new gallery on New Year's Eve. That was what she hadn't found yet—a centerpiece for his Druid Gold show. She couldn't help wondering how much more time he would give her. And who else he had looking.

Shane might have made his fortune gambling, but he never left anything to chance.

Two

"**Did the client agree** to having these objects manually inspected?" Risa asked, frowning.

Dana nodded. "Yes, but we've already photographed, x-rayed, and otherwise electronically scanned the pieces, including XRF and SEM."

Without waiting for Shane to ask, Risa translated. "X-ray fluorescence to determine the composition of the metal alloy and scanning electron microscope for all the fiddly little details."

"The results are digitized," Dana continued, "and can be reproduced in three dimensions, so if you would rather not take the risk of handling the objects yourself—"

Risa's laugh drowned out the rest of Dana's words. "I live to handle ancient jewelry, gold in particular. High-quality gold doesn't respond easily to the acids on human skin, which means I don't have to wear surgical gloves to handle gold for a brief inspection."

"Why would handling gold matter to you, other than pleasure?" Niall asked.

"No photo, no computer reproduction in 3-D, no hologram, no electronic scanning, no graphs or reports, nothing works for me like actual touch. In humans the only thing more sensitive than the fingertips is the tongue. The delicacy of the work on some of the objects I've handled is so fine it defeats human eyes and fingertips."

"So you lick it?" Niall asked in disbelief.

An amused, sideways glance was her only reply.

Shane's eyelids lowered almost lazily. It was his only visible reaction to the thought of something being explored by Risa's sensitive tongue. Certainly the idea was more interesting than any of the gold pieces on the table in front of him. While they had historic value, they left a lot to be desired in terms of pizzazz.

And that was what he needed. Impact. The kind of gold artifacts that could reach through ignorance and twenty-first-century smugness and shake the viewers to the soles of their casually shod feet. It might last only a few moments, but for that time the viewers would *know* that people just like them had lived for thousands of years—laughing, yearning, loving, crying, dying, and creating, always creating.

The fact that such an exhibit would also increase traffic through Tannahill Inc.'s resort casinos was nice, but it wasn't the reason he was pursuing all that was good and enduring in gold artifacts. Quite simply, he despised the looters and scavengers of ancient cultures. It was a passion and a pursuit that only two other people were aware of—Dana and Niall. Shane worked hard to keep it that way.

The less people thought of him, the easier it was to catch them off guard.

"Did you have anything else to show me?" he asked. "These aren't what I need. When I open the Druid Gold show, there will be press, media, and cameras until hell won't have them. Celebrities. Politicians. Socialites. The whole tacky tortilla."

"What Shane is trying to say," Risa offered, "is that in Las Vegas there's downtown, downscale, tasteless, and then there's uptown, upscale, ostentasteless. Nothing in this lot will make a jaded tourist blink."

Yet even as she spoke, her fingertips reverently brushed the cool, damaged surface of what could have been a privileged child's torc or a votive offering to one of the four hundred named deities the Celts had worshipped. To her, even the most awkward artifact deserved respect simply for having survived when so much else had been lost.

Dana waved off the explanation and looked at Shane. She had expected his impatience. That was why she had insisted that Rarities pay for Risa's time and travel. "Down, boy. She's here for us, not you." To Niall she said, "Why don't you take him to the basement and play with guns or something."

It was an order, not a question.

Shane laughed and held up his hands in mock surrender to the small brunette. "You rise to the bait so beautifully, Dana. Hard to resist."

"Fight it," Niall suggested, but the lines at the corners of his eyes gave away his silent laughter.

Dana said something that was either "men" or *"merde."* No one asked for clarification.

Smiling, Risa picked up the small torc. "From its

weight, it's hollow. This torc—neckring—is most probably grave goods or perhaps an offering to the spirit of a special spring or a marsh or a river. From the color, I might guess that the torc was made from a gold-silver alloy similar to the hoard found in Snettisham, England, which has been dated to mid-first century B.C. Even if that is the case, it wouldn't be definitive proof of origin for this object, because graves and treasure troves have been dug up and melted down and reworked for as long as people have been burying gold in the ground in the first place."

"But you would be comfortable with labeling that torc as British Celtic, approximately first century B.C.?" Dana asked.

"If that is consistent with your XRF results—"

"It is," Dana cut in. "None of the pieces match XRF graphs of modern nine-, fourteen-, or eighteen-karat-gold alloys."

Risa nodded without glancing away from the torc. "The technique isn't up to the standards of what has been published from the Snettisham hoards of the first century B.C. These terminals aren't even engraved. Maybe the torc wasn't finished. Maybe it was. We'll never know. We can only judge what we have in our hands, not what might have been."

"But the torc is similar to the Snettisham goods?" Dana pressed.

"Apparently this torc is made of electrum. So were some of the Snettisham goods. That's all I'm willing to say at this point."

Risa held the torc out and turned it so that the overhead camera would have a clear view. The awkwardness of the object leaped into high relief.

"This is a single hollow tube of gold shaped—

inelegantly—into a small neckring," Risa said. "As a golden survivor of the centuries, it has both extrinsic and intrinsic value. As an example of the jeweler's art of Iron Age Britain . . ." She shrugged. "Ordinary. Very ordinary. Any good museum has something like it in storage in the basement, waiting for a scholar to care."

Dana's nod made light shimmer over her short dark hair. The client had doubtless hoped for more, but that was his problem. Her problem was to buy, sell, appraise, and protect the constant stream of cultural artifacts that came through the door of Rarities Unlimited.

"The other pieces are of similar artistic quality." Deftly Risa replaced the torc in its nest and picked another piece of jewelry at random. "This penannular brooch—think of it as a broken circle—was used to keep robes, cloaks, and the like from falling off your shoulders. Many such brooches were made of iron or bronze. The Vikings preferred silver, because that's what they had the most of to work with. The Celtic tradition in earlier times and other places is rich in gold."

Niall looked at the brooch. There wasn't any way to fasten the piece to cloth. There wasn't even a sharp point to pierce fabric before coming to rest in the rudely formed clasp. "Don't see how it could hold up anything."

"That's because the pin part of the brooch was broken," Risa said, replacing it. "The destruction was probably deliberate and happened when the brooch originally was buried or thrown into water."

Niall opened his mouth to ask why something should be broken before it was buried or offered to a god. Then he caught Dana's slicing, impatient look and shut his mouth. There was no need to know. Not for him. It was enough that Risa knew.

Besides, he could always ask her later.

"Two of the remaining brooches are similarly broken." Risa skimmed three pieces with her fingertips. "These small armlets are from a later time, after the Romans began to influence British Celtic styles. They appear to be solid gold." She picked them up one after another and weighed them in her palm. "Not hollow. Again, the technique is frankly crude. It lacks the polish of the Mediterranean goldsmiths who came with the Romans to Britain. Nor do the pieces have the sheer . . . well, *presence* that the best of the Celtic goldsmiths gave their work."

"Define 'presence,' " Shane said.

Her first thought was that he should know all about presence. He certainly had more than his share of it. "It isn't definable. If it's there, you feel it. If it isn't . . ." She shrugged.

He started to ask another question, only to be cut off by his employee.

"I'll discuss it with you later if you wish," Risa said, "but until then, try looking in the mirror." At Shane's surprised expression, her chin came up defiantly. "Men. *Merde.*"

Dana's laugh was as smoothly tenor as her voice. "Anything else you want to add for the recorders?"

Red flared briefly on Risa's wide-set cheekbones as she remembered that every word and gesture was going into digital storage. "The overall crudeness, simplicity, and fragmentary condition of the pieces make me inclined to say that they aren't forgeries. They're just not good enough to generate the kind of interest and money that pay forgers for their skill, time, and materials."

"Would you be willing to put a verbal, nonbinding value on the collection if sold as a whole?"

"Are these being represented as a single trove found at the same place and time?"

"No," Dana said.

"In that case the value is considerably less."

"My client is aware of that."

"At this point, and assuming that the provenance is very good, I don't see more than seventy-five to a hundred and fifty thousand dollars in the whole lot. There's little in these pieces to lure a major museum. If you find a jewelry collector whose interest lies exclusively in Celtic gold work, you might get more money." Her vivid, dark blue gaze pinned Shane. "Collectors are an unpredictable lot. They pay whatever it's worth to them."

Shane's smile was all hard, gleaming teeth.

Niall coughed as he closed the case, exchanged it for the other spun-aluminum box and returned to the group at the table. The new box was half the size of the first. He opened the lid and turned the case toward Risa.

She sensed the stillness that came over Shane. She glanced at him and saw nothing different in his expression.

Yet she knew he had decided to buy the piece even before he heard his own expert's opinion of it.

Merde.

She really hated when that happened.

At least this was an artifact she would be proud to have in the Golden Fleece's collection of gold objects. Always assuming the artifact wasn't a fraud or had the kind of cobbled-together provenance that screamed of blood and theft. If the provenance was suspect, she and her boss would be in for some yelling matches. Her idea of solid provenance was too rigid, according to Shane. A lot of auction houses would agree with him.

Risa's childhood and youth were so spotted she required the cleanest of artifacts. Shane's background was of the driven-snow variety, which made him more tolerant.

He had never been caught red-handed with something he didn't legally own.

She shoved aside the unhappy memories of her childhood as an Arkansas orphan and concentrated on the artifact in front of her. There was an integrity to the piece that transcended whatever guilty or greedy souls might have owned it in the past.

"Visual only, or may I handle this?" she asked.

"Same as the other lot," Dana said.

Risa smiled even as she shook her head slowly. "No, this is very different from the other lot. This has presence."

Shane gave her a sideways look.

She ignored him and concentrated on the torc. To her relief the object felt only of cool gold and weight, none of the disturbing power that she sometimes felt with an artifact—and never more unnervingly than she had in Wales, amid standing stones, even though no artifacts had been there. But she didn't like thinking about that and the currents of awareness that sometimes reached out to her, telling her she was *different*.

With a long breath she forced herself to concentrate on the here and now rather than a lost childhood and an eerie oak grove in Wales.

The torc's circle was divided into three equal arcs. The outer curve of each arc was decorated by a spoked wheel balanced on the center of the arc. Each wheel was itself divided into thirds by three equally spaced gold knobs.

"Classic three-part design," Risa said. "The Celts loved their trinity long before Christian times." Carefully she lifted the torc from its nest. "From the weight, it's solid. Whether this is pure gold or sheet gold wrapped over iron, I can't tell visually. If it's a wrap, it's a thick one. I see nothing but gold."

Dana spoke softly into the microphone buttoned to her collar. "Research?"

"Iron core," said the ceiling grille. "Verified by Rarities."

"Excellent." Risa all but purred.

"Wouldn't it be more valuable as pure gold?" Niall asked.

"As metals go, pure gold is very soft," she said absently. "You can shape it any way you want without much trouble, but it gets out of shape just as easily. Worse, it might not stop a surprise sword blow from the back, which was probably the original reason torcs were worn. The fact that this is gold wrapped around iron makes it more likely that the torc was a badge of royalty or very high status that was actually worn by a woman or a pencil-necked man. Beautiful. Just beautiful." With sensitive fingertips she traced the whole of the circle. "Mmm. Yes. Here it is. And here."

Shane watched her fingertips and thought of her tongue. Irritably he pulled his mind back to the gold object instead of his increasing, damned inconvenient lust for his curator.

Risa looked at Dana. "I will assume a mortise-and-tenon joint at each end of this arc."

"English, please," Shane said.

The edge to his voice made Risa's eyes narrow. "Think of it as innie meets outie."

Niall snickered.

Risa turned back to Dana. "That kind of joint was known and used in the Iron Age. It would allow one arc in this torc to be removed so that the remaining two-thirds of the ring could slip—or be pushed—around the neck. Then the arc would be replaced, the torc squeezed shut at the joints, and God help whoever wanted to take it off."

"Sounds uncomfortable," Shane said.

"Status usually is."

He gave Risa an amused, approving look. Her combination of pragmatism and razor intelligence interested him as much as anything else about her, including her lush body.

And that worried him. Affairs weren't based on intelligence and pragmatism. They were fast, greedy, and hot. Anything where intelligence crept in was a relationship.

Bad idea.

He wasn't any good at relationships. The only ones he had were with family, and they could best be described as mutual combat in his father's case, mutual sadness in his mother's case, and mutual frustration all around.

If only you would try, you and your father could get along. Just try, Shane. Try. Please. For me.

His mother's often-repeated plea echoed like an unhappy ghost through Shane's memories. He ignored it with the ease of a lifetime's practice. Not even for his mother would he put up with his father's corrosive arrogance. End of argument. End of family life.

Beginning of Shane's true education.

There was nothing like being broke on the streets to teach a man all the things he hadn't learned while getting a master's degree in business at Stanford University.

"As for age," Risa continued, running her fingertips lightly along the cool, ancient gold, "I know of at least one torc that is similar in execution and style to this. It came from Marne, France, and dates back to the fourth century B.C."

"Provisional estimate of worth?" Dana asked.

"With good—very good—provenance, I would start asking at three hundred thousand dollars and hope to make considerably more. Up to five hundred thousand. Maybe even higher. Depends on whether it's a public auction, which tends to drive up prices just by the competitive nature of collectors, or a private sale to an interested individual."

"Is it for sale?" Shane asked bluntly.

"Yes," Dana said.

"May I?" he said, but he was already holding out his hand in silent demand.

Risa gave him the torc.

For a moment he simply closed his eyes and absorbed the weight, texture, and feel of the ancient jewelry. He couldn't have said why he approached collecting gold artifacts this way; he knew only that he always had. No matter how spectacular a piece might appear, if it didn't feel right, he didn't buy it.

When his eyes opened they were the clear, bottomless green of imperial jade. And he was looking at Risa, *into* her.

The hair at the nape of her neck prickled. She turned away from him so quickly she nearly stumbled. "Tell your client that, subject to verification of provenance, he has an offer of three hundred—"

"Four," Shane interrupted curtly.

"Four hundred thousand dollars," she said between her teeth. "If he is uneasy that I would be both appraiser and acquirer, Tannahill Inc. will pay for a neutral appraisal."

"Right," Dana said. Mentally she toted up the commission to Rarities and smiled. "He won't kick. He requested you by name."

"Probably because he wanted Shane's attention," Risa said with faint bitterness. On her own she wasn't well known enough to attract artifacts of the quality Shane was holding now.

"Doubtless," Dana agreed. "Anyone with a fine gold artifact to sell anywhere in the world has heard of Shane Tannahill and the Golden Fleece."

"It certainly makes my life interesting," Risa muttered.

"Buying all that lovely stuff, eh?" Niall asked.

"No. Dealing with all the 'lovely stuff' that elbows its way out of the world's sewers holding gold in both fists."

Three

The book in Virgil's lap was heavy, scholarly, and filled with beautiful drawings and color photos of Celtic art. He didn't need to look at the pages to know what was there. They filled his memory. The book was just one of many he had collected to educate himself about the nature of the gold artifacts that were packed in three World War II ammunition boxes under his bed. All of his past addresses were neatly stenciled on each box, a ritual recitation of all the places he had fled.

But no more. He finally understood that he couldn't outrun the unthinkable.

He had chosen the spirit-infused Southwest for his last stand. He had hoped that putting the boxes of gold in the center of the three leaning stones he had found at the base of the nearby cliff would somehow . . . return the gold.

And free him.

When that plan had failed, he stuck the boxes under his bed and read books in hope of finding knowledge that would allow him to control whatever lived in the gold. That hadn't worked either, but hope was as persistent as breath. And as necessary.

He had kept on reading and hoping to find the key that would set him free from the curse of Druid gold.

Once he had even tried to go back to the Welsh autumn, to the place where he had dug out the treasure more than half a century ago. Gold, sacred gold, three times three times three artifacts that were the core of Druid rituals—rituals where life ended and began again, where kings waited while Druids spoke to gods, where the very course of the sun and moon were assured. Beltane in May, when the time of warmth and hope returned to the land, and Samhain in November when the time of cold and desperation began once more.

Samhain, when what was real and what wasn't flowed together and created an eerie whole.

It had been Samhain when he returned to Wales to find again the nine hills, six oak trees, three leaning stones, one tiny spring. He hadn't taken a metal detector that second time. He wasn't after gold. He was after absolution.

He hadn't found it, nor the black spring in the center of the stones. The very place that he had discovered so easily in time of war eluded him in peace.

Defeated, still cursed, he had fled back to America. Here he remained, older and no wiser for all the books he had read. Nowhere in those books had he discovered anything to equal the twenty-seven objects he had found in the Druid grove. Nowhere in any of the modern fancies about white-robed Druids had he found anything to equal the power of the ancients whose minds had held the entire reality of a culture. Druids who cured the sick or made the healthy ill. Druids who talked with gods and held power greater than kings. Druids who knew no difference between themselves and a river or an oak or a stag; everything all of one piece, seamless, sacred.

And all that power was summed up and contained in the ritual artifacts he had stolen.

He was doomed.

Setting the book aside, he stared uneasily at the heavy gold torc whose circle of twisted gold chains gleamed coldly in the moonlight pouring through his open window. There was enough light to read by if you had young eyes, but not enough to bring out the red color in the huge rock faces that loomed just beyond his run-down little house.

Tourists paid big bucks to be hauled over the rugged land in pink jeeps or dusty open vans. He had never understood why. The sun was just as pretty lots of other places. The sky was just as blue. Yet visitors came here to Sedona to stand cheek by jowl with other visitors and shuffle along crowded vortex trails that already had been beaten hard by thousands of aging New Agers.

Virgil had even tried walking the vortex trails himself, back when he thought he could bleed off some of the bad luck that had hounded him since he went AWOL for a two-day trip to Wales. But no matter how many vortex sites he went to, no matter how hard he tried to open himself to that other reality, he always came back down the trail with the same old reality he had hauled up it in the first place.

In time he had discovered channeling. A one-hour session cost more than a trip to a fancy cathouse, but he hadn't had much use for whores after he turned seventy-six. Besides, using a channel was a lot easier than clawing his way alone to the most remote and powerful vortex sites—the ones that weren't listed in the flashy four-color pamphlets that sold for ten bucks apiece and weren't worth the paper they were printed on. Using a channel was a lot easier on him than touching the damned gold itself and hearing hell beckoning in his own screams.

The clock's hands stuttered and snapped together like the ends of a fan.

Midnight. Halloween.

Samhain, when all boundaries blurred.

It had to be now.

After two tries he forced himself to grab the torc. His skin rippled violently as it tried to crawl away from the cold gold. He was certain he heard thunder way far off, hell and gone to Wales, *lightning pouring through his clenched hand, searing, burning, destroying* . . .

The sound of his own screams shook Virgil out of whatever he had fallen into. Hell, as near as he could tell. He had seen it, touched it, and was terrified he would spend eternity with it.

"Can't do it alone," he said to the darkness. "Need the channel. Need her *now*."

For a few minutes he put his head in his hands, pushed trembling fingers through thick white hair, and gathered his strength to face the darkness again.

At least Lady Faulkner would be with him this time.

The thought gave him enough courage to call the number he remembered even when he forgot other things. But not everything. No matter how hard he tried, he couldn't forget the hell he would have sold his soul to forget.

If he still had a soul.

Motionless but for the tremor in his hands that never stopped these days, he waited for his channel to pick up the phone and answer questions about the state of his soul.

Four

The telephone's relentless ringing finally dragged Cherelle Faulkner from a drugged sleep. Naked, she sat up and peered groggily through eyelashes clogged with mascara. Outside the window whose only curtain was dust, the motel's faded neon sign blinked on and off, on and off, a slow heart beating in the darkness advertising rooms by the night or the week or the month.

The phone kept ringing.

She shoved her hands through the bleached length of her hair and kicked the man sleeping beside her. "Chrissake, Tim! Get the fucking phone!"

"Shit," mumbled Tim Seton. "Listen to you. And here you're always telling me to watch my mouth around the dumbs."

"The only dumb in this bed is you, and we all know that assholes don't have ears, so I don't have to watch my fucking mouth, do I?"

Tim turned his beautiful profile away from her and fell back asleep.

The phone kept ringing.

With a hissing curse Cherelle clawed her way across Tim until she could see the Caller ID readout.

"Virgil," she muttered. "Shit."

Virgil O'Conner was one of their best dumbs—*clients*, she corrected herself silently. Paid cash. Up front. No hassle, no bouncing checks, no credit card trail. She wished they had fifty more like him. Hell, even five. With that and a little luck in Vegas, a girl could do as well as her childhood pal Risa already had.

Thinking of Risa made Cherelle slide back toward the good old days, when two smart Arkansas orphans had stuck it to the—

The phone was still ringing.

She shook off the last of her half-sleeping memories, pulled her vortex persona around her like invisible robes, and picked up the receiver. When she spoke, her voice was hushed and gentle.

"Good morning, Virgil. I sense that you're having a difficult time."

"Gotta see you."

"Let me check my—"

"No," he interrupted. "Now, Lady Faulkner. It's gotta be now. While it's still dark. That gold is killing me."

She barely bit back the gutter words that were doing back flips on her tongue. "Gold, hmmm? Did you fall asleep over the pictures in one of your old books again?"

"Got things better than any damn book. You come quick. You'll see."

"Virgil . . ." *It's the middle of the fucking night, you moron.* She clenched her jaw, swiped hair out of her eyes, and said carefully, "All right, I'll come, but I'll have to ask for double the usual fee. I'm sorry, but that's the—"

"If you get here before dawn, I'll give you four hundred," he cut in.

"Cash?"

"Yeah." It was all the money he had left, but he wasn't worried. If this appointment didn't do the trick, he didn't think there would be any others. "But you gotta get here fast."

Cherelle swallowed. "I'll be with you before dawn. Peace and prosperity, Virgil."

Before the client could answer, she dumped the phone in its cradle and shook her partner hard enough to make his blond-streaked hair fly. "Up and at 'em, pretty boy. Virgil has four big ol' bills waiting for us."

Tim opened one beautiful blue eye. "Who do we have to kill?"

"Ha, ha. You can't even step on a cockroach. You have to have your jailhouse buddy do it for you."

The other blue eye opened. He smiled like a china angel. "It gets done, don't it?"

With a sound of disgust she dropped his shoulders and finished crawling over him to get out of bed. "Haul that sexy butt out of the sheets. We have to be at Virgil's before dawn."

"Socks won't like it if we aren't here when—"

"Socks can fuck himself."

"Hey, you're always down on my buddy."

"I never went down on him, not even when he offered me a hundred."

Snickering, Tim stretched. He liked jabbing at his lover. It was his way of getting even for not being half as smart as she was. Neither was Socks, for all his bragging. Next to Cherelle, they were both stupid. But that was okay.

Thinking was a pain in the ass.

So he left thinking to Cherelle unless it was more up his buddy's alley, like fencing the occasional TV or DVD player. He didn't tell Cherelle about that part of it. She would shit a brick if she knew Socks was burgling some of their clients. Not all of them. Hell, even *he* could figure out that would be stupid. Just a few of them when they left for the winter, the ones that had so many TVs they wouldn't miss one or two.

Anyway, it was Cherelle's fault. If she wasn't so tight with cash, he wouldn't have to moonlight with Socks. But she had a bug up her ass about saving enough money to get a place somewhere that nobody knew them and they wouldn't have to be looking over their shoulder all the time. That took money, and that meant he was lucky to see a fifty from her once a week so that he could have a few beers with Socks and—

"Timothy Seton, get your ass out of that bed!"

"Bitch, bitch, bitch," he said, but he made sure she didn't hear. "I'm up, I'm up!" Then he looked down at his early-morning woody and laughed. "Sure enough, I am. How about it?"

She gave him a look that took the lead right out of his pencil.

Rather wistfully he glanced down at his deflating glory. Oh, well. There was more where that came from. And if she didn't want it when it came around again, there were others that did.

Whistling, he headed for the shower that Cherelle had finally cleaned last week. About time, too. There had been enough crud on the floor to tickle his feet.

Five

The lobby of the Wildest Dream hotel/shopping/theater/gambling complex was decked out like a Halloween tart in black velvet and neon orange. The most photogenic of the Strip's gambling glitterati milled around the champagne fountain and dipped black crystal glasses into the fizzy orange wine. Gail Silverado, sole owner of Wildest Dream Inc., was famous for her yearly Halloween bash. It started loud and just got better. By 3:00 A.M. the party had developed a really shrill edge that would just get worse every half hour until dawn, when the bubbly fountain would finally run dry.

But that was several hours away. With a smile brighter than the shimmering faux pearl beads that outlined her figure in loving detail, Gail held her tenth glass of champagne—one sip from each, no more, no less—and looked at her watch without appearing to. She still had a few more minutes before she would be called away on business.

Even if a meeting hadn't been arranged, she would have wanted to get away. The high, sexy heels she was wearing had been designed for a younger woman, one who hadn't spent too many of her fifty-odd years strutting her well-kept butt in front of whichever man could afford it. Her feet were screaming.

Her smile never wavered beneath the exotic, pearlescent feathers that framed her face like loving fingers. There was too much young ass in Las Vegas for a woman over thirty ever to let down her guard. But even if she had been playing against a field of dogs, Gail would have gone through the same arduous workout and surgical schedule that she did now. She needed to look fifteen years younger than she was. Twenty would be better.

"Shane!" she called. Her smile tipped into the megawatt category. "I was afraid you wouldn't come."

With a wave, Shane slipped through a costumed throng of devils, some Hell's Angels—who may or may not have been in costume—more "showgirls" than had ever pranced down the Lido's runway, and some truly reptilian aliens with heads that would have made Medusa turn and run.

"I should have Carl throw you out," Gail said to Shane when he came to stand beside her, but her approving look said otherwise.

"Why sic your head of security on me?" Shane wasn't quite shouting, but it was a near thing. The volume of the party had reached frenetic. A lot of people relished it. He wasn't one of them. He was here for business, not pleasure, and all that noise got in the way. Almost shouting just to have a conversation wasn't his idea of fun.

"Because, honeylove," Gail said, hands on her narrow waist, "you're not in costume."

Shane looked down as though surprised to find himself in the same leather jacket, open-collar cream shirt,

and black slacks he had worn to the meeting at Rarities.
"I'm in costume."

"As what?"

"Normal twenty-first-century male of the species
Homo sapiens sapiens."

Gail laughed. "Point to you. The last thing anyone
would accuse you of being is normal."

He looked over the crowd with a practiced eye. No
matter how unlikely their costumes, he easily spotted the
security guards. They were the only ones not drinking. It
was the same upstairs, on the catwalks hidden behind
ceiling grilles and one-way mirrors surrounding light fix-
tures. Security people walked overhead and manned
each Eye in the Sky while the cameras worked. At the
Wildest Dream, as at other big casinos, every bit of the
action was captured and put into digital storage.
Though the records were accessed as bytes on minidrives
more often than on videotape, everyone still referred to
the records as "tapes."

"Great crowd. Who's on God duty tonight?" Shane
asked idly, referring to the security people upstairs.

"Whoever lost the toss."

Gail must have signaled a server, because one left a
hole in the crowd getting to Shane to offer him whatever
his heart desired. He waved off the leggy girl whose
breasts bobbed like waterlogged coconuts above her
low-cut neckline. Other than an eyeful, Shane couldn't
decide what her costume was supposed to represent.
Chartreuse and silver kitty-cat, maybe.

And maybe not.

"You're not going to stay long enough to eat or drink
anything, is that it?" Gail asked when he waved off the
server.

"I just got in from L.A. I'm way too tired for your crowd."

She didn't believe it for a second. She knew just how much energy and stamina the man had. What she wanted to know was how to get him back in her bed again. It had been too many years.

At first she had thought it was the age difference that made Shane stop calling her. Gradually she had realized it was worse than that. He simply didn't want any more from her than the enjoyable affair they had already had.

If there was no other choice, she could live without him in her bed. There were plenty of energetic males in Vegas. But it really chapped her ass that Shane couldn't see what a perfect business match they were. He was the only man she had ever met who could crunch numbers as fast as she could, whether or not the computer was up and running. He could speed-read a balance sheet and know instantly if things were kosher or in the toilet. So could she.

Together they could rule Vegas.

And whoever ruled Vegas controlled the biggest little money laundry in the world. When you controlled that laundry, all kinds of delicious opportunities came knocking on your back door.

The broad, powerful figure of a Celtic warrior in full—and quite imaginary—regalia appeared out of the crowd behind Shane. As though he had eyes in the back of his head, Shane turned and took in the full effect of helmet, leather shirt, gilded metal armbands, earrings, sword, and the hairiest thighs this side of a sheep pen.

"Hi, Carl." Shane held out his hand. "Nice helmet. You swipe those horns off a Texas Cadillac?"

Carl Firenze grinned as he shook Shane's hand. "Gail

picked it out for me. Said she wanted to be able to find me in a crowd."

"Crowd, hell. She could find you in a stampede."

With a bark of laughter Gail's head of security released Shane's hand and looked toward his boss. "Call waiting for you, Ms. Gail." He checked the window of the small computer unit that kept him in touch with the most important things that were happening in the Wildest Dream. "Berlin."

It was the signal Gail had been waiting for, but suddenly she was reluctant. Even when she was positive she wouldn't ever take a certain road again, she hated burning bridges behind her.

On the plus side, she was used to it. She had set fire to more than her share of bridges on the way to her present multimillionaire status.

"Thanks, Carl." She turned to Shane. "Still no chance of becoming business partners?"

Shane took one of her perfectly manicured hands in his. He liked Gail and respected her razor-edged business mind. Yet his instincts whispered that it would be a bad match. He had learned the hard way never to go against the voice that spoke so silently somewhere inside himself.

He brushed a kiss over her scented cheek. "You know we're better as friends and competitors than we would be as partners."

She almost closed her striking hazel eyes for a moment. It could have been a lazy reassessment. It could have been regret. Either way, both ways, nothing changed. "Yeah, I suppose. It's just . . . ah, hell. Can't fight karma, can you?"

He squeezed her hand and released it. "How about

selling your gold collection to me?" he asked. "It doesn't really fit in with the Wildest Dream's fantasy theme."

"Not a chance." Gail knew her gold was the only thing that really interested Shane, but she didn't admit even to herself that was the reason she competed with him whenever a choice gold object came on the market. She wanted his attention, pure and simple. And bitter as hell.

She kissed him soundly on the lips. "Catch you later, honeylove," she said. "Gotta fix my face for an international video conference."

It was only half a lie. She definitely was going to repair her makeup before she confronted the business waiting for her.

With a bit of nostalgic regret, Shane watched Gail glide into the colorful, blaring crowd. She was a hell of a woman, but she wanted more than he had to give, and he wanted more than sex and business from his woman, which was all she had to give him. He didn't know exactly what he wanted, but he knew there had been something missing when he was with Gail.

When he heard his own thoughts, his mouth curled at one corner in a sardonic smile at his own expense. He knew just what was missing. Something in him. In her, too, he supposed.

Maybe they were a good match after all.

The voice inside him whispered that he knew better. He didn't bother to argue.

Snagging some cold shrimp from a passing server, Shane munched as he walked toward the main casino, which surrounded the lobby the way a wheel surrounds its hub. When people called out to him, he greeted them whether he recognized them or not. He didn't like the public part of being the wunderkind of Las Vegas,

"Prince Midas," the "Man with the Twenty-four Karat Luck," "Golden Boy," or whatever else the chic media tagged him whenever they needed another splashy article to separate their ads. Nor did he appreciate the endless gossipy speculation that had him sleeping with every good-looking female east of the Pacific Ocean, but he knew that the prurient interest came with the territory of being the bachelor owner of the biggest, most successful resort casino in Las Vegas.

Besides, the constant speculation about his private life was free advertising for the Golden Fleece.

The electronic unit that had descended from the old personal data assistants vibrated discreetly at his waist. Since he had turned off his normal paging number, he knew this call was urgent.

He pulled out the hand-size unit and automatically decoded the message as it scrolled across the window. It was from the pit boss who oversaw the baccarat tables. One of the Japanese "whales"—someone who could and did drop a million dollars gambling—was riding a winning streak. Six hundred thousand and counting. Did Shane want to change dealers before the shift ended in hope of breaking the whale's luck?

Shane sent back a negative reply. It had been a while since the Golden Fleece had had a big winner from Japan. In the long run, the free publicity more than paid for the losses.

Letting the party shriek and gyrate around him, he continued scanning his call log. Risa had tried to reach him several times. She wanted to talk to him, but not enough to put in the override code.

Smart lady. But then he already knew that.

He opened his e-mail and saw that the Portuguese chef was having a fit over the shellfish that the Golden

Fleece's suppliers flew in daily from various seaports around the world. Too many of the Penn Cove mussels had cracked shells. The New Zealand green mussels looked gray. The Boston clams were too big. The scallops were too small. The raw oysters tasted like snot.

Shane snickered. He had always felt that way himself about uncooked oysters. In his opinion the only thing worse than a raw oyster was a cooked one.

A flick of his thumb brought up the next message. This time it was the wine steward who was complaining. The French supplier was gouging. The Italian supplier was sending inferior labels. Napa Valley wines were too expensive for the quality. Would he consider substituting some of the fine wines from the Southern Hemisphere?

Shane bit back an impatient curse. Part of the trouble with running something like Tannahill Inc. in general and the Golden Fleece in particular was that employees worked round the clock and expected him to do the same. But unlike his employees, Shane didn't put in only one eight-hour shift per day. He put in two and then some.

He should delegate more. He knew it. He just hadn't gotten around to it.

The third message made him smile. The new firewall he had recently set up around the computer nerve center of Tannahill Inc. had not only stopped four probes cold, it had sent a lovely little virus he had designed back along the same path the hackers had used to break in. Right now at least four hackers were looking at piles of trash that had once been expensive computers.

Rot in hell, he thought cheerfully. He should have put the redesigned firewall in place months ago, but he hadn't had time. He hoped nothing important had slipped through the old firewall.

The programming/hacking skills he had learned from his father—and pursued later to get even with the bastard—often came in handy. If Shane hadn't been more interested in people than electronics, he would have dived into a computer long ago and never surfaced. There was a Zen state about creating new ways to interface human and computer that fascinated him. The only things that appealed more to his restless intelligence were the quirks and pangs of humanity as revealed in timeless, eternal golden artifacts.

"Shane!"

Automatically he put away his hand unit as he turned in answer to Risa's call. She was pushing through the crowd toward him, wearing the same clothes she had in L.A., which meant she had been as busy since they landed as he had. With the humorous recognition of one Type A+ for another, he made a mental note to tell her to delegate more.

"What are you doing here?" he asked.

"My job. You're not answering your pager."

She had also been curious as to why her boss had gone to his former lover's Halloween party. Not that she would have admitted her curiosity aloud.

Especially to him.

"I turned it off," Shane said. "In case you haven't noticed, it's past working hours, even mine. What's wrong?"

"I've been checking the provenance on that elegant gold torc you bid on."

In disbelief Shane looked at his watch. Quarter past three in the morning on Halloween, and she was checking provenance.

"It must be bad news," he said. "You never hurry with any other kind."

Impatiently Risa ran a hand through her short, tousled hair. She knew she must look as rumpled and shopworn as she felt. Unlike the maddening Mr. Tannahill, she needed more than five or six hours of sleep a night. Seven was her minimum.

"Look," she said, pitching her voice over the irritating howl of the crowd, "you hired me to check on—"

"I know why I hired you," he cut in. "Spit it out."

"The torc might have been part of the museum goods that the Germans confiscated while they occupied Paris during World War Two."

"Might have? That's the worst you can do?"

"Give me more time," she said through her teeth.

"With enough time the provenance of damn near everything in any public or private collection in the world is suspect." Yet even as he was arguing, Shane was thinking. "All right, all right. You did your job. Now do the rest of it and get me that torc."

"But—"

As Shane had expected, several people were leaning closer to hear what the infamous Prince Midas and his often-photographed curator were arguing about.

"Provenance is only as good as the paper it's printed on," he said distinctly. "Show me the paper that says the torc was looted by Nazis from a French museum."

"I don't have any paper."

"Then don't waste my time. Possession *is* nine-tenths of the law, remember?"

"What if I find proof after you buy the torc?" she demanded.

"First find the proof. If you can."

From the corner of his eye Shane registered the knowing looks passing among the eavesdroppers. Along with the other headlines he had made, the Strip's premier poster boy had picked up some well-chosen blots on his reputation. He was rumored to buy gold goods of doubtful provenance. Hot enough to burn his hands, if you believed gossip.

Most people did.

Including, Shane suspected, his curator.

The thought both amused and irritated him. The amusement he understood. The irritation he didn't. With the exception of two or three people, he didn't give a damn what the world thought of him. He didn't like the idea that somehow, against every intention and shred of common sense he possessed, Risa had become one of the people whose opinion mattered to him.

His hand slid around her elbow in what looked like the polite gesture of an escort helping his date through heavy traffic. Risa felt the steely strength of his fingers and knew better.

He bent close and said in her ear, "Let's finish this in private. Or was it your plan to stand around and sling mud at my reputation in the most public place in Las Vegas?"

Red flared along her cheekbones—anger, not embarrassment. "Listen, Golden Boy, it's my reputation, too. I work for you."

"That could be remedied."

With an angry Risa in tow, Shane headed for the sliding walkways that connected the Wildest Dream and three other megacasinos. One of those was the Golden Fleece.

Six

When Gail Silverado opened the door of her private office, she was reminded that Las Vegas and Hollywood had two things in common. The first was that, one way or another, people gambled a lot of money. The second was that women had a place, and it was on their back beneath men. A few women managed to claw their way into the top position, but not many.

That was why Gail was the only woman at the meeting of the most powerful people in the Las Vegas casino industry—minus Shane Tannahill, of course. He was the reason for the meeting in the first place.

Prince Midas just wasn't a team player.

That made life unnecessarily difficult for the rest of the megacasinos in town. Instead of dividing the gambling industry among themselves for the greater profit of all, Shane had introduced a costly element of honesty and balls-out competition for customers. He was winning, too. As a result, the new kid on the Strip was by far the biggest earner in Vegas.

For the first year Gail hadn't particularly minded the

competition. She had been tied at a healthy second place. But now she was sliding into third place, and she had an expensive remodeling scheduled. That kind of outlay made stockholders nervous. Since she held only 45 percent of the Wildest Dream's stock, she had to start turning a higher profit or look for another job.

"Good evening, gentlemen," Gail said as she closed the door behind her and looked at her four guests. "Or should I say good morning?"

The men scattered around her plush office were in costume to the point that they wouldn't have been recognized by their employees or closest enemies, which was the whole idea.

French Henkle, manager of Say Paris!, was wearing the drab robes of a Franciscan monk. He had taken off his burlap mask and tossed the cowl back to reveal his thick blond hair. He was tapping the mask idly against the red Italian leather couch he was sitting on. At thirty-two he was the youngest man in the room and the only one with children. Shane Tannahill, along the way to becoming the most successful man in Vegas, had bankrupted French's father. If French resented or applauded what had happened years ago, he hadn't told anyone.

The man sitting closest to French was John Firenze, who was dressed like a magician—or maybe he was supposed to be Zorro. It was hard to be certain of anything except that the costume hid everything relevant to his identity. John was Carl's uncle, divorced, no children, and the CEO of Roman Circus, one of the first wave of huge resort casinos built in Vegas. Though the place had been revamped three times in the past thirty years, it never seemed to really click with the big money crowd. Roman Circus wasn't a downscale grind joint by any means, but it wasn't a primary destination for the national or international whales. Indelibly blue-collar, Roman Circus still made most of its money on slot machines and "feather shows" featuring women wearing nothing else.

Sitting alone, Mickey Pinsky was dressed like a hooker in skyscraper heels, a high-necked purple silk shimmy dress, major breast and butt prostheses, and a platinum wig that added inches to his height. Minus the costume and makeup, he looked like the graying world-class jockey he had been before his horse rolled over on him just out of the starting gate. Three times divorced, rumored to be hung like a mule and just as sterile, he represented the owners of a handful of "family resorts" that had bet serious money that family entertainment à la Disney World would be the coming thing in Vegas.

Pinsky and his backers had learned the painful way that you make more money on liquor, slots, and sophisticated big-city shows than you do on bubble gum, skateboard contests, and apple pie. At huge cost the entertainment complexes had resurrected themselves a few years ago as "destination resorts" for singles who were feeling lucky. Pinsky's bottom line was showing small signs of life, but he was still swimming hard to keep his head above the swamp of his past mistakes. Anything that sent some of the Golden Fleece's standing-room-only action in his direction would be fine with him.

The most powerful man in the room was also the oldest. At fifty-eight, Richard ("call me Rich") Morrison, had been on and off the marriage-go-round four times. His present wife was a rich Texas bitch with political credentials that Rich was putting to good use. Tonight he went against type and dressed like a hippie. He was almost trim enough to carry it off. The shoulder-length black rasta wig he wore wasn't quite 1960s, but it covered his own short silver hair admirably. A full and fully fake beard did the same for the rest of his recognizable features.

Rich was president and CEO of Shamrock, the resort casino that was currently tied for second in the Las Vegas profits race. He had tangled with Shane years ago on a business and a professional level. Rich had lost both ways. He hadn't liked it then. He didn't like it now. But tonight he was here for business. Nothing personal. If that same business chewed up Golden Boy and spit him out like a bad taste . . . well, sometimes you got lucky. Rich's only concern was that Gail had been reluctant to play her part in setting up Tannahil. Tonight he would see if she was still dragging her feet.

"Since you're all still here," Gail said, "I assume you decided that nothing is being recorded by me."

A variety of grunts and grumbles answered her. The men sure as hell knew that they weren't doing any recording of their own. None of them had liked being searched by Carl, but they had held still for it. No one wanted to be featured in a headline that shouted VEGAS BIGGIES CAUGHT ON TAPE CONSPIRING AGAINST PRINCE MIDAS.

Especially since a federal task force had been all over the big casinos like a rash, looking for dirty money from the Red Phoenix triad. The group had a lot of cash to launder. Rich—and, he hoped, Gail—was ready to help, but neither one of them wanted to get caught by the feds.

That was why Rich had organized this meeting.

"Anyone care to search me just to be sure?" Gail asked, holding her arms over her head. With the grace of the dancer she once had been, she turned slowly, insolently, in front of the seated men.

Rich looked at the tight dress and abundant curves

and was tempted to put his hands on her just for the hell of it. So were the other men. But no one got up.

"You have more to lose in this than we do," Rich said. "You're making more than most of us."

"And a lot less than Tannahill," she retorted. Tossing aside her mask, she leaned her glittering backside against the crescent-shaped black steel desk. She gave Rich a level look from eyes that had seen it all and done it twice. "This meeting was your idea. Deal the cards."

"I have a plan for breaking Shane Tannahill."

"So do I," Firenze muttered. "One bone at a time."

Henkle rolled his eyes. "Jesus, not another chorus of the good old days. They're gone, John. Shit, you're too young to even remember when the Mob ruled Vegas. Only Rich is old enough, and he wasn't even—"

"Shut up, French," Mickey Pinsky cut in mildly. "Let's hear what Rich has to say."

Henkle smiled and mimicked putting tape across his mouth.

"Every man has a weakness," Rich said. "Tannahill's is gold artifacts. He's all wrapped up in this new show he's going to open New Year's Eve to take the steam out of the Wildest Dream's Fabergé show."

"So?" Firenze challenged.

"It's not going well for Golden Boy," Rich said. "He's still looking to buy stuff. Gail has been getting in his way a lot, beating him to some really good pieces, buying before he even knows anything is on the market."

Gail's expression didn't change, but she wondered how Rich knew so much about what she had thought was her private competition with Shane. "What does that get us?" she asked.

"While he's chasing gold, he's not watching business

as close as he usually does. With a little nudge from us, he might get careless."

"How careless?"

"Careless enough to be set up for the feds on a one-two punch. First we see that he gets caught with hot gold artifacts."

"How do we do that?" Pinsky asked, smiling, liking what he was hearing.

"Gail should have a few ideas," Rich said blandly. "Some of the places she bought gold objects weren't exactly legal. They should know how to get more."

Her eyes narrowed at the extent of Rich's knowledge, but she nodded agreement. "I've thought of sticking Shane with some hot stuff, but his curator is a lot more rigid than his reputation suggests. Everyone talks about how Shane buys shady goods, but no one can nail him at it and no one will as long as she has the inside track."

It was Rich's turn to be surprised. "What's her name?"

"Risa Sheridan."

"I'll look into her. When we get a twist on her, we have leverage on him."

"Fine," Gail said impatiently, "but even if Shane is caught with burn marks from hot goods, he'll never get arrested, much less go to jail. He's had his hands smacked before. He just returns the goods, takes the loss, and keeps on hammering our casinos into the ground."

"Why wouldn't he be arrested?" Henkle asked.

She gave him a pitying glance. "You do remember what Shane's real last name is, don't you?"

Henkle blinked. "Uh, no."

"Chrissake, French, don't you ever tune in to anything but the porn channels?" Pinsky muttered.

"What does that have to do with—" Henkle began.

"Merit is Shane's last name," Gail interrupted curtly. "Tannahill is his mother's maiden name."

Henkle looked blank, then pained. "Yeah, now I remember. He's related to *the* Merit, as in Sebastian Merit."

"Jackpot," she said with a slicing smile. "Shane is Merit's kid. His only kid. Ain't no way in heaven or hell that America's premier billionaire would let his kid go to jail, even if they supposedly haven't spoken for years. Unless yelling at your son in public that he'll come crawling on his hands and knees, begging to be taken back in the family, counts as conversation."

Rich smiled thinly. That threat had made headlines around the world and fodder for tabloids and gossip news on Father's Day, when everyone dusted off the clip of Merit cussing his son out in public.

"Well, shit," Henkle said, frowning. "If Shane has all that money, why did he bankrupt the Blue Mare on his way to making a few million? He could have bought Daddy's casino outright for what Merit keeps in his safe at home."

"Shane walked away from his family money," Rich said, rubbing his scalp beneath the itchy wig. "Apparently the price of putting up with Bastard Merit was just too high. But some things breed true. Tannahill got a full helping of his father's business genius and a good share of the hard-ass, too."

"That's the rest of the reason why hot gold artifacts aren't enough to bring Shane down," Gail said. "He's not going to run away and hide from some bad press. All the publicity would probably just increase traffic through the Golden Fleece. Tourists love to think they're rubbing elbows with real live crooks. Hell, most of the people downstairs swilling free champagne believe we're all part of the Mob."

"Still, getting caught dirty would take a lot of the shine off Tannahill's Golden Boy image," Pinsky argued. "The press will shit on him instead of sucking up."

"He'll survive," she said flatly.

Rich nodded his agreement that bad press alone wouldn't get Tannahill out of their hair.

"You talked about a one-two punch," Firenze said to Rich. "What's the knockout?"

"Between us screwing up his big gold show and sticking him with some hot goods," Rich said, "Tannahill will be too busy to notice what's really happening."

"Yeah? What's that?"

"That's what he'll be saying when the feds swoop down and indict him for money laundering."

Gail shook her head. "He doesn't."

Rich smiled like the shark he was. "And I'm not a hippie. But if it walks like a duck and it talks like a duck, it's fair game during hunting season."

She looked at Rich with new interest. "I'm listening."

So were the rest of them.

Seven

SEDONA
HALLOWEEN NIGHT

Headlights jerked and bobbed. The ten-year-old Ford Bronco was making heavy work of the unpaved road. The ruts wound up a dry ravine that fed water into Beaver Creek when there was enough rain. There hadn't been lately. Runoff from autumn storms had barely slicked the streambed with mud.

As though squeezed out by the weight of the harvest moon, shadows flowed from every rock and hollow. Sycamores loomed up out of the night like white-skinned ghosts. A stone became a huge tooth poking through the sun-hardened dirt of the road.

"Watch it!" Tim shouted.

Cherelle was already swinging the wheel to miss the ragged rock. She had been up old man O'Conner's "driveway" often enough in the last six months that she had every stone and rut memorized.

Even so, the Bronco lurched and swayed hard enough to snap Tim's teeth together.

"Chrissake," Tim complained. "Slow down."

"He said four hundred if we got there before dawn."

"We'll be dead before then," Tim muttered, thinking his voice was too low for Cherelle to hear.

She heard it anyway. "Look, get it through that beautiful thick head of yours that we need money. The printer is yelling at us to pay for the pamphlets and business cards he ran off for us. Our credit cards are maxed, and no one is mailing us any new ones. The tires on this piece of shit are bald. The rent is overdue. We have a quarter tank of gas."

Tim made *yada-yada-yada* sounds.

"Virgil has money," Cherelle continued. "Cash in hand. If he wants us before dawn, we get there before dawn."

Tim yawned widely. "Y'know, lately you're sure pissy when you get into your channel role. Lighten up."

She wished she could. But she couldn't. It had gotten so that every time she pulled on her white channeling outfit with its long filmy shirt and skirt, her palms got cold and her heart started to beat too fast, like when she used to boost stuff from the convenience store back home as a kid. An adrenaline roller-coaster ride, fear and exhilaration combined.

She didn't mind that part. What she minded was the dead-cold scaries, the way her nightmares made her feel. Channeling was getting to her. Seeing too much. Hearing too much. Feeling too much.

It was one thing to run a con on the dumbs. It was a whole other thing to feel like the con was real.

Not all-the-time real. Just some of it.

And with Virgil, most of it.

Voices whispering. Chanting. Screaming. Fires burning and knives dripping blood.

Christ Jesus, it was enough to send her whimpering back to the nuns who had done their best to terrorize her into being a good little girl all those years ago.

Unhappily Cherelle decided that she was getting to be as crazy as Virgil. Maybe it was catching, like herpes.

The Bronco hit a pothole so hard that Tim whacked his head against the passenger window. "What in hell do you—" he began.

"Shut up," Cherelle cut in savagely. "You're not the one who has to do it. You just stand around and look smart and pretty and make nice with the females. I'm the one sleeping with the devil and hearing all the screams of the damned."

Tim gave her a startled, sideways look. "Uh, you feeling all right, Cher?"

"Fucking fantastic, why?" she asked through her teeth.

"You've been acting weird."

"Well, ding-dong, we have a big ol' winner. I'm a channel, remember? I'm supposed to act weird."

"You're doing a hell of a job of it."

She had started to tell him just what she thought of his half-wit, shit-for-brains comments when she spotted the glow of light from the old man's house. Fiercely she clenched her fingers around the steering wheel and gunned down the bumpy driveway.

There was barely the smallest hint of color along the eastern horizon when she got out, slammed the car door, and gulped air. Without waiting for Tim, she started up the dirt path lined with colorful river cobbles that looked black in the darkness. There was one light on in the old house. The position told her it was the living room, which often as not served as the old man's bedroom. He spent as much time pacing as sleeping.

The front door opened before Cherelle was halfway to

the house. Golden light licked out toward her like a rectangular tongue. With the determination of an actress stepping into the spotlight, she pulled her role more tightly around her.

Showtime.

A gaunt, angular man who was barely taller than Cherelle's five and a half feet stalked stiffly toward her. As usual, Virgil was wearing several old shirts, one over the other. On top of that he had on his customary flapping black jacket, army-surplus pants from the days when uniforms were still made of wool, and boots that were as hard and gritty as the ground itself. The only thing unexpected about him was the cheap wooden box he carried under one arm.

Before she could open her mouth to offer a bland, peaceful greeting, he shoved a wad of cash into her hand.

"Four hundred," he said.

It would have broken the mood to stop and count the cash. Besides, Virgil had never stiffed them with a payment. So Cherelle murmured something that could have meant anything and passed the wad off to Tim, who had just caught up with her.

"I see the need is very strong in you tonight," she said to Virgil. Then she bit the inside of her mouth to keep from laughing out loud. When you got right down to it, there wasn't much difference between hooking and channeling. In both jobs the whole point was to make the mark feel good no matter how pathetic he actually was. "Would you be more comfortable inside?" she asked without real hope.

"No good inside," he said impatiently. "Let's move on. Dawn's coming sure as hell."

Even before he finished talking, Virgil set off up the

rise behind his cabin. The steeply sloping, rugged trail led to the base of a bluff that was a wide swath of black against the stars and moon. His steps were short but not hesitant. He didn't bother with the pencil flashlight in his jacket pocket. He knew the way to the vortex spot Lady Faulkner had discovered on his property. At least, he let her think she had discovered it. He had led her there and then waited, seeing if she would pass the test. None of the others had.

Lady Faulkner did.

She knew right off he had himself a vortex place. A whacking good one, too. She told him she felt it like electricity the first time she touched the three big red rocks on the ridgetop. Like three men standing—leaning drunkenly, if you want the truth—the stones huddled at the base of a much bigger, much taller sandstone cliff that ran for several miles along a tiny creek.

Back when he had first moved here, he had poked around the ragged cliff face. He found old broken pottery, fallen-down walls, and mounds of stones that had once been houses. But he didn't go prowling anymore. It was hard getting around, and the ghosts in those places had nothing to tell him that he didn't already know.

People died. No one cared.

Eight

Grateful for the bright moon, Cherelle followed the old man's footsteps. Her white clothes shimmered in the moonlight. The skirt and loose blouse lifted and swirled and billowed at the least hint of movement. Nice and atmospheric for the dumbs, but the clothes didn't give her nearly enough warmth for predawn in the high cedar scrub forest around Sedona.

She had been going for angelic with her costume but had landed closer to winding sheets and goblins. God knew she felt cold enough to be a corpse. Her skin had roughened like the hair along a junkyard dog's spine at the sight of a thief. Cursing silently, she rubbed her palms over her arms and wondered if Tim had remembered to bring a jacket. She doubted it. He was worse than a kid. If she didn't think of it, it didn't get done.

She was fed up with being mama-chick to every pretty baby-chick she stumbled over.

Silently she reminded herself that being poor wouldn't last forever. Sooner or later she would make the big ol' score that was waiting for her. She didn't know what it would be, she just knew that it *had* to be. She wasn't going to spend her whole life one bad break away from turning tricks again. She had too many brains for that.

She was the one who had figured out that there was money in the channeling gig after Tim came back from an all-expenses-paid sex holiday in Sedona with a fistfull of cash and a lot of lame one-liners about talking to ghosts. It had taken a year and more work than either of them liked, but she and her pretty boy-chick had put together a channeling business. Not a great one. Not a lousy one. Just a business.

Everything had been going okay until Tim's old jailhouse buddy had showed up. Socks was a real pain in the ass. He kept wanting Tim to play when there was work to be done.

Not that she blamed Tim. This working all the time was for the dumbs. What kept her at it was the belief that someday soon one of the morons who came to Sedona looking for a vortex thrill would be a man rich enough to take care of her and young enough to still get it up. When that happened, Tim and the stupid channeling con were history. Or maybe Tim would get lucky first and find himself a nice rich old lady who believed in talking to Thunderballs or whoever the flavor of the day was. Then Cherelle could live off Tim while she looked over the old lady's rich male friends.

Thinking of that day was almost as good as doing crack cocaine. Both made her feel like she could fly. One day she would. She'd just step off the edge and fly and fly and fly.

Smiling, dreaming, Cherelle bumped into Virgil. She would have fallen against him if one of his thin, surprisingly strong hands hadn't clamped around her arm to steady her. Even with that help she had to brace herself on one palm against the cold surface of a man-high stone. Instantly she snatched back her hand as though she had touched a live rattlesnake. She hated those stones with a passion that came straight from fear.

"Thank you," she said in a low voice. "The energy is so strong here that I forget about the normal world." *Goddamn path could use a few lights, too.* But she kept that nonvortex insight to herself.

Tim came up behind her. "Everything okay?"

"Everything is perfect," she said, shivering and lying through her locked teeth.

She couldn't dream away the clenching of her stomach any longer, or ignore the cold slide of sweat down her spine. She had nearly peed her pants in raw kindergarten terror the first time Virgil had led her to this place. She didn't know what waited in the shadows between the three stones, but she knew to the bottom of her feet that she didn't want any part of it.

She watched Tim go over and lean against one of the big stones, waiting for her to get on with the act. He no more felt anything than the rock did. Less, probably.

The boy was beautiful and could fuck her blind, but he had the IQ of hominy grits.

Virgil gave her a little shake. "Dawn's coming, Lady Faulkner."

"Of course." Belatedly she realized that Virgil was no longer holding the wooden box. She looked around, then jerked. The box was in the center of the ragged circle made by the stones. Some trick of moonlight was making the cracks between the slats glow. "What—" she began, then cut off her own words. Scammers didn't ask the dumbs any questions. "I presume you wish to speak with Merlin."

"You got that right."

Mother Mary, not again. Cherelle bit back her irritation at doing the same old same old one more time. She wondered if that was how Broadway stars felt when they repeated the same performance night after night after night and twice on Wednesday and Saturday.

"Many people wish to communicate with Merlin," she forced herself to say calmly. "As we have discovered, he rarely wishes to communicate with them."

"Hell, I know that. Had more than one so-called channel claim he had a direct pipeline. It was crap. Not a one of them could tell me what was in the boxes under my bed."

When Cherelle understood what Virgil meant, she wanted to scream. He was after a mind-reading act, not a chat with a mythical magician.

And she was no mind reader.

"Someone else in Arthur's court would be eas—" she began.

"Merlin," Virgil cut in. "He's the only one with the power. Let's go. We're wasting time. It has to be before dawn, when they're all shooed back to hell."

For a moment Cherelle didn't know what he was talking about. Then she remembered it was Halloween, when spirits supposedly were let out after dark and then harried back into their dank holes at daybreak. She wondered if he also believed in flying broomsticks and dancing toadstools.

She bit the inside of her mouth again, forcing herself not to laugh in the old man's face.

"Mr. O'Conner has a point," Tim said, smiling.

Only Cherelle saw malice in the beautiful curve of her lover's lips.

That was one of the problems with being smart in a

world full of dumbs. You saw too much and most of the time couldn't do squat about it.

Tim barely smothered his yawn.

She wanted to kick him in his ever-ready balls. He always left it all up to her. She had to carry off the whole channeling act with him yawning in her face.

"Of course." Cherelle's voice was smooth despite her anger and the constant prickling of gooseflesh on her body.

She really hated this place. Somehow she had to figure out what was in the boxes under Virgil's bed, and then she could "channel" it to him straight from Merlin and get the hell out of here.

She shuddered. She couldn't wait to see this creepy place in her rearview mirror for the last time.

With a toss of her head that sent her pale, elbow-length hair flying, Cherelle stepped around the wooden box until she stood in the small area at the center of the three rocks. And she damned her overactive imagination for making it feel darker and colder between the stones, empty, bottomless, like she was falling down a well.

She had done that once as a kid. It wasn't one of her favorite memories. Lately channeling always reminded her of it. It was making her sick to her stomach.

Screw the past, she told herself. *I got out of that trailer park, and I'm on my way to real money. No motel clerk with bad breath and dirty hands will ever look me over and ask for cash up front or a blow job behind the counter.*

All she needed was one good break and she would be set for life. She wouldn't blow all her money like a dumb. She was way too smart for that.

One good score.

Just one.

Holding on to her dream with every bit of her determination, Cherelle ignored the sickening lurch of her stomach. She forced herself to close her eyes and go into her channeling performance. Gradually she changed her breathing, deepened it, held it until she was almost dizzy, and slowly, slowly let it trickle out between her teeth. Most people did the channeling gig sitting down, but she had never liked putting her butt on bare ground. The one time she had brought a blanket to sit on, her ass had started itching like she was on a nest of fire ants.

So she stood up and breathed in and out, in and out, until the sound of her own breathing became a kind of liquid rushing, a whispering of phrases that described a shaft of white light flooding down on her, sheathing her, surrounding her, telling her . . .

Come on, come on, Virgil thought with an impatient glance at the eastern horizon. *Get the damned channel open.*

This was the hardest part of the whole process for him. Waiting, waiting, waiting to find out if it was going to happen tonight, if he was finally going to be free of the Druid curse that had ruined everything he touched since he first found the treasure. He never should have believed his great-uncle, never should have gone to Wales, never should have dug up the damned gold. Nothing but grief. Not one damn thing.

". . . sense a presence," she said in a low voice that wasn't like her normal one. "Come closer, spirit. We wish no evil, ask nothing forbidden. We simply seek to . . ."

Pushing back a yawn with his fist, Tim tuned out Cherelle's patter. He never could figure out why she hated doing her act at this pile of rocks so much. Day or night, rock piles or classy condos, the gig was always the same. She put on her ghost outfit, muttered a lot, told the dumbs what they wanted to hear, and then went home with enough money to pay the rent and buy some beer. Big deal. He would do it himself, but he couldn't stop snickering long enough. Talking to Merlin or Melchizedek or Marilyn Monroe—what bullshit.

He clenched his teeth around another yawn. Man, this getting up in the middle of the night wasn't for him. That was one of the reasons he had never made it as a full-time burglar. Too much like work. At least the channeling scam was easier than prowling apartments, and it didn't bring the cops down on your ass.

Nobody had passed any laws against helping dumbs be as dumb as they could be.

He shoved his hands into his pockets and wished Cherelle had told him to bring a jacket. There wasn't much wind, but it was enough to make him shiver from time to time. Glumly he eyed the wooden box, blinked, and blinked again. Then he wondered when the crazy old fart had turned on his little flashlight and stuck it in the closed box. And why. Hell of a way to waste batteries, and batteries cost damn near as much as cigarettes.

". . . feel you, but I can't hear you," Cherelle whispered. "I sense how powerful you are. Please help me."

Tim swallowed a snort of laughter. As soon as they got off this shitty piece of rock, he would give her something to feel and something to hear, too. He had a heavy load to get rid of.

". . . don't know what Virgil wants," she said clearly. "Do you?"

The old man tensed and leaned forward. *Merlin knew just what he wanted.*

"Ah, of course," she murmured. "He has something of yours." The words stopped. Her teeth snapped together. She jerked once, twice, and then shivered from her head to her heels.

"Too dark," she said urgently. "Can't hear you. You're taking the light! Please, please help us!"

Virgil waited so tightly that he was afraid his bones would snap. She must be getting close. Never before had she sounded so . . .

Scared.

"Can't—hear—you," she said jerkily. "Please help me. Please. We mean no harm and want nothing forbidden. Help me clear the channel, Merlin. Help—me."

Virgil didn't wait to hear any more. This session was going the same way as the others, right into the toilet. With a few quick movements he took worn leather work gloves out of his back pocket and yanked them on. He had hoped it wouldn't come to this.

But it had.

She would get a clear channel now, tonight. He would make sure of it.

Eyes closed, Cherelle fought down the scream that kept wanting to climb up the clenched darkness of her throat. Each time she came here, it was worse. Now she felt like she was two people, one of them watching in amusement and the other one a terrified child wanting to run to Mommy. But there was no Mommy. There never had been. There was only darkness and fear and the kind of trapped-animal rage that made her want to—

A piece of metal so cold that it burned smacked down across her palm. Light and dark exploded into something that was both and neither. It was everything.

And then it was nothing.

She was nothing.

Nine

Cherelle was still screaming when Tim backhanded her hard enough to send her staggering out of the shadow of the three leaning stones. She stumbled and went to her knees. Shaking, bent over, she bit back the bile that was clawing up her throat along with all the screams she had spent a lifetime throttling.

"When you finally lose it, you really lose it," Tim said, eyeing her warily. He bent over, picked up the thick gold neckring Virgil had given to Cherelle, shoved it in the wooden box, and slammed on the lid. "C'mon. We gotta get out of here before it's light enough for people to see us."

"What . . . ?" She looked up, shook her head sharply, and glanced around. "Where's Virgil?"

"Where do you think? You hit him hard enough to knock him halfway down the trail." He dragged her upright. "Why'd you do it?"

She shook her head again, but nothing made sense. "Do what?"

"Kill him."

"I didn't!"

"Hell you didn't. I saw it. He handed you that chunk of gold, and you knocked him ass over teakettle."

"Chunk of gold? What the hell are you talking about?"

Impatiently Tim reached beneath the wooden lid and jerked out a thick circle of gold. The light of dawn flowed over the braided chains of metal, light flowed around gold, into it.

And it glowed.

"This," he said, shoving the gold under her nose.

Slowly Cherelle focused on the neckring. Her eyes widened. She had seen pictures of jewelry kind of like this in one of Virgil's old books. It was the sort of stuff museums loved, which meant it was worth money.

Maybe a lot of it.

Tim dropped the gold back beneath the wooden lid, put his hand between her shoulder blades, and shoved.

"C'mon. We gotta get out of here."

Together they hurried down the steep, narrow trail. All around them the first spears of daybreak were pushing away the darkness. The sunrise didn't make Cherelle feel much better. Between the fingers of bright light, stark pools of shadow remained. They were blacker than the bottom of a well.

"You sure about Virgil?" she asked.

Tim dragged her off the path, through the brush, and turned on the old man's pencil light. "What do you think?"

Pinned by the narrow beam, Virgil lay in a pool of shadow. He was on his back, eyes open, staring at the dawn he would never see. Brush surrounded him.

"I think he's dead," Cherelle said as she edged back toward the path.

One way or another, Tim had seen enough sudden death to know exactly what it looked like. "Oh, yeah. He's meat."

She blew out a hard breath and forced herself to think. *She really had killed Virgil.*

Shit.

On the other hand, he wasn't the first. She had skated on that other one. Cops wrote it off to a drug buy gone bad. She would skate on Virgil, too. Besides, she hadn't meant it, not really, not either time. It had just happened.

And by the time anyone stumbled over the body, there wouldn't be much left. Coyotes howled from every ridge and prowled all the shadows for food.

Oh, yeah. He's meat.

"What else is in the box?" Cherelle asked.

"Nothing. C'mon."

"There's gotta be something else. I know it."

"There's cops, that's what. You want to be caught with a corpse, you go ahead and hang around. Me, I'm gone."

"Wait. There's gold. Goddamn it, there's more gold!"

He started to tell her she was nuts, saw the flat look around her eyes and mouth, and knew she wouldn't listen to what he said.

Fine. Fuck her.

Tim headed off down the rest of the trail without looking back.

"Boxes," she muttered to herself. "Virgil said something about boxes. What was it? Think, damn it, think!"

Not one of them could tell me what was in the boxes under my bed.

Under his bed.

Cherelle took off down the trail, passed Tim, and kept going with a speed that left him scrambling. The front door to Virgil's cabin was unlocked. As far as she knew, it always had been. A man who rode an old bicycle to town and wore clothes a ragpicker wouldn't own didn't have any reason to lock his door.

She shouldered her way through the opening and went straight to the bedroom just off the living room. From the look of the bed, he hadn't slept in it last night. He wouldn't tonight either, unless death was another kind of sleep.

That thought was too close to her nightmares when she was surrounded by black nothing and yet still awake, still aware, screaming. With grim haste she went down on her hands and knees and peered under the bed. Shoes, a tangle of cloth that could have been underwear or a washrag, dust.

And two wooden boxes.

She pulled out the first one, opened it just enough to see the gleam of gold, and slammed it closed.

"What the hell do you think you're doing?" Tim said from the doorway. All he could see was Cherelle down on her hands and knees with her head under something and her ass sticking up in the air. "I've burgled enough places to tell you that you're wasting your time here. Chrissake, he didn't even wear a watch."

"Wasting my time, huh?" Cherelle asked. She lifted the lid of the second carton, caught her breath, and smiled. "Well, you waste time your way and I'll waste time my way."

She stacked the cartons on top of each other and lifted them. She had to make two tries before she could stand. The boxes of gold weren't as big as her greed, but they were plenty heavy.

Throwing back her head, she laughed and staggered toward the door. Finally, finally she had done it.

The big score.

Now all she had to do was figure out how to turn hot gold into cold cash without getting burned along the way.

Ten

With well-concealed impatience—her feet were screaming—Gail Silverado said her good-byes to Mickey Pinsky and John Firenze, French Henkle, and Rich Morrison. When Rich hung back from the other three, she gave him a dazzling smile.

"Forget something?" she asked.

"Just to call my wife, and I forgot my cell phone." He smiled slightly. "Would you mind if I used yours? I don't know which party to meet her at."

"Not at all. Good night, gentlemen. I'd suggest you take separate elevators."

She shut the door to her outer office on the other three men and turned to Rich. Saying nothing, she walked to her private office and closed the door after him.

"Did you really forget your cell phone?" she asked.

"What do you think?"

"I think I have some champagne on ice if you have something worth celebrating."

He laughed and regretted again that his present wife

with her very important political connections had made it clear that if he screwed around, she would cut off his cock and feed it to him. He knew that his cock was safe enough from her threat, but his chance to be head of the Nevada Gaming Control Board wasn't. He wanted power more than he wanted a piece of ass—even a very talented piece like Gail.

"I heard from my business associates earlier today," he said.

Gail kept walking toward the champagne in her office fridge. "Good news?"

"Golden Boy finally got around to putting in a new firewall."

She stopped and looked over her shoulder. Her pose was as elegant as it was unconscious. "Not good."

Rich scratched under his obnoxious wig. How women wore the damn things was beyond him. "Not bad, either. They had finished the setup and were just feeding in money from a Shanghai account every day into his hold for the slots and the baccarat tables."

"How much did they plant before they were shut down?"

"Ten million. Maybe fifteen." Rich shrugged. "Chump change, compared to what they're waiting to run through our casinos, but it will be enough to hang Tannahill. He probably won't do jail time, but the Gaming Control Board won't ever let him into Nevada again."

Gail bent, opened the fridge beneath the bar, and pulled out a bottle of Cristal. "You sure they left enough tracks to trace the money back to Red Phoenix accounts?"

"Hell yes. These boys were trained by the best hackers the U.S. had to offer. Tannahill has been paying state and federal taxes on that triad money for weeks and keeping the rest for himself as pure, sparkling-clean profit."

With an expert twist, Gail pulled the cork and inhaled the fragrant mist that rose from the bottle. "Then we have him." She poured two glasses of the fine champagne and handed one to Rich. "The only question is when we drop the hammer."

"I've put out a few anonymous feelers to the federal task force on the Red Phoenix triad. It shouldn't be too long. Eventually even the feds catch on."

The glasses met with a musical sound.

Eleven

Most of the big hotel/casinos had a focus in their lobby to lure and entertain walk-ins. The least imaginative of the resorts had gigantic floral arrangements. Others had an aquarium twenty feet high and sixty feet wide, or a chlorine-scented river sparkling with coins the guests had tossed in, or glass flowers growing out of a ceiling as long as a football field.

The Golden Fleece had . . . a golden fleece. A spectacular one. No matter what the time of day or night, there was always a wide-eyed crowd gathered around Shane's replica of the mythical gold sheepskin that had sent many an ancient treasure hunter on a chase to the ends of the known world.

With the soul of a poet welded to that of a pragmatist, Shane believed that the myth of the fleece had its roots in ordinary reality. Ancient gold miners had washed gold-bearing gravel in wooden sluice boxes. By the time the gravel reached the end of the sluice, everything heavy had dropped out of the water. Except the gold dust. It would have kept on flowing out with the waste water, and out of the miners' pockets, but for the sheepskin at the bottom of the sluice. At the end of a day's or a week's work, the miners shut down the sluice and shook out the gold dust that the fleece had collected from the rushing water.

As a centerpiece and crowd magnet for his new mega-resort/casino, Shane had bought the biggest sheepskin available and designed a sluice box such as might have been used for mining gold two thousand years ago. He had stretched the sheepskin crosswise to the water's flow so that the fleece would comb out the bucket of gold dust he had poured into the clean water. Then he put it all inside a big aquarium, turned on the pumps, and waited.

Through the minutes, hours, days, weeks, the sheepskin tirelessly filtered the almost invisibly fine gold from the water. When the fleece could hold no more gold in its dense wool, it glittered like a fantastic dream just beyond the reach of man.

And there it stayed suspended in a cage of clear water, a great shaggy sculpture of gold just waiting to launch new generations of treasure hunters into the Golden Fleece's casinos.

"Good morning, Mr. Tannahill."

Shane turned toward Susan Chatsworth, one of his four executive assistants. A former police officer, she was his liaison with the security department. Because she had school-age children, she took the day watch at his casino. Her husband, a captain on the Las Vegas police force, worked swing shift, yet somehow they managed a good marriage.

Susan wasn't in uniform, unless Las Vegas Casual could be considered a uniform. With her frothy shoulder-length brown hair, silk shirt, jeans, and strappy sandals, she looked like a guest who just happened to carry a big purse along with her big smile. Inside the purse her walkie-talkie, cell phone–computer link, and gun stayed safely out of sight.

"Morning, Susan," Shane said. "Have you combed the ice cream out of your rug yet?"

She laughed and shook her head. "It was quite a party. I'd forgotten how much noise a group of squealing twelve-year-old girls can make. And thank you— Amelia loved the CD you gave her for her birthday. How did you know that every preteen girl's secret desire is to shriek along with Swivel Jack and the Sweat Rats?"

"A wild guess."

Susan shook her head. She knew better. Her boss was anything but a wild guesser. "She told me to give you a kiss and a hug, so consider yourself kissed and hugged."

"Good way to start the day."

He began walking. She fell in beside him. Shane's unpredictable rounds through his huge entertainment complex were famous among the staff. Whether the toilet or VIP lounge, at any time—day or night, holiday or workday—Shane could and did appear. If his stone green eyes missed anything, no one had figured yet what it was.

"Any urgent problem areas?" He didn't look at her while he asked the question. All his attention was on the lobby activity, the check-in and check-out lines, the VIP escorts, the crowd around the glittering fleece, and the empty paper cup that better not be on one of the lobby's coffee tables when he came back.

"Just one at the moment," Susan said. "I don't know if you've gone over yesterday's hold yet."

"I have." Examining the hold—the gross profit the casino earned in twenty-four hours—was the first thing

Shane did every morning, even on the mornings when he had been up most of the night.

"Then you know we had six big jackpots yesterday on the wall of Solid Gold Slots."

"Yes." That was improbable, but not impossible. Gambling was a game of odds. Odds were quirky in the short run and utterly reliable in the long run.

"I went over the tapes," she said, referring to the digital record that was made of everything that went on at the casino. "I suspect we're getting hosed by a techno-team."

Shane made a note to look at the recordings himself. "Electronic? Magnetic? Mechanical?"

"I'd bet on a magnetic reset of the payoff."

He grunted. No matter how carefully they shielded the "brain" of a slot machine, some techno-geek could always find a way in—especially one who had worked on the casino's slot programs in the past.

He would have to check his personnel files.

"Did the team come back today?" he asked.

"I haven't seen them."

"Excerpt their photos and circulate them on the hot line."

She nodded. Technically the casinos in Las Vegas were competitors; in reality they cooperated on security matters.

"No more thefts on the fourth floor?" Shane asked, but his eyes were searching the excited crowd around the craps table. The pit boss was right where he should have been, able to see the craps crew and the crowd. The stickman—who happened to be a woman on this shift—was doing what she was paid for: watching the action in the center of the craps table, making sure the dice weren't crooked, and rounding up and returning dice to the shooter. Opposite the stickman was the boxman, who told the dealer—two dealers in this case, because the action was hot—who and how much to pay. An excited woman in mussed makeup and a white satin evening dress with drink stains on it was blowing on the dice, whispering to them, praying over them, and finally flinging them down the length of the green felt.

Les jeux sont faits.

"Another snake eyes!" called out the stickman. "The lady is hot!"

The woman shrieked, jumped up and down, and watched while the dealers doled out chips. The size of the stack of chips in front of her doubled. She let it ride and grabbed the dice as soon as they were swept back to her by the long curved stick.

The crowd leaned closer in vicarious greed and excitement.

Shane and Susan kept walking.

"No, sir," she said. "You were right. One of the day clerks was copying electronic keys and slipping them to her buddies. Stupid. Whatever they get from a fence won't begin to pay for the time they'll spend in jail."

"That's the thing with crooks," he said. "They always assume they're too smart to get caught."

"Yeah, well this wizard found the cops waiting for her in the employee parking lot."

Shane didn't ask if it had been handled discreetly. He paid his security people very well to make sure that the never-never land aura of the Golden Fleece wasn't disturbed by something as distasteful as reality. It wasn't an accident that there were no clocks, no radios, no television screens except in the sports betting lounge, no telephones to remind gamblers to phone home, not even so much as a weather channel on the TVs in the guest rooms to hint at an outside world. The silent message was overwhelming: *Everything you need is right here.*

"Anything else?" he asked as they walked down the center of a double row of blackjack tables. Depending on the demand for the tables, the ante varied from five bucks a hand to five thousand dollars. When the demand was high, the price of playing went up. Two of the tables had discreet RESERVED signs on them. They were for two brothers from Argentina who liked to gamble side by side for three thousand dollars a hand, preferred those two tables and two blond dealers manning them, and lost enough money that Shane was happy to accommodate their whims.

"Nothing else yet," she said.

"I don't like the sound of that."

She shrugged. "Those two whales from Japan got pretty loud about the time I came on this morning."

"Happy loud or mad loud?"

"Oh, they finally lost more than a million bucks apiece just like good little whales, but—"

"Lost?" Shane cut in. "Last I heard at least one of them was winning."

"The winning streak broke about four A.M. We're up two million now. But they were still whiskey-happy and ready for action."

"That's what our hospitality room is for."

The plush room was heavily soundproofed and out of the way. More than one VIP guest had slept off a long gambling or drinking streak in the hospitality room. For those who refused to leave a game, the game was moved right along with the drunks out of the casino's mainstream action.

"They wouldn't leave the table until their croupier offered to go with them for a breakfast of pickled fish, boiled rice, seaweed, and more baccarat," Susan continued. "And whiskey, of course."

"Where is everybody now?"

"Last I checked, the chef you assigned to the whales when they arrived was wielding a knife over something raw and putting it on top of sticky rice. The croupier was trying not to gag on pickled fish while dealing the whales yet another losing round of baccarat."

"Which croupier? Finnigan?"

"How'd you guess?"

"He's the only croupier we had on last night who has the skill to deal for whales, the charm to ease them out of public view if they get drunk, and the stomach to eat pickled fish at four A.M. just to keep them company. Slide one of my personal thousand-dollar markers into his pay envelope. Sometimes losers forget to tip."

Susan flipped open the side pocket of her purse and said a few quick words into the built-in recorder. "Anything else?"

"Find out why we weren't notified by other casinos about the presence of a new techno-team in town."

"Maybe we were the first they hit."

"Maybe. We'll know soon enough."

Susan spoke a few more hurried words into the recorder.

"What was the follow-up on the trash fire?" he asked.

"Busboy was sneaking a smoke and tossed a butt in the trash bin."

"Ex-busboy."

"As of this morning, six A.M.," she agreed.

Shane made another circuit of the casino, noted that the woman's hot streak at craps was holding and the crowd had tripled. Nothing attracted people like a big winner. Smiling, he headed toward the kitchen. Kitchens, actually; the Golden Fleece not only had its own perpetual all-you-can-eat buffet but also five world-class restaurants, each with its own kitchen staff and temperamental chefs.

Before the days of the megacasinos, food in Vegas was cheap and plentiful, a loss leader for the casinos. Not any longer. Not on the Strip. Here the restaurants, like the hotels, were expected to show a profit along with delivering four- and five-star cuisine. It was part of the luxury experience that the biggest resort/casinos delivered to a wealthy international audience. Because the average visitor to Vegas only stayed three days and only gambled two hours per day, it was necessary to ensure that a hotel/casino's guests didn't have to go anywhere else for anything else—food, entertainment, high-end shopping, opulent spas, everything under one huge roof.

And all corridors led back to the casino.

The Golden Fleece wasn't unique in its design. Every other megacasino funneled people into the gambling area. The profits from hotel, entertainment, shopping, and food varied with the season or the economy; the gambling odds didn't. No matter what the window dressing, Vegas, like Monte Carlo, was about gambling.

"What was the follow-up on the guest who claimed that the escalator jerked her off her feet?" Shane asked as they took a staff-only elevator down to the kitchens.

"About what you'd expect. We ran the tapes, saw her 'fall' two or three times until she managed to attract attention, and then the fun began."

"Fun." His mouth turned down.

He expected the card mechanics and the cons, the petty grifters and the big ones. It was Vegas, after all. But the carnival of ambulance-chasing lawyers and senior citizens taking well-timed pratfalls in hope of hitting a different kind of jackpot really annoyed Shane. No matter how many times it happened, people didn't seem to figure out that everything in the Golden Fleece but the toilet stalls and the guest rooms were under 24/7 camera surveillance.

Shane glanced at his watch, wondered what had happened to the time, and mentally juggled his schedule. No matter how he tweaked it, he couldn't fit in the kitchens this morning. In ten minutes he had an appointment with his curator. It wouldn't be a pleasant meeting. Or a short one.

It was past time for Risa to come up with a centerpiece for his Druid Gold show. He needed gold artifacts that could compete with the Fabergé exhibit that would open in the Wildest Dream on New Year's Eve. The fact that, once again, Gail was going to a lot of expense just to get in his face didn't change the reality of it. He needed a showstopper.

And Risa was damn well going to find it for him.

Twelve

Gold lay in gleaming array across the frayed chenille bedspread that Cherelle had jerked over the rumpled sheets. There were twenty-seven extraordinary and eerie pieces of metal art.

"What do you suppose they used this big ol' thing for?" she muttered, staring at the most impressive piece of gold.

It was a heavy gold sculpture shaped like a bent totem pole. Its base started out as a man's head repeated three times in a design that spiraled up from the bottom, which had a wooden core. At the point where the faces would have wrapped around each other to repeat the design, they flowed upward into another spiraling shape that suggested three long-necked birds or snakes, which spiraled into three wolves, and then the wolves flowed into a rutting bull three times repeated, always spiraling upward like a dream or a nightmare until the design ended in a bird's thrice-sculpted head whose staring eyes were human skulls and from whose thick beaks dangled limp human figures.

"Man, whatever they were smoking really fucked with their minds," Cherelle said, rubbing the goose bumps on her arms. "Hooo-*eee*."

But the eerie, bent totem pole was gold. Even though half of it was filled with some kind of wood, the gold itself had to weigh four, maybe five pounds. That, and the gold neckring she had belted the old man with, accounted for maybe a quarter of the weight of the whole treasure. The golden knife with the odd curved shape and the gem-set gold sheath were no lightweights either.

The rest of the gold was pretty much jewelry— armbands or bracelets, a finger ring for a woman with symbols incised inside its broad interior, fabulous pins as big as her hand. Only one of the pieces was set with stones. Others had enamel that gleamed as bright as any gem. Most of them had designs or symbols that made her head ache when she tried to follow them.

She didn't need that. Her head had been screaming like a pig since the channeling session with Virgil.

She was grateful that other than being creepy, handling the gold now didn't burn her the way she vaguely remembered being burned when she grabbed the biggest neckring and clobbered the old man. But she wasn't going to think about that. She didn't like remembering what had happened a few hours ago, so she concentrated on the treasure.

The six collars or neckrings or whatever could have been choker-type necklaces, but they would have been a bitch to put on and take off. Then there were the figurines of animals or demons or body parts or whatever. Each statuette could have fit in her hand, yet the detail

on some of them was enough to give her eyestrain trying
to figure out what it meant.

But the pieces of gold that really excited her were the
heavy sculpture that reminded her of a totem pole, the
piece that looked like a small gold jug with a hinged lid,
the oddly curved dagger in a golden sheath, and the
mask of a man or a god or a devil whose bleak, empty
eyes always seemed to be watching her no matter where
she stood in the motel room.

Creepy or not, it was quite a haul. As far as she was
concerned, the gold artifacts were as good or better than
anything in one of Virgil's books.

That meant money, pure and simple and very sweet.

Thinking about money, looking at the gold, she fid-
dled with a long blond curl that was part of her
painstakingly casual hairdo—three-quarters swept up
and the rest dangling, tempting a man to toy with the
locks and the skin beneath. The curl she was winding
around her finger usually lay in the shadowy cleavage revealed by the deep V neck of her red sweater, which
strained over her chest until her sheer black bra showed
through beneath the knit. The sweater was tucked into
jeans so tight they should have split. The soles of her
scuffed white sling-back heels were shadow-thin. She
swore if she stepped on a coin she could tell the date it
had been minted.

Absently her fingers tested her belly and her butt.
Gravity might be winning the battle of the bulge, but she
still had a body that turned heads and made men happy
to buy her a drink or a bit of blow. In fact, she could use
more of the white stuff right now. Her head was killing
her. Even some more cheap crack would be okay.

Too bad the cocaine was gone to the last speck. Not
that there had been enough of it for two anyway. Tim

wouldn't be happy that she had smoked it, but he would survive. He probably wouldn't even notice until it was too late to get mad.

She glanced out the window into the parking lot, where gaps in the pavement ran like thin black snakes across the sun-bleached macadam. Tim should be back with breakfast—and Socks—any minute. Then there would be hell to pay, and cocaine in any form wouldn't have anything to do with it. Socks would want a third of the action, and she was damned if he would get it. This was her score, not his. He hadn't been there.

He hadn't killed anyone.

Abruptly she turned away from the window and paced into the bathroom. She didn't want to think about that endless time when she had been screaming in the center of nothing, screaming and there wasn't any sound, just the certainty that she was screaming and screaming and screaming. A pipeful of crack and four fingers of vodka had chased the memories. For a while.

She hadn't meant to kill Virgil. Hell, she couldn't even remember doing it.

But he sure enough was dead.

"Well, nothing I can do about that now," Cherelle told her image in the dull mirror. "I have to think of me, and to hell with everyone else. Even Tim."

She went to the bed and began gathering up a generous half of the gold pieces, generous in both number and weight of the pieces. She was greedy in her division, but she wasn't stupid. She left twelve articles for Tim, including an eye-catching armlet, a necklace, the three smallest pins, and something that looked like a pecker and balls. Reluctantly she added four of the small figurines, because they were the kind of gold Socks would understand. Portable and a nice weight in the hand.

Tim's share fit easily into one of the small, battered wooden cartons. She wrapped the rest of the gold in dirty clothes and packed it inside one of her two beat-up wheeled suitcases. If she had thought she could get away with taking all of the gold, she would have, but she was smarter than that. Even if Tim would stand still for her holding everything until it was fenced, Socks wouldn't. He was a real junkyard dog.

So she would throw him a golden bone.

After she locked the suitcase full of gold in the trunk of her car, she stuck a spare key in her bra. She was forever losing keys, so she stashed spares everywhere. Carrying extras in her bra was easier than breaking into her own apartment or hot-wiring her own car every time she had a brain fart and forgot where she had left something.

She opened the second, smaller suitcase, set it on the floor next to a coffee table that wobbled, and looked around for anything important she might have forgotten. The first thing she saw was the stack of newly printed pamphlets advertising Tim as a spiritual adviser and herself as a "clear, clean" channel. With a smile of contempt she knocked the stack off the table. Pieces of paper flew and slid everywhere, including one that landed in her suitcase.

She dumped shoes and candy bars on top of the brightly colored pamphlet, then tampons, shampoo, underwear, makeup, toothbrush, everything she owned. When she was finished, she bounced on the suitcase lid until she could shut it. Only one of the wheels still worked, but it was better than nothing. With a squeak and a snarl the suitcase limped after her out the door and into the parking lot.

Tim and Socks drove up just as she was shoving the suitcase into the backseat of her car. Socks was driving the Pontiac Firebird that he spent more time underneath than inside of. It was neon purple, had fat tires, and could pass anything on the road but a gas station. Socks himself was less flashy—medium height, bulky, dark hair, dark eyes, and a firm belief that every female in the universe would benefit from a session with his dick.

Tim got out, balancing three coffees and a sack full of doughnuts. "Packed already?"

"My stuff," she said. "You want yours packed, you do it."

He gave her a hard kiss. "Knew I should have screwed you when we got back this morning. You get real bitchy when you go without."

She made a show of shoving him away, but in the process one of her hands just happened to slide down to his crotch. She squeezed him where he liked it, the way he liked it.

"Watch that coffee," Socks said, slamming the door of the Pontiac. "Paid five bucks for it."

If he hadn't said anything, Cherelle would have stopped at a playful squeeze. But Socks was forever trying to come between her and Tim, so she settled against her lover for a thorough rubbing. As always he responded with impressive speed. No doubt about it, the best part of this boy was below his belt.

"Gimme that." Socks grabbed the teetering cardboard tray of drinks out of Tim's hands and headed for the open motel door. "You wanna hump her in the parking lot, knock yourself out. I'm having breakfast."

Cherelle licked Tim's lips, gave him a slow stroke, and whispered huskily, "Wanna?"

"You ever know me when I didn't?"

"Nope." It made up for a lot, including his lack of brains . . . most of the time. With a final measured squeeze, she stepped back. "Soon as we unload Socks, I'm gonna suck you dry."

"Uh, he's coming to Vegas with us."

She wasn't surprised. She wasn't happy either. Eyes narrowed, she crossed her arms under her breasts. "You told him."

Tim shuffled from one foot to the other. Then he shrugged. "Hell, he's my buddy."

Sometimes Cherelle wondered just how close a buddy good old Socks was, but she didn't push it. Men as beautiful as Tim often were switch-hitters. The good news was that he had never been too used up to take her on, so maybe it was just the jailhouse thing with Socks, like fraternity boys or soldiers bonding because they all ate the same shit to get where they were.

"He wasn't with us last night," she said.

"We still owe him for the blow."

She let out a hissing breath and thought fast. Cocaine was the major reason she put up with Socks. He never seemed to have any trouble getting it, and he didn't charge them an arm and a leg. "He'll get paid. He always does."

Socks stuck his head out of the motel room. "Hey, I thought you said you had something good to show me."

"In your dreams," Cherelle muttered, but she started toward the room. It would be just like Socks to yell questions about stolen gold across the parking lot. Tim had his faults in the brain department, but Socks could be severely stupid. If he hadn't been connected, someone would have whacked him long ago.

"You coming?" Socks asked impatiently.

"You asking about our sex life?" Cherelle retorted.

"Huh?"

"Nothing," Tim said. "She's just being cute."

With a muttered word, Cherelle left Tim behind and stalked into the motel room. She lifted covered coffee cups until she found the only one that was still full. She took a sip and almost spit it all over Socks. No sugar, no cream, and he damn well knew how she liked it. Just because he and Tim drank theirs straight up didn't mean that she had to.

"So where is it?" Socks said. "Tim wants more blow, and I ain't doing nothing until I'm paid for the last time."

"In the box." She pointed toward the wooden carton that sat on the floor next to the rumpled bed.

Socks nudged it with his foot. "That all? Tim said there were three boxes."

"They weren't nearly full, so I put it together. One's easier to carry than three."

"Huh." Socks looked dubiously at the box. "Don't look like much from here."

Tim sauntered into the room and stuffed a doughnut into his mouth. He didn't know what was going to happen, but he knew it would be entertaining. He loved watching Cherelle rip someone a new asshole—as long as that someone wasn't him. As for the gold, whether she had it or Socks had it, Tim would get his share.

"How full is not full?" Socks asked.

"How full is not full?" she mocked. "Man, we have a fucking philosopher here."

"Huh?" Socks frowned.

So did Tim.

Times like this, she really missed Risa. The two of them used to fall on the ground laughing about things no one else was smart enough to get.

"Look," Cherelle said, pointing toward the box. "That's Tim's half."

Socks opened the box and started to dump it on the floor.

"Wait!" she shrieked. *What a jerk-off.* "You bang that stuff around, it won't be worth as much, so don't come whining to me about how Tim's half isn't worth what mine is worth."

Tim headed off an argument by taking the box and unpacking its contents one at a time on the bed. Twelve pieces. A couple of armbands, some little statues, a neck-ring, some pins with red in their designs, a woman's ring. It might have been half of the haul, but she hadn't let him touch the boxes she carried, so he couldn't be sure. Besides, it really didn't matter. Whatever she had, sooner or later he had. Even at her bitchiest, she couldn't wait to get her hands on his joystick.

"Weird junk." Socks eyed the pieces. "Gold?"

"Yeah," Tim said.

"You sure?"

Tim looked at Cherelle, who nodded curtly. He turned back to Socks. "If she's sure, I'm sure. It's gold."

"How do you know?" Socks asked her.

"I know a lot of things."

Socks couldn't argue that, so he went back to the gold. "Have to go to one of my uncle's connections to pawn this. That means Vegas. My Sedona connection only handles things that plug into a wall."

"Vegas, huh?" Tim said, as though Cherelle hadn't already been bugging him to leave this dump for the bright action of Las Vegas. "Sounds good to me. I haven't seen my mama in yonks."

Socks didn't give a damn about Tim's mama. "Pack it up and let's drag butt out of here."

"You'll get a better price if you wait until I can find out more about these pieces," Cherelle said quickly.

"What do you mean?" Socks said.

Tim started packing up the gold.

"I've seen stuff like this in books," Cherelle said. "It's worth more than its weight in gold all by itself."

Socks just looked at her.

"How long until you find out?" Tim asked.

"As long as it takes," she shot back.

"Listen," Socks said, "I ain't waiting until you go back to school and get a fancy degree to—"

"I don't have to. I know someone who has a fancy degree already."

"Who?"

Cherelle hesitated. Through the years she had kept in touch with Risa from time to time, but always alone. She didn't think Risa would approve of having a lowlife like Socks turn up on her doorstep. Especially not now, when she had turned herself into a classy nerd scholar. "Just someone."

Socks shrugged. "Do what you like. I ain't waiting for mine."

She turned to Tim, who looked uncomfortable. "This is our big chance," she said flatly. "I'm sick of getting two cents on the dollar because Socks doesn't know a single fence that won't hose him. Just give me a chance. You won't be sorry. When I'm done, you'll have enough to buy a big ol' bathtub packed full of blow."

Tim frowned. He hated it when he was in the middle of these two. He looked toward Socks. His friend had a stubborn line to his mouth.

"Tell you what," Tim said as he pushed two figurines away from the rest. "This is for what we owe you for the blow, plus you'll get us a few more ounces of pure, okay?"

Socks looked at the gold. "Gimme one more."

Cherelle made a wailing sound.

Tim picked up an armband and took back one of the figurines. "Here. This is worth two of them."

Socks sucked on his lower lip and eyed the rest of the gold. "Okay, but you ride to Vegas with me. I'm sick of following that sorry wreck she drives."

"Sure," Tim said. "Radio in her car doesn't work anyway."

Cherelle watched unhappily as Socks wrapped his two artifacts in greasy napkins and shoved them in his backpack. She really hated letting any of that gold go. Despite her brave talk, she wasn't certain just how much any of it was worth. She might need all of it to crawl out of the hole her life had become.

Humming, Tim wrapped his gold in shorts or socks or whatever came to hand from the garbage bag that was also his suitcase. As soon as he was finished, he began stuffing his ten pieces of loot into the backpack that went with him everywhere. Eight went in easy. The ninth was a struggle.

"Careful!" Cherelle said. "If you ruin that other armband, it won't be worth as much. Same for that pin. And—"

"Here," Tim said, shoving two of the underwear-wrapped packages toward her. "Now get off my ass, okay?"

"Hey!" Socks said unhappily. He already thought of that gold as his own, but he was just smart enough not to say it out loud. Tim wasn't as easy to lead around as he had been before he hooked up with Cherelle. She was one ball-breaking bitch.

"Relax, buddy," Tim said with an easy smile. "She's going to Vegas, too. Right, precious?"

"But now she's got most of it," Socks said.

It was too late. Cherelle had already grabbed the two pieces of Tim's gold and put them in the ratty backpack/purse that doubled as an overnight bag for her. "See you in Vegas, boys. Same place, right? Motel near your mama's house?"

"Yeah." Tim grabbed Cherelle, buried his face in her cleavage, and made bubbling noises. "Don't be late."

"No shit," Socks muttered. "The bitch has most of the gold."

"I won't," Cherelle said, ignoring Socks.

Tim scooped up his backpack in one hand and grabbed his buddy's backpack with the other. "C'mon. Let's go see that pawnbroker in Vegas. He's gotta be better than the one in Sedona."

"But the bitch has most of the gold!"

"C'mon, man," Tim said. "We do it your way and we have a real catfight. We do it her way and the worst that happens is we get some money now and a lot more money later. What's your problem with that?"

Socks was still trying to explain his problem when the car doors slammed and the engine revved to life.

Thirteen

The white-walled, Persian-carpeted room was quiet except for the occasional sound of paper when Shane turned a page in one of the catalogs Risa had given him to look through. There were no framed pictures from her past on the desk, no personal letters stuck in the belly drawer, no forgotten earrings tucked in among the pens, nothing to suggest her life outside of work hours. Her casino apartment was the same. There was nothing of the past she wanted to remember.

She had learned at sixteen that the way to get what she wanted was to shut out all distractions and focus her intelligence on her goal. She didn't begrudge a moment of her hard work. She had pulled herself out of the kind of southern poverty that made good jokes and lousy lives. Then she had discovered the world of ancient jewelry. It was her own personal paradise, a place where beauty lived and excitement was in every book she opened, every piece of new jewelry that came into her hands.

And if sometimes, just sometimes, she felt the cool,

unnerving breath of the past rushing around her when she handled a gold object, she could live with it just the same way she lived with some of her own past's more brutal memories. None of it mattered in the here and now. Only her work did, her key to a far more beautiful world than she had been born into.

Risa loved her job.

And she was worried about losing it.

Without moving her head, she checked the wall clock. Unlike most of the rooms in the Golden Fleece complex, her office actually had a built-in way to tell time. She knew that clock intimately; she had just spent the longest ninety minutes of her life waiting to be fired because she hadn't found the kind of crowd magnet Shane needed for his Druid Gold show.

Not that the beautifully made and fully alarmed glass display cases were empty. They held some very good—and even a few exceptional—artifacts from all across the area of Europe that had once supported the artistic style that the twenty-first century called Celtic. For the show Shane wanted to have, the emphasis was largely on objects found in Irish, Scots, Welsh, and English "hoards" through the centuries.

Unfortunately most of the hoards that had ever been discovered had gone to the Crown and from there to the royal smelter to make more coin of the realm. Wars were expensive, the English were ambitious, and antiquities weren't revered. Through the centuries the hoards that weren't declared to the Crown had been secretly melted down into anonymous gold ingots.

After the 1700s, when owning antiquities came into fashion, the owner of the land—nearly always an aristocrat—might keep whatever hoards were discovered in his family collection instead of melting the pieces down for their ore. Once collected, the objects might, just might, end up in a museum for people like Risa to study. More often they simply were passed from generation to generation in familial obscurity.

Her stomach grumbled unhappily. She tried to ignore it. It just growled louder.

Shane glanced away from the auction catalog he had been studying under the fluorescent lights. He would rather look at Risa anyway. Museum quality, but not ancient. Living, breathing, and . . .

"Hungry?" he asked.

"Gee, whatever makes you think that? The fact that I can't remember the last meal I ate?"

"Yesterday they threw peanuts at us on the flight from L.A."

"I know. You ate mine."

"You were asleep."

She didn't want to pursue that line of conversation, because she had awakened with her head on his shoulder and him looking at her with hungry eyes. At least she thought it was hunger. Whatever it was had been replaced with his usual shuttered watchfulness before she could be certain.

She really had to talk to Niall about another job. One with Rarities. Then she could get Shane Tannahill out of her system. An affair would be just what the doctor ordered. It had been a long drought for her in the male department. In some dark corner of her mind, each man who asked her out ended up being compared to Shane—and coming up short. Unfair to everyone involved, but there it was. Unchangeable.

When she finally dined on his forbidden fruit, she would find it tasted just like the supermarket kind. Then she would shrug and get on with her life.

"Is that glazed look a yes or a no to my suggestion of fruit?" he asked.

For a horrifying moment she was afraid he had read her mind. Then she realized that he'd been offering her a snack. "Yes. Definitely."

"Good. A few more minutes and we wouldn't have been able to hear each other over our growling stomachs."

While Shane phoned in an order to the chef du jour, Risa prowled around the long room where various gold artifacts lay gleaming within specially built display cases. Technically this room was her domain, but lately every time she turned around, Shane was taking up space in it. Since they had come back from L.A., he had all but slept in her office. He brooded over the display cases like a hen with too few chicks. Then he chewed on her for not coming up with anything better. In the last ninety minutes, particularly, he had made it clear that she had failed to supply him with a showstopper.

The only good news from her point of view was that so far none of his other contacts, formal or otherwise, had done any better.

Not that what she had found for him was inferior. The gorget she had purchased from a private estate sale was a lovely artifact. The decoration—perhaps a badge of high office—was fully eighteen inches wide and three deep. When worn across a man's chest, it must have been splendid, especially if it had been fastened in place with a magnificent gold brooch on either side. Granted, she didn't have said brooches, and the gorget itself wasn't intact, but the pieces that did exist were striking.

And the provenance had been of the highest.

If only better gorgets didn't exist in Ireland . . . But six or seven that did came immediately to mind. Shane just didn't accept second best, much less seventh or eighth. Most of the time she admired and understood that hard-driving quality. And sometimes it made her nuts. The past three months qualified for the made-her-nuts category.

Her stomach growled.

She told herself that was good. Her figure was already too lush for anything but men's magazines. She would much rather have had the willowy size-eight form that all the—male, of course—clothing designers had in mind when they drew their pencil-wide sketches or made slacks of fabrics and colors that fairly shouted, *Whoa, d'ya ever see a butt quite that wide?*

Unconsciously she smoothed the dark, man-made miracle fiber of her slacks over her hips, wishing they were less round. But they were what they were, *round,* and that was that. The best she could do was try to disguise the matter by choosing businesslike clothes and making sure nothing was tight or sheer. Loose blouses concealed the breasts that other women envied and she would have given away in a hot second, but only if the hips went with them.

Cherelle had always laughed at her for being self-conscious about a figure that a lot of women would have killed for, Cherelle included. If Risa had wanted a career stripping or dancing nude for hard-breathing men, then her figure would have been ideal. What she wanted was to be taken seriously by men and women alike, which meant toning down the physical and honing the mental. That was precisely what she had done. That was what she continued to do.

She must have succeeded, because Shane hardly seemed to notice she was a woman at all. She suspected that he liked the swizzle-stick-thin model type.

Without knowing it, she sighed.

The small sound broke Shane's concentration. Not that it was hard to do. When Risa was around, his attention was never far from her. It irritated the hell out of him. Maybe he should have taken Gail up on her offer of sweaty sex.

He dismissed the thought almost before it formed. He didn't want a bedroom marathon with Gail. He wanted it with Risa.

And he wasn't going to get it.

"What about Jenkins?" Shane asked curtly.

Risa blinked and brought her mind back from her growling stomach. "Mel hasn't called."

"Call him."

"I did. He's on a collecting trip in Ireland."

"Good. When is he due back?"

"Doesn't matter. He went on Silverado's nickel. She'll get first pick of whatever he finds."

Shane's mouth thinned. Gail's determination to beat him to every Celtic gold artifact worth having was becoming a real nuisance. Having her swipe his best Celtic buyer was just the latest in a long string of annoying little tricks. Knowing that she was doing it solely to irritate him didn't make living with the results any easier.

At least Rarities had turned Gail down, citing a conflict of interest with one of their "core" clients. Having an organization like Rarities working against him would have made acquiring good artifacts almost impossible. That was why he paid them a yearly retainer. If they heard of something good and golden, they let him know. As they had connections around the world, he often had first look at artifacts newly come on the market.

Often, but not always. If the source was the kind that wanted to hide from Rarities, Shane had a standing no-questions-asked reward of ten thousand dollars for information leading to the acquisition of museum-quality gold artifacts.

"Nothing new from any of the auction houses?" Shane asked.

"No."

Silence grew as he took a solid gold pen from his pocket and began "walking" it across the back of his right hand, weaving it between and around his fingers, turning it end over end with a motion that looked easy. It wasn't. It was a card mechanic's trick for limbering up fingers before dealing from whichever part of the deck would do the most good. When the pen reached Shane's middle finger, the metal made a distinctive clicking sound as it met his gold Celtic ring, which had belonged to one of his great-great-greats on his mother's side. From the crispness of the incised symbols, he was the first one to truly wear the ring in many, many centuries.

"Mr. Tarlov is still interested in working out a loan for his collection of Romano-Celtic fibulae," Risa said.

The only answer was a *click* when gold met gold on Shane's quick, elegant hand.

"Erik and Serena North agreed to let you display their magnificent gold carpet page from the Book of the Learned," Risa pointed out. "It will be the page's first public display. With all the death and mystery that surrounded its discovery, the page is sure to be a crowd magnet."

Click.

She hadn't really expected an answer from Shane. He wanted the Druid Gold exhibit to be owned entirely by Tannahill Inc. Insisted on it actually, except for that sole illuminated page. He had agreed to display the heavily foiled, intricately decorated manuscript page because it represented the final flowering of Celtic art. The fact that nothing else like that page had ever been found was the decisive factor for Shane. Nothing better of its type existed anywhere, at any price, and the Norths wouldn't sell; that left borrowing it for the show. Unsatisfactory, but better than nothing.

"Look," Risa said, rubbing at the headache that was gathering between her eyes, "what you already have in this room is a collection that a lot of museums would be delighted to find in their display cases."

He kept walking the pen. His eyes were focused on a horizon only he could see. She knew from experience that he wasn't ignoring her. Not really. He was simply sorting through available options with a speed, intelligence, and pragmatism that she admired even more than she did his long, athletic body.

Ring and pen clicked against each other once more. Then the pen vanished as swiftly as it had appeared.

She braced herself for whatever Shane had decided.

"If we have to," he said, "we'll go with Sotheby's gilded Late Iron Age helmet. Personally, I don't think it has enough 'presence,' as you put it, to carry a show, but coupled with the gold-inlaid iron sword hilt I bought last year, the two should hold everyone's interest for a few moments. Pity that the blade is rusted through in so many places. If the placard didn't say 'sword,' no one would know what it was."

"It's not that bad."

"Which? The helmet or the sword?"

"The sword."

"It's a delight for anyone who has made a study of Celtic artifacts. For the guy on the street, it's a frown and a shrug. Guess how many scholars there are in Vegas versus average guys."

Risa didn't bother to guess. Though she agreed with Shane's reluctance to feature the clumsily made helmet with its gold foil more missing than present. She knew that putting the helmet together with the sword from the age of King Arthur would give more impact to both items than either one apart.

"Properly displayed," she said, "the helmet will appear menacing rather than crudely made."

His mouth turned down at one corner in a sour kind of smile. " 'Crudely made.' Lovely. Do be sure that description appears in the catalog. They'll be lined up from here to L.A. to get a look."

She felt heat flare across her cheekbones. "I know my job, Mr. Tannahill."

"Shane, remember?"

"That's your good twin. I'm talking to the evil one right now."

He laughed. She was one of the few people he employed who didn't pull her punches with him. It was just one of the many appealing—and maddening—things about her.

"Assuming that we pay more than the helmet is worth—"

"It's an auction, isn't it?" she cut in dryly.

"—and end up owning it, how would you display it for maximum impact?"

"On you."

He blinked. "Excuse me?"

"At least for the catalog. I wouldn't expect you to stand around half naked wearing a gold-foiled helmet while groups of female tourists drooled on you."

"Just half naked? How disappointing. I thought Celtic warriors wore nothing but blue paint into battle."

"Only a few of them went naked. Probably a warrior

elite, like the SEALs or the SAS. Some people believe that the Celtic men in blue were Druids, but most people believe that the Druids were an intellectual elite rather than warriors."

"The Samurai were both."

"Good point. I won't stand in the way if you want to rub limey clay into your hair, strip naked, and paint yourself blue for—"

"No," he cut in quickly. "Not even for the catalog cover."

"Well, dang, sugah," she drawled. "It would have been a showstopper—you with your hair sticking up like an albino sea urchin, ice blue goose bumps all over your glorious body, and a gilded helmet held in front of your pride and joy."

Shaking his head, Shane tried not to chuckle. It didn't work. The image of himself in blue goose bumps and gold helmet held over his crotch was as ridiculous as he would have felt posing naked in the first place.

That was another of the things he liked about Risa. She made him laugh.

"Seriously, though," she said, tilting her head to one side and studying him. "Do you have chest hair?"

"What?"

"Do you have—"

"Yes," he interrupted. "Do you?"

She ignored him. "Okay. A shot from about here up"—she pointed to his breastbone—"elegantly inlaid haft of the sword placed diagonally across your hairy chest, the gold helmet emphasizing those stone green eyes and dark beard shadow . . . oh, yeah. It would have women lined up three deep around the parking lot."

"I'm beginning to feel like a side of meat."

"Now you know how a chorus girl feels."

"Never touched one of them, so I'll take your word for it."

Shane was famous for keeping his hands off the help, so Risa just smiled from the teeth out and kept talking.

"Of course, Celtic warriors usually sported a mustache that drooped over the corners of their mouth and trickled down their chin. But," she added, "we could always catch a shaggy dog and—"

Risa's phone rang, saving Shane from having to listen to the rest of whatever mischief she had in mind. He watched while she answered the phone with the quickness that fascinated him, because her movements always appeared easygoing, almost lazy. It must have had something to do with the southern upbringing that he heard in her voice when she teased someone.

"Risa here," she said. "What can I do for you?"

He saw the change that came over her, emotions crossing her face too quickly for him to read. Then nothing, as though a light had been turned out, leaving only a professional expression behind.

"Hey, it's great to hear from you, and I'd love to talk to you, but I'm working right now. Can I call you back?" Risa turned away from Shane. "Lunch? Sure." She looked at the clock. "One hour, the jazz bar off the lobby."

Carefully Risa hung up. Before she turned back to Shane, she made sure her game face was in place. Hearing from Cherelle was always bittersweet. They had so many years together as children, so many shared memories. Without Cherelle, Risa wasn't sure she would have survived to grow up.

Yet they had become such different adults.

The combination of love and guilt she felt toward

Cherelle made Risa ache for the childhood laughter that had been and could never be again.

"A client?" Shane asked mildly, yet his eyes were intent.

He knew in his gut it wasn't casino business she would be conducting in an hour. The thought of her meeting someone for lunch shouldn't have bothered him. After all, he was the one who had encouraged her to be active in the private-appraisal business, if only as another way to ensure that he kept tabs on what was new in the old-gold market.

Yet something about her reaction to the call made every fey instinct in him wake up and sniff the air for danger. Niall would have called it things that go bump in the night. Shane just called it a hunch.

Risa was hiding something.

From him.

"No, not a client." Deliberately she opened one of the seven auction books. "Have you looked at the figurine in lot 18B? Granted, it's only gilt rather than solid gold, but the design is exquisite."

Dutifully Shane looked at the figurine.

All he really saw was the moment when he would be alone with his own version of the Eye in the Sky, reviewing the input from the camera that covered the jazz bar just off the lobby of the Golden Fleece.

Fourteen

"You said you'd wait for Cherelle to—"

Socks didn't let Tim finish the sentence. "I didn't say shit. You did all the talking."

With a heavy foot on the accelerator, Socks sent the car shooting into an intersection just as the light went red. Cars on either side honked. Socks hung his middle finger out the window.

"You shouldn't bust lights when we have crack in the car," Tim said. "I ain't aching for any more time in the joint."

"What are you? My old lady? Bitch, bitch, bitch. Can't do anything but bitch. Besides, there ain't enough rock left to cover a cockroach's dick, remember? We finished it an hour ago."

The next light was dead solid red when they approached the intersection. Socks considered blowing through just to hear Tim's girly shriek, but there was a Budweiser delivery truck pulling into the intersection.

Folks around here would hang him if he got in the way of their brew.

Tim stared out the window and wished he had some more coke. This was the no-collar section of Las Vegas, the part between Glitter Gulch and the Strip, where the gutters were filled with trash and the windows and doors with iron bars.

"Home sweet home," Tim said bitterly.

Socks didn't care. In fact, he felt real comfortable on these dirty streets. A man knew the score here: do unto others before they thought of doing it to you. He had grown up not far from this neighborhood.

So had Tim, but he didn't like it nearly as much as Socks did. The five-year difference in their ages had kept them from meeting each other until Tim checked into the same prison cell as Socks. Tim had been in for card-sharping and humping a fifteen-year-old. Socks had been in for sticking up a 24/7 convenience store. Both of them had complained of their bad luck in getting caught doing what everyone else was doing.

Across the street a hooker spotted the shocking purple car. She was wearing a crotch-length leather skirt, mountainous platform sandals, and a stretchy midriff blouse that once had been white. She swung her hips in an improbable figure eight as she crossed the street and leaned in the open driver's window.

Socks gave the goods a thorough once-over, then passed. She looked fifty and was probably twenty-five. He could see the needle tracks on her dirty toes and the dead space in her eyes. The emptiness and dirt didn't bother him, but he wasn't nearly horny enough to take on a whacked-out hype. Not after watching a ripe number like Cherelle rub all over Tim. Socks might not be as pretty as his friend, but he was damned certain his equipment was just as good. That was one thing you did a lot of in jail—seeing how you measured up against other inmates.

The light changed to green. Ignoring the woman, Socks gunned the engine and turned off the main street. After a few blocks he cranked the wheel over and zoomed to the curb in front of two sun-beaten bungalows whose curtains were drawn as tight as the bars over the windows. Both houses had a small front porch shaded by an awning. The bungalow on the left had an old man in a wheelchair and a dog flaked out at his feet.

Tim would have noticed the old man only if he *hadn't* been on the porch. For as long as he could remember, Mr. Parsons had been parked in that spot with a dog nearby. It was the same for the weeds and dust. Just there. Always.

The tiny cottages were crouched between a two-story apartment building that had seen better years—a lot of them—and the kind of single-level, low-rent strip mall that never seemed to go completely bankrupt, probably because there was a liquor store in the center of it.

Two middle-aged men sat in the apartment parking lot and sucked on bottles wrapped in brown paper. A thin, nervous old lady walked down from the second-story stairway with a mutt on a leash. The way she circled around the drinkers said that she thought alcoholism was contagious.

Tim looked at the unshaved men and told himself that at least his father wasn't one of them. Maybe he had never seen his father up close, but he knew who he was. That was more than Socks could say. The only family he ever talked about were some broken-down lowlifes who had worked for the Mob way back when it was big in Vegas.

"Gimme your stuff," Socks said as he fished a used-up cigarette pack out of his T-shirt sleeve. He lit the last wrinkled cigarette, tossed the trash out the window, and blew smoke at the dashboard. "I'll meet you back here after I've talked with my fence."

"I'll keep mine until I see what you get for yours."

Socks made a disgusted sound. "Pussy-whipped, that's what you are. Just plain pussy-whipped."

"Fuck you."

"Like you could. You were the queen of the cell block."

Tim grabbed the cigarette and took a quick drag. It tasted as bad as it looked, but the nicotine hit just fine. He wasn't hooked on it like Socks was, but he enjoyed it from time to time. He sucked hard and deep before surrendering the cigarette to Socks again.

"Cherelle has more brains than both of us put together," Tim said, blowing out a long stream of smoke. "If I was you, I'd wait and get more money."

"You ain't me."

Tim shrugged.

"Why'd you let her keep some of your share, too?" Socks asked in a voice that was real close to a whine. "There were three fucking cartons, and all I have is two shitty little pieces."

"She's tired of taking pennies from your fences when the stuff I give you is worth thousands." It wasn't quite true, but what the hell. If Cherelle had known about all the fancy electronics he and Socks had stolen for pennies on the dollar, she would have screamed.

"Price of doing business," Socks said. That, and a

really sweet cut for himself, of course. What Tim didn't know wouldn't hurt him. What Socks knew pissed him off. He was broke, and whatever he got for the gold likely wouldn't be enough to change that for long. "Gimme what you have in your backpack."

Tim shifted uncomfortably, as though the backpack sitting on his lap had suddenly gotten heavy. He reached for the door handle.

"Hey, buddy," Socks said, grabbing Tim's arm. "Just a piece or two, okay? I'm broke, and even a room a cockroach wouldn't want costs fifty bucks a night here. I want a good-looking woman and five lines of white and a bottle of bourbon and a steak and a dessert some waiter with an attitude sets on fire, you get it? We been living like burger-flipping, minimum-wage jerks. I wanna rave."

Tim thought of what Cherelle would say. But that was in the future, and he might find a way around her. Socks was here and now, and Tim hated fights.

"Well, shit," Tim said. He reached into the backpack and dragged out two lumpy socks. He didn't know which pieces he was handing over. He didn't care. There was more where it came from, and it would shut Socks up. "Don't come back with less than four hundred bucks for me."

"Four hundred! You crazy?"

"Four hundred, you hear me?"

"Yeahyeahyeah." Socks had heard it all before and hadn't listened then.

"I mean it." Backpack in hand, Tim climbed out of the car. He leaned in the open door and snagged his garbage bag from the backseat. "Cherelle thinks we're onto something big. I don't want to screw it up. Woman's got a mean tongue."

Socks held up his hands in surrender and smiled genially. "I hear ya, buddy."

"And bring back my socks," Tim added, straightening. "Nothing wrong with them my mama's washing machine won't cure."

"What the hell would *I* do with your socks?"

Tim laughed. Socks had gotten his street name because he never wore any. If he had a real name, Tim had never heard it. For men like Socks, a street name was the only kind that mattered.

"When will you have the cash?" Tim asked.

"I'll call your mama."

It was the answer Tim had expected. He waved and headed for the front door of the shabby bungalow.

Socks watched for a moment. He might not have been university smart, but he was gutter clever. Tim had been easygoing and eager to please before Cherelle. There hadn't been any change at first. But now . . . now Socks was getting the short end of the triangle. Tim was taking the bitch's orders and ignoring the buddy he used to listen to. Half the time he and Tim were arguing like old marrieds.

What really bothered Socks was that he couldn't shake the feeling he was losing.

Fifteen

For long minutes Cherelle stared at the Golden Fleece's namesake suspended in a tank full of water. While crowds of people eddied around her and oooohed and murmured over the golden sheepskin, all she could think about was how much she'd like to break that tank and roll in the gold dust until she was a solid gold woman. Even her eyes. It would be really cool to have them gold instead of the boring pale blue she'd been born with.

"Hey, Max, look at this! They're having a big gold show New Year's Eve. We'll have to come back."

Cherelle gave the middle-aged couple a cold look for interrupting her fantasy. Then she saw the pamphlet the woman was waving at her husband. Gold flashed hypnotically from color photos.

"Where'd you get that?" Cherelle asked.

The woman pointed toward the holders placed around the big square pedestal that supported the tank and the fleece.

Cherelle elbowed forward, grabbed a pamphlet, and began reading eagerly. Then she looked at the photos again. They weren't exactly like the gold she had, but they weren't *not* like it either.

A note at the bottom next to a classy photo said RISA SHERIDAN, PH.D., CURATOR.

Cherelle shoved the pamphlet into her purse and chewed on the inside corner of her mouth. She should have changed clothes, something fancier. But she didn't have anything clean and didn't want to go hang out with all the busted-up street people at the Laundromat near the motel while she watched her clothes do somersaults in the dryer. She was classier than that.

Well, screw it. She wasn't the only woman in the Golden Fleece wearing jeans and high-heeled sandals.

After a last longing look at the fleece, Cherelle sauntered off toward the bar called Gabriel's Horn for the golden trumpet that hung over the back mirror. The bar itself stuck like a glittering toe into the casino that wrapped around the lobby. She knew that Risa hadn't wanted to meet her old friend inside the Golden Fleece, but she'd given in when Cherelle had done what she used to do while they were kids—roll right over Risa's halfway objections like they didn't exist.

Cherelle had pushed the matter because she didn't want Risa to see her in a roach palace like the motel she'd left her clothes in. She had always let on that she was doing real well, better than Risa in fact. Up until a few years ago, that had been close enough to the truth.

Soon it would *be* the truth. Hell, she would be doing better than Risa. She would get classy clothes like her old friend, and some sexy underwear, and some shoes that didn't kill her feet. Then she and Tim could fire up the crack pipe and screw each other blind.

As soon as Cherelle sat at the bar, the bartender came over. She waved him off. She didn't have five bucks for a glass of soda water. A well-dressed working girl farther down the bar sent her a hard look. Cherelle just shook her head slightly, silently telling the other woman that she didn't need to worry about any poaching. Cherelle wasn't in competition for a horny john.

"Sure I can't get you something?" the bartender asked, giving Cherelle a knowing once-over.

"Sugah, I wish you could." She leaned forward and gave him a good view of what he wasn't going to get any of. "But I'm not working. I'm waiting for a friend."

"You change your mind, ask for Slim John."

She looked at the bartender. Tall, thin, in his forties, he seemed more like a schoolteacher than a bartender. "Well, you sure are one long drink of water, and that's a fact."

He winked at her and went down the bar toward a man who'd just sat down.

Cherelle wondered what time it was. Her watch didn't work, and there wasn't a clock anywhere in sight. Then she saw Risa crossing the lobby, headed toward Gabriel's Horn. She was wearing the kind of soft gray slacks and jacket and intense blue blouse that fairly shouted money and class. Some kind of ID card swung on a silver chain around her neck. Just before she left the lobby area, a bellman ran up to her. She turned back toward the registration desk, where someone instantly handed her a phone.

As Cherelle watched people scurry around for Risa, it became obvious that her old friend was a well-known and important employee in the fancy casino. And she looked good enough to leave a sour taste in the back of Cherelle's throat.

That was why she had stopped visiting Risa a few years back. She hated being jealous of what the big-eyed, scrawny, defiant orphan had grown up into.

She couldn't have done it without me, Cherelle reminded herself bitterly. *I fought her fights. Now she has everything, and I have shit.*

She owes me.

Sixteen

Miranda Seton's blue eyes were as faded as her dreams. Other than alcohol, there was only one source of pleasure in her life, and he was standing in her garage with an empty stomach and a garbage bag full of dirty clothes. She hugged him again and again while she fed clothes into a washing machine that was almost as old as her son.

"I can't believe you're here, Timmy! You should have called. I would have bought some pork chops to fry for you and made your favorite cookies."

Tim patted his mother's narrow shoulder and kissed the top of her head. He kept forgetting how small she was, how old she looked. And what a gray place she lived in. Even the Siamese cat curled up on the kitchen counter looked down on its luck.

Anger flared. "Mama, you should make that stingy bastard treat you better."

Her smile quivered and flipped upside down. Tears stood in her wide-set, childlike eyes. She had a savings account just full of money given to her by her son's father, but she was waiting for Timmy to grow up before she turned it all over to him so that he could take care of both of them.

Even half drunk, she knew it might be a long wait. But right now that didn't matter. Her beautiful boy was back in the house.

"Don't you talk about your daddy like that," she said. "I'm happy here, and he gave me the best thing in my life. You."

Tim's anger slipped away. He had never been able to hold on to it for long. The one time he'd worn his mother down enough to reveal his father's name, she spent the next four days drunk and crying and making him promise over and over again not to contact his father, not for any reason, *not ever*.

She might have loved the man once, but he had always frightened her.

After Tim had learned more about who his father was, he knew why his mother didn't want to rattle that cage. Once you got past the public face, that was one cold, mean son of a bitch his mother had spread her legs for.

"Aw, don't start in," Tim said, hugging Miranda. "As soon as Socks gives me what he owes me, we'll go out to dinner at that cafeteria you like so much. How about that?"

Though she said instantly, "Don't waste your money on me," she was smiling again.

When the garbage bag was empty, she opened up his backpack, knowing that he usually stuffed dirty clothes in there, too. Her groping hand found cloth wrapped around something hard. She grabbed it and hauled it out into the glare of the naked lightbulb just above the washing machine.

"What's this? You carrying shotgun shells or something bad?" It was her greatest fear that Tim would end up in jail again. That first time, his father had ripped her up one side and down the other for letting his son go bad. But he hadn't threatened to stop paying her.

The nice thing about the statute of limitations on murder was that it never ran out. Not that that was the only thing that kept the money coming in. Tim's daddy didn't have any children. He might not be real good when it came to loving and all that, but he sure did like owning things—even a son he couldn't brag about.

Tim snatched the sock before his mother could upend it on her palm and shake out the figurine. "This is just some shit Cherelle picked up from a friend. Why don't you go and scramble me some eggs or something, and I'll put the rest of the stuff in the washer."

Miranda hesitated, smoothed her hair uncertainly, and drew her faded rose housecoat more closely around her body. If she had known that her son was coming, she would have dressed up a little. Or at least changed out of her pajamas.

"You sure?" she asked. "You know how much soap and everything?"

"Mama, I'm over thirty. I can wash a few clothes." He just didn't like to. Most of the time he could sweet-talk Cherelle into doing it for him, along with the rest of the cleaning.

"That lazy girl of yours is making you do your own wash, isn't she?" Miranda's voice was laced with a mixture of irritation and triumph that no woman treated her son as good as his mother did. "You're out working two jobs to put food on the table, and she's lying around eating chocolate and watching daytime soaps."

Tim ignored his mother.

"Huh," she muttered. "You should kick her out on her no-good ass and find a woman that knows how to take care of a man."

"They don't make 'em like you anymore, Mama."

"Huh."

Smiling, Miranda hurried into the house, shooed the cat off the counter, and began cooking for her boy.

Seventeen

Risa hung up the house phone, cursed under her breath, and headed for Gabriel's Horn before another person with the wrong kind of gold artifacts to sell could interrupt her. She didn't want to keep Cherelle waiting. Not only would it be rude, it would give Cherelle a chance to do what she did best—attract attention.

Risa hoped that her friend would look better than she had the last time they met. She'd looked so poor that guilt had closed around Risa's throat like a fist. She wondered if Cherelle had ever connected the hundred dollars in twenties stuffed into her car's ashtray with the childhood friend who had taken her to lunch that day.

If Cherelle had made the connection, she hadn't ever said anything.

"Hey, baby-chick," Cherelle said, standing up with a wide smile when she spotted Risa. "How the hell are you?"

Risa grinned, hugged her, and stepped back. "I'm just fine, mama-chick. Hey, you look"—*worn, hard, angry*—

"just like you did the last time, and that was almost four years ago. What's your secret? Women our age are supposed to *look* over thirty."

"Well," Cherelle said, smoothing invisible wrinkles out of her tight jeans and winking at a nearby man whose eyes followed her hands, "the sex diet works for me."

For a moment Risa's smiled dimmed, then notched up again. Cherelle had never made any secret of her men. Quite the opposite. It was as if she believed that every man she'd had made her that much better than any other woman. When they were younger, it hadn't mattered so much. But that was many men ago.

Risa wished that just one of them had made Cherelle happy.

"I'll have to give that diet a try," Risa said lightly. She hooked her arm through Cherelle's. "Come up to my office. I ordered some lunch for us, but I've got several calls out that I don't want to miss. You want anything from the bar?"

Cherelle hesitated.

"My treat," Risa said, signaling the bartender. If Cherelle's wallet was as used-up as her clothes, she didn't have money to spend on luxuries like eating or drinking in a restaurant.

"Cosmopolitan. A big ol' double," Cherelle said to Slim John. When she'd first started drinking in bars, a Cosmopolitan had been the ultimate in sophisticated drinks. She knew that something else must have taken its place among the young and flashy, but she didn't know what it was.

The bartender nodded and looked at Risa. "What can I do for you?"

"You're new, aren't you?"

"This week," he agreed.

She smiled. "Welcome aboard. I'm Risa Sheridan, Shane Tannahill's curator. Send the order up to my office. Sally"—she gestured toward a woman dressed in 1950s beatnik costume who was chatting up a customer— "knows the way."

"What about your drink?" Cherelle asked. "Or do you have a bottle stashed somewhere?"

"I've been on short rations of sleep. If I had anything alcoholic, my face would be in my salad."

"Oh, baby-chick, what's happened to you? Time was you could match me drink for drink."

"You were right. Education rotted my brain."

Cherelle snickered. "Told ya."

"You sure did." Many times. *Forget that nerd shit, baby-chick. Mama-chick will teach you all you need to know.*

For a while she had.

But after Cherelle turned seventeen and left town with a drug salesman, Risa had discovered that she loved books, and especially loved learning about the world beyond Johnson Creek, Arkansas.

At sixteen Risa had a lifetime of schooling to make up. She did it in one year, thanks to her own unusual intelligence, newfound discipline, and a dedicated schoolteacher who had no family. Ms. Stinton's tutoring, faith, and encouragement, coupled with fourteen-hour study days and advice about clothes and makeup, had speeded Risa's transformation from tag-along hellion with no future to solitary, gifted scholar.

That change created a chasm between Risa and the one person who had truly cared about her during childhood, the person who had protected her when no one else answered her screams: Cherelle Faulkner.

So many shared memories . . .

She and Cherelle had been sisters in everything but blood. And in the end, how much did blood count? Their own blood had given them away before they were even born. Cherelle had taught Risa how to ride a bike. Cherelle had taught her how to put on lipstick and eye shadow. Cherelle had told her where babies came from and how to make sure none came from you. Cherelle had imitated the class snob so perfectly that Risa had wet her pants laughing, and in doing so got over the pain of being called trailer-park trash for having hand-me-down clothes and charity lunches and holes in her sneakers.

Cherelle also had taught her how to ditch classes, forge notes from home, and boost stuff from the 24/7 store by the highway.

And it was Cherelle who had hauled a college boy off a fifteen-year-old Risa and then kneed that boy where it would do the most good, all the while screaming that just because *she* did it for money didn't mean her friend did it for free.

Shortly after that miserable night, Cherelle had left town with one of her "dates." Risa had cried like she had lost her whole family.

Because she had.

Her adoptive mother had died before Risa was six. The man she called "Daddy" hadn't wanted a child in the first place. Risa had gone to her dead mother's sister. Stepsister, really, but the girls had grown up together, and Sara Lisa really needed the child-support payments she got when she took Risa in. Not that Sara Lisa had been a bad mother. She didn't beat Risa or refuse to feed her. It was just that Sara Lisa was too busy waiting tables and getting drunk on weekend "dates" to have much time or energy left for Risa.

Then Cherelle's foster parents had taken over the trailer next door to Risa's. In a matter of weeks Risa had gone from a lonely nine-year-old to Cherelle's quick-witted shadow. Together the girls conquered the world with giggles and long legs that could outrun any trouble they got into. At least, for a while.

Silently Risa led Cherelle to an inconspicuous door marked EMPLOYEES ONLY. She punched the proper code into a keypad next to the door. It swung open.

"Here we go," Risa said.

The door closed behind them. They were in a quiet, plain hall. Equally plain elevators lined both sides of the hall. After the lush décor and cheerful noise of the casino, the beige paint and silence were almost shocking.

Risa took the plastic ID card on its long chain and shoved it into a slot next to the elevators. After the doors opened and they were inside, she put the card into the slot next to a keypad and tapped out the code to her office. Only when a valid code had been entered did the doors close and the elevator rise. There were no lights, no numbers, nothing to indicate the floors as they whipped by invisibly.

"Hooo-eee, baby-chick. You work in the money room or something?" Cherelle asked.

"What?"

"All the cards and codes and crap. Not even a floor number."

"Oh, that. The artifacts I work with are quite valuable."

"Yeah? You'll have to show me."

"No problem. We'll be having lunch with them. I'm working on a show for my boss."

Cherelle almost purred. She'd been wondering how to raise the subject of her golden goodies without just plopping them out on the table like a dead bass. "Like the one in the pamphlet?"

"Pamphlet?"

"You know. The ones around that sheepskin downstairs."

"Oh. I forgot about those. Actually, I'd *like* to forget about them. My boss is chewing my tail because I haven't found anything special enough for his upcoming gold show. What's in the pamphlet is just a cross-section of gold objects we've displayed in the past, plus a few teasers about the wonderful Druid Gold show to come."

"Druid gold? What's that?"

Risa paused and thought quickly, trying to find a way to explain without making Cherelle self-conscious about her own lack of education. "Remember in school when we were studying England?"

"Baby-chick, I never studied nothing. That was for the dumbs."

"How about Stonehenge? That ring a bell?"

"That big ol' stone circle where people dress up in sheets and dance around pretending to be witches or wizards?"

Risa laughed. "Close enough." The fact that Stonehenge had been built long, long before Druids came on the scene didn't matter. It was enough that Cherelle had some point of reference, however vague. "After the original builders of Stonehenge vanished, a people we know as Celts arrived. They started in Europe a long time before Christ was born and spread in all directions until they reached the British Isles about three thousand years ago."

"Yeah?" Cherelle rummaged in her ragged purse/backpack for some gum. She had a taste in her mouth that would gag a maggot. The Cosmopolitan she'd ordered would go a long way toward cutting the scum, but the drink wasn't here right now and the taste sure as hell was.

"Mmm," Risa agreed as the elevator began to slow. "The Celts were master metalworkers. In fact, some scholars believe that the Celts taught the Greeks how to work gold. Others, of course, shriek at the mere suggestion that anyone could have taught the Greeks anything. We live in a very Eurocentric culture."

Cherelle unwrapped some gum.

"Sorry, mama-chick," Risa said. "I forget that not everyone loves the same stuff I do."

And talking about it deepened rather than built a bridge over the chasm separating her from her childhood friend.

The elevator stopped. The door opened onto a hallway that was as quiet as the other had been, but not as plain. There was wood paneling on one side, framed art of various kinds on the other, and a dense, colorful carpet underfoot.

"This way." Risa gestured to the left. "My office is next to the 'museum.'"

"Museum." Cherelle's tone of voice said she would sooner have her toenails pulled out one by one.

"Not really," Risa assured her. "I just call it that because we have a lot of things scattered around while we try to figure out what would go best in the show."

"Gold?" Cherelle asked, focusing on Risa.

"Gold."

"That's more like it, baby-chick."

Laughing, Risa gave Cherelle a one-armed hug. Her friend's cheerful greed was refreshing after spending hours on the phone with auction-house representatives who sounded as though they would choke if someone asked what an item was worth. This was *culture*, after all.

It was also commerce, as anyone in the business knew. The more the auctioneers flogged culture, the higher the price went.

"So show me something," Cherelle said, looking around.

"Jewelry?"

"Oh, yeah. Big ol' hunks of gold."

"Right this way."

Cherelle followed Risa eagerly toward a long, glass-topped case. Risa gestured at the articles within.

"These are some of the things Shane has collected in preparation for the Druid Gold show that will open New Year's Eve."

The thought of time slipping away made Risa's stomach knot. The only good news was that none of Shane's other searchers had done any better than she had.

So far anyway.

Cherelle bent so close to the case that her breath fogged the glass. With a muttered word she retreated a few inches and stared intently. This stuff was more like what she had than the pictures in the pamphlet. Except that a lot of these pieces looked beaten up, as though they had been hauled around in backpacks and dumped on cement floors.

Silently she counted. Eighteen pieces. One more than she had locked in the trunk of her car.

"What do you call those?" Cherelle asked.

Risa looked beyond the pointing finger. "Those are torcs. Like bracelets for your neck."

"Solid gold?"

"Some torcs are. These aren't. They're hollow, but their history is very . . ." Risa stopped talking for the simple reason that Cherelle had stopped listening.

"And those?" Cherelle asked.

"Armbands."

"Solid?"

"Thick gold foil over iron. The design is simple but exquisitely done."

Cherelle wasn't interested in design of any kind. "Those?" she asked, pointing again.

"Fibulae. Like fancy safety pins for fastening clothes," she added quickly. "They didn't have zippers or buttons in those days."

"Those pins are solid gold?"

"The two on the right are."

"Kinda small, aren't they?"

"They were probably a votive offering—a way of giving something to the gods so that the gods would listen to your prayers."

Cherelle chewed on the corner of her mouth and wondered what the bits and pieces in the case were worth.

Risa watched her friend's expression. In many ways Cherelle was a good test audience for the articles. "What do you think?"

She shrugged. "This stuff is like an old whore. Same equipment as a young one, but with the kind of mileage that really cuts the price."

Risa looked at the battered metal arc that probably had been damaged by the same farmer's plow that had unearthed the treasure in the first place. The other items showed nicks, dents, bends, warps, irregularities, and outright breakage that troubled modern eyes accustomed to new, machine-made jewelry.

But to Risa's eyes every mark was priceless, for it told

of each artifact being made, worn, passed from one generation to the next, buried, and dug up again. Each piece had a tantalizing history. She'd often daydreamed of what stories the jewelry could tell.

"When you're between fifteen hundred and three thousand years old," Risa said, "you show it."

Cherelle's head snapped around toward Risa. "What?"

"Fifteen to thirty centuries."

She swallowed her gum in surprise. "Holy shit."

Risa smiled wryly. That was one way of putting it. "Yeah. A long time."

"I suppose that makes it worth more, huh?"

"More than its weight in ordinary gold? Oh, yes."

"How much more?"

"It depends on a lot of things."

"Like?" Cherelle pressed.

"Age, rarity, artistry, and provenance—that's where it came from and how well documented it is."

"Documents, huh?" Cherelle chewed the corner of her mouth some more. That could be a big ol' bitch of a problem. "All this stuff came with papers?"

"Actually, most of it was dug up at some time in the past by the ancestors of the titled men and women who sold off parts of their inheritance in order to keep the rest. Others came from museums that were cleaning house. Some were probably stolen by people who found them and didn't tell the landowner." Risa shrugged. "But it all happened so long ago in the past that it doesn't matter anymore."

"How long does that take?"

Risa smiled. "At least a hundred years. The more hundreds, the better the provenance, the higher the price."

Cherelle went back to chewing on her mouth. She

didn't have a hundred years. Hell, she probably didn't have a week before Socks wheedled Tim's gold out of him. "So who bought the stuff before it had all the paper to go with it?"

"People who wanted the objects more than they wanted to display them publicly. Collectors, in a word."

"Like your boss?"

Risa's mouth turned down. "Not if I can help it. Everything I show to him is legal."

A small smile played around Cherelle's lips. "But you're not always the one showing stuff to him, right?"

Risa shrugged.

"Hey, baby-chick. Take the frog-sticker out of your ass. This is your mama-chick, remember? We used to boost more stuff in a week than this here glass box could hold."

"Yeah. And I was so scared the whole time that I couldn't spit."

Full, husky laughter poured out of Cherelle, making her look almost young again. "Those were the good times, weren't they? Heat thick enough to walk on and cold drinks swiped from Old Man Burlington's cooler. We'd shinny up that big ol' oak in front of your aunt's trailer and freeze our brains slugging icy Coke, and we'd stay up there till dark wishin' we was boys so we didn't have to come down to pee."

Risa laughed at the memories. Cherelle was right. Those were the good times, when life was a long, hot summer filled with mischief and laughter and dreams.

"But we always had to come down, didn't we?" Cherelle asked with a hard twist to her mouth. She looked through the smudges she had left on the glass and sighed deep enough to haze the surface. "So how much is this all worth? A couple hundred? A thousand?"

"Dollars?"

Cherelle gave her a look from the old days, the one that said, *Baby-chick, if you so smart, why you so dumb!*

Risa smiled. "Lots of thousands."

Cherelle's breath hitched, then smoothed. "Like twenty?"

"More like hundreds."

It was an effort to breathe. After a moment, Cherelle managed it. "Help me with this, baby-chick. She gestured to the case. You saying that this is worth hundreds of *thousands* of dollars?"

"That's what I'm saying."

"Hooooo-*ee*!"

"And I've got a piece arriving in a few days that we just paid four hundred thousand for."

"One fucking piece?"

"It's in excellent condition. High artistry. Very old. Very, very special. We were lucky that we found out about it before Gail Silverado."

"Who's she?"

"She owns the Wildest Dream casino. She loves beating Shane out on everything gold and Celtic. He's had to pay ridiculous prices to keep her from outbidding him for good pieces."

"Like four hundred thousand dollars?" Cherelle asked without really caring about the answer. She was still trying to wrap her mind around that much money in one piece of gold.

"Actually, that price was fairly reasonable," Risa said. "A few years ago a single Celtic fibu—er, pin—sold for one million pounds at auction. That's about one and a half million dollars."

Cherelle's breath rushed out. "Christ Jesus. Hold me

down and beat me like a stepchild." She closed her eyes and fought a wave of dizziness. "A million and a half dollars. *One pin.*"

"One very unique pin. Most aren't worth a tenth of that. Or even a hundredth."

"A tenth."

"Yeah. About one hundred and fifty thousand dollars. A hundredth would be fifteen thousand dollars."

Cherelle leaned against the case because she didn't think she could stand up without help. *A second-rate or even a third-rate pin was worth more cash money than she had seen in her whole life.*

And she had a trunkful of stuff that looked better than anything she saw in Risa's fancy case.

"Are you okay?" Risa asked just as a knock came on her locked door. "That's lunch. Or maybe your drink."

Cherelle blew out another long breath and started grinning. "Baby-chick, I hope it's the drink. It's been a long life, but it's worth every bit of shit I ate just to kiss the asshole it came from."

Throwing back her head, Cherelle laughed and laughed. She had done it. *She had really done it.*

And it was one hell of a big score.

Eighteen

Shane's fingers sped over the keyboard of his specially modified computer. No one at the casino had the access he did to all the various television eyes that recorded every corner of the casino, lobby, public hallways, and employee rooms.

Usually Shane let security watch over the casino, but not this time. He didn't want to ask them to spy on Risa. He didn't even want to do it himself.

While he called up the digital sequence from Gabriel's Horn, he thought of all the more useful ways he could spend his time than seeing who his curator was meeting for lunch. If his instincts hadn't sat up and howled over Risa's reaction to the phone call, he would be spending his time doing something more productive—working to put together an even fancier firewall to protect his computer or going over the casino's electronic books, for example.

Normally he spent at least one day a week matching every department of the casino's hold from one week to the next, comparing it to the hold for the same week the year before and the year before that, all the way back to the first week the Golden Fleece opened. It was a time-consuming job and, lately, not as interesting to him as it once had been. But it was the way he picked up trends for specific games, for cards versus slots, for sports betting versus baccarat, new scams or new variations on old favorites, and which insurance fraud was going through Vegas like a flu. Juggling figures was also the best way to pick up the trail of employee theft, dishonest dealers, and the occasional brass-balled hacker.

The success of the Golden Fleece owed a great deal to Shane's ability to draw truths and trends from the complex database of numbers that made most people roll their eyes and head for the nearest bar. While he was beginning to feel the same way about massaging the data, the job still had to be done.

Eventually.

No. *Soon.*

With an unconscious sigh, Shane promised himself that he would take the electronic books apart byte by byte just as soon as the Druid Gold show was launched. At least he had put in an updated firewall last week. Two months late, to be sure. The good news was that none of the data suggested that the Golden Fleece was losing money thanks to a computer mole. But he still should be working on designing a new firewall right now.

Where the hell did the time go?

One way or another, whether fretting or doing something useful, most of his working and waking hours had been taken up with the upcoming Druid Gold show. Not to mention the curator who both intrigued and annoyed him. What little was left over of his time or energy went into the countless small, urgent business decisions that had to be made, the ones that weren't covered by training manuals. Those decisions were bucked up the management line to him every day, day after day.

He had to learn to delegate more.

And he would.

Eventually.

One of the forty flat screens that provided real-time wallpaper on the south side of his office flickered and then steadied. The picture was exquisitely clear. The time-and-date strip across the bottom blinked monotonously, a signal that this wasn't a real-time display. There wasn't any sound.

Gabriel's Horn looked pretty much the way it always did, night or day, holiday or workday. A handful of the barstools were occupied by several men and one woman in sleek resort wear. The men followed one or all of the pro sports that were featured on the bar's six TV screens. The well-dressed woman whooped and hollered when the man two stools down did. Every time the man shifted, a gold necklace and pendant—a heavy, diamond-encircled gold coin—glittered against his shiny black shirt. The whole package might have looked more impressive if the buttons weren't straining over his hairy belly.

The more dedicated gamblers played video poker while sitting at the bar. Six couples lounged at the tables, smoking or sipping or watching the TVs or munching on bar freebies. The really skillful people managed to do it all at once. A keno runner cruised through in long black stockings and a knee-length dress, looking for any betting cards that had been filled out by patrons who didn't understand odds or didn't care.

A woman in spray-paint jeans and a tight red sweater strolled into the bar and sat down. With a smile and a toss of her blond hair, she waved off the bartender. Her makeup was like the clothes—not subtle. If the woman wasn't a hooker, she was sure dressed like one. But then a lot of amateurs and weekend party girls dressed like that. So did some otherwise-bright women who thought the only taste men had was in their dicks. It made life real interesting for casino security, because one of their jobs was to keep prostitutes out of the casino's bars.

The men at the bar gave Red Sweater a long look. She ignored them and headed for a barstool that was away from the crowd. When the bartender came right over, she waved him off.

Shane settled back in his chair and waited for Risa to appear. The bartender made another try at selling Red Sweater a drink. Big smile and no sale. Red Sweater turned her back to the bar and watched the casino and lobby action.

With a few quick motions Shane keyed in the fast forward. Eventually Red Sweater slid off her barstool with a wide grin and outspread arms.

It was Risa she was so happy to see.

Shane's finger stabbed on the electronic brake. The two women were only on-screen for a minute or two. Then, arm in arm, they set off across the lobby.

His hands danced over the keyboard, calling up the stored memory of various cameras. He watched Risa and Red Sweater go through an employee entrance, up a secure elevator, and then into Risa's office. He called up the cameras that hovered above the valuable artifacts in her office rooms.

This time there was sound. It was part of the security system that always surrounded the people who worked with gold.

Settling back again, Shane watched.

And listened.

Then he turned off the sound and ran through the sequence again. And again. And again. No conversation to distract him, just the expressions that came and went like heat lightning over Risa's face, expressions he could freeze with a flick of his finger.

For a long time the only sound in Shane's office was the occasional *click* of gold against gold as he walked his pen across his fingers, back and forth, back and forth, watching his curator and the woman she called Cherelle.

The contrast between the two of them was enough to make every one of his instincts quiver. Cherelle looked like she made her living on her back and knees. Risa looked like an executive who was doing everything she could to minimize her female appeal.

And yet . . .

When they laughed together, he could see the children they once had been and the bond that had survived the years. At least on Risa's part. There was none of the calculation in her eyes, none of the bitterness in the line of her mouth that the woman called Cherelle showed whenever Risa wasn't looking.

Abruptly Shane slipped the pen back into his pocket and went to work. First he excerpted five of the clearest shots of Cherclle and sent them, along with possible variations on the spelling of her name, to his head of security. Cherelle would be entered into the security computer and picked up whenever she was within range of one of the cameras. It was just one of the many ways the casino protected itself against cheaters, card counters, and known criminals.

Then he called Rarities Unlimited, using one of Niall's private numbers.

"What's up, boyo?" Niall asked immediately.

"I want a full search on two people. I've already loaded the pertinent digital sequences onto your security computer."

"Bloody hell! You hacked your way in again."

Shane made an impatient noise. "If I had, I wouldn't be asking you, would I? I only accessed the file you have on me and dumped the stuff in."

"You accessed the . . . Shit. You're a menace. Good thing you're on the side of the angels."

"Yeah, but don't tell anybody. I hear much more when people think I'm dirty."

Niall gave an evil chuckle and called up Shane's file. A picture of a woman popped onto the screen. "My, she's a real bit o' work, isn't she? Name?"

"Cherelle. No last name. No definite spelling on the first."

"Lovely. What did she— Bloody hell, that's Risa with her!"

Shane grunted.

"You're asking for a full search on Risa Sheridan," Niall said neutrally.

"Wouldn't you?"

"I— Hell, we're both paranoid."

"My daddy is Bastard Merit. What's your excuse?"

"Experience. Even—"

"—paranoids have real enemies," Shane finished in a disgusted tone. "That joke is older than you are, which makes it older than the combined ages of—"

The sound on the line told Shane he was talking to himself. He punched out and went back to the sequence in the bar before Risa arrived. Something was nagging at him.

This time he didn't watch Cherelle. He watched the other woman at the bar. This time he caught the bartender's signal. Immediately the well-dressed woman got off the barstool and headed for a nearby slot machine. About ten seconds later one of the casino's plainclothes security personnel went through the bar. As soon as he left, the woman returned. This time she sat down right next to the guy with the belly and the gold chain. She ordered a drink and paid for it with a twenty.

The bartender gave her fizzy water and no change.

She didn't ask for any.

Shane hit the button on his phone that called the head of security for this eight-hour stretch. It was answered instantly.

"This is Ned, what can I do for you, sir?"

"Check out the eye in Gabriel's Horn for the last hour. If you see what I think you'll see, show the bartender to the door and make sure the hooker goes with him."

"I'm on it, sir."

Shane's other phone rang as he hung up. The ID number was the daytime casino manager.

"Now what?" he muttered. "Can't anyone decide to sneeze without calling me?" He picked up the receiver and said curtly, "Tannahill."

"I'm glad you're in, sir. Bob Fairweather is pushing against his maximum. Will you want to extend his credit line?"

"No." Fairweather was Gail Silverado's executive casino manager. Unlike most managers, he liked to gamble. Like most gamblers, he didn't admit he was riding a losing streak until the money ran out. "Comp him to a nice meal in the VIP lounge. And make sure he's sober when he leaves."

"He isn't drinking."

Shane grunted. Fairweather usually drank. But then

he usually gambled *after* he finished his shift with the Wildest Dream, not before. He must have felt lucky.

He wasn't.

"Anything else?" Shane asked.

"No, sir."

Shane punched off, sat back in his chair, and pulled out his pen. He looked at the freeze-frame picture of Risa and Cherelle hugging on one TV screen. The only sound in the room was the rhythmic, relentless click of gold meeting gold.

Something didn't fit, which meant that something was wrong. Very wrong. It was the kind of hunch that Shane didn't want and couldn't ignore.

And whatever was wrong, Risa was dead center in the middle of it.

Nineteen

Socks left his neon purple baby in a parking space at a burger joint two blocks away from Joey Cline's pawnshop. Backpack over his shoulder, jeans sagging around his ankles, Socks strolled past businesses whose windows were about as clean as the gutters outside.

A wadded-up cigarette pack blew along the cracked sidewalk, driven by a hard, dry wind. The cloudless sky was taking on a brassy sheen that would have been smog in Los Angeles but was just dust in Las Vegas. Socks didn't really notice any of it. He'd seen it all before, too many times. He'd grown up four blocks from Joey's pawnshop. Nothing had changed since then except the number of cracks in the sidewalk.

Nothing much was different in the pawnshop's windows since his last visit to Joey either. Behind the dusty glass and iron bars there were guitars, amps, Indian jewelry, rifles, TVs, VCRs, DVDs, dirty handguns, and a violin with three strings waiting for someone to get lucky again. Socks gave the pawned handguns a look, but they were all small-caliber. He didn't want a girly gun. He wanted something a man would be happy to stuff in his pants.

A friendly little bell tinkled when he opened the front door of the pawnshop. Experience told him that a much less friendly bell was going off in the back room and a video camera in front of the store had started running just to make sure a guy didn't help himself before Joey came out of the back room to greet the customer.

The front part of the shop was clean but otherwise like the sidewalk display window—narrow, dingy, and unwelcoming. The light was bad, the counters were old, most of the glass was chipped or cracked or both, and the goods inside the cases were exactly what a cop would expect to find pawned by losers riding the downward curve of their luck into desperation.

Socks wandered off to the left side of the shop, where he knew the camera couldn't reach. He leaned over a scarred wooden counter and pressed a button. Two things happened at once. The camera stopped recording, and a panel no wider than his butt opened at the end of the counter. He slid through before the panel could close again.

"Hey, Joey, it's Socks!" he hollered.

A sound came from the back.

Socks took it as the invitation it probably was. He opened a man-size cabinet that held racks of shotguns and rifles so dirty they would have jammed or blown up on anyone fool enough to load and fire them. He reached between two worn stocks and pushed. A concealed latch at the rear of the cabinet snapped open, the back panel swung aside, and Socks walked into the real business center of Joey Cline's pawnshop.

The weapons here were clean, modern, and large-bore. The best of them were cold—untraceable by any cops from city badges all the way to the FBI. Next to a case full of shiny weapons there was a bulletproof display table whose contents would have done credit to Tiffany's. More than one second-story man had discovered just how little money on the dollar stolen jewels would bring from Joey Cline. On the plus side, Joey paid in cash and didn't talk to anyone about anything that went on inside the back room, not even his wife.

Dressed in a dark, oil-stained denim shirt and jeans, Joey emerged from behind a worktable covered by the various lubricants, rags, and tools of a gunsmith's trade. Joey's first love was fixing guns until they were as oiled and eager as a hot woman.

"Hey, Cesar, been a long time," Joey said, pushing his magnifying goggles up on his head and smiling big enough to put creases on either side of his wispy mustache. "You got something for me?"

Socks winced. He hated his given name. Everybody called him by his street name except people who had known him before he did time. Joey was one of those people. He and his father and his grandfather had fenced stuff for Socks's family for years. Ripped them off for years, too, but that was the way it was in this part of town. If you couldn't steal from strangers, you stole from friends. When it got down to the really short strokes, you stole from kin.

"Yeah, I got something," Socks said. "If you make me a good offer, I won't shop it over at Shapiro's."

Joey shrugged and wiped his hands on a rag that was as black as his hair. "I give you the best deal I can and still stay in business. You know that."

"Uh-huh." Socks knew that Joey gave him as little as he thought he could get away with. Nothing personal. Just the way things were.

Joey knew the game, too. Dumb lumps like Socks were a big part of the pawnshop's profit margin, but the lumps came back again and again because they were just clever enough to want to stay out of jail. Joey had never snitched off anyone. Well, maybe once or twice, but that was only to stay out of jail himself. Nothing personal. Just the way things were.

Socks shrugged off his backpack and reached inside. The first thing he pulled out was one of the figurines that looked kind of like a buck with a nice spread of antlers. The designs on the body were so tiny they made Socks dizzy trying to figure them out. So he didn't look at them.

He held the figurine about a foot above Joey's oily palm and opened his fingers. "What do you think of this?"

Joey grunted as the surprising weight of the metal smacked into his palm. He knew right away it was either lead or gold. Nothing else felt that heavy for its size, yet almost soft to the touch. His heart quickened. He pulled the goggles over his eyes and flipped the figurine over in his fingers, looking for any sign that it was a gold-plate job.

Even magnified, the etched designs were so dense that he felt like his eyes were crossing when he tried to look at them.

He repeated the inspection. Slowly. It was like looking into one of those fractal screen savers his nephew loved, with a design repeated in smaller and smaller sizes but never ending, never still, and always staying the same. No beginning either. Just . . .

He swallowed and closed his eyes so his head stopped spinning. Just plain weird was what the figurine was. But there wasn't any sign of gold plate rubbed thin enough to show base metal beneath. Nor did he see any sign of the bubbles and pits bad plating often showed as it wore down over time.

"So someone plated a lead figure with low-karat gold," Joey said finally. "Big fucking deal."

But he didn't offer to give back the piece.

"Blow it out your ass," Socks said. "That's solid gold."

"How do you know?"

"I just know."

"You just know. Uh-huh. Like when did you get to be a big-deal gold expert?"

Socks had expected this. It was part of the bargaining process. And because he was just smart enough to know that he wasn't as smart as Joey, Socks had lined up his arguments ahead of time. No way he was going to be sent off with a hundred bucks for all the gold and a pat on the head for free.

"If you can't tell real gold, that's your problem. Gimme that. Shapiro knows real gold when he sees it."

Joey's fingers closed over the figurine. Shapiro was a few short steps up out of the gutter. Joey often resold really high-end stuff to him at a hefty markup. Shapiro resold it to Nance or Cochran or maybe even Smith-White, who traded it off to New York or Dallas or L.A., where he could turn it around in one of his fancy shops for ten or fifty or a hundred times what the original thief had been paid.

"Don't go off half-cocked," Joey said. "Maybe you better tell me what you think Shapiro will pay you that I won't."

Satisfaction rearranged Socks's dark features into the kind of smiling geniality that made his surges of brutality all the more unexpected. "Oh, I think he'll go a yard on this."

"A thousand dollars for this?" Joey scoffed. "Man, you're smoking crack."

"A yard," Socks said.

" 'A yard,' he says," Joey mocked. "Kiss mine. I'll go three hundred, but only because we're old friends."

That was three times what Socks had expected, but he was already reaching for the figurine and couldn't pull back in time.

Joey had no such problem. He jerked the piece beyond the other man's reach. "Okay, okay. Four hundred."

Socks was so surprised at the price he couldn't even talk.

"What do you say?" Joey asked.

Silence came while Socks tried to wrap his brain around the idea of four hundred dollars for this crap. Maybe Tim's bitch knew what she was talking about.

"Man, you're killing me here," Joey said. "Six hundred, and not one fucking cent more, and only because we go back so far, understand?"

Socks nodded.

The figurine vanished into Joey's pocket. "Got any more, or was it a one-off?"

Socks started to say he had been talking about all the gold, not just the one piece. Before he could be that dumb, he shut up and pulled another figurine out of his backpack. Then a pin. Then the armband.

"This is worth twice any of the others," Socks said, remembering what Tim had told him.

Joey wanted to disagree, but his mouth was dry. He knew just enough about old jewelry to realize that the heavily decorated gold band was likely worth an arm and a leg and a testicle if you had access to the right market. He didn't. Smith-White wouldn't even return his calls. Half the time Cochran wouldn't either.

But Shapiro could get through to Cochran.

Visions of that South Seas cruise his wife had been bugging him about swam delightfully in Joey's mind. "Two and a half yards for the lot of them."

That was more cash than Socks had ever held in his fist at one time. Robbing convenience stores was a hand-to-mouth way to live. Most of the time he was lucky if he got a hundred bucks plus all the booze he could carry for a night's work.

Twenty-five hundred dollars.

And lots more gold where that came from.

"I need a cold gun," Socks said. "Forty-five."

"Only got a nine-millimeter now. Try me in a few weeks."

"The nine is cold?"

Joey nodded.

"Guaranteed?" Socks pressed.

"Hell yes. You think I'm dumb enough to piss off someone that whacks guys for a living?"

"I don't whack guys. I just stick 'em up."

"I wasn't talking about you."

"Oh. How much?" Socks said.

"A thousand."

"What! Fuck, you'd think the gun was made of gold!"

"Gold would melt if you used it for a gun barrel," Joey said impatiently. "Look, just for you, just this once, I'll throw in the silencer and sell it for five. That leaves you with two thousand bucks in your jeans. We got a deal?"

Arithmetic had been one of the many subjects Socks

flunked on his way out of public schools, but the figure sounded about right to him. Best of all, he would have the gun, too. With that he could get more money.

"We got a deal."

Twenty

Cherelle licked up the last bit of shrimp cocktail off her fork, mopped steak juices from her plate with the final bite of her third French roll, finished her second double Cosmopolitan, and sighed happily. "Now, that's *food*. And it's free! How can you work here and not weigh two hundred pounds?"

Risa smiled. Watching her old friend eat her own lunch—and half of Risa's—had left her with a good feeling, as though she was giving back to Cherelle some of the help that she had given to Risa when they were much younger.

"Usually I'm too busy to eat lunch," Risa said. "Otherwise my butt would be a yard wide."

"Nah." Cherelle stretched. "*Two* yards."

Risa laughed, but her amusement faded as soon as she noticed the ripped seams under Cherelle's arms. Along with her friend's worn jeans, run-down shoes, and outright hunger, it added up to a woman who was on the ragged edge of poverty. Motels, even the worst of them, weren't cheap in Las Vegas.

The thought of Cherelle sleeping in her car or picking up some man in a bar just to have a place to spend the night made Risa feel angry and guilty at the same time. She was sure it wouldn't be the first time Cherelle had traded a "ride" for a bed to sleep in.

But it was the first time Risa had been able to do something about it.

"Hey, I have a great idea," she said. "I've got to get back to work right now and don't have any vacation time coming, but there's no reason we can't get together and play at night, is there? One of the perks of this job is an on-site apartment, complete with maid service. I'll call the front desk and tell them to leave a key to my casino apartment for you. You get your stuff and go on up and enjoy the man-size bathtub, order more food from room service if you're hungry, another drink from the bar, whatever. Take the bedroom on the left and treat it like your own hotel room."

The two potent drinks Cherelle had gulped made her wonder if her hearing was going. "You mean it?"

"Absolutely. I'll call down to the desk right now. They'll program a passkey for you."

"Well, go do it, girl! I can feel that steaming bathtub already. Uh, you mind if I borrow some of your clothes?"

"No problem. They might even fit. I've lost a little weight."

"Yeah, I saw that. Why you'd want to dump those inches . . ." Cherelle shook her head. "Baby-chick, don't you know that men like to grab a big ol' double handful of what's good?"

Shaking her head, Risa said, "You have some ID on you, or should I walk you down?"

"Driver's license."

"Perfect. My boss is a fiend for security."

Risa went to the phone, called up the front desk, and began giving instructions.

Smiling, Cherelle ran her fingertip around her steak plate and waited for the key to the magic kingdom to arrive.

Twenty-one

The phone rang on Shane's desk. He ignored it and kept on frowning at the computer screen. Considering all the payoffs that the Golden Fleece had made on slots, the machines were showing a surprising profit margin. Most slots earned a profit of between $100 and $125 per day. Not much, but when you had four thousand slots, it didn't take long to add up. Yet if the figures in front of him were correct, the machines were taking in an extra $18 per day, for no reason that he could discover. He expected some variation, a few percentage points over or under expectations. Under, usually, because cheats took money rather than depositing it. But here was a consistent high-end variation of more than 10 percent.

"Excuse me," Susan Chatsworth said, sticking her head in the doorway, "but Mr. Smith-White insists that you'll want to speak with him personally and privately."

Irritation warred with curiosity. Curiosity won. Smith-White owned a series of very upscale decorator stores, the kind that supplied genuine antiques and antiquities to wealthy clients and the interior decorators who decked out wealthy houses. Since Shane wasn't in the process of remodeling anything, there could be only one reason Smith-White was so insistent on talking to him privately.

Gold artifacts.

Shane picked up his phone. "Good morning, Jason. What can I do for you?"

"I understand you're still looking for outstanding Celtic artifacts. Gold."

"I'm always looking. That's why you called me."

Smith-White gave the breathless, liquid laugh of a lifetime smoker. "I have four pieces for you to look at."

Shane settled back into his black leather chair. "How old?"

"Hard to tell. Gold doesn't date. But my guess would be they're part of a hoard. A Druid hoard."

Excitement kicked in Shane. Antiquities normally came complete with papers describing them precisely, most especially on the subject of provenance. Obviously the four pieces of gold Smith-White was peddling didn't have paper pedigrees.

"Druid? What makes you say that?" Shane asked.

"When you see them, you'll know. They're quite extraordinary. Only high priests or kings would have possessed them."

"Sounds expensive."

"The best always is. These are museum quality, which is why I thought of you."

And the reward, Shane thought dryly as he glanced at his watch. Early for lunch and late for coffee. "How soon can you bring them here?"

"An hour, maybe more. Depends on how long my ten o'clock takes."

"Have the front desk call me when you arrive. A guard will meet you and bring you up."

He disconnected and buzzed Susan. "Have someone meet Smith-White at the front desk anytime after ten-thirty." He hesitated and gave a mental shrug. Even though he had called Rarities and given them the information from Cherelle's driver's license, Niall hadn't called back yet. "Anything more on the Faulkner woman?"

"She went out an hour ago. She hasn't returned."

"Suitcases?"

"Still here."

"What's the tab so far?"

"Seven thousand seven hundred and change."

Shane whistled. "How can anyone eat that much lobster and caviar?"

"She didn't. She discovered the salon and the boutique."

"Transfer the charges to the comp account," Shane said, referring to the account that paid for the comps, or freebies for people who bet a certain amount of money every hour for at least three hours a day. "But call down and tell them to draw the line at real jewelry. Sure as hell she'd go for the fancy yellow diamond solitaire."

"The one that's worth three-point-four million?"

"You noticed," he said, laughing.

"Are you kidding? Security is sweating bullets over it, not to mention the matching necklace and earrings."

"If the Wildest Dream is going to have a Fabergé show on New Year's Eve, the least I can do is bring in some fancies from De Beers. Let me know when the Faulkner woman comes back. I'll nail shut all the boutique doors."

"You could just close down the apartment's credit line."

"Not yet." He was curious to see just how far Cherelle Faulkner would go.

He was also curious about Risa's reaction when she realized that her old friend was hosing her.

Twenty-two

As far as Socks was concerned, Miranda Seton's house smelled like a bakery and sounded like a catfight. Cherelle was screaming at Tim and kicking the furniture around. The faded rose couch cushions and the chipped white wicker frame sat drunkenly askew. The table lamp with the rose-beaded fringe was lying on its side. A framed picture of Tim at his middle-school graduation was facedown in a corner, its glass shattered.

That was when Socks had retreated to the kitchen. The metal frame on that photo had damn near brained him.

The furniture had taken the first hit of Cherelle's fury when she finally pried out of Tim the information that he'd hocked two of his gold objects for four hundred dollars.

Total.

"You have the brains of dog shit!" she yelled, kicking out at the couch again, making the light framework jump. "How could you be so stupid! I told you they were worth real money!"

Tim held his hands in front of himself, palms out, and watched Cherelle warily. He had seen her pissed off before, but never like this. She could have sucked up bullets and spit molten lead.

"Hey, precious, take it easy. There's more gold, right? We'll make plenty. And four hundred isn't exactly chump change."

Cherelle was still screaming—*"Fucking moron!"*—when Socks came back into the living room with a double handful of peanut butter cookies.

"Put a cork in it," he told Cherelle around a mouthful of cookie. "You're upsetting Tim's ma. She's hiding in the kitchen with her hands over her ears, and the cookies are burning."

"Yo, roadkill," Cherelle said, rounding on Socks. "How much did you get for your two pieces?"

"The same."

"Lying sack of shit. Empty out your pockets."

"Hey," Tim said, "no need to call Socks names."

"I'm not calling him names," Cherelle said without looking away from Socks. "I'm describing him. Roadkill. Lying sack of shit. Cocksu—"

"Shut up, bitch," Socks yelled over her words. "Just shut the fuck up! We *were* broke, and now we *ain't* broke. So *shut up!*"

Cherelle considered kicking him in the crotch he thought so much of. Instead, she took a few deep breaths and tried to think past her rage at so much money slipping from her grasp. Hurting Socks would be satisfying, but it wouldn't change anything. Roadkill would never get any smarter.

Tim wasn't much when it came to brains, but he was better than roadkill. She turned back to her lover. "How much money do you have left of the four hundred?"

He shifted uneasily. "Uh, I bought a little blow, some booze, this shirt—nice, isn't it?"

She ignored the change of subject and the impressively loud Hawaiian shirt he'd showed up wearing a few minutes ago. "How much?"

"Two fifty. It's a nice shirt. You got new clothes," he added, gesturing to her pale green silk slacks and shirt. "Why shouldn't I?"

"I didn't pay for these!" Her eyes closed while she struggled against the rage that came more and more easily lately. She really should cut back on the crack, but there wasn't much else in life that felt good.

She was surrounded by morons.

With a raw sound she sucked in air. "Take the rest of your money and buy back the armband."

Tim looked at Socks, who shrugged and said, "Joey was doing me a favor. He'll probably be glad to get some money back." Especially after Socks leaned a little. He was beginning to think he'd been hosed by Joey. Not just a bit like always. A lot. "I have to do it for you, though. He don't like strangers."

And Socks didn't want Tim to find out what he really had been paid for the four pieces of gold.

"Roadkill," Cherelle whispered on a wild, shuddering outrush of air. "Fucking roadkill thinks pawnbrokers do favors. Christ Jesus deliver me from such *morons*. I'm going to tell you a little secret, roadkill. Those four chunks of gold you sold for eight hundred bucks are worth at least a million."

"Oh, yeah, sure they are." Socks laughed and remembered a line from a talk show. "You're a real funny girl. You ever think of getting your own show on cable?"

She just shook her head. Despair replaced the rage. So much money lost . . .

The tears shimmering in her eyes shocked both men. Neither of them had ever seen Cherelle cry. Not once. Not even when her car broke down and she was picked up by a guy who beat her, raped her, and dumped her out by the side of the road.

Socks and Tim looked at each other uneasily. Both were thinking the same thing.

What if she's right?

What if we let a million bucks get away?

Socks resettled his jeans, which were riding unusually low because of the gun stuffed beneath his bright new Hawaiian shirt. "Think I'll go see Joey."

"I think I'll come along," Tim said.

"Think. You *think*." Cherelle started laughing wildly. Then she wept without a sound. "Tim."

He turned back to her. "What is it, precious?"

"Don't come back without that armband. Ever."

It was a voice neither man had heard from her before. Neutral. Deadly neutral.

Both men sighed with relief when the front door of the little house shut behind them.

Twenty-three

In the midst of the cheerless cries and smoky desperation of one of Las Vegas's old-style, downscale grind joints, Slim John stared at his Golden Fleece paycheck stub and wished he could shove it up the head of security's ass with a wire brush.

"Who do they think they are, Mother Teresa?" he asked Merry Clare, a blackjack dealer at Say Paris! "Firing me because I help out a working girl, and then Mr. Godalmighty Tannahill's latest punchboard waltzes in and gives a big hug to another hooker and they swing their butts all the way to the employee elevator."

Merry shrugged and shifted so that the rump-sprung booth poked into a different part of her ass. The beer in front of her looked as flat as she felt. Anyone who thought dealing cards was an easy way to make a living was welcome to her job. Other casinos let their women dealers work in slacks and flat shoes. Not Say Paris! The boss insisted on French-maid gear complete with fishnet stockings that cut into the soles of her feet like wire.

"Yeah, life's an unfair bitch." Merry leaned forward and took a quick drag on Slim John's cigarette. Her heavily colored lips left a pink ring around the butt. "So who's Tannahill dicking these days?"

"An employee." Slim John swiped his cigarette back. He hated the taste of lipstick, which was why he screwed Merry but he rarely kissed her.

"Which one?" Merry asked.

"Risa Sheridan."

"Yeah? Hadn't heard that."

He snorted. Lipstick and gossip were Merry's passions. She hated being without either one. "You don't hear everything in Vegas. You just think you do."

"Yeah? Buy me another drink and I'll tell you how you can get even with Shane Tannahill."

"Even with Tannahill? Oh, yeah, sure, right after I become a billionaire."

"I'm serious."

Slim John hesitated, held up a five-dollar bill to catch a cocktail waitress's eye, and watched Merry. Another beer appeared with remarkable speed. Merry poured, savored the bite of frisky beer, and swallowed.

"Okay," Slim John said. "Tell me how."

"Word is that a lot of important people have a hard-on for Tannahill. He won't play their game, and that makes it tough for some of the biggest casinos."

"You're breaking my heart."

Merry's pink mouth curled up. "Yeah, I can see you're bleeding. Anyway, if you drop a whisper in Firenze's ear, he'll be so happy I bet he finds you work in his casino."

"What the hell could I tell Carl—"

"Not him," Merry cut in. "The uncle. Not that it matters. Either one would get the job done."

"So what am I telling John Firenze?"

She gave him an amused look. "Slim John, you really should listen when people talk about what's happening on the Strip under all the glitter and shine."

He grunted. "So talk."

"Some people want a handle on Risa Sheridan."

"Why?"

"Who cares? The pay is the same no matter what the reason. The fact that Sheridan's chummy with a hooker might be just what they want to hear. You know the hooker's name?"

"One of 'em."

Merry pulled a cell phone out of her purse. "Make the call."

He looked at the phone and shrugged. "Hell, why not? What do I have to lose?"

Twenty-four

Shane's computer screen was displaying the information on the hold for baccarat last week and every week before that. Frowning, he ran through the graphs again. Like the slots, the baccarat tables had been unusually profitable recently. The increase was under 10 percent, but it was there. And it added up to millions in extra profits. A few million he could have written off to the Japanese whales, but even they couldn't account for the extra seven million.

His fingers were poised to begin a probability scan on the baccarat numbers when his private phone rang. His very private one. He tried to be annoyed. He didn't succeed. Each time he started running the Golden Fleece's numbers, he realized how little he was enjoying what used to be meat and wine for him.

He picked up the receiver. "Yeah?"

Niall asked, "You recording?"

"Just dump all of it in my Rarities file at your end and give me the high points now."

"I don't like having you in my computer, boyo."

"Get used to it. Just like I'm used to the idea that Factoid spends every spare second he has trying to get into my computer. Thank God you keep that boy real busy."

At the other end of the connection, Niall laughed. Shane's genius with computers irritated the hell out of security-conscious Niall, but he liked Shane anyway. Probably because he trusted Shane not to use his gift against Rarities.

"Sauce for the goose and so on," Niall said, winking at Dana as she walked in his office door.

They were alone in his office, except for a wall of screens keeping track of Rarities Unlimited, much as Shane's "eyes" kept track of the Golden Fleece. She locked the door behind her, walked over, ruffled Niall's hair, and blew in his ear. Then she bit it.

Niall's concentration took a dive.

"I'd like a few facts with my cooked goose or gander or whatever," Shane said. "Forget the age, hair color, weight stuff type of information, unless it goes against anything in Risa's employee file."

Niall's right arm swept out and dumped Dana onto his lap. The office chair skidded a bit, then held.

"As kids, Cherelle and Risa were trailer-park neighbors in Johnson Creek, Arkansas," Niall said as his right hand glided over Dana's firm thigh.

She smacked his fingers.

He ignored her. She knew the rules—bite his ear and take the consequences whenever and wherever.

Now, for instance. Right here.

"The place was as big a dump as it sounds," Niall said. "Cherelle is either two or four years older than Risa, depending on whose foster-child records you believe." His hand kneaded over Dana's belly to her breasts. "Both girls showed up as bright lights on the early IQ tests, but it was Risa who really smoked the curve. That is one very intelligent woman."

"Tell me something I don't know."

"I'm trying." Niall's thumb and little finger spanned the gap between Dana's nipples. Circled. Flicked. The break of Dana's breath made him grin like a pirate. "Cherelle took Risa under her wing."

"Mama-chick and baby-chick."

"Yeah." Niall unbuttoned Dana's slippery blouse and slid his index finger inside her bra strap. A quick tug and one of her breasts was bare. Without knowing it, he licked his lips. The nipple rose as though he had stroked it. He closed his eyes, but he kept his hand right where it was, teasing her, making her back arch and her hips move slowly in his lap. "Anyway, they were thick as thieves. Apt phrase, that. Cherelle got caught boosting stuff several times but always got off with a tap on the wrist. Risa was nailed once."

"How old?"

"Eleven."

"I thought juvenile records are sealed."

"Same way the Rarities computer is sealed, boyo, until some bright computer jockey comes along."

Shane chewed on that in silence.

Niall peeled down the other bra strap.

Dana tried to steady her breathing.

"Up until Cherelle took off with a man, she and Risa ditched school, stole candy bars and such, painted words on walls, the usual ass-off delinquent thing. After Cherelle left—Risa was barely sixteen—Risa's record is spotless," Niall said. And stroked Dana's pouting breasts. "She settled right down under the tutelage of a maiden-aunt schoolteacher, made up all the academic work and then some. National Merit finalist. Not bad for a girl whose adoptive mother died when she was five and her mother's stepsister took her on but never really cared one way or another about the child."

Niall switched to speakerphone and slid his newly freed hand under Dana's skirt. She gave him a look that promised she would get even when he least expected it.

He smiled.

"Risa went to UCLA," Niall continued. "Challenged most of the undergraduate courses at the end of the first year and passed. Two years total for a B.A." His fingers traced lazy upward circles on Dana's thighs. "A few more years for a combined master's and Ph.D. Top one percent of her class. Worked at the L.A. County Museum as an intern—"

"And the museum loved her like a little flower, did handsprings to bring her along, and wept buckets when I stole her away," Shane interrupted. "Tell me more I don't know."

Niall's finger slid beneath delicate underwear, found sultry heat waiting, and he barely managed to bite back a husky sound of satisfaction. "That's just it, boyo. Once Cherelle blew out of town, there's nothing you don't know about Risa. After age eighteen, everything we found and everything Risa volunteered on our employment application match. It adds up to a checkered childhood and saintly adulthood. She pulled herself out of poverty with raw intelligence and will."

"Okay. What about the lovely Ms. Cherelle?"

"Ah, yes." Niall slid one finger in beneath the lacy underwear, felt the helpless clench of Dana's response, held her close, hard, deep, withdrew, returned, and smiled as she arched to drive him deeper still. He wanted his dick where his fingers were, but he wanted to torture her more.

"Niall?" Shane prompted.

"Just checking something."

Dana bit back a sound and tried to squirm off Niall's lap. He didn't let her. He simply kept her pinned between his chest and his hands, pleasuring her.

"After Cherelle left Arkansas," Niall said, "she was picked up for vagrancy, small shoplifting, hooking, underage drinking, petty grifts, that kind of thing."

"Drugs?"

"Never made it stick. She took up with several men, one at a time, mostly, and—"

"Pimps?"

"Unknown." Slick fingers probed, plucked, teased, until Dana gave up trying to get away and settled in to finish what she had started. "I'm guessing not. Cherelle only got busted for hooking once. If she'd been a full-time pro, she'd have been busted more often."

"What's she doing in Vegas?"

"Ask Risa."

"What do *you* think Cherelle is doing in Vegas?"

With one arm Niall lifted Dana off his lap so that he could reach his zipper. "At best, she's borrowing money from an old friend."

"At worst?" Shane asked.

"She's a petty thief, a grifter, and a part-time whore. You do the math."

"Risa seems pretty tight with her," Shane said neutrally.

"Question is, how tight?" *Just bloody perfect*, Niall thought as he filled Dana.

"The kind of friend you do things for?" Shane asked.

Fiercely Niall held himself still, held Dana still, felt their mutual pulse beating thickly. "Are you saying you don't trust Risa?"

"I'm saying Risa might have her loyalties divided between her childhood pal and her adult responsibilities."

"I'm voting for the adult to win that race."

"So am I," Shane said. "But the child can trip you up every time. Dump the stuff in my file."

"It's done."

Shane disconnected.

Niall didn't bother. He just started driving into his lapful of woman until they were hot and slick and came in a wild kind of silence that was filled with the hammering of their hearts.

"Bloody hell," he said against her neck when he could talk again, "what got into you?"

"Besides you?"

He started to laugh, then groaned as she clenched around him, released, and sighed in the aftermath of climax.

"The Kama Sutra ivories arrived," she said, shivering. "Exquisite. Simply exquisite. As soon as I cataloged them, I knew I had to . . . tell you about them."

"I'm all ears."

"Not quite," she said, clenching around him again.

His breath broke. "Learn anything new?"

"Did I mention that each position is demonstrated not by a single carving of a man and a woman but rather by interlocking carvings?"

"Interlocking?" He smiled slightly. "How?"

"Guess."

He moved.

"Good guess," she said. "Now let me show you an interesting variation on that theme. First I turn this way."

"Here, let me help." He lifted her just enough to give her wiggle room.

"Perfect," she said, half facing him. "Now this leg goes here, and that one goes up there, and then I pull up your leg and lean this way and . . ." Sensation shot out from the pit of her stomach, taking her to the edge of climax in a single instant.

He sucked in a breath past the raw lust exploding inside him. "Bloody hell, but that feels good. How many figurines are there?"

"Enough to kill us."

His eyes gleamed. "What are we waiting for?"

Twenty-five

Shane sat in Risa's office, going through museum catalogs and art books that featured Celtic gold artifacts. Just to watch her cheekbones get red, he had brought in a popular magazine with a breathlessly misinformed feature about the fabled Druid hoard. The article was on the bottom of the stack of material to be reviewed, but he was working his way down to it quickly.

Yanking her chain kept his mind off the overbright, undermoral Cherelle Faulkner.

"Now, take this torc," Shane said, pointing to one catalog.

"I'd love to," Risa shot back, wanting to pull on her hair. Or his. "But then the British Museum would raise hell with Uncle Sam. The Snettisham torc you're lusting after is considered one of the finest examples of Iron Age British Celtic gold working. It is a bona fide cultural treasure."

Though her voice was sarcastic, the fingertip tracing the outline of the torc in the photograph was almost reverent. Shane watched and wondered if she would touch a man like that, awe and appreciation combined. The thought had an immediate effect on the fit of his pants. Because of that, he was more impatient than usual.

"In case you forgot," he said coldly, "I'm holding the Druid Gold catalog cover for something this spectacular."

Risa's dark blue eyes narrowed. She decided she would rather pull his hair than her own. Definitely.

"Let's go over it again," she said. "Nice and slow. I'll try to keep the words short so I won't lose you. Ready?"

He was more than ready, which really irritated him. He nodded curtly.

"Goods like that torc are cultural treasures along the lines of, oh, the Liberty Bell," Risa said with fierce calm. "No one sells cultural treasures like that unless he steals them first. If you buy a stolen cultural treasure, you can't show it in public and you damn well better never show it to me. Are you with me so far?"

Shane watched her mouth. As always, it was worth watching. Lush. Female. Made for pleasure.

Damn, but he was tired of wanting her from a distance.

"Treasures like this torc are kept at home, wherever home might be," she continued with teeth-gritting restraint. "That's why there are great exhibits in national museums like the British Museum and the Hermitage and the Louvre. And they aren't for sale!"

"That's your problem," he said. "Mine is to get a centerpiece for my show before it opens. So far all I have is one good torc on the way and a million bucks in artifacts that will take a lot of explanation before the average person can appreciate them. As a show to compete against Fabergé, it's a nonstarter. I'm holding the cover of the catalog for you. Don't let me down."

"What about your sharks?" she asked, exasperated. "Go chew on them instead of me."

Shane looked at her oddly. "Sharks?"

"The other, less scrupulous people you have scouring the gutters for you."

He smiled almost lazily. "The thing about sharks is they're so hard to chew on. You're much more tender."

The way he was looking at her and the slow, almost drawling quality of his words made Risa feel like she'd been stroked. Her thoughts fragmented. With something close to desperation, she started thumbing through the next catalog. Nothing in it inspired her. Nothing in it made her forget the look in Shane's beautiful jade eyes.

When she looked up, he was still watching her like a man with tasting on his mind. Nervously she wet her lips, saw his eyes narrow, and knew she was getting in way over her head.

And it wasn't nearly as deep as she wanted to be.

She had to ask Niall about another job. Soon. Really soon. Like the instant Shane left her office. She could only pray that would be soon enough. She had never seen that particular smoky quality to his eyes. They burned.

So did she.

"What about this?" Shane asked, sliding the magazine out from the bottom of the pile.

She stared blankly down at an artist's rendering of life among the Druids. The Druid in the picture was imposing, dark-haired, dressed in white robes, wore a gold gorget that covered most of his chest . . . and he had eyes the exact color of Shane's. He was looking at her, into her.

And he was Shane Tannahill.

She had a dizzying feeling of something turning under her feet like loose stones, throwing her off balance.

"Risa?" His hand waved in front of her face. "Where are you?"

She shook her head sharply. "Guess I shouldn't have drunk that second Cosmopolitan last night. I feel a little odd. So, what about this Druid?"

"Not this Druid, the Druid hoard."

"Have you taken up smoking crack?" she asked impatiently.

"No. Just a little light reading. The Druid hoard—"

"Doesn't exist," she cut in. "There is no treasure hoard of sacred golden objects buried by Merlin in sixth- or seventh-century Wales or Cornwall just before Druidic learning was finally and forever trampled into the mud by Christianity. There are other hoards that have been found and melted and sold and hidden and buried and found and kept and passed from family to family. But—listen closely, this is important—*there is no Druid hoard*."

"It would be a great casino attraction," Shane pointed out, deadpan. "Just what I need for the show."

"If it existed, it would be wonderful." She took a breath and spoke with great care. "If. It. Existed. It doesn't."

"It does."

"Shane—"

He talked over her. "A guy just offered to sell some of it to me. Two million. Cash. And that's a minimum bid. Plus my ten thousand reward, no questions asked. For that I get first look and last bid."

She put her head in her hands. "Please, God. Not again. How many times have you been offered Druid sacred objects in the last year? Three? Five? Eight?"

"Nine, but who's counting?" he said. "Given the fact that I'm rich, collect gold artifacts, have a Celtic name, and am opening a whole new gold gallery based on

Celtic gold, I'm offered Celtic objects more often than I'm offered sex."

"Bullshit," she muttered into her hands.

She wasn't quiet enough.

"It works better if you look at me when you tell me you think I'm sexy and irresistible," he said.

Her head snapped up. "I didn't say that!"

"Sure you did. Think about it."

"But—"

He kept on talking. "And while you're thinking about that, think about this: I've got a feeling about this tenth offer. A Druid hoard kind of feeling."

She thought he was jerking her chain. Then she took a better look at his eyes.

He wasn't teasing her.

"Oh, shit," she said on an outrush of air.

He smiled. "Now you're getting it."

She thought fast. She was good at that. It had gotten her out of trouble in the past. Maybe it would keep Shane out of trouble in the future.

"Okay. Great," she said quickly. "I'm not going against your gambler's instincts. Hell, who would?" It was the truth. Those instincts had made Shane a million-aire many, many times over before he was thirty. "But consider this. Are you listening? Really listening, gambler's instincts and all?"

His smile shifted and warmed. "I love it when you go all big-eyed and appealing."

"You aren't listening."

"Right now I'd have to close my eyes to listen to you."

"Stop," she said, throwing her hands up in the air. "I'm not trying to jerk your chain, so stop yanking mine and *listen to me.*"

He closed his eyes.

She let out a soundless, relieved breath and asked bluntly, "Does the word 'provenance' mean anything to you?"

"Yeah." He opened his eyes. "It means you have your work cut out."

She wondered if screaming would help. A single look at his level, too-intelligent eyes told her that she should save her breath for the discussion that was coming.

Discussion. She almost laughed out loud. Lord, what a neutral word for the verbal donnybrook that was shaping up between them. No matter how dubious the provenance of an artifact or how regularly Shane ended up very quietly returning the wrongly purchased artifacts to the country or person who had a better legal claim than mere possession, she had never talked her boss out of anything he really wanted.

But she had to win this time. She couldn't let him smear his reputation—and hers—by buying something whose ownership wouldn't be legally defensible even if you had all nine Supreme Court justices lined up on your side.

What a pity Shane was so rich. Anyone else would have been stung badly enough by returning stolen artifacts in the past not to keep on buying dubious ones in the present.

The man simply had too much money.

"Let's assume that the Druid hoard exists," she said. "Just for the sake of . . . discussion."

"Sure."

The careless tone of his voice made her want to grind her teeth. Yet when she looked into his eyes, they were serious and utterly focused on her. It was unnerving to most people to be the center of such intensity, but she was used to it. Besides, she'd caught herself with the same look on her face when her brain was fully engaged, focused to the maximum on some project.

"Let's assume that the Druid hoard was buried in the sixth century and the secret of its location kept for fifteen centuries," she said.

"It could happen," he said easily. "Oral knowledge is passed down through families and secret societies all the time."

"Uh-huh." *Not bloody likely.* "Now we assume that someone recently—"

"Why recently?" he cut in.

"Because if it wasn't recent, the hoard would already be in someone's museum."

"Or private collection."

"Possibly," she conceded. "Just barely. I can't imagine it being kept a secret. Collectors are a gossipy, rumor-mongering lot."

"Which is why we keep hearing about the Druid hoard."

She abandoned that line of argument. It wasn't getting her where she wanted to go, which was the hell away from having to watch while her boss bought a stolen national treasure.

"All right," she said carefully. "We have a Druid hoard recently discovered—"

"I'll concede the recent part," he interrupted, "but I reserve the right to revisit it."

Her teeth clicked together. He should have been a lawyer. "Fine. You have revisiting privileges. May I continue?"

His smile said he was enjoying the color that flared along her cheekbones when she was angry. Lately, around him, that was about 99 percent of the time. She really had to look for another job before she killed him. Or jumped him.

Right now she wasn't sure which she would enjoy more.

"Sure, go ahead," he said. "I love watching you talk."

"If you make a crack about my mouth, I'm walking out."

"Your mouth?" Shane hoped he pulled off the feat of looking surprised. A lot of men must have told her that she had a mouth that made them think of the kind of sex that left everything it touched hot and wet and totally sated. "What about your mouth?"

Risa decided she would enjoy killing him more than jumping him. Definitely.

"We have a recently discovered Druid hoard," she said with outward calm. "Chances are said hoard came from Wales, Ireland, or the south of England, possibly northwest Scotland. Agreed?"

"With revisitation privileges, yes."

"To speed things up, I'll assume that unless you reject something outright, you agree. With revisiting privileges, of course."

"Good idea."

His tone of cool reason made more heat burn along her cheekbones. All that kept her from walking out was his eyes. They were as serious as death.

She couldn't help wondering what it would be like to be the center of such intense concentration . . . and then to make those same eyes go blind with pure passion.

A hot thrill curled out from the pit of her stomach.

Tonight, she vowed silently.

She would call Niall just as soon as she reached her apartment. No more putting it off.

The time to get out was now.

"So we have a recently discovered Druid hoard," she said huskily.

"Solid gold."

Her eyes narrowed briefly, but in speculation rather than anger. "Anything else?"

"Sacred objects. Possibly votive offerings, more probably objects used in high rituals. Fantastic etched designs. Merlin's private collection."

This time she didn't bother to muffle her response. "Bullshit."

"Which part? Solid gold, sacred, possibly—"

"Merlin's private collection," she cut in. "Can't swallow it. Did the items come with a bloody label: 'Made in Wales for Merlin'?"

"He didn't say." Shane's voice was bland.

Risa's voice wasn't. It was cold enough to freeze alcohol. "The Druids couldn't—wouldn't—write. That's how they kept their secrets secret."

"That doesn't prevent a well-traveled court scholar who is also the adviser of a fifth-century Welsh king from knowing how to write Latin or Greek or even a version of the local Celtic language using the Greek or Latin alphabet, or even runic symbols."

"Granted. With—"

"Revisitation privileges," he interrupted. "Gotcha."

"Not yet," she shot back. "Assuming this well-traveled, scholarly adviser was a Druid—"

"Safe assumption," he cut in again. "The Druids were advisers to kings and chiefs. That was their job. No revisitation privileges on that one. It's as close to established fact as it gets about the Druids."

Maybe she wouldn't bother calling Niall. Maybe she would just kill Shane now and be done with it.

He lifted his dark eyebrows in silent query. "Something wrong?"

"Is anything right?" she retorted. "Oh, the hell with it. I'll grant it all. That still doesn't mean you can legally own the Druid hoard, much less show the damn gold on New Year's Eve! Unless you have a previously concealed desire to spend time in jail?"

"Nope. Finished?"

Her mouth opened, then shut. She licked her lips and knew she had to talk fast. Really fast. "Look, if it exists, the Druid hoard is the legacy of a time and a place when magic was real. Supposedly it was gathered and/or held by the greatest Druid of all—Merlin. No!" She held up her hand to prevent Shane from interrupting. "Supposedly the hoard was composed of solid gold objects inscribed with supernatural designs. Some sources say the objects magically vanished at Merlin's death. Others say they went into the Druid hoard, which had been passed down from the head Druid priest to the next leader for a thousand years or more."

"You read the article," Shane said, lifting the magazine.

"I read its source material in Latin when I was on my way to a Ph.D. I read pretty much the same thing in a translation from a seventh-century Welsh poem. I read it in a precursor to English so old it couldn't be told from ancient French or ancient German. I read it in a scholarly text from Chaucer's time. Ditto for the Shakespearean era. And I read reams of codswallop from the end of the nineteenth and twentieth centuries. Something about ending a hundred-year cycle brings out every nut in the fruitcake."

"I'm impressed. I didn't find the reference from Chaucer's time."

She blinked, absorbing the fact that for all his careless manner, he had researched the subject thoroughly. "It's in a locked collection at UCLA."

"I'll get a copy."

She didn't doubt it. "No need. I kept copies of all the information I ever came across about Merlin's gold or the Druid hoard."

Even as his instincts shivered up and down his spine, Shane became unnaturally still. "Why?"

"I wanted to find it," she said simply. "I went to Wales and the south of England and northwest Scotland and spent months . . ."

Her voice died. She wondered how she could describe it to him, the time-deep silence of standing stones, the elusive whisper of hidden springs, the unbearable beauty of a crescent moon balanced in the arms of an ancient oak.

"I chased legends," she said. "It was great for my dissertation, but all I found were some places that made the hair on my arms stand up."

"Stonehenge?"

"No. Oh, it was impressive and all, yet . . ." She shrugged. "It excited me intellectually but not here." She held her fist against her belly. "Other things I found went straight to my gut. They were more real than my own memories." Her hand opened as though to hold or to share something that no words could describe. "There were hill forts in Wales, standing stones, burial platforms, grave markers. All of them were too old to have been built by the people whose artistic style we call Celtic, but these places had been *used* by Celts. By Druids. These places were . . . different."

Shane waited, wondering what she saw with unfocused eyes that were as clear and deeply blue as a Welsh lake. When she didn't speak, he asked softly, "What are you seeing?"

"Midnight harvests in modern oak groves where the harvester wore white and cut sacred mistletoe with a silver knife. A black spring surrounded by an ancient stone ring, and the bush shading that spring decorated with ribbons, coins, fresh flowers, and carvings of hands or feet or genitals—whatever the modern supplicants wanted cured. But most of all I remember falling asleep in the center of an oak grove and standing stones that leaned like old men supporting too many memories."

"You dreamed."

It was said so softly that she answered before she knew what she revealed. "Yes. I dreamed."

Then she heard her own words. She rubbed her own arms briskly, driving away the gooseflesh that rippled over her like a pool disturbed by the wind.

"Big deal," she said crisply. "People dream all the time."

Shane didn't bother to argue. He was too busy understanding why Risa interested him as no other woman had.

She dreamed.

And, sometimes, so did he.

"What did you dream?" he asked.

At first Risa thought she wasn't going to answer. Then she decided it didn't matter. She was going to be looking for a job anyway.

"The Druid hoard," she said, "the treasure I had been looking for, was gone."

His eyes narrowed. "Lost forever?"

"No. Just gone. Like so many Celts. Gone to another place. That's what the Celts were best at. Moving on.

One extended family at a time. Occasionally a whole clan. Settlers, not soldiers. Celts neither had nor wanted nations and states and standing armies. They were far-seeing, civilized, bullheaded, courageous individuals who loved art and wine and wild places."

She gave him a sidelong glance that was both wary and wry. "Rather like someone I know."

"Yourself," Shane said.

She looked startled. "I was thinking of you."

The smile he gave her was unlike anything she'd ever seen from him before, like moonrise in a sacred grove. She didn't know whether to bask in the unearthly brilliance . . . or run.

Before she could decide, the phone rang. She grabbed it like a lifeline.

"Curator's office," she said.

"This is Milly at the front desk. Is Mr. Tannahill with you?"

Risa handed the phone to Shane. "Milly at the front desk."

"Tannahill," he said briefly. "What is it, Milly?"

"Mr. Smith-White is here with a box he refuses to allow security to open."

"Send him up."

"Your office or Ms. Sheridan's?"

"Risa's."

"Yes, sir."

"And, Milly?"

"Yes?"

"Send security with him. Armed."

Twenty-six

Uneasily Tim glanced around the public part of Joey Cline's pawnshop. It was only two blocks down and one over from his mother's place. Jesus, she lived in a dump. No wonder she drank so much. Or maybe she lived there because she drank. Whatever. The place sucked.

He shifted his shoulders, missing the weight of his backpack. Socks had made him lock it in the trunk, saying that Joey would freak if someone he didn't know walked into his private space with a backpack.

"Man, from the look of this shit," Tim said, "your fence is lucky to have two dollar bills side by side. Where'd he get the cash to buy the gold?"

"Follow me," Socks muttered. "And don't say nothing. I'll handle Joey."

With a shrug, Tim followed his buddy through the opening in the counter. He laughed out loud when he saw the door hidden in the cabinet full of busted, rusted guns, and then he whistled when he walked into the real workplace.

"Nice," Tim said, looking at the rainbow of gems and gold in the locked jewelry display.

"Yeah. He does okay. Hey, Joey! Where the hell are you?"

"On the can. Be out in a minute."

Socks started pacing along the display cases, looking for gold. He found a lot of it, but not the stuff he wanted.

"You see it?" Tim asked.

A grunt was Socks's only answer.

Tim started searching cases, too. "How long was the ticket good for?"

"What ticket?"

"The pawn ticket you got when you hocked the gold."

"Never got one."

"What? How the hell do you expect to get it back when—"

"Shut the fuck up," Socks cut in, his voice a low snarl. With the speed of a seasoned nurse or a burglar, he snapped on nearly transparent surgical gloves. "I said I'd take care of it, didn't I?"

Joey walked in from the bathroom, zipping up his fly. "Hey, Cesar, my old buddy. You got more gold for me?"

"Cesar?" Tim said under his breath, looking at Socks.

"Maybe," Socks said, ignoring Tim. "It depends."

Joey thought of the fast fifty thousand he had made on the four gold items and smiled. You never knew when you were going to hit the jackpot twice in a day. "Depends? On what?"

"My buddy's old lady cut him off unless we get back that bracelet or armband or whatever the fuck it was. Five hundred was the price, right?"

Joey laughed, saw that Socks wasn't laughing, and cleared his throat. "Cesar, hey, my boy, you didn't tell me you were going to want anything back. I turned it around already."

Tim started to say something but ended up making a strangled noise when Socks reached under his shirt, jerked out the silenced gun, and pointed it at Joey.

"Hey, Cesar, whoa, buddy," Joey said, backing up with his hands held out to show they were empty. The gun was bad enough. The thin shine of the gloves he had just noticed on Socks made Joey sweat. When a man wore that kind of protection, he meant business. "We're nearly family. Family don't pull guns on family."

"Who'd you sell my gold to?" Socks asked.

Tim started to say it was his gold, too. A glance at his friend's flat, dark eyes changed his mind. The last time Socks had looked like that was in prison, when he shanked an old man because he didn't get out of the way quick enough. Socks might not be real bright when it came to school things, but he knew how the gutter worked. The boy was cold and fast as a snake.

"That's private business," Joey said. "You understand that, right?"

"How much?"

"Hey, you know I can't tell—"

Socks shot him in the right knee. The bullet made less sound than a dropped glass. He watched while Joey flopped around on the cement floor, screaming and bleeding.

"Who'd you turn them to?" Socks said. "Tell me or I'll blow off your other kneecap."

Joey managed to say, "Shapiro."

"He still have 'em?"

"Don't—know," Joey gasped.

"How much you sell them for?"

"Fifty—five."

"Thousand?" Socks asked. "Fifty-five yards? You're telling me you got—"

"Yes!" Joey cut in desperately. "Jesus, Cesar. Call an ambulance! It hurts!"

Socks kicked the pawnbroker in the throat, which stopped the conversation.

Tim grimaced as his stomach flipped. He really didn't like this part of being Socks's buddy. Tim was a born con artist, a smiler and a soother, not a leg-breaker or hit man. Socks was a born enforcer. He didn't mind hurting people.

"Fifty-five thousand!" He kicked Joey in the balls. "That's for hosing me, asshole." He kicked him again. "Still think you're smarter than me?"

Joey didn't answer. He couldn't. There was too much vomit, too much pain, darkness like a mountain falling down on him.

Socks turned his back on the moaning, retching pawn-broker and began ripping through desk drawers and filing cabinets.

"Uh, Socks, maybe we should—" Tim began.

"Shut up and smash open that jewelry case."

"What about an alarm?"

"Not back here. The last thing Joey wants is nosy cops hard-assing him over the merchandise."

Tim selected a cleaning rod from the gun-repair bench and started whacking at the thick glass of the case. Cracks shot like lightning through the panes, but the special high-impact material hung together no matter how much he beat on it.

Socks slammed shut the last of the desk drawers. "Fuck! Where'd he keep it?"

"What?"

"Cash, asshole, what do you think I'm looking for?"

Tim slammed the rod down end first. The shattered glass bent but didn't break. "He have a safe?"

"Yeah. I can't open it. Already tried once a year ago."

Socks returned to Joey and went through his pants pockets, then his underwear. Sure enough, there was a wad of cash in a security pouch that hung down over his pitiful dick.

Impatiently Socks yanked at the knot that fastened the pouch's ties around Joey's waist. The knot tightened. A quick swipe with a pocketknife took care of the problem. It also cut a thin line of red across Joey's groin, but he didn't complain. He was too busy trying to suck in air past the pain and vomit to notice a little scratch.

Cursing in a monotone, Socks counted the money. A few thousand. An hour ago he would have danced in place with glee over that amount. Now all he could think of was Cherelle's scream bouncing around in his mind.

Those four chunks of gold you sold for eight hundred bucks are worth at least a million.

Angry at the whole world for screwing him yet again, Socks kicked Joey as hard as he could.

The pawnbroker barely groaned.

Tim slammed away at the high-tech glass and tried to look anywhere but at the floor where Joey was curled up like a boiled shrimp.

Still cursing, Socks went to the workbench where Joey spent most of his waking hours. He yanked out the first in the row of belly drawers that lined the long, scarred table. With a flip of his thick wrist, Socks slammed the drawer into a bench leg. Small tools scattered every which way.

No money.

The second drawer held a bunch of rags and lubricants. The oilcans made a nice clanging sound when they hit the wall.

Still no money.

The third drawer had a cell phone, some cash, and a gun with silencer attached.

For a moment Socks forgot about the missing gold. He shoved the cash in his pocket and checked out the gun. Clean, loaded, ready to go, and either cold or registered to Joey. Whichever, it was a really sweet piece.

Whistling soundlessly through his teeth, Socks unloaded all but one bullet from his own gun. Feeling much better about the world, he went to Tim and handed him the nearly unloaded gun.

"Forget the glass," Socks said. "We got what we need. Here, whack the jerk and let's go."

Tim looked unhappily at the gun and at Socks's nicely sheathed hands. "You didn't tell me I'd need gloves. Let's just go and—"

"Uh-uh, buddy," Socks cut in. "Stick it in his mouth and blow his fucking head off."

Tim started to argue, saw the flat look around his jailhouse pal's eyes, and knew he wasn't going to get out of it. It had been the same way the first time he went along while Socks got a case of tequila for them at the end of a gun; whatever Socks did, Tim had to do. It was a good way to make sure your buddy didn't snitch you off to the cops.

Tim sighed. "If I blow his brains out from this close up, we're going to have shit all over our new shirts."

"Jesus. Who could tell?"

Tim looked stubborn.

"Just whack him, okay?" Socks said. "Just do it."

Tim sighted over the barrel. A heart shot, not one in the head. Much neater. He squeezed the trigger.

Joey jerked once, gave an odd, bubbling sigh, and went still.

Socks checked him with a good kick. No reaction. *Bye-bye buddy, and here's for hosing me all those years.*

Still smiling, Socks turned to Tim and shot him with Joey's gun. Even with the silencer on, there was still enough impact to send Tim spinning and crashing face first into a tall metal filing cabinet. He started sliding down it, grabbed the top to hold himself upright, and ended up pulling the cabinet over on himself instead. Man and metal landed on the cement floor with a racket that drowned out everything else.

In the sudden silence following the fall, the wailing of a siren was too loud, too clear. And it was coming this way.

Socks jumped and swore. Some nosy bastard must have called the cops. Or else Joey had an alarm he hadn't talked about.

He bent over the pawnbroker, grabbed lax fingers, and forced them around the butt of the gun he had used on Tim. When Socks let go, the gun just fell out of Joey's hand. He tried again. Same thing the second time.

The siren screamed around a corner so close that he could hear the tires cry.

Sweating, Socks made one last try at stage setting. This time the gun stayed put. He let out an explosive breath and looked over where Tim was. Nothing moved under the cabinet except a trail of blood snaking across the floor.

And the siren was making Socks want to scream.

Not even noticing the blood on his shoes, he turned and sprinted out the back door.

Twenty-seven

Smith-White didn't look like his name. Instead of being tall, thin, and distinguished, he was short, bald, and round as Santa. But there was nothing particularly jolly about his eyes. They were the kind of opaque gray that reminded people of old snow.

With barely concealed impatience, Risa waited for Smith-White to finally get down to business.

Knowing his guest's tastes, Shane had sent for Turkish coffee and sweets. The fact that Smith-White was still smacking his lips and choosing among the fruit tarts and candied fruit slices told Risa that she would have to wait a little longer to see the gold. It also told her that Smith-White was toying with them because he had something really superior to sell.

That didn't make waiting any easier.

Neither Shane nor Risa glanced at the locked spun-aluminum box Smith-White had set on the low table next to the coffee service.

The guard barely looked away from the box. Anything

that was allowed into the upper reaches of the Golden Fleece without being searched made him unhappy.

"Lovely," Smith-White said, blotting powdered sugar from his upper lip. "Your dessert chefs are simply the best outside of Manhattan. Probably inside, too."

"I'll be sure to pass along your pleasure," Shane said. "More coffee?"

Risa wanted to kick him for offering.

Smith-White hesitated, realized that Shane wasn't going to open the subject of business, and mentally gave the owner of the Golden Fleece high marks for his poker face. If Shane had anything more on his mind than a pleasant conversation with a visitor, it sure didn't show anywhere, even in his body language. With a tiny sigh, Smith-White accepted that he would have to open the negotiations. Shane Tannahill could teach patience to a statue.

"Thank you," Smith-White said. "I know that both of us have many demands on our time. It was gracious of you to see me on such short notice."

Shane nodded pleasantly as he poured another dark, syrupy dollop of liquid into Smith-White's dainty cup, which was too small even to be called a demitasse. When Shane finished, he reached for his own coffee. Rather than slamming it in one slurping swoop like a native, he took a bare taste of the thick, incredibly sweet Turkish coffee. Between caffeine and sugar, the stuff had a kick like a crazed camel.

Smith-White's compact, well-manicured fingers caressed the aluminum box.

Shane took another sip of coffee.

Risa thought about the joys of homicide.

The guard shifted his suit coat slightly and watched the visitor's hands. He sincerely hoped the prissy visitor didn't have anything more than gold inside the box. It was real close quarters for any kind of gun work.

The sound of the four-dial lock being manipulated was quite loud in the silence. Smith-White was making long work of what should have been a familiar combination.

"Has the torc arrived yet?" Shane asked Risa in a lazy voice.

"I'll check."

She stood and walked over to her computer. The fact that Shane was watching her with eyes that were anything but lazy made her wish she had worn a head-to-heels burlap bag. Not that her slacks and jacket were tight—indeed, they were fashionably loose and unstructured—but he made her feel every bit of her ample female curves as though he had run his hands over her. Not for the first time, she wished she was thin and cat-sleek. But she wasn't and never would be.

Get over it, she told herself curtly.

She keyed in a familiar URL and waited.

"According to their tracking system," she said, "the torc left the airport at ten thirty-six this morning and is on the way to us as I speak."

"Good. Thank you."

Something in the quality of his voice made her look at him. It was there in his eyes, too.

Heat.

Smith-White realized that his attempt to create suspense had failed. He cleared his throat and finished opening the lock with nimble fingers. Then he held the lid up so that he was the only one who could see inside.

And the guard, of course. Smith-White didn't really notice him, because he wasn't a buyer.

While Smith-White pulled on surgical gloves, the guard took a good look inside the box, then another one just to be sure. Finally he hitched a hip against one of the sturdy display cabinets and relaxed. If anything inside the guest's aluminum box shot bullets, had a cutting edge, or exploded, he would eat a yard of plastic poker chips—no salt, no ketchup.

Risa settled into her chair and checked her nails for problems. Nothing ragged. Nothing torn. Nothing chipped. And if that dear man didn't pull something more than his hand out of the aluminum box real quick, she was going to go right over the coffee table after him and ruin a perfectly good manicure ripping his smug face off.

"Here we go," Smith-White said blandly. "A rather nice bit of jewelry, don't you think?"

First impressions flooded through Risa as she looked at the circular, hand-size brooch resting in a shallow box lined with black velvet. Celtic, no doubt about it. Fine. A sun symbol shaped in gold to hold a chief's or Druid's robes. Probably fourth to seventh century A.D. Possibly Irish. Possibly Scots. Gold with red champlevé inlay repeating the sinuous lines etched in the metal itself. Apparently intact.

And she had never seen a gold brooch like it. Bronze, yes. Silver, yes. But never gold.

She looked at her boss. From Shane's expression, Smith-White could have been holding out a tuna sandwich, no mayo.

Risa hoped that her poker face was half as good as Shane's. It was all she could do not to snatch the pin from Smith-White and examine it more closely.

"May I?" Shane asked, holding out his hand.

"Of course. Would you like gloves?" Smith-White held out a pair. "Extra large, like your hands."

"I'd prefer not to," Shane said. "That's why I collect

gold. High-karat gold doesn't tarnish with brief handling. But you know your gold. If this won't take any contact with bare skin . . ."

Smith-White wasn't about to say that he thought the gold was inferior. Nor was he going to remove his own gloves. Saying nothing, he dropped the spare gloves on the table.

"Would you like me to lift the brooch from the tray?" Smith-White asked evenly.

"Please," Shane said.

With no wasted motions, Risa snapped on her own surgical gloves. The less the surface of the gold was contaminated by handling, the easier it would be to answer questions in the lab. And she had a feeling there were going to be lots of questions.

She only wished the answers would be what she wanted to hear.

With narrowed eyes she watched Smith-White pass the brooch over to her boss. She looked at Shane, not at the object itself. Though she couldn't point to any single change that came over him when he held the brooch, she knew that he would buy it.

He glanced at her, saw that she understood, and didn't know whether to be annoyed that she saw what no one else could or pleased because it saved time. He studied the brooch, turned it over with a deft motion of his hand, and passed the gold on to her.

Even through gloves, the feel of the gold was almost hot against her skin rather than cold. An odd whisper of sensation went up her arm. She hadn't felt anything like it since Wales. She hadn't wanted to feel anything like it ever again.

She pulled a jeweler's loupe from her pocket and examined the brooch. At 10x magnification the integrity of the etched designs leaped into high relief. Curving, abstract in places, startlingly real when curves became bird heads and took flight in a series of diminishing inverted Vs. The spaces between repetitions of the central design flared bloodred with an enameling technique that hadn't lost color or crispness to the passing centuries.

"I'd like better light," she said after a moment. "And, Mr. Tannahill, my job will be easier if you wear gloves in the future."

Only Risa saw the flicker of surprise on his face. She had never insisted before. Without a word he took the spare gloves Smith-White was holding out to him again.

"May I?" she asked Smith-White, gesturing toward her work area.

He waved his hand, giving her permission to examine the brooch under any light she wanted.

On one of her worktables there was a bright, full-spectrum light framing an oversized ten-power magnifying glass on a swing arm. She used it when she wanted to have her hands free for drawing or taking notes while examining an artifact. What she wanted now was the binocular 10x to 30x zoom microscope that was on the second table. She pulled over her rolling chair, positioned the brooch, adjusted the zoom . . . and felt time flowing over her in a soundless rush that stole her very breath.

An artist holding the brooch, dreaming the designs, incising the symbols in solid gold. Every stroke a prayer to the gods who ruled sky and lightning and sun-blaze, the burning wheel of life turning and returning, and man so small, so weak, so weary . . .

Risa blew out a breath, shook off the waking dream, and forced herself to concentrate on the here and now.

The artifact was handmade. Definitely. The irregularities were reassuring. They gave the piece a feeling of warmth where so much machine-made jewelry could be cold. The design was classically Celtic—a series of abstract, sinuous lines that "flowered" periodically into a three-part design that evoked bird heads. Throughout the circle of the brooch there were three such flowerings with three "leaves" each, and the second of each of the three leaves was intricately enameled in red glass. A zigzag of raised gold separated the enameled from the plain gold in a design that suggested both a wheel and an eye. The bird head on either side of the enameled design had a smaller version of the complex, three-part design cut into the metal itself.

The long, tapering pin was decorated with the same design. Somehow the artist had managed to adjust the design so that the proportions remained balanced along the narrowing length of the fastening itself, all the way down to a point that was still keen enough to penetrate cloth. The complexity was staggering, as was the skill. The ancient artist had had only his own eyes and prayers, yet a modern curator needed a microscope to appreciate his work.

The sound of Shane's dainty Turkish coffee cup being returned to its equally dainty saucer told Risa that she had been quiet long enough.

"Yes," she said blandly without looking up, "a rather nice bit of jewelry. It's in excellent condition. Rather too excellent for my comfort. Most items that have been around since the sixth or seventh century A.D. show more wear. A lot more."

"Not if they have been someone's prized possession," Smith-White said smoothly. "Think of the pope's ritual items, sacred symbols in gold lovingly stored and passed from generation to generation, used only on occasions of highest ceremony."

Then how did they end up in your hands? Risa asked silently, sardonically. Doubtless Shane was thinking the same thing. Problem was, he didn't care as much about provenance as she did.

Saying nothing, Risa took another long look at the brooch. She made sure when she finally swung the lamp away that she gave the security camera a good, unimpaired view of the piece. She had a mountain of research to do and damned little time to do it in.

She would have given a lot for the database at Rarities Unlimited.

Casually she turned the brooch over to give the camera a shot at the other side—also beautifully incised—before she picked up the gold and returned it to Smith-White.

He put the brooch in its velvet-lined tray, then left it on the coffee table for Shane to admire and, hopefully, desire enough to pay half a million dollars for. Minimum. Deliberately Smith-White refilled his tiny coffee cup and sip-sucked noisily in the approved Turkish manner until only the grittiest dregs remained in the cup.

The guard shifted to his other hip.

Risa waited and thought again about ruining her manicure on Smith-White. She glanced at her watch.

So did Shane.

Smith-White took the hint. He reached into the aluminum carrying case again.

"This is another nice bit," he said. "It's a votive offering presented to a very, very powerful Druid or made at his behest for an important religious ceremony. My guess would be winter solstice, when those poor shivering bastards prayed for the sun to return on its appointed rounds."

He didn't wait for Shane to ask for the object. He simply held out the stylized horse figurine in its velvet-lined tray. Shane picked up the figurine, then almost dropped it at the jolt of energy that sizzled through his hand.

"The weight of gold is always surprising, isn't it?" Smith-White said with a satisfied smile.

Risa knew it was more than that. Shane had handled enough gold that its heft didn't take him by surprise.

But something certainly had.

When Shane glanced from the horse to her, she knew he would be buying it along with the brooch.

Bloody hell, as Niall would say.

With rapidly failing patience, Risa waited for Shane to pass the object over for her to inspect. Instead of simply giving it to her, he slid one hand under hers before he put the object in her palm with the other. She didn't know which shocked her more—the heat of his hand or the bolt of sensation that went through her when the horse met her palm. She did know one thing: if he hadn't been bracing her hand, she would have dropped the priceless figurine.

A look at the infinite green of his eyes told her that he knew it, too.

"Thank you," she said in a husky voice.

His smile said that it had been his pleasure.

Without a word she got up and stalked over to her worktable. She held on to the horse with both hands the whole way. The original burning sensation had subsided, but the tingling of her palm went clear to the back of her eyes.

It was Wales all over again.

Dizziness like dark lightning, the soundless cries of

people long dead worshipping gods who had also died . . .

Ruthlessly she crushed the thought and the sense of time swirling around her in a silent storm. Letting out a breath, she focused the microscope on the horse.

Like the brooch, the horse was handmade, probably cast through the lost-wax technique, incised with symbols, and undoubtedly Celtic. Unlike the brooch, it was of very early Celtic design, rather than late. The decorations didn't cover the available surface. Instead, they were concentrated along the barrel of the horse. The major symbol was the wheel of the sun inscribed on both sleek sides of the figurine. Each wheel had three equally spaced smaller wheels etched around its rim. In place of hooves a sun wheel grew at the base of each leg. The effect was both elegant and powerful. Whoever had created the figurine had been an extraordinary artist as well as a skilled craftsman.

He had also lived at least four hundred years before Christ and had been influenced by the culture archaeologists called La Tène, after the site where this particular style of art was first found and studied. The wheels/hooves owed more to a time two hundred years earlier, called Hallstatt after a different archaeological site.

She made sure the hidden, overhead camera had a clear view before she walked back to the waiting men.

"Remarkable" was all she said as she set the horse in its velvet-lined tray. "There's almost no blurring of the incised design after twenty-five hundred years. It might have been made yesterday."

She only wished she could believe that it had. A fraud would have been easy to dismiss. But she was very much afraid that the artifact was as real as it was powerful.

"Next?" she asked flippantly.

Smith-White frowned. He had heard that Shane's curator could be difficult, but this was the first time he'd encountered it personally. Saying nothing, he pulled a third artifact from the aluminum box.

"Another votive figurine," he said to Shane. "Excellent condition."

"Why am I not surprised?" Risa asked no one in particular.

Shane cut her a sideways look out of stone green eyes before he took the figurine. This time he was prepared for the searing jolt of recognition and power. His hand didn't so much as quiver. Even as he admired the astounding complexity of the designs incised on the obviously potent stag, he passed the gold over to Risa. The challenging look in her eyes told him that if he braced her hand again she would dump the artifact in his lap. Smiling slightly, he placed the stag on her palm.

Other than a subtle jerk that only he noticed, she appeared to have no reaction. But the flare of her pupils told him that she had recognized the artifact on some primal level, just as he had.

That realization was as staggering as the densely inscribed designs on the figurine.

She dreamed.

She recognized.

And she was running from it as fast as she could.

Silently he vowed to find out why.

Risa put the stag under the microscope. When the artifact came into focus, she didn't know whether to celebrate the extraordinary beauty that lay on her palm or to put her head on the table and weep for all that had been lost to time and could never be known again.

"Celtic," she said huskily. "At least fourth or fifth century A.D. I'm looking at the beginning of the golden age of Celtic art, which culminated in the illuminations of the Book of Kells. The style of designs on this stag are closer to those of the Lindisfarne Gospels, at the beginning of the flowering of the illuminator's art. It would be the work of a lifetime to decipher the complexities and interconnections of the symbolism on this figurine. And even after that lifetime I would enjoy only a fraction of the understanding, of the sheer emotional and intellectual impact, that someone from that time and place would experience in the stag's presence. The context has been lost. So much . . . lost."

Smith-White heard the reverence in Risa's voice and wondered if he hadn't made a mistake by showing the stag third instead of last. To him, the armband had been the most spectacular of the lot, which was why he had chosen to show it last. The stag was a nice piece, indeed very fine, but the designs were so intricate that they were dizzying to the modern eye. As far as he was concerned, the armband was much more imposing.

It remained to be seen if Shane's curator would agree.

After positioning the stag for the ceiling camera, Risa reluctantly returned it to Smith-White.

"Again," she said to Shane, "I have to point out how unlikely it is that gold work that detailed would retain its crispness through so many centuries."

"Noted," he said.

Before that line of discussion could continue, Smith-White pulled out the fourth and final artifact. "This is, quite simply, spectacular."

Risa wanted to argue, but there was no point.

The piece was incredible.

Shane mentally braced himself to take the armlet. The jolt came hard and deep, then eased. He had felt other instants of recognition with other artifacts, but nothing to match this; it was like grabbing a bare electrical wire.

He stood and walked over to Risa, putting himself between her and Smith-White's shrewd gray eyes.

"Brace yourself," he said too softly for the other man to hear.

Warily she took the armlet. A flash of heat, a whirl of time, a rush of light-headedness, and then the present settled into its accustomed place.

Except that the look on Shane's face told her it had taken her longer to come back than the few seconds of disorientation she remembered experiencing.

She didn't object when he came with her to the worktable. She put the armband under the microscope and willed herself not to be drawn into its sinuous, potent designs. She told herself she was successful.

The gooseflesh rippling up her arms told her she was lying.

Designed for either muscular biceps or a very thin neck, the heavy gold band was perhaps three fingers wide and incised in such a way that light flowed over it as though the gold was constantly shifting, breathing, *alive*. Without magnification, the background designs had suggested the symmetrical basket-style decoration of the Snettisham hoard, but what caught the eye—and the breath—was the face that stared out at her through the mists of time.

Almond-shaped eyes of blue enamel and jet pupils, eyes that were empty yet all-seeing in an eerie way. High brow fit to wear a crown. Thin shadow line for a nose, no mouth. The face—or perhaps it was a skull—dominated the dense designs it sprang from. The designs themselves were highly abstract, interlaced lines symbolizing geese. A thick-beaked raven bracketed either side of the head/skull.

Raven of death, immortal geese, and man caught between, living through death to eternity.

She would have sworn she hadn't spoken aloud, but beside her Shane said, "Yes."

Risa grimly shook off the spell of the art. When she spoke, her tone was neutral. "The artist who created this was aware of every style from Hallstatt through all variations of La Tène and prefigured the avoidance of empty space in a design that became the hallmark of Celtic work as seen in the Book of Kells."

"Are you saying he was alive in the ninth century A.D.?" Shane asked.

"Or she. I simply use the masculine form for convenience." Risa made a swift movement of her hand before he could say anything more. "To answer your question, I would have to compare many artifacts, particularly ones that had been found in situ. Otherwise, dating is rather arbitrarily decided upon stylistic details. Unfortunately, styles remain static in one geographic area of the Celtic civilization and surge forward in another, which leads to all kinds of assumptions about age and source of a given artifact that are little more than educated guesses. Highly educated, granted, but still guesses."

"Could this be sixth century?"

"Are you going to buy it?" she asked very softly.

"What do you think?"

"I think we should talk about provenance."

"We'll get to that."

"Before or after the sale?" she shot back in a furious undertone.

He didn't answer.

Rather bitterly she turned back to look at the gleaming armband that should have been malevolent but was simply, deeply powerful. Staring at it, she wondered why Shane bothered to pay her at all. Half the time he ignored her. The other half they fought like hell on fire.

The longer everyone avoided the subject of provenance, the more certain she was that she and her boss were about to have their last battle. There was absolutely no way in heaven or hell that these artifacts weren't stolen. The only question was when and where.

And how many had died along the way.

Twenty-eight

The silence in Miranda Seton's house was thick enough to walk on. That was what Cherelle was doing, pacing back and forth, back and forth, living room to kitchen, kitchen to living room, a tense ghost wearing lime green silk.

Tim should have been back by now. If he was coming back.

If you don't get that armband, don't come back. Ever.

She had meant it then. She meant it now. But she really wanted that armband. The more she thought about giving away any part of the gold, the more she was afraid that there wouldn't be enough left to get her where she wanted to be in life.

She didn't know exactly where that was, but she knew it sure as hell wasn't *here*.

Even dressed in a frayed leopard-patterned tunic over tights and ballet slippers, Miranda Seton was adept at fading into whatever room Cherelle wasn't occupying. Bit by bit, a few moments at a time, Miranda had managed to do two things since the men left. The first was to put the living room back together. The second was to sip at a teapot full of vodka until the world took on its customary reassuring haze.

Unfortunately, there wasn't enough vodka in all of Las Vegas for Tim's mother to feel good about sharing space with her son's grim, hard-bitten girlfriend, so Miranda just did her best to be invisible. After a lifetime of practice, she was good at it.

But it annoyed the hell out of her the way Cherelle scattered her things around like some kind of princess born to be waited on. Car keys, lipstick, a comb, a scarf, shoes, mascara brush, crumpled paper towels she had used for napkins, and God knows what else. It was a wonder the silly bitch ever found anything again unless someone followed her around picking up after her.

Finding herself back in the kitchen, Miranda took a healthy hit directly from the teapot spout. As she put the chicken-shaped pot down, she spotted yet another piece of Cherelle's life scattered on the counter just behind the place where the teapot's "nest" usually was. There was a wad of tissues there, too, as though Cherelle had been pawing through her huge new backpack/purse looking for something, throwing things right and left in her hurry to get to the bottom of the soft leather bag.

With the vodka streaking courage through her veins, Miranda grabbed the plastic room key and tissues and hurried out to the living room. She nearly ran into Cherelle when the girl turned around with a cat-quickness that startled Miranda. She was used to life lived at a slow and dreamy pace.

"What," Cherelle snapped, a demand rather than a question.

"I'm tired of picking up your stuff, that's what." Miranda held out the evidence. "Look what I found in the kitchen."

A swipe of Cherelle's hand sent the electronically coded plastic rectangle and the crushed tissues flying over the back of the couch. The wadded tissues wedged between the wall and the top of the couch. The key kept going to the floor.

"That was dumb," Miranda said. "How you going to get into your fancy hotel room now? You damn well aren't staying here."

"I'll get there just like I did before, in the employee door by the east parking lot, turn left, employee elevator, fourteenth floor, turn right, six doors down on the right."

The biting singsong mockery of Cherelle's voice etched itself on Miranda's brain. Just like that other voice, the sneering insults that even vodka couldn't dim, Tim's father telling her just how worthless she was. Now there would be more words to remember, more echoes of her own uselessness.

"Oh, aren't we just soooo smart," Miranda said with false awe. "Too bad it won't do you any good without the key."

Before Cherelle had a chance to tell Miranda just where she could shove the key she was so worried about, both women heard the bubbling, farting exhaust of Socks's purple car pulling up along the curb in front of the house. As one, the two women rushed to the front door. Because Cherelle was bigger and quicker, she got there first and flung the door open.

Socks levered himself out of his low-slung car and swaggered up the walkway to the small house.

Tim was nowhere in sight.

"Chickenshit is probably hiding behind the front seat," Cherelle muttered.

"What?" Miranda asked.

Cherelle didn't answer. She was watching Socks approach, seeing all the small changes in him that warned of an unholy cocktail of drugs, testosterone, and adrenaline. Face both tight and flushed, eyes jumping around like spit in a hot skillet, dark splotches of sweat under his armpits.

She hadn't spent a whole lot of months trading sex for cash, but she had spent long enough to learn how to judge men. Right now Socks was bad news. The worst kind.

Without a word she spun away from the door, grabbed her oversized purse, and headed for the door that led to the garage from the kitchen.

Socks pushed past Miranda so hard she staggered against the couch and went to her knees. He ignored her and lunged after Cherelle. His grasping fingers latched on to her backpack strap. She spun toward him before he could rip the bag out of her hands.

"Hey, where you going so fast?" he said.

"Where's Tim?" she asked.

Dark eyes jittered. Along with the rank odor of fresh layers of sweat over old, Socks had a feral, jungle smell. It came off him in a wave that made every survival instinct Cherelle had scream at her to get away, *get away now!*

But she couldn't. Not unless she gave up her purse, and with it a few more precious pieces of gold. Tim's gold, given to her to shut her up.

"He'll be along," Socks said roughly. "Had some business to take care of, you know? Man business."

Now she recognized the smell beneath the sweat. Blood. She looked at the broad male hands that were gripping the straps of her new backpack/purse. No blood under the nails or in the creases of his knuckles.

But there were smudges halfway up his arm, like he had rubbed an itch with bloody fingers. Or bloody gloves.

"Man business?" she asked, forcing herself to relax. Or at least to look like it. "You telling me he's out getting laid?"

"You told him not to come back." Socks smiled. "He ain't."

Her stomach sank. Socks was way too certain about Tim staying away. "So you didn't get the armband back."

"What's the big fuss? You got lots of gold. You got me. Way I figure it, this is your lucky day all around. Where is it?"

Cherelle knew he meant the gold, just as she knew she would probably have to have sex with him in order to get away without a beating. Seemed like no matter how hard she worked, she always ended up under some sweating, grunting, stupid son of a bitch just to survive. Sure as hell he would ruin her new clothes before he was done.

"It's in a safe place," she said in a low, husky voice. Then she smiled and leaned closer to the man she would rather have knifed. "You sure Tim won't be coming back?"

"Yeah, and don't point the finger at me 'cuz he's gone," Socks said, looking at the lime green button straining between Cherelle's breasts. "You're the one who's so bitchy."

She forced a sigh that shifted her cleavage.

His breathing hitched. Her body made it hard for him to keep his mind on what he really wanted—the gold. Especially when he could see her nipples clear as headlamps beneath the pale silk. How was a man supposed to think when a braless woman with a good pair of tits shoved them under his nose? He swallowed hard and forced himself to concentrate on something besides finally getting a little of the great ass that Tim had spent so much time bragging about.

"So where is it?" Socks asked hoarsely.

"In my pants, sugah pie, just like always."

He dragged his glance down to her crotch. It was covered by thin, pale silk that barely concealed what lay beneath. He saw the cushy dark shadow that told him she wasn't wearing enough underwear to get in a man's way. He pushed one hand between her thighs and dug in. Hard. "You got a great pussy, but even you can't put all the gold in there."

She looked over his thick shoulders to where Miranda stood in the door, watching them with a cynical smile and eyes that were glazed by vodka. As Cherelle undid the button between her breasts, she envied Miranda her drunken haze.

Reality sucked.

"Oh, were you talking about gold?" Cherelle asked, tilting her pelvis toward Socks as though she just loved having him grope her like a steel gorilla. *Take a good feel, asshole. It will be your first and last.* "Like I said, it's in a safe place."

Socks grunted. "How safe?"

"All the locks and alarms and guards the Golden Fleece can provide, that's how safe."

The sexy purr of her voice and the female heat surrounding his hand made it real hard for Socks to concentrate. Then her nimble fingers had somehow undone his fly and slipped inside to stroke him. Blood rushed from his brain to his crotch. He shook his head like a dog coming out of water.

"Whoa. We got—" The words became a sucked-in rasp of air as she ran her fingernails around him, digging lightly into each dip and crease. "Business," he finished in a strangled voice.

"Sugah, I've got the only business that matters right here in my little ol' hand."

Socks gave up trying to think. A hand job was his idea of foreplay. Then, when he was really ready, he would yank off her fancy green pants and hammer in.

Cherelle measured his surrender in the glaze of his eyes and the quickness of his breathing. She judged her moment with all the care and coldness of the sex worker she once had been. Without warning, she dug her nails deep into his dick, twisted, jerked as hard as she could, and slammed her knee up into his crotch.

He managed to deflect most of the knee shot, but not all of it. Whooping for air, staggering, retching, he went to his hands and knees. He wasn't in any shape to hang on when she yanked her fancy purse free of his fingers and ran out of the house.

Thanks to Miranda the Mouse, Cherelle found that her car keys were handy for once. She grabbed them out of her purse, flung herself into the front seat of her car, and jammed in the ignition key.

By the time Socks pulled himself to his feet, she would be long gone.

Ignored by both the fleeing Cherelle and the wretched Socks, Miranda waited through the man's cursing and retching by retreating to the living room and watching warily. When the color of his skin was closer to white than green, and sweat no longer stood out on his forehead, she figured that Socks wouldn't belt her just because she was there and he was hurting. She reached down behind the couch and walked over to him, or at least as close as the kitchen door. If she was wrong about his state of mind, she wanted a head start.

"I'll kill her," Socks gasped, leaning against the counter.

Miranda sincerely hoped so. Cherelle was the first woman Tim had stayed with for more than a few months. Her boy deserved better than a hard-edged whore.

"You'll have to catch her first," Miranda pointed out. "I can help with that."

Socks straightened some, winced, and straightened some more. It would be a few days before a woody felt good, but he'd been through worse and still beaten the hell out of the guy who kicked him. "Yeah? How?"

Miranda held out the plastic coded key and recited Cherelle's mocking description of just how to get to her room at the Golden Fleece.

By the time Socks left, he could recite it too.

Twenty-nine

The sound of groaning woke Tim up. Vaguely he realized that he was the one making the low, ragged sounds. He opened his eyes and tried to focus. It didn't work. All he saw was a big gray stripe with light kind of shining down either side.

And he hurt. God, he hurt.

Memory slashed at him like knives. A glass case full of gold and jewelry. Greasy gun rags. A spitting sound and Joey flopping around on the floor. Socks kicking him. Handing Tim a gun.

"Oh, shit," Tim groaned. "I killed him."

Then Socks shooting Tim.

His old jailhouse buddy.

He tried to kill me.

Spinning and falling and grabbing at the file cabinet.

Jesus, that's what's in my face.

With a shove and a twist of his lean body, Tim slithered out from under the metal file. He would have worried about the crashing and scraping noises, but his chest was a pulsing fire that shot waves of agony and nausea through him. If he hadn't already been on the floor, he would have fallen there.

Joey lay less than six feet away. Mouth slack, blind eyes open, skin white as only the dead can be, stinking of death.

And Tim had killed him.

Gotta get out of here.

After a struggle he got to his hands and knees and from there to his feet. The pain made him whine like a whipped puppy, but there was no one to comfort him. He staggered toward the back door, the one that led to an alley. From there it was just a few more alleys over, and he would be home.

It felt like miles of walking naked over burning coals, only the fire was in his chest rather than his feet. All that kept him going was the same animal will to survive that had made him team up with Socks in the first place. In jail, if you didn't have a strong buddy, you were everybody's bitch.

It was pretty much the same on the outside.

He fell on his hands and knees again when he reached his mama's back door. Opening it, he went full length onto her kitchen floor.

Miranda shrieked before she realized that the intruder was her son. "Timmy! Oh, my God! What happened?"

"Shot." He flopped over on his back and passed out.

Even Tim's wild Hawaiian shirt couldn't entirely hide the spreading patch of blood. With a sobbing prayer, Miranda went to her knees. The one joy of her life was lying bleeding on her kitchen floor.

"Timmy?" she cried.

He didn't answer. His breathing was hoarse.

The world went cold and very clear around her. Without hesitation she went to the phone and dialed the number she never wanted to remember and never could forget. When someone answered, she didn't waste any words.

Very quickly she was put through to the man at the top. She didn't waste any words with him either.

"Your son has been shot. Send help to my house *now.*"

Thirty

Almost reluctantly Risa watched her office door close behind the smiling Smith-White. With quick, ripping motions she stripped off her exam gloves and fired them into the nearest wastebasket. She wasn't looking forward to what was coming next, but it had to be done.

"You do realize that you have just spent two-point-four-seven million dollars on goods you can't exhibit?" she asked Shane.

"Plus the ten thousand no-questions-asked reward, and who says I can't exhibit them?"

"I do." She held a palm out as though pushing him away. "No. Don't interrupt. You hired me to advise you, and now you'll damn well listen to what I say. The provenance Smith-White offered is a joke. A bad one."

Expressionless, Shane looked at the provenance Smith-White had provided for the incredible gold artifacts. "Purchased from an unnamed South African private collector during World War I by another private collector, James Madison, an American on a world tour.

Said transaction not validated by paper but by recollection of Madison's great-grandson, who sold the gold to J. E. Shapiro last week to cover a gambling debt. Shapiro sold it to William Covington, who sold it to Smith-White. All three recent transactions duly recorded."

"Do you believe that?"

"What do you think?"

"I think I want an answer!"

Shane smiled slightly. "I'm sure you do. So do I. Until we find out who is going to answer first, plan for a trip to Rarities ASAP. I want these artifacts put through every scientific wringer they have. I'll leave it to you to sort out what we can of their stylistic history. Tell Dana that we want special care with the photos they take. One of them is likely to be the cover for the Druid Gold exhibit catalog."

"You call Dana." Risa's eyes were narrowed, furious. "I quit."

Shane's dark brows lifted. "Everybody will assume you slept with me."

"So my reputation as Ice Goddess takes a hit. So what? Better that than being linked in print with stolen goods."

"Prove it."

"I will, just as soon as I can afford a full Rarities search on the objects."

"You'll have to be working for me for that to happen," Shane pointed out with a thin smile. "Rarities won't look at shit for you unless you own said shit and request its examination by them."

Risa wanted to scream. He was right. *Damn him.*

"However," he added, throwing Smith-White's record of past sales on her desk, "if you're still working for me, you won't have to pay for a thing. And you can always quit later, when you have the very proof that I will have thoughtfully, and at great expense, gathered for you."

Risa had the uneasy feeling that Shane was both laughing at her and pleased that she was willing to quit over provenance. "I don't get it."

"You will. That's a promise."

"If I don't, my resignation will be retroactive to this moment."

"Agreed. Now, call Dana."

Risa was reaching for the phone when it rang. She picked it up and said curtly, "Sheridan."

"This is security at the front desk. Ms. Cherelle Faulkner would like us to make another key for her. Apparently she lost hers."

"Some things never change," Risa muttered, thinking of her friend's lifelong lack of interest in keeping track of keys and other small things. "Make her another key."

"Should I change the electronic combination?"

"Hell," Risa said through her teeth. The last thing she needed right now was to be running around getting new keys for her own apartment every time Cherelle lost another one. "No. Same combination."

As she hung up, she met Shane's questioning green eyes. She could see that he wanted to know what was going on, but she was out of patience with him, herself, and the world. Worse, there was no short explanation for Cherelle, lost keys, and an old friend's bittersweet presence in Risa's Golden Fleece apartment.

"I don't have time to go into it now," Risa said as she punched in Dana's number.

"Later, then."

She moved her shoulders, trying to loosen knots tied by Cherelle and guilt and impatience and stolen gold. She really didn't want to talk about it.

Any of it.

"Risa?" Shane pressed.

"Sure. Later. Whatever," she muttered as she gripped the phone. "No, not you, Dana. My boss. Sorry."

Shane listened while Risa set up an immediate courier delivery of the four gold objects for a complete Rarities search. But it wasn't gold he was thinking of. It was Risa's unwillingness to talk about the woman whose tab was at $9,678.23 and counting.

It was one thing to give an opportunist like Cherelle Faulkner a place to stay and permission to play with the charge account. It was quite another to give her the key to the Golden Fleece's secure floors.

Thirty-one

Cherelle smiled at the earnest young man behind the guest-services section of the front desk. It was the kind of smile that was guaranteed to raise male blood pressure and hope, among other things. Though balancing packages in both arms, she still managed to caress the hairy fingers that were holding out her new key.

"Thanks, sugah," she said as she took the key.

"Let me help you up with your packages."

"Oh, I can't take you away from your work." She brightened her smile and backed away before he could point out that helping guests *was* his job. "But I'll be sure and look you up the next time I come in from shopping."

"You sure?"

"It's a big ol' promise," she said over her shoulder.

The instant she turned away from the man at the desk, her smile vanished. She knew that Socks would be after her. She just didn't know how soon he'd be in any shape to stake out the Golden Fleece and watch for her.

Before I rang his chimes, I should have asked him what he did to Tim, she thought bitterly. *Then I could have called the cops and sicced them on Socks.*

Too late now. Oh, she still could call the cops and report a missing person and mention Socks as the last one who'd seen Tim alive, but the cops wouldn't do dick until two days or two weeks had passed. That was way too late to do her any good.

Unless a body turned up.

Cherelle's rapid steps jerked, then steadied. She wanted to believe that Socks wouldn't kill his old jailhouse buddy, but she hadn't believed in fairy tales since . . .

Never.

She had always seen pretty stories for the con they were. *Here's some candy, little girl. Get in my car and we'll take a nice little ride. Oh, yeah, baby, I love you.*

If Tim was still alive, he would just have to take care of himself. The candy he handed out was great, the ride had been the best she ever had, and whining about losing either one was a waste of time she didn't have. Besides, maybe he was fine and just hiding until she cooled off.

And maybe dogs shit diamonds.

She pushed thoughts about Tim away to the dark corners of her mind. With the gestures that had quickly become routine, she balanced packages, keyed elevators and doors, and hurried down hallways until she reached Risa's apartment.

Even as worried as she was, she still felt a spurt of surprise laced with pleasure that she was actually walking into a place with city views, plush carpets, vivid colors, a bathroom you could host a football team in, and not a lick of work to be done by her except to enjoy it all. No cleaning, no cooking, no laundry, no picking up Tim's crap, no cracked bathroom floors laced with black slime, and no cockroaches crawling out of rusty drains.

No cocaine either. She hadn't had time to make a connection. Yet even without blow, living here for a day sure had been fun. Too bad it was over. But it was.

She dumped her packages on the bed and began going through them with quick, raking fingers. Short brown wig. Sports bra guaranteed to turn mountains into molehills. Golden Fleece T-shirt, triple-X large. Really baggy jeans. A variety of nylon security pouches. Tennis shoes. Oversized man's heavy nylon windbreaker. Enough safety pins to hold up a building. Baseball cap and generic sunglasses. Big maternity cushion.

The last item made her snicker. She would bet every bit of gold she owned that she was the first woman to boost a "full-term" pad from a maternity-store dressing room.

With one eye on the clock, Cherelle emptied out her two suitcases. She jammed all she owned except the gold into one of Risa's nifty little suitcase trolleys. Everything fit but the big lime green purse. With a stab of regret, she tossed it aside. She couldn't carry it openly. Even someone as dumb as Socks would recognize that purse if he saw it again, no matter what the woman looked like who was carrying it.

Carefully she wrapped each of the gold pieces in toilet paper so that they wouldn't clank. Then she put the objects into the various nylon pouches that had been designed to carry cash, credit cards, and small jewelry against a person's body and away from pickpockets. Safety pins flashed as she fastened straps to other straps, pouches to other pouches, and straps to neighboring pouches.

By the time she was satisfied, she had rearranged the gold around herself five different times and was down to her last card of safety pins. Carrying all the gold on her body was turning out to be a big ol' bitch of a job. Even after she took out the two heaviest gold pieces and hung them under her arms, she still waddled instead of walked. When she finally had everything strapped into place, she felt like a mule and looked like a burrito.

"How do they do it?" she muttered, balancing her weight over her hips by leaning slightly back. "Pregnant women gain, like, fifty pounds and still walk around. Shit, I'm not carrying near that much and I'm staggering."

She jiggled up and down experimentally. Nothing clanked. Everything stayed put, more or less. After a last jiggle she grabbed the maternity cushion and strapped it on over all the lumps.

The jeans barely fit over her bizarre "pregnancy," but the tough denim helped to keep everything in place, especially after she used the last of her pins. She yanked the sports bra on, swore, and shifted herself cautiously until the bra stopped pinching and the gold stopped biting her tender underarms. The gaudy black and gold T-shirt hid a multitude of strange bulges. So did the blue nylon shell.

Five minutes in the bathroom took care of all her makeup and got the wig pulled into place. She dumped her huge leather purse upside down on the bed. Driver's license, car keys, cash, cell phone—all went into the jacket pockets. The rest went into the trolley.

She settled the baseball cap gently into place over the wig and her own hair stuffed up beneath it. The hat was almost as gaudy as the casino shirt, but she wasn't going for invisible. She just didn't want to look like a well-dressed blonde with great tits.

Two more minutes at the mirror assured her that nothing showed that wasn't supposed to. She grinned at herself in the glass and then laughed out loud. There was nothing she liked more than conning the dumbs.

Too bad Risa couldn't come along for the fun, but her old friend would just have to do what Cherelle was doing.

Take care of herself.

Thirty-two

All the way down the hall to her apartment, Risa told herself she was dragging her feet because she was tired, not because she simply didn't feel up to a second night of playing Remember When with Cherelle. The shared memories only made the present distance between herself and her friend more obvious, more painful.

The discreet magnetic card that requested NO SERVICE PLEASE was stuck on the door above the lock to Risa's room. She let out a relieved breath. If her luck held, Cherelle would either be out shopping or adrift in another sea of bubble bath. Whichever, Risa would have a chance to get her second wind before she had to be sociable.

For the space of several breaths she stood and savored the quiet elegance of the carpeted hall, the fragrance of fresh flowers in their bronzed wall niches, and the gilded yet simple frames of the botanical drawings that dotted the long, peaceful hall. But she couldn't put off going inside forever. With a muted sigh she shrugged out of her sensible business jacket, kicked off her high heels, tucked everything under one arm, and slipped her key into the lock.

"Cherelle?" she called out from the doorway. "It's just me. Don't—" Her words stopped abruptly. "My God, what happened?"

Everything had been ripped apart. The contents of drawers, cupboards, closets—everything that could be lifted and thrown had been. The mess was incredible.

She started to call out to Cherelle again before old habits of fear kicked in. Her friend might have had a fit and trashed the place, but not likely. Which meant that someone else had been here.

Might still be here.

Waiting.

Risa started to spin away. She wasn't fast enough. A thick hand closed around her wrist and yanked her through the doorway into her own apartment. The door started to close automatically, only to hang up on the shoes and jacket she had dropped when he grabbed her.

"Where is it?" the man demanded through the opening in his black ski mask.

"Where is what?"

Socks glared at the pale lady with the big blue eyes and trembling lips. What did she think he was, stupid? "The gold," he snarled. "Where's the fucking gold!"

"I think you've mixed me up with someone else. The only gold I know about is locked in the casino's safe along with—"

Fingers closed like steel cables around her wrist. "The gold she got from that geezer in Sedona."

Risa wanted to think she was in the grip of a madman wearing surgeon's gloves and a ski mask. She had a sickening, spreading fear that he wasn't crazy. He was mad, period, as in furious. "Look, I'll be glad to help you find whatever you lost—"

"The bitch stole it," Socks cut in. "I didn't lose it. What kind of dumb fuck loses millions in gold?"

"Which bitch?" Risa asked, and prayed she was wrong.

"Cherelle Faulkner, who else? You know any other dumb bitches that live here?"

Just me, Risa thought bitterly.

"So where is it?" he demanded.

"If you could describe what she took," Risa said with aching control, "I might be able to help you."

Socks looked the offer over from all sides, searching for hidden traps. While he was at it, he looked his captive over, too. She was worth the effort. Classy but not a stick. Really nice tits under that loose shirt. Hard to tell about the ass under her straight dark skirt, but it showed promise. Too bad his dick wasn't up to that kind of workout yet.

Risa didn't like the greasy, dark-eyed appraisal. She had seen it in too many men's eyes once she grew breasts. But none of her fear or disgust showed. That was another thing she had learned as a kid. Show emotion, especially fear, and you're dead meat.

"Are you Cherelle's man?" Risa asked, trying to get his eyes back up above her collarbone.

Anger and something a lot darker tightened his mouth. "I coulda been, but the bitch stole my gold."

Risa wondered if that had been before or after he had swiped Cherelle's key to the Golden Fleece's secure apartments, and what had happened to Cherelle and her new key in the meantime. But those were questions Risa wasn't going to ask.

She might not like the answers.

But no matter where Cherelle was now and in what condition, Risa couldn't help anyone until she got free of this jerk in the explosive Hawaiian shirt and scary ski mask. Gently, very gently, she tested the man's grip on her wrist. Not as tight as it had been. The fact that cold sweat was slicking her skin helped.

"What kind of gold?" she asked. "Coins? Jewelry? Watches?"

"I didn't see all of it."

Risa didn't point out that if he hadn't seen the gold, how could it be his? Her captor might not have been particularly bright, but he was plenty strong.

Just like the old days, Risa thought savagely. *My brains against their brawn.*

"Can you describe what you did see of the gold?" she asked, letting a subtle whine creep into her voice. "I really want to help you, mister, but I can't unless you tell me what you're looking for."

Socks frowned. "Well, there was two little statues that looked like a dog or a buck or something. Then some freaky kind of pin. And an armband that was pretty cool. Looked kind of like a skull. The other stuff must have been the same."

Risa's stomach turned over, then clenched. It couldn't be a coincidence.

And it sure explained why Cherelle had been interested in Risa's work for the first time in memory.

"Cherelle stole those from you?" Risa asked.

"Yeah, and a bunch of others."

"A bunch," Risa said neutrally, yet her head was spinning. *Jesus, Joseph, and Mary. There are more Celtic artifacts.*

The thought was staggering, but she was careful not

to show it. Instead, she let her voice and her words slide backward into the time when she and Cherelle prowled their rural world like healthy young animals, a time when men like this one were all too common in the girls' lives.

"So . . . a bunch," she said. "Is that a big ol' bunch or just-a-few-more-than-four kind of bunch?"

Brawny fingers tightened on her wrist again. "What do you care how many?"

"Jeez, I'm just trying to help. If it's one or two, then she might have left them in the powder room in my office. If it's a big ol' bunch, then they're somewhere else."

"From what Tim said, there gotta be at least twenty."

Holy Mary, Mother of God. "Okay. A big ol' bunch, so we forget the powder room in my office." She made a show of looking around the shambles that was her apartment. "I'm thinking she didn't leave them here or you'd have found them."

"Unless you got some secret place?"

"Is that what she told you?"

"Bitch wasn't here."

Relief flickered through Risa. Cherelle wasn't somewhere underneath all the mess, hurt or beaten or worse.

"I don't have a secret place except . . ." Risa let her voice trail off. It was a long shot, but sometimes you didn't have any choice but to bet the odds that the game handed you.

Socks jerked on her wrist hard enough to stagger her. "Where?"

"Downstairs in the public restroom by the auditoriums."

"Huh? Why'd ya use a dumb-ass place like that?"

She shrugged. "It works."

Socks muttered and looked around again. No inspiration came. He lifted his big shirt enough to show her the butt of a gun. "Don't get wise with me."

She swallowed hard. "Hey, I'm with you on this, okay? No need to get snake mean."

"Just so you know."

He shouldered her out the apartment door. Side by side, her wrist clamped in his fingers, they walked to the elevator. He had an odd hitch in his stride. Not quite a limp, not quite a roll. More like a creaky old man than a young one.

But there was nothing weak about the grip on her wrist.

She prayed that whoever was on "God" duty at the cameras would be experienced enough to understand that if some guard barged in right now with his gun blazing, a lot of people would get hurt.

And Risa would be first.

Getting caught in that kind of crossfire was a guaranteed trip to the emergency room. Or the morgue.

It took her three tries to get the passkey into the tiny slot near the elevator. Her hand wasn't as steady as it had been before Bozo the Hawaiian Clown had grabbed her.

When the door opened, he crowded her in and watched while she punched buttons with fingers that were a breath away from shaking too much to be useful. What was making her really nervous now was the fear that he would spot the discreet camera in the elevator ceiling and panic. Being locked alone in a falling metal box with a twitchy gunman wasn't her idea of fun—and that was exactly what would happen if she triggered any of the obvious or subtle alarms on the elevator panel.

As the elevator slowed, the man yanked off his mask and stuffed it in his back pocket. She was careful not to look at him. There was no point. The cameras could do a better job and not make him nervous.

When the doors finally opened on the lobby floor and Risa stepped out, she wasn't a whole lot happier than she had been in the elevator. She didn't want her captor to go nuclear in the middle of the crowded casino. What she needed was a distraction, just a second or two, just long enough to wrench her sweaty wrist free and run for cover.

Across the room a long buffet line of hungry tourists waited for the chance to spend fifteen dollars each for a place at the all-you-can-eat trough that was one of the Golden Fleece's big attractions. To either side of the room the flash and glitter and strike-it-rich noise of the slots called out a siren song of instant wealth. The loudest—and best-paying—slots were parked near the street doors of the Golden Fleece, where everyone who came inside would be tempted to drop a little change into the pretty machines that seemed to pay off every third roll. And then drop a little more money farther inside the casino, and a little more at the tables, and then a little more . . .

Gotcha.

The slots were Risa's target, but not the high-traffic ones. She wanted the less popular slots, where only the bleary-eyed and dedicated pumped smudged coins into the Las Vegas equivalent of a cosmic black hole. At the end of the row of quiet slots were the two auditoriums, closed now between shows. Between the auditoriums was a restroom that the employees called the Maze because people got lost in it so often. There was a west door and a south door to the restroom, but almost nobody read the signs on the way in, so they found themselves in the wrong area of the casino when they came out.

Risa was counting on her captor being one of the people who didn't read. If he wasn't, at least she might get a chance to body-slam him against one of the vacant slots. Then she could get away without endangering crowds of people.

Socks looked at the icon on the bathroom door. A skirt. "Where the hell do you think you're going?"

"To look for the gold." Risa gave him a clear-eyed glance and prayed she hadn't lost the skills Cherelle had taught her. Among them was how to lie: always meet their eyes. "Just like I told you. There's a big ol' vanity in there with a drawer she could have—"

"But that's a women's can!" Socks cut in.

"She wouldn't hide it in the men's, now, would she?"

Socks chewed on that. "You got one minute to get back with the gold. Then I'm going to come in there and beat the shit out of you. And forget hiding in the stalls. I'm onto that bitch trick."

A look at Socks's flat, dark eyes told Risa that a minute was fifty-nine seconds more than he wanted to give her.

Sixty seconds wasn't much, but it was better than what she had now.

The instant his grip loosened on her wrist, she shot through the fancy gilt doors. By the time the doors closed behind her, she was sprinting toward the west entrance to the bathroom. She had only one thought—getting to the nearest employee elevator without attracting any attention, closing the doors behind her, and hitting all the alarms at once.

She went out the other door with a long-legged stride that was almost as fast as a run and attracted a hell of a lot less attention.

She might have made it all the way to the elevator if

one of the slots hadn't hit a big one just as she got close to it. Like everyone else in the place, Socks turned to look at the lucky jackpot winner. The first thing he saw was Risa quickstepping away from him.

"Hey!" he yelled, yanking out his gun.

Risa knew the layout of the casino by heart. The bozo in the Hawaiian shirt was between her and the doors leading to the street. The closest employee elevator was through the heart of the baccarat and craps tables, which lay like obstacles directly across her path.

At least the action was light around the tables now.

She hiked her skirt above her hips and ran flat out. Forget about going around. She vaulted up onto a craps table and then down the other side, darted between two other tables, missed her next vault, and scattered baccarat bets, bettors, and dealers in every direction. The fact that she was yelling the whole time—"He's got a gun! Get down! Get out of the way!"—might have had something to do with the near absence of people in front of her.

Socks's first shot shattered a slot machine. His second one gouged a fist-size hunk from a craps table. His third exploded a drink glass on the baccarat table Risa had just hurtled over. She cut right and vanished behind steel ranks of slots.

"*Fuck!*" he snarled.

He might not have been an IQ wonder, but he was plenty street-smart. He knew if he wanted to spend the next few years of his life smoking crack and screwing women, he had to leave.

Fast.

With surprising speed for a man who had trouble standing up all the way straight, he turned and raced for the front doors. People ran in all directions to clear a path for him. None of the casino guards fired their weapons, because their orders from Shane—and the Las Vegas PD—in situations like this had been direct and unmistakable: don't put civilians in danger.

Before the first sirens started screaming toward the Golden Fleece, Socks was sitting in his purple baby, sweating and breathing hard. His abused crotch ached like a bitch. So did his head from trying to think. But no matter how hard he thought, he couldn't see any way to get to the gold. One gun just wasn't enough.

But he was damned if he would let a bitch—two bitches—make a fool out of him.

It was time to cut his uncle in on the action.

He cranked the car to life. The radio came on at the same instant. A hot new retro-rap group was shouting their syncopated bile over the airwaves.

Grinning and snarling along with the *fuck-them-kill-them-eat-them* music pounding out of the radio, Socks headed down the Strip.

Thirty-three

Risa leaned against the wall next to the employee elevator and tried to get enough oxygen into her lungs. As she did, she silently vowed to take advantage of the employee gym more often. She should be able to sprint a few hundred feet without feeling like steel bands were squeezing her lungs.

Then again, fear might have had something to do with it.

"You sure you're all right?" asked one of the uniformed guards.

She nodded because she didn't want to waste breath on words.

"The police are on their way," another guard called out.

She nodded again. "I'm going up to my room. I need . . . a minute."

"Sure," the guard said. "Want me to walk you there?"

She shook her head.

Shane's voice cut through the babble in the casino. "Where is she?"

"Over here."

Risa shot the helpful guard a bleak look. She knew she was going to get the cutting edge of Shane's tongue for putting everyone in the casino at risk. Even though she had tried to avoid doing just that, it had happened all the same.

Bloody hell.

She straightened up, drew a slow breath, and watched Shane come toward her like a thunderstorm looking for a place to break. Without a word he crowded her into the elevator and keyed in the override. The doors shut. The car stayed put.

"Sorry," Risa said before Shane could start tearing a strip off her. "I tried not to involve the casino, but someone hit a jackpot and he—"

"Are you all right?" Shane cut in.

"Yes."

"I'm not."

"What—" she began.

With one hand Shane covered the ceiling camera lens. With the other he grabbed her and stopped her question with a kiss that made her forget that she needed to breathe.

She had wondered what kissing him would be like. Now she was finding out.

Hot.

Urgent.

Addictive.

With a husky sound she wrapped her arms around him and gave him back the kiss taste for taste, heat for heat, need for need. He was better than wine, sweeter, wilder. She wanted to be inside his skin, to wrap him around her, to taste all of him, to sink into him until she forgot who she was, where she was, knowing only him until the stars burned out and the universe went black.

"Risa," Shane said raggedly. His free hand swept up and down her back in caresses that were more inciting than calming. "Hush, darling, you're killing me. *I want you the same way.*"

Dazed, she realized that she had been whispering her thoughts aloud while she poured frantic kisses over every part of him she could reach. She leaned her forehead against his chin and fought to breathe without jerking. The slam of passion right on the heels of fear had sucked everything civilized out of her.

"Sorry," she said.

"If you apologize about running through the casino again, you're going to piss me off."

She shook her head. "For jumping you."

His laughter stirred the hair at her temple. "I jumped you first."

She drew a ragged breath. "Oh, yeah. That's right. I thought maybe I dreamed that part."

"I'd refresh your memory, but the cops are probably arriving about now."

"So?"

"The next time I kiss you, I'm not stopping until we're naked and I'm so deep in you we don't know who's doing what to who until the stars burn out and the universe goes black."

She knew she was blushing. "I shouldn't have said that. I didn't mean . . ." She stopped before she got in any deeper.

"You didn't mean it?"

A full-body shiver was her only answer.

He put his hand under her stubborn chin and tilted her

face up to his. Her lips were lush, flushed, wet, hungry. He nearly lost it just looking at her. "Did you mean it?"

The roughness of his voice was like being licked by a cat's tongue. She wished she could feel it all over. "Yes. Did you?"

He crowded her against the wall until she could feel every inch of him. "What do you think?"

Thick with heat and need, he pressed against her, silently proving just how badly he wanted her. The purring, approving noise she made deep in her throat had him reaching for his zipper.

Then he remembered.

Shit.

"If I boost you up, can you smash the camera lens?" he asked.

She blinked, looked at his hand braced against the ceiling over the grille, then shook her head as though recovering from a bucket of water flung in her face. "Camera. Shit."

"My thoughts exactly."

He removed his hand from the grille, keyed in a floor, and watched Risa with heavy-lidded eyes. When the doors opened again, he pulled her almost gently into the hallway.

"This isn't my floor," she said.

"I know."

Before she could ask another question, she was inside one of the casino apartments with a locked door behind her back and Shane molded to the length of her front.

"Now," he said, "where were we?"

"We were jumping each other."

"Show me."

He watched her eyes while her hands slid down his chest to his thighs. When she kneaded the heavy, flexed muscles, breath backed up in his throat. She was so close . . . and not nearly close enough.

"I was going to take it slow and thorough," he said roughly. "You're changing my mind."

"Your mind, huh?" Deliberately she unzipped his pants and found him hot and ready. She stroked the full length of his erection. "I was always told that men thought with their dick, but I didn't believe it."

"Believe it." His deft, clever hands went from her collarbone to her breasts to her thighs, opening buttons, pushing up her skirt, lighting fires. "What do women think with?"

"You're getting close."

His hands moved.

"You're there." Her breath hitched, and she melted in a shivering rush. Her hips pushed helplessly against his teasing hand. Her eyes closed as a small climax ripped through her.

Before the heat shot to her fingertips, she was on the carpet and he was pushing sleekly into her until he filled her. Stretching around him was the hottest pleasure she had ever known. And then he started moving. Sensations coiled inside her like a spring, tighter and tighter, until everything let go and she was flying, shivering, crying, and saying his name with every broken breath.

The first clench of her release pulled him over the edge with her. He kept sliding into her because it felt too good to stop, each hot pulse better than the last until his whole body was hard, shaking with the violence of his release. He felt another climax hit her, and he gave himself to it, driving both of them higher, until the world went black and pulsing around them.

Finally he caught enough breath to say her name and roll onto his back, taking her with him. She tightened around him, telling him without words that she liked having him inside her even when she lay limp and spent on his chest. He flexed his hips and felt more shivers take her. Fresh arousal prowled through him on hot claws.

"Jesus, we're going to kill each other," he said hoarsely.

"Are you bragging or complaining?" she said against his neck.

"I'm taking rain checks. A whole fistful of them."

"Okay. As long as I don't have to move real soon."

"Define real soon."

"This century." She sighed. "What the hell is tickling my thigh?"

"My pager is vibrating."

"Well, that's a relief. I thought maybe you had two dicks or something."

Laughing, he reached into the pocket of the pants he was still—mostly—wearing and pulled out his casino remote. Susan Chatsworth's number was in the window. Without shifting his position, he dug his communications unit out of the small of his back and keyed in Chatsworth.

"Tannahill," he said.

"The police have arrived. Would you like the interview to take place in your office?"

His executive assistant's carefully bland tone told Shane that whoever was on the elevator security camera must have put the word out real fast that Shane had probably jumped his curator in the elevator. And vice versa.

"My office," he said.

"Yes, sir. Right away?"

He bit back a curse at the laughter that lurked just beneath the question, as in *Sure you don't want time for a quickie?* But he felt much too good to be irritated.

"Send them up," he said. "Anybody follow the guy who grabbed Risa?"

"Sorry, sir. He was waving a gun, and your orders—"

"Fine," Shane cut in. "Was anybody hurt in the casino?"

"No. Most of the people are gathered around the slot machine he blew a hole in. Some are admiring the gouge in the baccarat table made by another bullet. A few folks headed straight for the bar. And here come the cops."

"While we talk to the police, settle up with the gamblers whose games were interrupted. If you have any problems getting the people to accept who owes what, run the security tapes to make your point."

"Yes, sir. Is Ms. Sheridan all right? Med techs are on their way, too."

"I'll check." Shane caressed down the length of her back to her lush hips. "You okay, Risa?"

"Fine as frog's hair," she said, and blew against his chin.

Laughing, Shane took his thumb off the receiver and said, "She's fine."

Really fine.

And somebody had just tried to kill her.

Thirty-four

John Firenze stared at his nephew and wished his sister had exercised better taste in men. The guy who had sired Cesar had been muscle, pure and simple. Mostly simple. Cesar was his father's son in every way that mattered, except one: he was Firenze by blood. Family had to be protected from stupidity for as long as possible. When it no longer became possible . . . well, his dear sister was dead, and his sainted mother would never have to know what happened to her only grandson.

Socks shifted uneasily from one foot to the other and moved the weight of Tim's backpack on his thick shoulders. He felt like a kid called into the principal's office for pinching a girl's tit. Firenze even looked like a principal. Dark suit and white shirt, dark striped tie, thinning hair combed straight back, hands that still showed the scars of a youth spent as a bare-knuckle brawler in the waning days of Las Vegas and the Mob. When he thought about it, Socks had a hard time believing that Kid Firenze had grown up to be a suit with a thin mouth.

But he had.

Firenze leaned back in his big leather executive chair and watched his nephew with unblinking black eyes. "Let's see if I have this straight. You just killed two men—"

"I didn't do Joey," Socks cut in quickly. "Tim did. So I killed him."

"Whatever. Two men are dead."

Socks shrugged. "Yeah."

"Where's the gun you used?"

"Down a storm drain. Hated to do it. Cost a lot."

Firenze grunted. "You wore gloves?"

"Shit, yes. I ain't stupid."

"Where are the gloves?"

"Flushed 'em in the men's room."

"Here?" Firenze asked sharply.

"Nah. An all-night gas station by the interstate. I told you, I ain't stupid."

That was a matter of opinion, but at least the boy was trainable. He hadn't forgotten how to do a clean job of dirty work.

"Are the cops onto you?" Firenze asked.

"Far as I know, they don't even have a body yet. I hocked my police-band radio, so I can't be sure."

One of the five phones on Firenze's desk rang. He ignored it, just as he ignored the subtle beep of his computer every time a new e-mail arrived.

"Anybody see you?" Firenze asked.

"I went out the alley and then down to the burger joint where I parked. I always remember what you told me about not parking near a job."

Thinking of Socks's screaming purple car made Firenze wince. He could park it on the far side of the moon and someone still would notice. One of these days

Delia's dumb little boy was going to get into the kind of trouble even his well-connected uncle couldn't get him out of.

This had all the earmarks of just that unhappy day.

"Did *you* see anybody?" Firenze asked.

Socks frowned. "A drunk pissing in the alley over from Joey's pawnshop. Does that count?"

Firenze sincerely hoped it didn't. "Okay. You got away clean."

Eagerly Socks nodded.

"Then why did you come to me?" Firenze asked.

"Well, it's kinda about Joey. He really hosed me."

Firenze waited. Getting hosed by a pawnbroker wasn't the type of news that would lift his heart rate.

"I mean, *really*," Socks insisted. "Stuff I had was worth a million, at least, and he only—"

"A million?" Firenze cut in, leaning forward sharply. "What the hell were you doing robbing jewelry stores? How many times do I have to tell you that those high-end places aren't—"

"No jewelry," Socks interrupted, talking fast. "I remember what you taught me, Uncle John. And this shit didn't come from no high-end place."

Firenze settled back again. "What were the goods?"

"Gold."

"You're strong as a bull, I give you that, but even you couldn't carry a million in gold."

Socks didn't quite follow what his uncle meant, so he stuck with what he did understand. "Tim's bitch said the stuff was worth a million, and it was gold—little statues like toys and stuff—and she's so fucking smart she oughta know, right?"

Firenze felt a headache coming on. A big one. Its name was Cesar. "Tim, the guy you whacked, right?"

Socks nodded.

"So where's his bitch now?" Firenze asked.

"I was getting to that," Socks said, his voice close to a whine.

"Get to it faster."

"Okay. Right. She killed the old man, took the gold toys, gave ten to Tim and kept more for herself. We sold four to Joey and he hosed us big time. We went to get the gold back and he had already turned it to Shapiro and Tim shot him and I shot Tim and then I went to see the bitch to get the rest of the gold and she damn near yanked my dick off and ran, so I went to her room and she's gone but another bitch comes in and says she knows where the gold is and so we go downstairs to the casino—"

"*Casino!*"

Socks just kept talking. "—so she goes to the women's can to get the gold but the bitch double-crosses me and cuts out so I shot at her but she's running like a fucking racehorse and I miss so I ran out and here I am."

Firenze didn't bother to ask how many people had seen Socks. It didn't matter. The whole thing had been recorded digitally and was now in the belly of a casino computer. "Where?"

"Huh? Here, just like I said."

"You did this in the Roman Circus?" Firenze asked, shooting upright with a furious snarl.

"Nah. *I'm* here. The bitch was at the Golden Fleece."

The pounding in Firenze's head settled into a steady, vicious stabbing.

"Remember what I told you about security cameras?" Firenze asked softly.

"Uh . . . yeah. I wore a ski mask." *Most of the time.* But he wasn't going to talk about that part of it. Even his tight-assed uncle wouldn't expect him to wear a ski mask on the main floor of the Golden Fleece, would he? Socks yanked the mask out of his pants pocket. "See?"

Firenze gave the limp mask a look. "Anything else you want to tell me?"

"Like what?" Socks said.

"Like what you want me to do about any of this."

Socks brightened. "I figured you could unload the rest of the gold for closer to what it's worth, see? Then—"

"Wait." Firenze held up his hand. "You said the bitch had the gold and she got away."

"With most of it, yeah." Socks rolled one thick shoulder and caught the backpack as it dropped. "But Tim had some more in his backpack."

For the first time since Socks started talking, Firenze looked interested. "Bring it here."

Socks hurried up to the big, ultrasleek black desk, which looked like something out of a *Star Trek* rerun. No papers littered the shiny surface. A single ebony pen lay across thick, creamy paper that was decorated with the Roman Circus logo: two roaring lions flanking a bare-breasted chorus girl.

"I ain't had time to really look at this shit," Socks said as he yanked impatiently at Velcro and buckles.

"Where are your gloves?" Firenze snapped.

"Huh?"

"Listen and listen good. You don't want your fingerprints all over stuff that goes straight back to the guy you killed."

"I made it look like Joey killed him."

Firenze's headache just got worse at the thought of his numb-nuts nephew trying to concoct his own alibi. "Wear gloves."

"I tossed my last ones."

"Buy more. Until then don't touch the goods. Got that?"

"Yeah."

Glumly Socks poked a hand around in the backpack. One at a time he fished out six lumps wrapped in socks or underwear and laid them out on the polished desk. Firenze watched like a vulture trying to decide if his next meal had finally given up and died. When Socks started to shake out one of the pieces, his uncle gestured him back with a slicing motion of his hand.

"I'll do it. I don't want you scratching up my desk."

With a delicacy that was surprising in a man as thick-bodied as Firenze was, he eased the first gold piece out onto a creamy sheet of paper. Despite his care, the figurine thumped audibly when it hit. His eyes opened, then narrowed. He unwrapped the other five pieces one after another.

And then he just stared at them. Two figurines, a ring, some weird kind of pin, a choker-style necklace of braided chains, and what might have been a four-inch-wide armband that made his skin crawl to look at it. "What the hell are they?"

"I told you. Gold."

"I can see that. What kind of gold?"

"Dunno. Joey said Shapiro paid him fifty thousand for four pieces like that. And we have, what, six? That should be worth, uh, more."

Jesus, the boy can barely count. Firenze dragged his mind away from his nephew's shortcomings to the problem at hand. Shapiro was a hustler who chiseled and whined over every penny he paid out of his pawnshop.

"If he paid fifty," Firenze said, "it's gotta be worth five times that. Hell, maybe even ten."

"That's what I thought. But Joey ain't gonna do nothing dead and I don't trust Shapiro and the bitch probably has a buttload more gold and I can't get it without help. So I come here to my favorite uncle. I can trust family, right?"

"Sure you can," Firenze said absently. "Does the bitch have a name?"

"Cherelle Faulkner."

That kicked up Firenze's heart rate. He opened the folded piece of paper on his desk and looked at the information that had been passed up the line after a blind phone call came in from someone who didn't want to do Tannahill any favors.

Risa Sheridan and Cherelle Faulkner know each other real well. Look into it and you'll have Tannahill where it's short and curly.

"Tell me about her."

"Great tits, an ass that won't stop, and—"

"I don't give a shit about her body," Firenze said, talking over his nephew. "Is she a hooker, a thief, a hype—what?"

"She don't hook no more. She and Tim run a channeling scam out of Sedona. Gets them into rich houses and then Tim and me clout them when no one's home. She loves smoking crack and snorting blow, but she don't do the needle thing."

"Has she done time?"

"Dunno. Not in the last few years, for sure."

"How did she get onto Risa Sheridan?"

"Who?"

"The bitch you tried to shoot in the casino," Firenze retorted. Christ, he knew more about Risa from a blind phone call than Socks did from kidnapping her. "Didn't you even know her name?"

Socks shrugged. "From what Tim said, the two bitches grew up together. Like, sisters or something."

There was silence for a moment while Firenze sorted through what he had and didn't have.

"Anyway, Tim's bitch whacked the old man that owned the gold."

His nephew's casual afterthought made Firenze's blood pressure rocket. Cherelle was a murderer, and she and Risa were like sisters—Risa, who knew all about old gold art.

Firenze chuckled. Right now, in his hands, was a lever against Tannahill's in-house gold expert. Risa could tell Firenze what his nephew's gold was really worth. Then she could sell it to her boss, who just might find himself an accessory after the fact to murder one.

Socks looked uneasily at his uncle. He hated it when Firenze laughed that way. Usually it meant someone was going to get the shit kicked out of him. Socks, for instance.

For a few gorgeous moments Firenze thought about what a coup it would be to bring Shane Tannahill down without the help of the other casino bosses. It would make him a big man around town, just the way his father and grandfather had been. Men of respect. But Firenze didn't want to end up the way they had—one murdered, one serving life for murder. No, the smart thing to do would be to use the information to trade up the ladder of power. Not as much fun, but a whole lot safer.

Unlike his nephew, John Firenze was smart enough to know when he was in over his head.

Even so, Firenze's hand hesitated as he reached for the phone. If he had more information, he would get a bigger piece of the pie. Not the whole pie. But a great big juicy chunk of it. At a minimum he needed more than his dumb nephew's estimate of the gold's worth.

Settling back in his chair, he played with ways to get hold of Risa Sheridan for a fast, very quiet appraisal. He could go to her openly, but that would bring in Tannahill.

Firenze shook his head. Not smart.

"Uh, Uncle John?"

"Shut up."

After a few more frowning minutes, Firenze decided that the quickest, cleanest way to Risa was just to grab her. If she wouldn't cooperate . . . well, there was always the desert. She wouldn't be the first person to go out there and not come back.

Thirty-five

Shane closed his office door behind the LVPD detective who had asked more questions than Risa could answer. When he turned back, Risa was still sitting in the informal conversation area that adjoined his office. Sagging against the sage green cushions, she looked exhausted. Pale skin, smudges under her beautiful eyes, hands lax, even her saucy cap of dark hair looked dull. He suspected he knew why.

And it pissed him off.

"You did everything you could to cover Cherelle's ass," he said roughly. "That's a hell of a lot more than she did for you."

Warily Risa lifted her chin and looked at Shane. "What do you mean?"

"Your pal turned her key over to a—"

"No," Risa cut in. "Cherelle loses stuff like keys. She always has. It's just the way she is."

"So you're saying some jerk finds an electronic key somewhere in Las Vegas and just happens to know that it belongs to your room and how to get to that room without asking directions?"

Her mouth opened, then closed. "I can't explain that part."

"Then maybe you can explain why you're so eager to put a halo of innocence around a piece of work like Cherelle Faulkner."

"That 'piece of work' is as close as I come to family," Risa shot back. "We're sisters in everything but blood. She wouldn't set me up like that."

"You keep saying it often enough, you might convince yourself."

Risa came to her feet on a surge of adrenaline and rage. "What do you know about friendship? You don't have any friends! You're too cold and calculating to know what it's like to need—" Abruptly she stopped talking and turned away from him. She didn't want him to see the tears that burned beneath her anger. "I'm sorry. That was way out of line. You go ahead and believe the worst of Cherelle because she dresses sexy and doesn't spend her time doing good works for charity. Just don't ask me to sing along with the chorus."

"You didn't think I was cold in the elevator," Shane pointed out with deadly calm. "I'll concede the calculating part, because I remembered the camera and didn't fuck you blind for the entertainment of the men on God duty."

Risa winced at the cutting edge of his voice. Angry, impatient, thoroughly irritated with her. Part of her agreed that Shane had a right. Another part of her wanted to scream that Cherelle was her friend. Her only friend. They'd been through too much together to ever betray each other.

"I can't believe she sicced that thug on me," Risa said.

The stiff line of her back and the strain thinning her voice made Shane feel like slime for pushing her. She'd been through enough in the last few hours without him hammering on her about what a double-crossing bitch her childhood friend was.

Silently he walked over and put his hands on Risa's tense shoulders. She jerked with surprise, then didn't move again.

"Do you have any idea what went through my mind when I saw that goon pointing his gun at your back?" Shane asked quietly.

She shook her head.

He bent until his lips were a whisper away from the nape of her neck. "If I could have killed him, he would have died where he stood."

The warmth of his breath as much as the certainty in his words sent a quiver through her.

"And that was before we were lovers," Shane said. "I don't know why you have such a hold on me. But you do."

She took a shivering breath. "Lust. That's all. Just . . ." Her voice died when she felt the warm tip of his tongue touch her nape once. Lightly. ". . . lust."

"If I thought that, I would have slept with you before I hired you," he said. "You wanted me the first time we met at Rarities. I wanted you. Easy math, right? A hot week in the sheets, handshakes all around, and off we go on our merry, separate ways."

"R-right."

"Wrong." He tasted her again. Lightly again. He didn't trust himself to really kiss her. He wanted her now even more than he had earlier. A lot more. Now he knew exactly how good it would be. "It's deeper than lust. You knew it. I knew it. And we both ran like hell. Can you at least admit that much?"

She wanted to refuse. She couldn't. "It scares me."

"Me, too. Then I looked at a monitor and saw that son of a bitch trying to shoot you. I went crazy. I don't even know how I got to you. All I know is that I'm through running away from whatever it is that pulls us together. I want to . . . help you."

The thought of Cherelle casually screwing her old friend made Shane want to splinter every bone in Cherelle's high-mileage body. But he didn't think Risa was ready to hear that. She might never be.

It was too bad Risa didn't feel that kind of bone-deep attachment to her lover.

Not that Shane was surprised about the lack of feeling on her part. According to his father and mother, he just wasn't the lovable sort. So, like his father, he had settled for being rich. Unlike his father, for Shane rich wasn't enough.

But Shane hadn't learned that about himself until he saw a thug in a Hawaiian shirt setting up to kill Risa.

"How do you feel about it?" he asked. "Still want to run?"

"No. Yes." She gave a broken laugh. "I don't know."

He could have slid his hands over her, kissed and stroked her until she was the way she had been in the elevator—hot, mindless, ravenous for him. He knew she would burn for him as no other. He wondered if she knew, if that was what she feared as much as she wanted. From what he'd seen of her childhood background, she'd spent as much time denying her feelings in order to protect herself as he had.

"All right." Shane lifted his hands and turned away.

"It's almost dinnertime. Do you want to eat before we check out your apartment?"

"No." The word came out raggedly, so she cleared her throat. "No, thanks. You don't have to come along. No one will be hiding in the closet this time."

"Too bad."

She turned around and saw the ghost of a hunter's smile still on his lips. It wasn't a pleasant smile. It was as cold as a winter moonrise. For the first time she understood, truly *understood,* that he would have killed for her without a second thought. The idea made her feel odd.

No one, not even Cherelle, had been that protective of her. Ever.

"In any case," Shane continued, "until the cops catch the man who tried to kill you, you're not going anywhere alone. Especially to your apartment."

"He won't come back."

"He shouldn't have been there in the first place."

"He must have followed Cherelle."

"If he did, he was invisible. Security has run the data from your hallway camera for every hour from two days before Cherelle got the key right up to the present. He only showed up twice. Once on the way in today and once on the way out with you."

Risa opened her mouth to defend Cherelle again, then realized it wasn't necessary. Shane wasn't attacking her friend. He was simply pointing out an unpleasant truth: the man hadn't followed Cherelle to Risa's apartment.

My God, Cherelle. What happened to the children we once were?

"Okay." Risa let out a sighing, hitching breath. "Okay. I'll try not to take it out on you because I'm scared and angry and full of adrenaline. But . . ." Her voice faded to a whisper. "God, it hurts. I was just trying to give back to her some of what she gave to me when we were kids. A place where no one harmed you. And I still think—I still *believe* that she didn't set me up. I believe that she's out there somewhere, running scared, just like we used to do. Only now she's alone."

There was nothing Shane could say that would make Risa feel better, so he simply squeezed her shoulders. "Ready to do that inventory for Detective Wilson?"

Without thinking, Risa turned her head and brushed her mouth over one of Shane's hands. "Okay. Maybe Cherelle left something for me. A note or . . . something."

Shane traced the line of Risa's jaw with his fingertips and reminded himself of all the reasons he shouldn't seduce her right here, right now, right where they stood. And the best reason of all was the fatigue showing beneath her beautiful eyes.

"I want you again," he said. "I never stop wanting you, even when I can't get any deeper in you."

She laid her head against his chest. "It's the same for me. I don't know what to do about it." She sensed as much as heard his laughter. "Okay, I know about that part just fine. It's the rest that . . . you know."

"Yeah, I know. Ready for the inventory?"

She blew out a breath. "Sure. At least that's something I understand."

Taking her hand, Shane led her to his private elevator and punched in the code. The doors opened and then swiftly closed around them. The thick, specially woven rug was a medley of muted colors that absorbed all mechanical sounds. The paneling was an exotic wood with subtle gold streaks through its grain. The air was fresh, smelling of high mountains and swift streams.

Sighing, Risa felt some of her sadness slide away. The elevator was a soothing oasis in the middle of business and fear and uncertainty. All too soon the doors opened, and she found herself staring out at her own hallway. She blinked, orienting herself.

"Isn't this marked as a service elevator?" she asked.

Shane smiled. "Yes."

"Sneaky."

He laughed and released her hand to nudge her out into the hallway. He felt the tension return to her spine when a man dressed in casual clothes walked toward them.

"Don't worry," Shane said in a low voice. "I've put extra security on this floor. He's one of ours."

"Evening, sir, ma'am,"

Shane nodded to the guard. "How's it going?"

"Quiet."

"Good."

The plainclothes guard ambled off down the hall, looking for all the world like a man with nothing on his mind but a night gambling in the casino.

"Is it evening already?" Risa asked, then glanced at her watch. "Yes, I guess it is." Her mouth turned down as she thought of the cops going over and over her story. "My, how time flies when you're having fun."

"Yeah. Don't know how much more of it my heart can take."

She stopped in front of her apartment, reached into her narrow skirt pocket, and came up empty. "I don't have my key. I must have lost it when I tried to get away from him. Or in the other apartment when we, uh . . ."

He gave her a smoky, remembering kind of glance.

Heat shot through her.

Without a word he pulled a slim plastic rectangle

from his wallet. The electronically coded key fitted neatly into the slot. The door opened. He handed the key card to her.

"New code. If you lose or loan it, let security know," Shane said. "Anybody using that card who isn't with you will get a lot of armed attention real quick."

Risa started to answer, then saw the mess beyond him. She walked into the room and stood with her fists on her hips. "Well, hell. I was hoping I was wrong."

"What do you mean?"

"I thought my mind was playing tricks and no mess could be this bad. Wrong again. How am I supposed to find out if anything is missing when nothing is where it's supposed to be?"

The fact that she was already striding toward her bedroom told Shane that she didn't expect an answer. She did a lightning check of electronics and found the TV, DVD, CD/radio/clock, and computer all in place. Mostly. The computer apparently had been thrown across the room. Clothes—ripped and wadded—covered the TV and made a big mound in the center of the bedroom floor. Shoes were scattered like confetti throughout the rooms.

She did a swift turn through the bathroom and kitchen. Big mess. Nothing obvious missing. Her grocery list was still stuck to the refrigerator with a grinning, bright green frog magnet.

Shane was in the bedroom, surveying the chaos.

"All the electronics are here," she said.

He plucked a midnight blue lace bra off a lampshade. He had discovered matching panties in the bathtub. *Next time I'll definitely take it slow. Sliding lace off her skin is worth going slow for.* He carefully folded the silky underwear and set it on top of a dresser that was missing all its drawers. They were facedown where they'd been thrown.

"What about jewelry?" he asked.

She shook her head. "The stuff I want is too expensive."

"So you go without?"

"I spent my childhood with second and third best and hand-me-downs from charities. If I can't afford what I want today, I wait until I can."

"What do you want?" he asked quietly. He would get it for her.

"It's all in museums." She looked at the upended mattress and for the first time noticed the slash marks where the man had taken a knife to the fabric. "I'm thinking he was pissed off."

Shane followed her glance and felt both ice and anger slide into his veins. "I'm thinking you're right."

"He was looking for something I didn't have."

"Celtic gold."

She stared at the mess. "Much as I don't like it, I have to agree."

"While you're being agreeable, think about trusting me a little more."

She turned and gave him a startled glance. "I trust you."

"Do you? Then why didn't you tell me that Cherelle had some knockout Celtic gold artifacts for sale?"

"Because she didn't tell me."

"Interesting." Without knowing it, he got his gold pen from the pocket of his sport coat and began walking the slim gold over his fingers while he sorted through possibilities and probabilities with a speed that had made more than one person uneasy.

Risa wasn't bothered. She liked knowing that he was

more than a pretty face and a fine body. Next time she would have to get more than the essential parts of him naked. She bit her mouth against the smile that wanted to settle in. A few minutes with Shane had been better than hours with any other man. It would have made her nervous if it hadn't felt so damned right.

"Did she know what you do for a living?" Shane asked finally.

"Yes. But until this last time she never asked me any questions about my work."

"So we can assume she came to you because of your knowledge about ancient gold artifacts rather than an overwhelming desire to touch all the childhood bases."

Risa didn't like admitting it, but it made too much sense for her to deny. "I guess so. I hadn't actually seen her in several years. We kept in touch by phone."

The gold pen hesitated. "You have her number?"

"She moved around too much. She'd call me collect."

"From a pay phone, no doubt."

Risa shrugged. "I didn't ask. The last time we talked, it sounded like a cell phone."

"Moving up in the world."

She thought of Cherelle's clothes when they first met and said nothing. If that had been moving up, her friend had been a long way down.

"She didn't call anyone the whole time she was in your room," Shane added. "At least, not from your phone."

"You checked?" Risa asked, irritated.

"Everything on this room comes out of the comp account."

"Since when?"

The gold pen vanished back into his pocket with startling speed. "Since your friend put about ten grand on the tab."

Risa's jaw dropped.

He pulled out his pocket unit and keyed in a file number. Silently he handed the unit to her. The list of charges Cherelle had put against the room was startling.

And long.

"I'll pay you back," Risa said grimly.

"No."

"Yes. It's—"

"Not worth arguing about," he cut in. "I have a standing reward of ten thousand dollars for information leading to the purchase of museum-quality artifacts. As far as I'm concerned, Cherelle collected it. Or are you going to argue that she had nothing to do with the Celtic gold we bought and it's all a beaut of a coincidence?"

Out of habit, Risa started to argue, then stopped herself. "I'd like to, but even fuzzy feelings from childhood can't make that one fly." She scrolled quickly through the list of purchases and handed the unit back to him. "Well, now we know why the camera didn't see her leaving the room before Bozo got here."

Shane hadn't kept track of Cherelle's charges for today. He gave the list one fast look, took the unit back, and flipped it into communicate mode. Before he was finished talking, fifteen people were scanning stored camera data, looking for a hefty woman with short brown hair, baggy jeans, and a blue nylon wind shell.

"Tell them she's probably dragging a black rolling suitcase," Risa added. "Mine. It's not in the closet."

Shane added the information and disconnected. When he turned around, Risa was digging through the heap of clothes in the center of the room. At the bottom were two ratty suitcases.

"Cherelle's?" he asked.

"Yes."

He went to Risa, took one of the suitcases, and began feeling the seams with a gambler's sensitive fingertips. All he found was old grime and a new rip. It was the same for the second suitcase. He glanced over to Risa. She was sorting through the mound of clothes on the floor with the swift, confident motions that had always fascinated him. That kind of cool precision was unexpected in a woman who looked—and was—as lushly sensual as Risa Sheridan.

"Are all the clothes on the floor yours?" he asked.

"So far," Risa said.

"No notes in lipstick on the bathroom mirror?"

She snorted. "Cherelle wouldn't waste good makeup."

"No notes on the grocery list in the kitchen?"

She gave him a startled look.

He smiled. "No, I haven't been snooping. Most people have a list going somewhere in the house. Kitchen, usually."

"No note."

"How about the list?"

A smile flickered over her face. "It's there. Every word in my handwriting."

She picked up a robe and shook it out with a hard snap that sent a crumpled piece of paper shooting out of the folds toward Shane. He snatched the paper out of the air with a lightning motion, smoothed out the page, and began reading silently.

"I didn't know you were into the vortex thing," he said, looking toward her.

"What vortex thing?"

"You know. Red-rock country and holding hands at the solstice. Talking to the dead through a channel or having the dead talk to you. Expanding your psychic—"

"Bullshit," she muttered, then froze, trying to remember something Bozo had said. Not red-rock country, but something like it.

"—powers," Shane finished. He turned over the colorful page, which had apparently been torn from some kind of pamphlet. "Well, well. She was doing the Sedona channeling scam."

Risa looked up. "What?"

"Cherelle. Or should I say Lady Faulkner?"

"In Sedona?" Risa stood up.

"Looks like it. 'Lady Faulkner will be your guide in all matters Druidic. Speak with King Arthur, Queen Guinevere, and the Master Druid, Merlin himself. Through Lady Faulkner you will know the most intimate practices of the ancient and powerful—' "

Risa snatched the paper from Shane's hand, scanned rapidly, and grimaced. "So that's what Bozo meant."

"What?"

"He said something about the gold she got in Sedona from an old geezer." Risa glanced up and found his eyes intent on her. "There's more Celtic gold out there somewhere."

"You didn't mention that to Detective Wilson."

"I was tired of his questions." And she hadn't wanted to implicate Shane in trafficking in hot gold artifacts. "You know they're stolen, don't you?"

Shane smiled. "Never doubted it. Question is, how long ago?"

"Not long enough," she said succinctly.

"No. Not long enough."

"You sound quite certain."

"Factoid hasn't found even a whisper of them on anybody's hot sheet. Not Interpol, not Scotland Yard, not the stolen archaeological treasure data bases, not museum thefts, not private collectors—not one damn thing.

If those gold objects ever existed in any public record, we can't prove it."

"Well, hell," she said. "If Rarities' top researcher can't find anything, it's not there to be found. Which leaves us with a problem."

"No, it leaves *me* with a problem."

"What are you talking about?"

"You're fired."

Thirty-six

S. K. Niall sat in his Rarities office and gave the view screens on the far wall a quick, comprehensive glance. Dana stood next to him, her hand on his shoulder, kneading his muscles with the absentminded sensuality of a cat. He didn't take it personally. Yet. That would come later, when they ate dinner at his cottage on Rarities Unlimited's parklike grounds. The riots of color he managed to achieve in his November gardens were quite beautiful by moonlight. So were the lights of L.A. spread out below. From his bed they were incredible.

And so was Dana.

"I thought that damned meeting would never end," Dana said. "Some people just don't understand that they're paying for an expert opinion, not an advertisement for their goods. Did Risa call back?"

"No. Want me to call her before we leave?"

Dana sighed, stretched, and began tracing the strong lines of Niall's neck with delicate fingertips. "If it can wait until morning . . ."

"That's what I was thinking."

"Big surprise. You're always thinking of sex."

His smile was quick and primitive as a love bite. "That's one of the things you like best about me."

She laughed as he lifted her over the arm of the chair and onto his lap. "Not again! One of these days we'll get caught."

"Promises, promises." But he kept his hands out of the danger zones while he gave the security screens a final scan. "Looks good. All buttoned up for the night except for number-two clean room."

Dana focused on the screen displaying the clean room that was still in use. Lawe Donovan, a part-time consultant with Rarities Unlimited, was checking out the emeralds in an early-Renaissance reliquary a dealer was hoping to sell. Ian Lapstrake was with him. They had formed a kind of rough-and-tumble friendship, probably because Lawe was missing his twin Justin, who at last communication was somewhere in Madagascar. The harsh illumination of the room turned Lawe's hair from chestnut to gold and Ian's black hair into a shiny kind of midnight.

"Like a study in darkness and light," Dana murmured. "Beautiful in a masculine way."

"Quit drooling. You'll wound my manly feelings."

"It would take a fifty-caliber round to wound your manly feelings."

"Which is the second thing you like about me," he retorted. "I don't fold up at the first sign of your royal displeasure."

"Then I'll try my temper on Lawe. I'm ready to lock up and go home."

"Go ahead. I'll—"

"With you," she cut in.

He glanced at her dark eyes. Their lazy, sultry gleam told him all he needed to know. Like him, she viewed their earlier play as a snack—and she was ready for a full meal. He lifted her to her feet and activated the audio for the third clean room.

"How's it going, boyo?" he asked.

Lawe didn't look up. At Rarities he had become accustomed to ceilings speaking to him without warning. "Depends on which outcome you prefer."

"Happy clients are always good," Dana said.

"Then it's going badly."

Dana tilted her head and studied the screen. "Why?"

"I'm ninety-nine percent sure that two of the emeralds are laboratory gems that have been stressed to reproduce the kind of fracturing that is common in natural emeralds. I can't be a hundred percent certain without removing a stone and sacrificing a tiny bit of it for testing."

"But the emeralds are fake?" she asked.

"Technically they're quite real. Just man-made. Very nice color. Perfect for this kind of primitive cabochon setting and quite in line with early usage of gems, when stones were chosen for their depth of color rather than their brilliance."

"Could they be replacements of earlier stones that were lost?" Dana asked.

"Could be. But I suspect at least some of the gold is a modern eighteen-karat alloy," Lawe continued, pushing back from the table. "It just doesn't have the feel of some of the old gold I've handled. If I'm right, at best you have a heavily repaired object. At worst a fraud. I'm not a gold expert, so I can only suggest that you do more tests."

Dana looked at her thin platinum watch. "Tomorrow."

"He has a ten A.M. flight to Seattle," Ian said.

"We don't need Lawe for lab tests," Dana said. "Write up your preliminary report. If the client wants more tests on the emeralds themselves, we'll take care of it."

"It's a lovely piece," Lawe said.

"It's a joker," Ian said.

"So it's a lovely joker."

"Why would anyone put all that work and expensive raw materials into making a fake?" Ian asked, shaking his head.

"Because there aren't any modern churches, kings, czars, or emperors who pay artisans to create gorgeous dust-catchers," Lawe said. "But museums and collectors will pay high dollar for history with crowd appeal. So you create the history and get very well paid at the same time." Lawe ran sensitive fingertips over the piece. "Either of my sisters would love this."

"We'll offer that fact to our client as a consolation prize," Dana said. "Good night, gentlemen."

"I believe that's a hint," Ian said, standing and stretching.

"Ya think?" Lawe asked, nudging the other man toward the door. "C'mon. You owe me a beer."

"Huh? What are you talking about?"

"You bet a beer that Factoid wouldn't try the chocolate syrup thing twice on Gretchen."

"So?" Ian asked.

"So she came back from lunch with a chocolate smear on her majestic cleavage."

"That doesn't prove that—"

Niall hit the audio switch. "Let's go before something—"

His phone rang. One of his very personal numbers. The one very few people had. "Bloody hell."

"Amen," Dana muttered.

Niall checked the caller number, said "Tannahill" to Dana, and put the call on the speakerphone. "Niall here. What's wrong?"

"Risa was attacked by a thug who thinks she has more Celtic gold artifacts like the ones I sent you."

"Is she all right?" Dana and Niall asked simultaneously.

"Hello, Dana," Shane said. "Risa outsmarted the guy, so she wasn't hurt. Her apartment in the Golden Fleece was trashed and slashed."

"Who did it?" Niall asked.

"Don't know yet. The cops took a good photo off the camera data, and his fingerprints are all over the apartment, so we should have an ID pretty quick. I need Lapstrake here by tomorrow morning to help me persuade an artifact trader to tell the truth about where he got the goods."

"He'll be there," Dana said. "He can protect Risa, too."

"He'll get real bored on the job," Shane said.

"Why?"

"I fired her after her attacker got away."

"You—" Niall began.

"I want her out of the game," Shane said, talking over Niall. "One of her childhood friends is in this up to her dirty neck, and there are more gold artifacts floating around out there. Until they're all accounted for, things could get lethal."

Dana and Niall exchanged looks. Now they knew why Risa had called.

"I'll be at Rarities by six A.M.," Shane continued. "I'd appreciate a preliminary report on those four pieces. The gold is coming back to Vegas with me."

"No need. Lapstrake will fly out with the artifacts and

the preliminary report." Dana paused. Her fingers moved fluidly on the cool desktop, as though playing notes on an imaginary flute. "Do you think Risa's attacker will be back?"

"Doubt it."

"Then why did you fire her?" Dana asked quietly.

"I told you. I want her safe, and the only way to keep her safe is to get her off the playing field."

"What about your big New Year's show?" Niall asked.

"What about it?"

"Who will be your curator?"

"I'll worry about it later. Right now all I care about is keeping Risa from getting shot."

"Ian can do that very efficiently, and we still would have the benefit of her expertise in tracking down the rest of the gold artifacts," Dana said. "If her childhood friend does indeed have a part in—"

"No." Shane overrode Dana. "I want Risa out of it. I'll expect Lapstrake at the casino by seven A.M."

There was the clear sound of a disconnect.

Niall made a grumbling sound. "Well, I'd better start checking out job possibilities for Risa. I'm sure he gave her a nice severance package, and I'm equally sure she told him to shove it up his arse."

"Men," Dana muttered. "What on earth possesses them to make decisions for fully capable women?"

Her partner ignored her. He'd heard her view on the male of the species before. Most of the time he was exempt. But not always.

It made life interesting.

"Well," Dana said, "looks like Rarities will soon have a full-time consultant on ancient jewelry and Celtic gold artifacts."

Niall shot her a look from amused blue-green eyes. "You're putting her back on the Celtic gold?"

"Of course. Our motto is 'Buy, Sell, Appraise, Protect.' We exist for the artifacts, not for the clients. Someone out there has some extraordinary pieces of human history and art hidden away. We're going to find them and return them to their rightful guardian. Risa is our best hope of doing it before some brainless piece of shit melts down the gold and crawls back into the sewers to hide."

"Shane will be pissed off when he finds Risa back in the game."

Dana smiled like a cat. "Yes, I rather think he will. It will do him good to be reminded just what money can and cannot buy."

"What about the danger to Risa?"

Dana gave Niall the kind of look that said he was no longer exempt from her jaundiced view of men. "Did she ask to be packed in cotton and put on a high, safe shelf?"

He had the losing end of this argument and knew it. "Let's get out of here before the phone—"

It was already ringing. Swearing, he hit the ID button. "It's Risa."

"I'll take it," Dana said, nudging him aside with a well-rounded hip so that she could reach the speaker button. "Hello, Risa. Dana here. How would you like to go to work for Rarities full-time?"

"Took the words right out of my mouth. I'll pack tonight and be there tomorrow morning."

"No need to relocate yet."

"I'd rather, if it's all the same to you."

"It isn't."

Niall winced. Dana could be tactful when she wanted to be. This wasn't one of those times.

"Okay," Risa said. "Where do you want me?"

"Stay where you are until Ian Lapstrake gets there. Remember him?"

"Tall, dark, moves well, smarter than he lets on."

"You remember him." Dana smiled slightly, knowing that Shane wouldn't like having Ian underfoot with Risa around. "He's your bodyguard until—"

"I don't need one," Risa interrupted.

"If you work for Rarities, you take orders from Dana and me," Niall said. "We say you need a bodyguard. Subject closed."

There was a pause. "Right. I need a bodyguard. Like hell, but I promise not to kill him. Then what?"

Dana's smile was like a stiletto sliding out of a sheath, thin and deadly. "Then you find your childhood friend and get the rest of the Druid gold."

Thirty-seven

Rich Morrison's office took up half the top floor of the Shamrock's tall needle of a building. Two stories below, a rooftop swimming pool and garden lured the high rollers and whales who took advantage of the VIP spa. Men from several countries lounged like beached albino sea lions around the glittering turquoise water. Showgirls—minus feathers—served drinks, canapés, and themselves to anyone who was interested.

Rich certainly wasn't, not even as a voyeur. He was a lot more interested in the conversation he and John Firenze had had a few hours ago. Stolen gold and murder. Thanks to a blind tip, the police had found a pawnbroker called Joey Cline faceup on his workroom floor, along with a lot of merchandise that had made the cops' eyes bug out.

Then there was the matter of the second man's blood on the workroom floor. Rich wondered when the cops would tumble to that. If they had already, nothing about it was appearing on the twenty-four-hour news channel.

Rich's intercom buzzed, cutting across his thoughts. He stabbed the button. "Yes?"

"Ms. Silverado is here for your dinner appointment."

"Send her in."

He stood up just as the outer door opened and Gail swept into his spacious office. She looked edible in a pantsuit the color and airiness of meringue. An assistant shut the door behind Gail and vanished like the discreet nonentity he was. A very well paid nonentity. Rich wasn't stupid or stingy when it came to people who could cause him trouble. He didn't want them to be bribed by a few hundred dollars waved under their noses.

"Stunning," Rich said, holding out both hands to Gail. "As always."

Smiling, she gave him her fingers while they exchanged a cool kiss on the cheek.

"I'd tell you how handsome you are," she said, pulling back and winking at him, "but you said something about an urgent matter regarding techno-thieves."

"Apparently someone forgot to warn the Golden Fleece. They hit Tannahill for several big jackpots recently."

"Gosh, how do you suppose that happened," Gail said without inflection. "We'll have to go over the notification protocol again. Can't have things falling through the cracks, can we?"

Rich's smile almost reached his eyes. "It's a shame we're so much alike, Silver," he said, calling her by her old nickname. "We would have made a great team. But as it is, we'd—"

"Kill each other before dawn," she finished. "We're too smart to go partners. Just like I'm too smart to buy the line about rushing over here to find out about techno-thieves in the Golden Fleece."

"You want to sweep the office before we talk?"

She shook her head. "You're not the kind of idiot or egomaniac that records every word for future generations to swoon over. You know that kind of record keeping is like having a loaded gun in your bedside table—chances are better you'll get shot with your own weapon than you'll manage to take down a burglar."

"Or as my mother used to say, once the shit hits the fan, everybody gets dirty."

Gail laughed. "I could have used a mother like that." She strolled over and looked down at the pool. "Poor bastards."

"The whales?"

"The girls. They think they're going to land a rich one."

"You did."

"Several times," Gail agreed. "But not by serving drinks with my titties hanging out. I used my head more than my body." She turned back to him. "What's up?"

"Has anyone approached you with a number of Celtic gold artifacts for sale?"

"No."

Rich was watching closely. He saw nothing to indicate a lie. "Then Tannahill probably has them by now."

"Are they hot?"

"Oh, yeah."

"How did he get them?" Gail asked.

"That's the problem. I don't know."

"That'll make it tough to tie a big red bow on his cock." She narrowed her cool hazel eyes. "How do you know he has the gold? And don't bother with the 'little birdie' crap. I didn't come here for a bedtime story."

"One of the thieves told Firenze."

"Carl? Why didn't he—"

"John, not Carl. Otherwise *you* would have called *me* and we'd be holding this conversation in your office, because neither one of us trusts phones worth a damn."

Her sleek eyebrows raised. "Only a fool expects phone conversations to be private."

He smiled.

She waited for him to start talking again. As she waited, each breath she took made light shift and shine over the breasts filling out the tailored white silk suit. She could tell he was looking at her and enjoying the view. She also could tell he wasn't going to do anything about it.

Too bad. Men were so much easier to control once you got hold of their dumb handles.

"As far as I can tell, some small-time stickup artist got lucky," Rich said. "He scored at least twenty, maybe more, Celtic gold artifacts."

Gail's rosy lips pursed in a soundless whistle.

"He and a buddy pawned four of the pieces to Joey Cline."

"Never heard of him."

"You wouldn't. He's at the bottom of the food chain. You feed at the top."

"So do you."

"But I never forget there's a bottom." Rich watched his words sink in, saw the faint frown between her big hazel eyes, and congratulated himself for getting under her pampered skin. "Cline turned over the merchandise to J. E. Shapiro."

"Shapiro. Shapiro . . ." She tilted her head. "That name doesn't chime either."

"Another pawnbroker who's pretty low on the food chain."

"Then it would be too low to have access to Shane."

"Probably. That's why I called you."

"Sorry to disappoint you. I gave up slumming before I was old enough to drink."

Rich ignored her. "J. E. Shapiro isn't answering calls, so for now it's a dead end. He probably heard about Cline's murder and—"

"Murder! You didn't say anything about that."

He shrugged. "What's one pawnbroker more or less? Vegas is full of them, like maggots on a carcass."

"Shit. Murder brings too much heat."

"Not if we can connect Tannahill to it. Then it would be just the right amount of heat."

Gail grimaced. "I'm not wild about tagging Shane for a murder he didn't commit."

"What makes you think he didn't commit it?"

"If he whacked somebody, you'd never find the body. That's one very, very smart man." She moved closer to the wall of glass and looked out at the sprawling, loud, grasping desert city that had made her fortune. But the world had changed since then. Las Vegas had changed.

She had changed.

Like the world and the city, she was older. A lot older. She didn't have it in her to start all over again if Wildest Dream stopped being a cash cow. And it would happen. Her profits were declining. Not steeply, but with the slow, steady bleeding that screamed of future disaster when massive remodeling was required to keep the casino/hotel up-to-date. Too many new casinos. Too many mega–entertainment complexes. Not enough tourists to keep everybody fat.

Damn it, Shane. Why couldn't you see how perfect we would have been together? We could have fucking owned this place.

But Shane couldn't see.

Rich Morrison could.

Life's a bitch and then you die.

She turned toward Rich, smiled, and wondered which one of them would survive their partnership.

Thirty-eight

Shane stood in Risa's office, growing more frustrated by the moment. "The apartment and office are yours for as long as you want them," he said impatiently. Again. "It was all in the severance package."

"Haven't read it." Risa didn't look up from the desk she was emptying as rapidly as possible into one of Cherelle's battered suitcases.

"Then you don't know that you have a year with full pay and benefits to find a new job."

"Don't need it."

"Don't make this harder than it already is."

The warning in his voice made Risa grateful that her hands were busy. Shane didn't lose his temper often, but he was closing in on it right now. Part of her was bitterly pleased to know she could upset him that much. The part of her with brains wished she hadn't fallen asleep at 4:00 A.M. and not awakened until 8:00. Maybe then she could have cleaned out her office before her ex-boss discovered that not only was she leaving her job, as soon as possible she was leaving the casino, the city, and most of all Shane Tannahill.

"Risa."

The yearning in his voice had her looking up before she knew what she was doing. Then it was too late. The heat and shadows in his green eyes took the ground out from under her feet.

"It's the only way to protect you," he said simply.

"Did I ask for protection?"

He hesitated. "No."

"If the positions were reversed, how would you feel?"

He opened his mouth, closed it, frowned. "I'm a man."

"I'm a woman. So what? Do you defend yourself with your dick? Zippers at dawn?" Still in her chair, she bent over and went back to cleaning out her files. "I've been taking care of myself since first grade."

"Against a murderer?"

"Bozo? He never left a mark on me."

"A bottom feeder called Joey Cline was murdered in his pawnshop yesterday."

Risa stopped stuffing journals into the suitcase. Her head snapped up. "Does he deal in stolen antiquities?"

"Probably."

"Did he have more gold pieces?"

"No."

"Then how do you know he was connected to the Druid gold?"

"Call it a hunch."

"Call it baloney and serve it with mayo." Journals slapped together as she slammed them into the suitcase. "Excuse me, I'm in a hurry. I'm supposed to meet someone at the airport."

She stood up. Too late she realized that Shane had

moved in. He was so close to her now that her mouth was all but tasting the green nylon windbreaker he wore.

"You're not leaving here without an armed guard," he said.

"No worries," Ian Lapstrake said from the doorway. "I caught an early flight."

Shane spun around with a lethal quickness that startled Risa. What shocked her even more was the gun that had appeared in his fist.

Ian smiled and held his hands in plain sight. "Hey, Shane. Long time no see."

"You sneak up on me again and you won't see anything for a long time, period." The gun disappeared beneath Shane's windbreaker. "What are you doing here?"

"Protecting Rarities Unlimited's newest employee," Ian said.

"Who?" Shane asked.

Ian glanced at Risa. "Didn't tell him, did you?"

"You've heard of 'don't ask, don't tell'?" Risa said. "He didn't, and I didn't."

"Beautiful," Ian said, watching the other man warily. No wonder Dana had been smiling when she gave him the assignment. Shane was looking mean and territorial, and Risa was mad enough to slip a knife into a man where it would do the most good. "You'll both be happy to know that, despite Risa's sexy mouth and never-quits body, I don't date fellow employees."

"I'm devastated," Risa said indifferently. "Especially considering your great shoulders and trust-me smile."

Ian snickered.

She went back to packing journals.

"Tell me why I shouldn't throw your great shoulders and trust-me smile out of my casino," Shane said to Ian.

"Simple. Until I find out what the hell is going on,

Risa is safer here than she will be anywhere else except headquarters in L.A."

"So take her to L.A."

"In case it has escaped your notice," Risa said without looking up, "I'm not a package to be picked up and dropped off when the whim takes you. I'm an adult fully capable of taking care of herself."

"Works for me," Ian said easily. "I'm going to have my hands full finding the rest of the Druid gold for Dana."

"I'll find it for her," Shane said.

"Not alone, you won't," Ian said. "Or do you think Risa's childhood friend will take one look at you, swoon, and spill all the golden secrets on your manly chest?"

"Money makes a lot of people talk. I have a lot of money."

"I'll keep it in mind." Ian looked at Risa. "Do you have your friend's address in Sedona?"

"No."

"Telephone number?"

"No."

"License plate?"

"No."

"Make and model of car?"

"No."

"Whoopee. I always did like a challenge." Ian reached into his denim jacket, pulled out the communications unit that Rarities gave to all high-level employees, and keyed in a number on the cell phone. "Research? Lap-strake. You have anything on Cherelle Faulkner yet?"

"We've only been working on it a little more than a day, and—"

"You've had it for a day?" Ian shot a look at Shane.

"—we already sent a brief to Tannahill on Sheridan and Faulkner, as you would know if you ever checked your e-mail."

The last words were said in a rising tone. Ian's refusal to waste time on bureaucratic junk like e-mails was legend at Rarities. It was just like Dana and Niall to let him find out for himself.

More interesting yet was the fact that Shane had ordered an investigation of Risa along with Cherelle Faulkner. Ian wondered if Risa knew. It would explain why she was so furious with her boss. Ex-boss. Come to think of it, getting fired was enough reason to steam her.

"So give me the good parts," Ian said into the phone.

"Sheridan was easy," the voice on the unit continued. "She fills out forms with real information. The Faulkner woman lives on the edge where bureaucrats don't go. She hasn't changed her driver's license, home address, or car registration since Johnson Creek, Arkansas."

"Most recent being?"

"Tannahill has it. That's where you are now, isn't it? Vegas?"

"Yeah, I'm here. I don't know if he feels like sharing."

"Shit. Why not?" Shane said, understanding the half of the conversation he hadn't heard. "You can have both profiles, Risa's and Cherelle's."

Then he waited for the explosion when Risa put two and two together and discovered he had put in a recent request for a complete Rarities background on Cherelle.

And on Risa.

The narrowing of her eyes and the flattening of her lush mouth told him that she'd made the connection very quickly. If she'd only been mad, he could have accepted it. But there had been a flash of raw hurt in her brilliant blue eyes before she lowered her head and resumed emptying out the bottom drawer of her office files.

He went and sat on his heels in front of her. "In my place what would you have done?" he asked quietly. "Someone from your childhood appears, someone who isn't anything like you, someone you don't want me to know about. Someone, in fact, that you hide from me."

Risa tilted back her head, furious with him but most of all furious with herself for the tears burning her eyes, her throat. "So you sicced Rarities on her. On me."

"Yes."

"You don't trust me."

"Risa—"

She made a sharp gesture with her hand to stop his words. "Never mind. Why should you trust me? I didn't trust you enough to tell you who Cherelle was because she was where I came from, where I could have stayed, where she . . ." Risa swallowed and fought against the tears that wanted to fall.

The back of Shane's fingers caressed her cheek once, lightly. "I was wrong. Your past isn't any of my business. All that matters to me is where you are now. Unless I had badly misjudged you because I wanted you so much, Cherelle didn't belong in your 'now.' That's why I called in Rarities. I didn't trust myself. And that's a first."

He stood and met Ian's dark, wryly sympathetic glance. "Unless research has something new, the data is in my office," Shane said.

"Anything since you sent the files to Tannahill?" Ian said into the cell phone. "Right. If and when you do, we want it yesterday. Yeah, same to you, sweetheart."

He switched off and put the communicator back on his belt. The supple leather straps of a shoulder holster gleamed briefly, then vanished beneath the denim jacket again.

"So Rarities flew you in," Shane said, seeing the harness.

"The longer Dana looked at your Druid gold, the more she wanted to find the rest of it. She said there was something both otherworldly and all too real about the art."

"Did you bring my four pieces with you?" Shane asked.

"You requested them, the lab wept and screamed, and I brought them. It would have been easier if you'd stuck with pictures for show-and-tell and questioning strangers."

Shane didn't accept the opening to explain why he had insisted the gold be returned.

Risa did. "Pictures don't have the same . . . feeling."

If Ian noticed that her voice was unusually husky, he didn't comment. "That's exactly what Shane said to Dana."

She glanced quickly at Shane, then away. Being reminded of how much they thought alike wasn't what she needed right now. "Where are they?" she asked Ian.

"With security downstairs. I refused to open the locks on the box, and they refused to let me upstairs until I did."

"How far did the Rarities lab get with them?" Shane asked.

"Dana put everything in your Rarities computer file. Said you could bloody well hack your way into it."

"My pleasure."

Ian shook his head. "One of these days you're going to push Niall too far."

"Not if I can help it," Shane said. "He's got more than a decade on me, and he hasn't slowed down a bit."

"You still work out with him?"

Shane smiled ruefully. "Every chance he gets. He just loves thumping on me."

"And here I thought he liked coming to Vegas to gamble." Ian laughed. "Getting thrashed on a semiregular basis will do you good."

"That's what Niall says."

Beneath black, lowered eyelashes, Ian glanced at Risa. Her eyes no longer looked on the brink of overflowing. Her hands were steady as they shuffled journals into the suitcase. But then her hands had been steady when she was fighting tears.

"According to Dana," Ian said to Risa, "our first priority is finding Cherelle Faulkner, because we're assuming she has the rest of the gold."

Risa nodded.

Shane didn't. "Our first priority is Risa's safety."

Ian's smile was all teeth. "Look, you don't like my orders, yell at Dana. In the meantime get the hell out of my way."

"No."

Ian sighed. It had been worth a try. "Niall said you would jump salty. So here's the fallback position. You work with me. That way Risa will be twice as safe."

Shane nodded. "The first thing you and I need to do is rattle William Covington's cage. According to the written provenance, he's the one who supposedly bought the gold pieces from a descendant of the original finder."

"What about me?" Risa asked with false calm.

"You stay here," Shane said.

"Because it's safe?"

"Yes."

"Bullshit. I was attacked here, remember? I'd be better off somewhere else. With two charming and manly bodyguards by my side, for instance. Lacking that, I'll settle for you and Ian Lapstrake."

Ian snickered.

Shane started to argue.

"Get over it," Ian advised, turning toward the door.

"That sounds like Dana," Shane retorted.

"Straight from her mouth to your ear." Ian smiled and winked at Risa. "Damn, but I love seeing Shane tangled up like a mere mortal. Does my peon's heart good."

"I don't want you to go," Shane said to Risa.

"Get over it." She smiled. "Besides, I'm the one who just remembered the name of the motel Cherelle was staying in."

"What is it?" Shane and Ian said together.

"I'll drive you there" was her only answer.

Shane started to object, saw both the determination and the shadows in Risa's beautiful eyes, and shut up.

"It gets easier with practice," Ian said quietly as they followed Risa out of the room.

"Says who?" Shane muttered.

"Niall. And if he can learn, anyone can."

Thirty-nine

LAS VEGAS
NOVEMBER 4
MORNING

The nurse poked his head around one of the wide hospital-style doors that were about the only sign that Timothy Seton wasn't staying at a small, expensive hotel. The Bateman-Molonari Clinic of Cosmetic Surgery was nothing if not exclusive. Discreet, too. Especially when their normal fee was tripled.

Miranda Seton would have preferred a real hospital, but as Tim's father had curtly explained, real hospitals had to report real bullet wounds to real cops.

"Your son just woke up," the nurse said in a hushed voice to Miranda. "You can talk to him as soon as the doctor leaves, but only for a few moments."

Miranda whispered a prayer of thanksgiving to a God she had stopped believing in when she found herself pregnant by a man she hadn't known was married. A man who not only could kill, but did. Her thin, almost frail hands clutched each other, pale but for the bleeding cuticles she picked at absently, constantly.

As soon as the nurse left, she opened her handbag,

took a stiff drink from what was left of a pint bottle of vodka, and stuffed an industrial-strength mint into her mouth. Fortified, she pushed herself to her feet and hurried down the lime green carpet to Tim's room. Perfectly framed pictures of perfectly sculpted faces smiled perfectly down at her from the cream-colored walls.

The door was numbered in brass, like that of a hotel room. And like a hotel room, its décor was both inviting and subdued, with framed Impressionist prints, soft colors, and lots of cushions on the furniture. The only jarring note was the patient laid out on pale rose sheets with monitors, machines, and tubes attached to parts of his body that Miranda didn't want to think about.

He looked worse than he had when covered in blood.

She wanted to rush to the bed and cuddle him, but she didn't. Her orders were quite specific: find out who had shot Tim. As soon as she did, there would be suitable vengeance.

"Oh, Timmy," she said in a strangled voice.

He grunted and kept his eyes shut. The last thing he needed right now was his mother fluttering around him like a wounded moth.

"Who did this to you? Cherelle?"

His eyelids flickered open, then settled at half-mast. Even the room's filtered, soothing light was more than he wanted right now. Speaking was an effort, but he managed. If he could send any trouble his old buddy's way, he would be happy to do it.

"Socks," Tim said painfully.

"I'm sorry. I didn't bring any with me. Are your feet cold? Maybe one of the nurses will have a heating pad or something."

Slowly, wearily, Tim moved his head from side to side. "Shot me."

She hesitated. "Socks? Your friend shot you?"

". . . yeah."

"Why?"

Tim let out a thready breath, then another one. He wasn't real sure of the answer. "Dunno." He paused, swallowed, "Gold, I guess."

"What gold?"

He ignored the question. It was too much effort to explain. The only thing that was worth the pain of talking was sending some bad luck down on Socks. "His name—Cesar."

"Another man?"

"*Socks.*" The word was a desperate exhalation.

"You mean that Socks's real name is Cesar?"

A groan that might have been yes was Tim's only answer. Then another groan. "I killed him."

"Socks?"

"Cline. Don't want prison. Never."

"Don't worry, Timmy. Your father will take care of you. He loves you."

Tim would have laughed, but he was trying to find a place on his body that didn't hurt. He was still trying when black closed around him again. He welcomed it like a lover.

Miranda picked at her cuticles and looked down at her frighteningly pale son.

Soon there was a light knock followed immediately by the door opening. The nurse looked in. "I'm sorry, Mrs. Seton, but the doctor wants your son to rest as much as possible. Please come with me. Dr. Wells can answer your questions."

She started to object, saw that Tim had slid back into unconsciousness, and sighed. "How long before I can visit him again?"

"Several hours at least." The nurse's broad, hairy hand gently gripped Miranda's elbow as he steered her out of the room. "Dr. Wells is waiting. There will be plenty of time for all your questions before your son wakes up again."

And, the nurse thought cynically, plenty of time for the worried mother to slip out and buy more booze and mints. From what he'd seen on the clinic's discreet surveillance cameras, she was about at the end of her bottle.

Not that the nurse really cared. He was used to alcoholics and their games. When the Bateman-Molonari Clinic wasn't tucking up sagging skin, it was drying out and feeding up rich patrons so that they could go forth and drink themselves back into a coma. Between vanity and booze, the clinic always had a waiting list. Still, he couldn't help feeling sorry for the lady. The patient might wake up a few more times, maybe even have a real lucid spell . . . but that would be it.

The lady's son was dying.

Forty

Ian pulled his car up near Shane in the cracked parking lot of the Jackpot Motel. He noticed that Shane was doing the same thing Ian had been since they left the casino—looking over his shoulder.

"Where is he?" Shane asked as Ian walked over.

"Who?" asked Risa.

"The guy who followed us," Shane said.

"The blonde in the red car?" she asked.

Shane gave her a quick look. He hadn't thought she noticed.

The look she gave back to him said that there were a lot of things about her that *he* hadn't noticed, and number one of all was that she could take care of herself.

"That's the one," Ian agreed, drawing their attention to him. "He's half a block down."

"You get his plate?" Shane asked.

"Already called it in to Rarities."

"If they can't access Nevada's state license bureau in a hurry, I can."

"Yeah, Niall said something about you learning to be a world-class hacker at your daddy's knee."

Risa said, "I'm not listening to this. I haven't just heard my boss—my *ex*-boss—say that he can hack into government computers. Think of the blackmail possibilities. But I'm not listening."

"Good call," Shane said. "Let's go."

Armed with photos taken from the security cameras of Cherelle and "Bozo," the three of them walked into the Jackpot Motel's office door. The office reeked of smoke and the contents of an overflowing ashtray the size of a soup plate. The woman behind the fake wood counter looked old enough to have kids on Social Security. She was wearing a scoop-front, thigh-length orange sweater and black tights. Her hair was improbably black. Her face looked like it had been slept in for eighty years.

"Sorry to bother you, ma'am," Risa said, "but I'm trying to find my friend, Cherelle Faulkner." As she spoke, Ian slid a photo onto the counter. "She was staying here a few days ago and might not have checked out yet."

"You lose your friends often?" the woman asked in a raspy voice.

Risa smiled from the teeth out. "No. But Cherelle is a little careless about things like checking out and paying bills. So I kind of go along behind her and see that nobody ends up short. How much did she owe you?"

The woman glanced briefly at the photo. Then she lit a cigarillo and took a long, considering pull on it while she studied the three people in front of her. None of them looked down on their luck, and one of them looked vaguely familiar, like someone she might have seen on TV. She took another long nicotine hit while she decided how much money she could charge for information about the slut in the red sweater. Exhaling, she thought about going for a hundred. Two, if she played it right. Then she could kick back with the nickel slots downtown until her butt went numb and her hand ached too much to hit the play button again.

As smoke streamed around Risa, she wondered if holding her breath would do any good. In the end she went for breathing through her mouth. It didn't make the air any better, but it didn't insult her nose as much.

"A hundred," the woman said.

Ian made a disgusted sound.

Shane reached for his wallet. Two fifties appeared in his fingers. He put one of the bills on the counter.

With startling speed one fifty disappeared into the woman's wrinkled cleavage. She watched Shane with watery, demanding eyes.

He kept the second bill out of her reach.

"She checked out a couple days ago," the woman said.

"Did she say where she was going?" Risa asked.

The woman hooted. "We weren't pals, dearie."

"Did she leave anything behind?"

"Dirty linen and fast-food trash."

"Room number?" Shane asked.

"Five. Check it if you want."

The fact that she was so willing to let them into the room told them there probably wasn't anything worth seeing.

"Later maybe," Ian said. "Was she driving a Ford Bronco, about ten years old, Arkansas plates?"

The woman shrugged and watched the fifty that Shane held just out of her reach.

"You're supposed to write down a vehicle and license when people register," Shane reminded her.

"Yeah, it was a Bronco. Didn't notice the plates."

"What about him?" Risa asked, putting Bozo's picture on the counter.

"Our deal was for her," the woman said.

Shane got out a third fifty, but he didn't give it—or the second fifty—to the woman. "This covers everything."

She drew smoke in and then shared it with her visitors in a coughing exhalation. "You cops?"

"No."

"Mob?"

"Sorry," Shane said.

She treated them to another round of dragon breath before she shrugged again. "Can't blame a gal for hoping. I liked the Mob. They were real men, you get me?"

"What about this one?" Risa said, tapping the photo of Bozo. "Was he staying with Cherelle?"

"No, the other one was. This one just tagged along with his tongue hanging down to his pecker."

"Either of those men have a name?" Risa asked.

"She called the other one Tim. He called that one"— she tapped the photo—"Socks."

"Last names?" Risa asked.

"She's the only one who ever registered."

Ever. Implies more than once. "How often did Cherelle come here?" Risa asked quickly.

"Couple times a year maybe. Had friends or kin nearby."

"How near?" Ian asked.

She looked at the two fifties in Shane's hand. He passed one of them over the counter to her. She stuffed the bill down the front of her bra, on the opposite side this time. One crisp bill for each limp boob. The hard edges of the money poked out against the sweater.

"Walking distance," she said. "At least he walked

some of the time. Whined about it, too. Car wasn't his, I guess."

"He?"

"The tall, pretty one. Tim. There's some apartments a few blocks over to the north and a few old houses just beyond. That's the direction he went when he walked. Wouldn't go there at night, if I was you."

"Did they make any phone calls?" Risa asked.

"No phone in the room."

"Any visitors?"

She shrugged. "Didn't see any."

Risa looked at Shane and then at Ian.

"Did Socks drive a car?" Shane asked.

"You got another fifty?"

"Only if you have a description and a license plate."

"No plate. Don't see real good that far off."

"You see the state?"

She nodded.

Shane reached for his wallet. "Talk to me. Make it good and I'll make you good."

"Purple coupe, the kind of purple that glows in the dark, you get me? Nevada plate."

"Foreign or American car?"

"American. Big engine. Sounds like a street racer and tricked out like a whore's Christmas. Lemme think a minute." She nursed a long drag and sorted through recent memories. "It's a Fire-something. Old American carmaker, like Ford or Chevy, but not that."

"Pontiac?" Ian asked.

"Firebird?" Shane said at the same instant.

"That's it. Glad you boys remembered. Things like that drive me nuts at four in the morning." She squinted at Shane. "Hey, ain't you that rich gambler fella?

Prince Midas? Saw your picture on the news after that shooting."

"A lot of people think I look like him," Shane said. He moved his fingers, and three fifty-dollar bills fanned out.

A wide, yellow grin split the woman's face. She grabbed the money and started shoving it down her sweater.

As the door shut behind them, Risa said, "You should have given her another fifty."

"Why?" Shane asked.

"Two doesn't go into five evenly, which leads to the question of where she stashed the last fifty."

Ian snickered.

Shane said, "Want to ask her?"

"No, thanks. I'm thinking I don't want to go there."

"I'm thinking you're right," Ian said.

Shane gave a long look around the parking lot of the motel and the street beyond. So did Ian. The roof of a red car was just visible halfway down the block, parked between two pieces of road iron that looked like they hadn't moved since the last rain.

Shane lifted his eyebrow in silent question.

"Not yet," Ian said. "First we'll see if we can find out who's following us without tipping our hand."

Risa said, "He picked us up when we came out of the employee parking lot."

"Is he the one who chased you through the casino?" Shane asked.

"Wrong color hair. Bozo's was dark."

"Too bad. I'm looking forward to meeting him."

Shane's smile made Risa uneasy. "Do we search for the kin he visited," she asked, "or do we go yank Covington's chain?"

"We could divide up," Shane said. "Ian can go door-to-door with the photos, and we can do Covington."

"Why don't you do the door-to-door thing?" Ian asked without real hope.

"Two reasons," Shane said. "The first is that, thanks to the camera-happy media, a half-blind old lady can ID me. The second reason is simple. Covington wouldn't give you the time of day, but he'll roll out the red carpet for me. Nothing personal. Just money."

"Figures," Ian muttered, reaching for his communications unit. "If Niall buys it, I'm out of your hair. Otherwise, get used to making like a dune buggy."

"A what?" Then Shane laughed. "Got it. Three wheels and you're the third."

Risa put her hands on her hips and turned her back before she said something rash about not needing one bodyguard, much less two. But she was afraid she did. Bozo's rough question kept echoing in her mind.

Where's the gold?

She didn't know. But she knew one thing. That kind of money on the loose brought out human predators. Cherelle knew it, too.

That was why she was running scared.

Forty-one

John Firenze grabbed his private phone like it was a winning lottery ticket. "Yeah?"

"Sheridan left with Tannahill and another man. They haven't returned."

"Where did they go?"

"Out."

"Jesus Christ, I could have guessed that!" He glared across his office to a window that overlooked the construction of another huge resort/casino. The problem with hiring relatives was that not all of them were real bright. At least his cousin Frankie had more wattage than numb-nuts Cesar. "Out where?"

"Place called the Jackpot Motel. The old bag there said they asked questions about Cherelle, Tim, and a dude called Socks. Cost me fifty bucks to find out that she didn't know anything so they didn't learn anything useful."

Socks. Shit. They'd made his fucking stupid nephew. "What are they doing now?"

"They split up. The second guy is going door-to-door with two photos."

"Who of?"

"I didn't get close enough to see. Want me to?"

"No. Get Sheridan alone and give her the message I gave you. Got it?"

"Yeah, but it won't be easy. Tannahill's all over her like a rash."

"Don't tell me your problems. I got plenty of my own."

Firenze disconnected and punched in the number he'd memorized simply by using it so many times in the last hour. The answering machine picked up again. He didn't wait to hear the message. Like the number, he had it memorized by now: *Mr. Shapiro of the Second Chance Loan Exchange is with a customer. Please leave a message, and he will get back to you as soon as possible.*

Firenze looked at his watch. He couldn't stall much longer. Another hour and he'd have to settle for a smaller piece of the pie.

Or none at all.

Forty-two

William Covington's business establishment looked like what it was, an upscale antique-consignment store that was rumored to lend money for short terms at ruinous rates with antiques as collateral. Brown furniture loomed everywhere, set off by crystal chandeliers and Tiffany-style lamps. The only weapons in the place were more than a hundred years old and mounted on the wall like trophies. Glass cases displayed smaller items whose value and portability might tempt a browser into crime.

"Thank you for seeing me on such short notice," Shane said when Covington came hurrying out of his office toward them.

"My pleasure, Mr. Tannahill, Ms. Sheridan." Covington smiled at each in turn, displaying brilliant teeth. "Come back to my office, please. I have coffee waiting."

Neither Shane nor Risa was interested in coffee, but they followed Covington anyway. The office promised more privacy than the front salesroom, where high-end bargain hunters and hungry decorators prowled among the dark furniture.

After everyone had sipped coffee and made appropriately meaningless remarks about the lack of weather in Las Vegas, Covington looked at Shane expectantly.

"I understand you sometimes do business with Mr. Smith-White," Shane said.

"We pass business along to each other, yes." Covington smiled. "We're friendly competitors."

Shane nodded to Risa. She took an envelope from her purse, pulled out glossy photos, and began spreading them across Covington's nineteenth-century mahogany desk. Shane watched the store owner, not the photos. There wasn't any flicker of eyelids, any shift in his mouth, any increase in the pulse beating visibly above his white collar.

Not one sign that he recognized the photos.

"Quite unusual," Covington said. "Are they for sale?"

"How much do you think they would be worth?" Risa asked quickly.

"Heavens." He frowned. "I'd have to think about that. I deal more in furniture than in decorative arts and antiquities. I haven't any idea what these items might be worth."

"Really?" Risa lifted her eyebrows. "Then how did you decide what to charge Smith-White for them?"

Covington absorbed the fact that apparently he had sold the gold. "Smith-White. Really. Was it a recent sale?"

"Early July, according to the receipts."

With a wave of his pale hand, Covington dismissed the matter. "Well, there you have it. My shop sells many things that I don't personally handle. This was probably part of an estate consignment or a consolidation consignment from another dealer which I sold to Smith-White because it suited his clientele more than mine."

"According to Smith-White's records, you purchased these gold artifacts from a Mr. Shapiro," Risa said.

"Then I or one of my representatives undoubtedly did just that."

"The provenance provided was sketchy," Risa said, watching him closely. "Second-generation descendant of a now-dead purchaser."

"Distressing how little the modern world cares about the past, isn't it?"

"So you've never seen these before?" Risa asked.

"Never. Sorry." Covington smiled and stood up. "Now, unless there's anything else I can do for you, I really must be off. So much to do." He turned to Shane. "I have a lovely new consignment from Italy to price. If you ever decide to open a gambling museum, there is a particularly remarkable roulette wheel I would like you to see. Gold rails, ebony and ivory insets, with a solid gold ball. It was used by Italian aristocracy for their own amusement."

"Send photos and particulars to my office," Shane said, standing and helping Risa to her feet, squeezing her hand in a warning for her to be silent. He gathered the pictures of the gold artifacts and slid them into his breast pocket. "If you remember anything else about the provenance of this gold, or if you have gold antiquities of a similar quality, my ten-thousand-dollar reward still stands."

Thin gray brows twitched. "Indeed. I shall check my inventory quite carefully."

Shane smiled like a wolf. "You do that."

As soon as they were outside, Risa said, "That lying sack of shit."

"We can't prove it."

She blew out an impatient breath. He was right and she knew it. She just didn't like it. "Now what?"

"Shapiro."

"Another lying sack of shit?"

Shane didn't answer. He didn't have to. His thin smile said it all.

Forty-three

Ian had seen enough dried blood to know what it looked like. Not that you had to be some kind of twenty-first-century Dick Tracy to figure out that the partial handprint on the side wall of the shoe-repair shop was organic and fairly recent. Even though the blood was dark rusty red and sun-struck, the flies were all over it, so he was sure it wasn't some graffiti artist's sprayed statement of urban anomie. There was a palm-size puddle of dried blood on the cracked pavement of the alley, too, as though someone had leaned there, gathering strength to cross the street.

Six doors down the alley, a uniformed cop was stringing yellow tape over the back of a crime scene. The bad news was that Ian couldn't track the blood back to its source without giving himself away. The good news was that the crime tape didn't leave much doubt about the source.

Since the cop didn't notice Ian looking down the alley, Ian just kept on walking until he reached the end of the block and could see down the main street. There was yellow tape all over one storefront. Several squad cars were double-parked in front. So was an ambulance. A white news van with a satellite feed sitting on its roof like a big soup dish waited curbside in front of the ambulance. Two plainclothes cops talked with a cameraman and a reporter who were leaning against the news van, waiting for a photo op.

Ian walked up to the uniformed cop who was guarding the front entrance. "Heart attack?" he asked.

The cop gave him a look. "What's it to you?"

"Nothing, so long as it isn't one of these two people." Ian pulled out the two photos. "Is it?"

The cop glanced down at the photos. "What do you want them for?"

"Missing person, nonsuspicious disappearance. Left her husband and kids back on the farm and came here to make her fortune. Her grandmother won't give up looking for her, which is fine for me." Ian flashed his trust-me smile. "Pays the rent. The guy may or may not be her most recent live-in."

The cop took another look at the photos. "This part of town is my beat. I know the hookers and the drunks and the regulars. Don't recognize either one of them."

"Thanks anyway. I'll try up and down the street. Maybe I'll get lucky."

The rattle of gurney wheels announced the ambulance crew a few seconds before they rolled out into the streaming sunlight. A dark body bag was strapped to the white sheet over the thin mattress. The way the bag moved announced that rigor mortis wasn't a problem any longer.

"Hey, wait!" called the cameraman, hurrying over. "Back it up and come out again, okay?"

One of the detectives yelled after the cameraman, "You think anyone in Vegas gives a shit about slime like Joey Cline?"

"It's a corpse, ain't it?" said the cameraman. "Give us a minute and do it again, okay?"

The ambulance crew shrugged. It wasn't like it made any difference to their patient. "Yeah, sure. Dude's been dead for probably a day. Few more minutes won't matter."

Ian waited near the satellite truck, hoping to overhear something else useful. No such luck.

By the time he faded into the edges of the thin knot of people that had gathered, the ambulance crew was making its third run-through for the "live film at six o'clock." The on-air reporter checked the smooth blond helmet of his hair, straightened his suit coat and tie, took his place by the front door of the pawnshop, and began talking into a mike for the third time. One of the detectives stood to his right, not blocking the camera's view of the scene and the reporter.

"This is Ralph Metcalfe at the scene of a brutal murder just moments away from Glitter Gulch. According to the police, Mr. Joseph Cline was found in a pool of his own blood in the back of his store. Another bloody spot indicated that a second man, possibly his attacker, had been lying on the floor. The whereabouts of the second man is unknown." He turned to face the cop. "Detective Yarrow, does the Las Vegas Police Department have any leads on this bloody and terrible murder?"

Ian was around the corner and out of sight before the detective got his fifteen seconds of fame. As soon as Ian was sure he'd faded away without attracting any official attention, he sent an update to Rarities and to Shane's voice mail. Then, just in case the cops checked, Ian worked his way through the storefronts, showing photos and asking earnest questions. No one recognized Cherelle or Socks.

Casually Ian eased down the side street and crossed over to the continuation of the alley leading away from the pawnshop. If the cops hadn't discovered the blood spoor back in the other alley, they would soon.

It took a few moments to pick up the trail of brown drops again. It led him down the alley and across a different street, up two half blocks . . . and vanished.

He thought about the back trail and the old woman at the motel. *There's some apartments a few blocks over to the north and a few old houses just beyond. That's the direction he went when he walked.*

Ian headed north, taking alleys, looking for more blood. He didn't find any until he was within sight of the back of one of the two old houses that huddled together against the onslaught of apartment buildings and strip malls. There were bloody handprints on the back door of 113 Oasis Lane.

No one answered Ian's knock on the rear door. The possible entrances were barred. Ian could have gotten through the metal, but he preferred to do it in the dark.

He went around to the front. To one side there was a wall of run-down apartments. To the other was another bungalow. A man old enough to be God was sitting on the front porch. He was so still Ian wondered if he was alive.

"Looking for something?" the man asked in a cracking voice.

Ian shaded his eyes from the relentless sun and walked up to the porch. Stretched out at the man's feet was a hound so old that it was gray from its nose to the back of its floppy ears.

"Good afternoon, sir," Ian said, smiling as he climbed the two low steps onto the porch. "Perhaps you can help me. I'm searching for a young lady by the name of Cherelle Faulkner. The woman in the apartment across the street and down a ways said that someone at 113 Oasis Lane might be able to help me."

As he spoke, Ian pulled out the pictures and presented them to the old man, who took a long time to fish half-glasses from his shirt pocket and settle them onto his nose.

The hound didn't stir at the interruption. Not so much as a quiver.

Ian wondered if it was stuffed.

"Ay-ah. She comes around a couple times of year," the man said in a scratchy Northeast accent. "Lives with that sweet lady's no-good son."

"The sweet lady next door?" Ian asked, gesturing toward 113 Oasis Lane.

"Ay-ah. Mrs. Seton."

"Is this her son?" Ian asked, tapping the photo of Socks.

The old man shook his head. "He's the bastid that drives the fahting purple car."

Ian swallowed a laugh by clearing his throat. "Do you know when Mrs. Seton will be back? Cherelle's grandmother really wants to see her granddaughter before she dies."

"Mrs. Seton didn't say. Just dumped Pitty Pat on me and took off in that black limousine yesterday afternoon."

Ian was almost afraid to ask. "Pitty Pat?"

"My Siamese. Cat likes the Widow Seton better, 'cause old Barks A Lot chases her, so she's always going and hiding next door."

"Barks A Lot?"

"My hound." He nudged the big animal stretched out at his feet.

The hound didn't move.

"Chases Pitty Pat," Ian said.

"Ay-ah."

"Cat must have a helluva long memory."

"Ay-ah."

"Did you see anyone with Mrs. Seton?"

"Can't say. Car pulled around to the back to pick her up. I know she's gone, though."

"How?"

"Pitty Pat stayed here. Soon as Mrs. Seton comes back, Pitty Pat will run off again."

Ian folded a twenty-dollar bill and put it into the old man's pocket along with a business card that had Ian's cell phone number on it. "If anybody comes back here, I'd appreciate a call."

"Don't want to bring trouble down on the widow. She don't much like that Cherelle. Heard 'em arguing more than once." He shook his head. "Poor Mrs. Seton. Cherelle is what we used to call coarse."

Ian bet people still called it that.

Forty-four

Risa and Shane drove by Shapiro's business, which was located close to the failing downtown and its downscale casinos. It was an area of small businesses that aspired to middle class and didn't quite make it. Shapiro's show windows were barred, the blue neon sign advertised payday loans, and the storefronts on either side were taken by a travel agent and something called Woman's Needs, which could have been anything from a sex shop to a free clinic.

Shane darted into a parking spot on the street a block away from Shapiro's business. The red Lexus that had been following them had no place to hide, no choice but to roll on by while Shane memorized the license plate. Without taking his eyes off the car, he keyed a number into his cell phone, waited until someone answered, and read out the plate number.

A slanting sideways look was Risa's only comment, but curiosity got the better of her. "Was that Factoid or one of your own computer moles?"

"Factoid. No point in duplicating his efforts. He's cracked every motor-vehicle registration bureau in every state of the union. Canada, too. He's working on Mexico but claims the system is so corrupt that no one drives the vehicle the plate is issued to. I told him he just doesn't understand the system yet."

Shane looked back toward Shapiro's business. If there were any lights on inside, they didn't show up against the glare of daylight.

"It looks closed to me," Risa said.

"Yeah."

He keyed in another command on his hand unit, checked the numbers that had called him, and accessed Ian's message. It wasn't chatty, but it was long. Phone to his ear, he listened with growing intensity.

Watching Shane's face, Risa wondered what had gone wrong. She knew something must have. Other people might not be able to see past Shane's impassive expression, but she could. With rising impatience she waited until he put the cell phone down.

"What?" she demanded.

"Joey Cline was murdered."

"Do we know him?"

"Not directly, but whoever killed him left bloody marks from the pawnshop murder site to 113 Oasis Lane, and whoever lives at that number knows Cherelle. My guess is that Cline bought the gold and turned it to Shapiro, who turned it to Covington, who turned it to Smith-White."

Risa forced herself to breathe. "You're sure about Cherelle. She's linked to a murdered man."

They weren't quite questions. Shane answered them anyway. "A neighbor on Oasis Lane recognized Cherelle from the photo. A man called Socks—the one you call

Bozo—was also recognized. Mrs. Seton, who is probably related to the man who killed Cline and left bloody marks in the alley, lives at 113. Her no-good son visits occasionally, according to the neighbor. Cherelle comes with the no-good son."

"Seton," Risa said, remembering the brochure Cherelle had left behind. "Tim Seton. He's Cherelle's partner in the channeling business."

"What about Socks?"

"Bozo?" Risa laughed shortly. "He wasn't mentioned in the brochure."

"He drives a purple car with a loud muffler."

Risa's fingers drummed on her thigh. She didn't like what she was hearing. She liked what she was thinking even less. "All right. So we have Socks in a purple car, Cherelle probably in an old Bronco, and Tim at the motel and then at the house on Oasis Lane. What does Mrs. Seton have to say for herself?"

"She isn't home. A black limo came for her yesterday afternoon. From what Ian could gather, Cline was probably killed yesterday. Rigor mortis had already come and gone."

Risa grimaced. "What about the guy who left bloody marks? Where is he?"

"Ian will check the house tonight, but I've got a hunch it was Tim who was hurt, so his mama loaded him into a limo and took him somewhere for some real quiet doctoring."

"A hunch, huh?"

"Yeah."

"The kind that made you into a multimillionaire?"

"Yeah."

She blew out a breath so hard her hair shivered. She couldn't think of a single comforting reason for Tim crawling away from the site of a murder covered in blood. The memory of Cherelle's full, wild laugh when she found out how much Shane's collection of Celtic gold might be worth was equally uncomfortable.

Damn it, Cherelle. Why didn't you come to me? I could have helped you. You didn't have to get tied up with . . . whatever it is you're tied up with.

Then Risa realized that Cherelle had come to her, and in doing so had sicced a thug on her.

Maybe she didn't have any choice.

Risa's mouth turned down. You always had a choice.

And sometimes the choice you made was bad.

"Why wait for night to check the house?" she asked.

Shane looked at her with jade green eyes that had both comfort and shadows in them. "Because Ian doesn't have a key."

"Then why not phone in an anonymous call for help from that address? Or tell the cops that whoever killed Cline went there?"

"Ian will do just that after he makes sure there aren't any more gold artifacts inside the house."

"But—"

"Dana's orders," Shane said, ignoring the interruption. "She doesn't want the artifacts scooped up or lost in the bureaucratic shuffle by a system that doesn't have the faintest idea of the gold's cultural worth."

" 'Buy, Sell, Appraise, Protect,' " Risa said, remembering Rarities's motto. "The art comes first and the client second."

"I knew that when I signed on. It's *why* I signed on."

Smiling faintly, she leaned her head against the leather upholstery. "But you work very hard to look like a sleazy collector. You aren't."

"Would crooks approach a Boy Scout with stolen cultural artifacts?"

"No, but most people care too much for their reputation to ruin it by looking dirty."

A lift of Shane's shoulder told her how much he cared about his good name.

Risa went back to drumming her fingers against her thigh. "What if someone comes back to the house before dark?"

"Ian is watching it."

"Do you think Cherelle is there?" Risa asked before she could stop herself. "Do you think she's hurt? If she is, shouldn't we . . . ?" Risa closed her eyes and took a careful breath. No matter what Cherelle had done, it was hard to sit and do nothing while her friend might be in pain. Or worse. "Shouldn't we break in?"

Shane took Risa's hand to still its restless motions. Her fingers were cool. He warmed them between his palms while he waited for her to settle. He knew what was worrying her. She was imagining her friend on the run, hurt, hiding, needing help. All those warm and fuzzy feelings left over from childhood running smack up against the cold edges of adult reality, and not a damn thing to be done about any of it.

"I'm okay," she said on a sigh. "Really." Her attempt at a smile turned upside down. "But one way or another it's been a big ol' bitch of a day. What really grinds on me is that it's not over yet."

Slowly he smoothed her fingers against his cheek. "The neighbor didn't see anyone but Mrs. Seton come or go. If Cherelle and Mrs. Seton didn't get along—and, according to the neighbor, they didn't—it's not real likely that Cherelle would go there if she was hurt." He kissed

Risa's fingers and released them. "Especially when she had a friend like you to go to."

"You mean stupid?"

"No. Generous." More generous than Cherelle deserved, but he wasn't going to add to Risa's unhappiness by saying it.

She shifted and raked her fingers through her short black hair. "Damn, I hate not knowing. Wondering. Waiting. She could be hurt."

"It's far more likely that no-good Tim is the one who left his blood on the pawnshop floor."

Risa knew that was true. It just didn't make her feel any better.

"Come on," Shane said. "Let's see if Shapiro is home."

"The sign says 'closed.' "

"Shapiro lives above the shop," Shane said.

"How do you know?"

"You don't want to know," he said, thinking of a spectacular piece of Mayan gold he had bought from Shapiro in his upstairs quarters. After hours, of course. Shapiro did his most profitable work then.

"You sure I don't want to know?"

"Yes."

Risa shut up and followed him toward the shop that was closed up tight in the middle of the business day.

Without so much as looking around to see if anyone was watching, Shane sauntered past the shop, around the corner, and into the alley where full trash bins awaited pickup. In addition to a secondhand-clothes store, a used-office-furniture store, and a shoe-repair shop, there were two cafés and a taco stand opening onto the alley. The trash bins gave off odors that flies found irresistible.

Shane wrapped his hand in his jacket and tried the

back door of Shapiro's Loan and Pawn Shop. It wasn't locked. He pushed it open, pulled Risa through, and shut the door again. Voices came from somewhere overhead.

The smell wasn't any better inside. If anything, it was worse.

"Shit," Shane said very softly. "Stay here."

"But—" Her objections dried up when she saw the gun in his hand.

The stairway risers were covered with linoleum that had been worn through to the black underlayer and from there right down to the boards. He went up them quietly, keeping to the side of the steps where they were less likely to creak.

Shapiro was in front of the TV. A tipped-over, empty quart of expensive bourbon lay on the couch next to him. The actors on the afternoon soap opera were humping tastefully beneath the sheets. When their choreographed cries faded, the action cut to an ad for toothpaste. Shapiro didn't react.

Shane thought the man was dead. It certainly would account for the smell. Then he heard the faint bubbling of a snore and realized that Shapiro was dead, all right.

Dead drunk, so out of it that he had filled his pants like a baby.

Forty-five

Shane's office was cool, well furnished, and smelled like glory after hours spent on the dusty streets and in the ripe alleys of Las Vegas. Risa sat with her head resting on the back of a sea green brushed-leather couch and tried not to worry about Cherelle.

"So far," Shane said to Ian and Niall, "we've got one dead bottom feeder, and he's the only one that matters. He's the point where the gold entered the system. We're assuming it went from Cline to Shapiro but can't prove it because Shapiro says his computer crashed and took all his records, and that's why he got drunk."

"Do you believe him?" Niall asked.

Shane laughed.

"Want me to squeeze him?" Ian asked.

"Short of beating the crap out of Shapiro—"

"Dana frowns on that method," Niall cut in.

"—we're stuck. Like Covington, he has deniability, lawyers, and has been around this track before," Shane finished.

"Don't forget Frank Firenze," Ian said.

"The one who was following us in the red car?" Risa asked.

"Yeah. By the time I got his name, he wasn't following you anymore. I called and asked him why he was following you. He didn't know what I was talking about, his car had been in the shop, he wouldn't follow you in the future, good-bye."

"If you see him tailing you again," Niall said to Ian, "let me know. Otherwise . . ." He stretched and rubbed his short, dark hair. Even the corporate jet cramped his long frame, but Dana wanted the gold and that was that. "We'll concentrate on the three other bottom feeders who are running around with the kind of treasure that the British Museum is screaming is rightfully theirs."

Risa was still flinching at the description of Cherelle as a bottom feeder when the rest of Niall's words sank in. She sat up in a rush. "What? I missed that part. When did the British Museum get in on the act?"

"As soon as we put out pictures on the Net," Niall said, "the Brits jumped on them with both feet, yelling 'Mine, mine, mine!' The Irish leaped in right after, then the Austrians and—"

"The Austrians!" Shane interrupted.

"Hallstatt and La Tène," Risa said. "Right?"

"Right," Niall said.

Shane snorted. "Nice try. Doesn't fly."

"Hey," Ian said, "when it's an international pissing contest, all that matters is volume, not quality."

"You're brighter than you look, boyo," Niall said to Ian.

"That wouldn't be hard," Shane muttered.

Ian flipped him off without real interest.

"As Dana would say, 'Shut it, children.' " Niall bent

down and pulled a sheaf of printouts from a battered canvas map case that was older than he was. "Rap sheet on Timothy Edgar Seton, Cherelle Leticia Faulkner, and Cesar Firenze Marquez, street name Socks."

"Firenze?" Shane said. "Interesting."

"Any relation to Frank Firenze?" Ian asked.

"Probably. The Firenze family was supposed to be Mob in Vegas back in the bad old days," Shane said. "But they're superclean now. The Gambling Control Board wouldn't have it any other way. John Firenze—the head of the family—has a business degree and all the right political connections."

"Maybe that's what Frank was after—Socks and the gold," Ian said to Risa. "When he saw you looking in all the wrong places, he gave up on you."

She barely listened. She was still reeling from hearing Cherelle's middle name for the first time. "I didn't even know she had one."

"One what?" Niall asked.

"Middle name," Shane said before Risa could. "Cherelle's. Leticia."

Ian looked from Shane to Risa and shook his head sadly. "It's already started."

"What has?" Niall asked.

"Finishing each other's sentences. Reading each other's minds." He glanced at Niall. "Like you and Dana. Enough to make a man swear off women."

"Your sentences could use some finishing," Niall retorted, scanning the first printout for the highlights. "This Socks is the kind of boy who keeps the penal system in business. In and out since he was ten. He's been on the streets a whole eighteen months now."

Risa rubbed her temples. "Will wonders never cease."

"Hey, it's a record," Niall said. "Most time he's spent on the outside since he graduated."

"High school?" Ian asked.

"Juvie," Niall said. "Once he turned sixteen, he started going away for longer times as an adult. Hard time."

Shane went to the wet bar, pulled a bottle of sparkling water out of the small refrigerator, and handed it to Risa. She gave him a surprised look that told him she'd just figured out she was thirsty and wondered how he'd known.

Ian gave her an I-told-you-so smile.

"Is that where Socks picked up Seton?" Shane asked. "In jail?"

Niall nodded and scanned the page rapidly. "Cellmates. Socks is suspected of shanking an old guy in prison. No proof. No charges."

"Shanking?" Risa asked.

"Killing him with a homemade knife," Shane said.

She grimaced as she unscrewed the bottle top. "Nice guy."

"Oh, he's a sweetheart," Niall agreed. "Armed robbery the last time out. Assault and battery before then. Burglary. Attempted rape. And after his dance through the Golden Fleece, you can add kidnapping, burglary, assault, and attempted murder. Car registered in Nevada. Nevada driver's license suspended for driving under the influence. No wife. No kids to speak of. No home address. Mother dead. Father a drunken small-time crook whose specialty was drying out in county jails in between running cigarettes from Indian reservations and selling them out of his trunk at swap meets. But that was only when he wasn't breaking legs for loan sharks."

"Hard to see someone like Socks having the contacts to steal the kind of high-end antiquities Smith-White sold us," Risa said. Water gurgled lightly as she raised the bottle to drink. A lemony tang spread over her tongue. She gave Shane a grateful look and decided she might forgive him for being overly protective. "Where would Socks find that quality of goods? Ditto for Cherelle. What about Tim?"

Niall grunted. "I doubt that Timothy Edgar Seton had them lying around the house. A really pretty face and a badly spotted soul. Underage drinking and gambling. Statutory rape and accessory to armed robbery. No high school graduation, but he went to the Gentleman's Deal, an expensive training ground for casino dealers and 'escorts.' Dealt blackjack, slept with women who paid his bills, buddied around with the hard-asses. His mother is Miranda Caroline Seton, never married, lives at 113 Oasis Lane in a house registered to a rental company. Father not listed on birth certificate. No other relatives. Seton lists his mother's place as his home address. Driver's license. No car."

Ian made a sound of disgust. "I'm not seeing any road to gold in Tim's background."

"Does credit count?" Niall asked. "Seton has four active credit cards. All maxed and late."

"I'm shocked," Shane said. With a sharp motion he twisted off the top of another bottle of water. "Where are the bills sent?"

"His mother's place."

Shane took a long swallow of water. He was still trying to wash the taste of Shapiro's apartment and Cline's death out of his mouth. By tomorrow, cop reports would be entered on the central computer. Whatever the cops knew, Shane would know, thanks to a boyhood spent trying to please—and surpass—Bastard Merit, king of the hackers.

"Cherelle Leticia Faulkner," Niall said, picking up another sheet of paper. "She's done a few nights with the county mounties for vagrancy, prostitution, shoplifting, petty grifting. The kind of childhood that a muckraking tabloid would love to cry croc tears over. Foster homes, abuse, more foster homes, suspected abuse, finally landed in an Arkansas trailer park and stuck for almost eight years. She ran away at seventeen with a drug salesman who sold illegal stuff along with the legal. After that she dropped off the scope. No marriage license. No known kids."

Risa didn't realize she was rubbing her temples again until Shane stroked his hand over her hair. Listening to Niall's deep, slightly rough voice recite the bare statistics of Cherelle's life made Risa's throat ache. Nowhere did she hear the laughter or see the sparkling mischief and lightning quickness of a much younger Cherelle.

"I'll go back to the Seton house at dark," Ian said. "I don't expect to find anything, but it's a base we have to cover."

Niall looked at Shane. "You're sure these three jokers were the source of your Druid gold?"

"Yes."

"Would it hold up in court?"

"Not with Cline dead. But I'm sure."

Niall's mouth turned down. *Things that go bump in the night.* He had learned not to question them. "Right. So we're sitting here with four gold pieces the Brits are screaming at Uncle Sam to hand over."

"What's their proof of ownership?" Risa asked.

"They're cobbling it together as fast as they can."

"They better cobble up a beaut," Shane said. "In the

absence of clear provenance, possession counts for a lot."

"I'll let you explain that to April Joy."

Shane's dark eyebrows went up. April Joy was one of Uncle Sam's up-and-comers in the murky sphere of geopolitics. She was intelligent, pragmatic, beautiful, and utterly ruthless when the job required it. Given the people she played with, that was most of the time. A few months ago she had tried to recruit him for a sting against the Red Phoenix triad that involved using Tannahill Inc. as a laundry for dirty money. He had declined. She hadn't liked it, but she didn't have any leverage on him, so she'd taken his refusal like an adult.

"I thought she was working on Asian gangs that were penetrating the U.S.," Shane said.

"She is."

"What does that have to do with Celtic gold?"

"Good question," Niall said. "Be sure to ask her if you see her."

"Thanks, but I'll pass," Shane said. "I'm not getting in that tiger's face unless she gets in mine first."

"Your mother didn't raise any dumb ones," Niall said, grinning.

"Actually, it was my father who taught me how the world really works."

The careful neutrality of Shane's voice made Risa wince. She had always felt she'd missed something by not knowing her parents. Then again, from what she'd heard about Shane's father, maybe she was better off.

"What's the basis of the British claim on the gold artifacts we bought?" Risa asked.

"Probability," Niall said. "For damn sure they didn't originate in, say, Africa."

"If origin was the only requirement for ownership, the

contents of the world's museums would undergo massive redistribution," Risa said.

"That's why we have politicians and bureaucrats—they swap favors and tell us peons where to send the goodies."

"Speak for yourself," Shane said. "I'm not sending that gold anywhere on the say-so of some D.C. political hack who wants a free tour of London in return for sticking it to me over the gold."

"That's why you wanted me to bring the goodies back, isn't it?" Niall asked, smiling.

Shane's answering smile would have looked good on a crocodile with a full belly. "From time to time Rarities Unlimited has to trade favors with governments in order to survive. I don't."

"Sure you do, boyo. You just haven't been brought to it yet. Hell, even your old man finally learned to bend his knee to Uncle Sam."

"I'll savor that image all the way to Sedona."

Risa sat up suddenly. "Sedona? I'm going with you."

"I never doubted it." Shane's mouth turned down. He didn't want her to go, but his instincts said not only that she would go but that she *should*.

"What's in Sedona?" Ian asked.

"The last known address for Cherelle Leticia Faulkner."

Forty-six

From the air, Sedona looked like a jeweled spiderweb flung across the black velvet land. The small airport was on top of a mesa, connected to the town by a steep, zigzagging road. While Shane discovered the limits of the local cellular connections, Risa drove the rental car—truck, actually—down the narrow road to the main highway.

"Right," Shane said into his cell phone/computer. "We're on our way to Camp Verde. No lights followed us down from the airport."

"Keep looking, boyo," Niall said. "I don't want a second dead body to turn up with your name on it."

"I'm touched. Is Ian checking out the Oasis address?"

"Been there. Done that. Nobody home. He vetted the place from stem to stern. Nothing except signs that she left in a big hurry."

"Anything else?"

"Cesar Firenze Marquez, aka Socks, is the lead on

everyone's news show. The TV folks are especially proud of their footage."

"Why do you think I had the copies made?" Shane asked. "TV news would lead with a dead cow rotting if they had film of it."

Niall laughed. "The cops are getting calls right and left from people claiming they saw Socks. If our boy is still in town, he'll be walking real small to avoid attention."

"What's the official police take on Cline's death?"

"Officially they're exploring all leads with great diligence."

"Unofficially?"

"They wouldn't give a shit if a TV crew hadn't been there to record the body," Niall said. "Cline wasn't on the cops' Ten Most Loved list."

"Do you want me to send the plane back to Vegas?"

"No. Dana said to pull out all the stops on this one. Having a pilot and plane at your beck and call is just one of the stops."

Shane grunted. "Good thing I can afford it."

Niall's laughter was clear in his voice, "We're keeping that in mind."

With a flick of his thumb, Shane disconnected. Another flick shifted his unit to computer function. He pulled a slender stylus from a clip on the side of the unit and went to work on the information that Rarities, via Factoid, was funneling into his computer as fast as they uncovered new data.

"I didn't know you were allergic to goldenrod," Shane said after a moment.

Risa gave him a slanting sideways look that told him to go to hell.

He grinned. "And scallops."

She stomped down on the accelerator to pass a polished new SUV whose driver still hadn't figured out where the metal monster began and ended.

"You're behind on your lockjaw vaccination," he continued, scrolling through whatever forbidden records Factoid had found.

"If you access my yearly gyn exams, you're limping back to the plane alone."

Laughing, Shane ran his fingertips over Risa's cheek and brushed the corner of her mouth. "Your teeth are in fine order, too."

She showed him a double row of perfection as she nipped at a fingertip that kept trying to burrow into her smile. He threaded his fingers through her short hair, safely out of reach of her teeth.

"You're distracting the driver," she said.

He caressed her ear, felt her shiver.

"*Really* distracting," she added.

Reluctantly he shifted his attention back to the computer. In silence he read computer files while the town's colored lights slid over the windshield and left bright reflections on the computer's small screen. He sensed the darting glances Risa gave him, but she didn't disturb his concentration by asking questions before he had a chance to discover the answers.

The colored lights ended when the highway wound through a stretch of national forest. A faded ribbon of red hung just above the rugged western horizon, silent testament to the sun's dying power. The waning moon was a radiant white force against the blue-black sky. Stars shimmered, but only where night lay thickly beyond the reach of sun or moon.

The village of Oak Creek slid by on either side of the car in a flurry of lights clustered along the highway. Beyond the lights, night waited darkly, patient as night is always patient. Soon darkness ruled but for the sword beams of cars whipping over black pavement.

Risa followed the sign for getting on the interstate and romped down on the gas pedal to match the ambient speed of the Arizona freeways—eighty miles per hour in the slow lane. When she cracked the window a bit, air as cold and perfect as a high mountain stream rushed around her. She drank it in, better than water, more vivid.

"Want me to drive?" Shane asked without looking up from the screen.

"I'm fine. I just wanted to find out if the air was as clean as it looked. It is."

"Yeah, I keep forgetting how beautiful the red-rock and cedar desert can be."

"I've never been here before tonight, so I have nothing to remember or forget."

He looked up from the computer. In the light reflected from the dashboard, her eyes were gleaming, mysterious, beautiful enough to squeeze his heart. "You don't get out often enough."

"I work for a slave driver."

"Remind me to thump on him for you."

"How about I thump on him instead?"

Shane grinned. "You must have mistaken me for my stupid twin."

"No way I'd ever suspect you of being stupid, despite your million-dollar looks," she said.

"Darling, I'm worth more than a million."

His expectant expression said that he was waiting for her to cut him off at the knees. She opened her mouth to oblige, only to be distracted by someone who was passing her as though she had her foot on the brake.

"Idiot," she muttered. "What does he think that piece of crap is, a fighter jet?"

The ponderous RV wallowed as its owner dragged the vehicle back over into the slow lane.

"Hope the tires are up to the driver's ambition," Shane said.

"Whatever. As long as he augers into the landscape well away from me."

Shane noticed her constant glances into the rear and side mirrors. "Anybody following?"

"If they are, they're staying far enough back that their lights blend with other traffic."

The sign for Camp Verde loomed out of the night. Risa didn't bother with a turn signal. She simply whipped over to the off-ramp, hoping to catch any follower by surprise. Just after the stop sign at the bottom of the ramp, she pulled way to the side of the road, shut off the lights, and watched the mirrors.

Nobody turned off for Camp Verde.

Nobody passed them.

Nobody cared.

"Wanna neck?" Shane said.

"Sure. You strip first."

He laughed out loud and thought how comfortable he was with her, how right it felt to have her within reach. "You make me wish I was good at the one-on-one thing."

"Is this where I tell you that you're better than good at the one-on-one thing?"

"Not sex. Relationships."

"Oh. That. I haven't had much luck in that department either. Guys seem to cramp my possibilities rather than expand them." She looked in the rearview mirror. "I suppose I do the same to them."

"So far you've been running away too hard to cramp anything but my ego."

She gave him a disbelieving look. "What are you talking about? I tripped you and beat you to the floor."

"Is that what happened? I thought I cornered you and jumped you."

She tried not to grin, then gave up and laughed. "It was . . . something. Each time. Every time."

Shane's eyelids lowered and his eyes gleamed.

Random sparks of memory sent heat through Risa's belly. She wanted to crawl into Shane's lap and start licking just to see if he tasted as good as she remembered. She blew out her breath and started up the truck before temptation got the better of her.

"You sure?" he asked huskily, watching her lush mouth.

She groaned. "Do you harbor a secret desire to be arrested for lewd and dissolute conduct in a public place?"

"Not until I met you."

"Shane."

"What?"

"Shut up."

He was still laughing when she turned onto a surface street.

The Cedars Motel was just off the main street and looked older than the bluffs rising against the stars. A tired neon sign blinked and sputtered, advertising rooms by the night, week, or month. Though the word below said VACANCY, the office was closed. It looked like it had been for a long time. A handprinted card stuck inside the window told anyone who really cared about a room to call a local number and inquire about rentals.

There were twelve units and two cars. Each car was parked in the center of its half of the dirt parking lot, as if afraid that the other patron might be contagious. Two units showed a knife edge of light behind tightly drawn curtains.

"Friendly place," Shane said.

"You sure this is it?"

"The reverse directory pegged Cherelle's phone to this address. The map I pulled off the Net led us right here."

"I thought cops and emergency services were the only ones with access to the reverse directory."

"You thought wrong."

Risa drummed her fingers lightly on the steering wheel. "Which unit?"

"Lucky number seven."

She grimaced. If unit number seven represented luck, she would stick with hard work. "No car. No lights."

"No key."

"No problem."

Shane's eyebrows lifted. "Is my upright, uptight curator suggesting a bit of breaking and entering?"

"No need. Cherelle always stashed keys all around, so when she forgot one—and she always did—she wouldn't have to break a window to get in."

"Damn. And here I was going to shock you with my black-bag technique. I get hot when you go all starchy on me."

She started to ask if he would really have burgled his way in. Then she decided she didn't want to know.

"Starch does it for you, huh?" she asked instead.

"Every time."

With a roll of her eyes she got out and started prowling for likely hiding places for a key. It took her about twenty seconds to find the key beneath a broken chunk of concrete on what passed for the walkway from parking lot to the entrance of number seven.

Shane took the key. "I'll go in first."

"Why? Do you think she's—"

He bent and cut off Risa's words with a quick, hard kiss. "I think I'm bigger than you, that's all. Wait until I give the all clear, okay?"

"No." She rubbed her arms against the biting night air. "But I'll do it. This time."

The key was gritty with dirt and worked just fine.

Shane stepped into the dark room and drew a cautious breath. Stale smoke. Something bitter. Dust. Unwashed clothes.

Old smells, not new. Not ripe.

Not death.

"Shane?" Risa asked softly.

"So far, so good. Shut the door behind you."

The first thing they saw was an old wooden box. Shane sat on his heels near it and started memorizing addresses.

Forty-seven

Cherelle pumped another quarter into the slot machine and hit the button. Reels spun, colors flashed, and her quarter disappeared forever.

"Shit."

"Not your lucky night?"

The man who had asked the question was sitting two slot machines down and would never see the young side of sixty again. While smoke drifted from the cigarette stuck in the corner of his grin, he gave her an allover look that said he could guess her price within a dollar. The whiskey in his voice was like sandpaper on cement.

If you only knew, asshole, just how much the stuff I have is worth, she thought savagely.

But all that gold wouldn't buy her a place to stay tonight, unless it was a jail cell. She could sleep in her car or she could take the senior citizen up on the business proposition that would likely be the next thing out of his mouth.

Not yet, damn it. Not until I'm dead fucking broke.

She stuck another quarter in, then another. The machine climaxed and gushed a nice pile of quarters. It wasn't a big ol' bell-ringer, but it was enough for a safe place to sleep and maybe even a few beers. She scooped the quarters into the plastic coin tub and headed for the cashier without looking back to see if the sandpaper man was disappointed or relieved.

Ten minutes later she had checked in to one of the cheap motels that lined the highway from the interstate to the razzle-dazzle of downtown Vegas. She dragged Risa's luggage into the room, locked the door, and turned on the TV. The only channel that came in was the all-news station. With a disgusted sound she threw the remote control on the bed and started to unzip her suitcase. She left the TV sound on, because she was tired of being alone. The talking lamp wasn't much for two-way conversation, but it was smarter than most people she met.

"It's the second murder of a small-business person in as many days," said the earnest female newsreader. *"Police have asked anyone who was in the area and saw something suspicious to call the number at the bottom of your screen."*

"Oh, yeah, that'll help," Cherelle said. "Some old granny that can't find her own skinny ass with a magnifying glass is gonna look out the window and come up with a murderer. Jesus, there really is one born every minute."

From the corner of her eye she watched the TV. A part of Vegas rolled by on the screen that looked familiar. Frowning, she turned and stared at the TV.

"Hey, that's close to Tim's house."

The news station ran the clip of its reporter interviewing a detective while a gurney rattled by in the background with a body bag strapped down tight. The same clip had run every half hour since yesterday.

Cherelle bit the inside of her mouth. She had a bad feeling that she was watching what was left of Socks's fence. She turned up the sound. Socks wasn't mentioned, but the second bloody spot on the floor was.

"Oh, man. Oh, shit. Is that what happened to Tim?"

She listened. All she heard was what the cops didn't know.

The solemn newsreader picked up as soon as the tape ran out. *"Since then the police have found a bloody trail down the alley and across the street. Then the trail vanished. No knife or gunshot wounds have been reported at local hospitals. None of the people nearby have been able to help the police."*

"Yeah, ain't it just a bitch how no one wants to help the cops do their job," Cherelle said.

She flipped back the suitcase top and hesitated. Part of her wanted to unwrap the gold, to be sure it was all there, to hold it and know that her dreams were finally going to come true.

And part of her went clammy at the thought of touching any of the artifacts.

"That gold creeps me out," she told the TV.

The TV tried to sell her a time-share condo in Hawaii.

Cherelle kept talking. "I'll be glad to see the last of it, and that's a fact. All I have to do is figure out how to sell it off without attracting the cops. Or Socks. That ol' boy has a streak of mean in him that makes a cottonmouth look cuddly."

"The crime wave in Las Vegas heats up. A gunman ran rampant through the Golden Fleece this morning."

At the mention of the familiar casino, Cherelle spun to

face the TV. Her mouth dropped open as she saw Risa sprinting down rows of gambling machines, her skirt hiked up to her butt, her long legs flashing as she ducked, spun, leaped, and rolled across tables, scattering chips and patrons in all directions.

"Christ Jesus," Cherelle said. "What—"

Socks came into view, his eyes flat, his hand steady as he tried to bring Risa down. The contrast between his deadly intent and his cheerful Hawaiian shirt was shocking.

"Acting on standing orders from the management, the casino guards didn't return fire, as that would have endangered innocent bystanders. The gunman fled out the front doors and vanished into the crowd."

A freeze-frame close-up of Socks filled the screen. His eyes were narrowed, his lips thinned, and his teeth showed in a snarl.

"Oh, yeah, that's Socks. Whoooo-eee! He's riding a big ol' mean." Cherelle grinned and flexed her right hand like a cat. "Bet his dick still hurts."

"Anyone having information leading to the arrest and conviction of this man will receive a fifteen-thousand-dollar reward from the Golden Fleece. Call the number at the bottom of your screen if you have information.

"Next up, the Santa Claus bikini contest draws crowds to the Blue Mare. If you know a portly"—sound of off-screen snickers—*"jolly old gentleman who would like to enter, there's still time."*

Cherelle barely listened. She was still looking at the number on the bottom of her screen. She couldn't collect the reward, but she didn't want to pass up a chance to send some bad luck Socks's way. As long as he was running around loose, she would be smart to hide. But she didn't want to hide. She wanted to sell that gold and spend the rest of her life living like the Hollywood star she should have been.

For that she could wait a while, until they nailed Socks.

Smiling, jiggling a handful of quarters, she went out to the pay phone down the hall by the Coke machine. Within minutes she was telling a recorder all about the make, model, and license plate of Socks's screaming purple baby.

She didn't leave a callback number.

Forty-eight

Dry-eyed, Miranda watched while the nurse wheeled the crash cart out of Tim's room. The cart hadn't helped. Nothing had.

The light and joy of her life was dead.

Feeling brittle and very old, she picked up the phone, punched in a number, and waited. Very quickly she heard the familiar voice.

"He's dead," she said. "Now there's only one thing I want from you. You do to Socks what Socks did to him. I mean it. You understand?"

He didn't like it, but he understood. He had been planning to do it anyway. He just didn't want to be rushed. Too many mistakes that way.

"I understand," he said. "Are you going home?"

"I don't have a home anymore. Timmy's dead. Don't you understand? *He's dead.*"

"A car will come for you at the clinic. He'll take you to another place. Stay there."

Before Miranda could agree or disagree, he hung up.

Forty-nine

Shane missed the rural mailbox the first time. It was easy to miss, because the "road" that led off toward the hills and cliffs was dirt, rocks, and weeds.

"Maybe the last address on that box was wrong," Risa said as they bumped off the paved road and into Virgil O'Conner's "driveway."

"You have a better idea of where we should look for the gold?"

"No." Nothing valuable had been left in the dump that was Cherelle's last address.

Sycamore trees with pale bark and branches twisted and shimmered like ghosts in the moonlight. Risa had more time than she wanted to admire the trees' eerie beauty, because Shane was driving the rental truck over the miserable excuse for a road. She winced as a rock leaped out and attacked the right front tire.

"Sure you don't want me to drive?" she asked.

"You think you could do better?"

She started to say yes, then held her tongue when she

saw the pile of rocks he had avoided by swerving over to the right. "No, but then I'd have the steering wheel to hang on to."

Shane grinned like a raider.

After she checked over her shoulder—stars, moon, no headlights—she said, "You're enjoying this, aren't you."

It was more of an accusation than a question, but he answered anyway. "Yeah. I'd forgotten how much I enjoy the backcountry."

"Speaks someone who never lived in East Bumble-fart."

"I thought you were from Arkar sas."

"Same difference."

"Hey, I happen to know that there are some grand places in—"

"I never saw them," she cut in. Then she blew out a rushing breath. "Oh, hell. You're right. The countryside is beautiful, all shimmery with heat and secrets. It was my life that sucked."

"Yeah, funny how that sours you on a place." He checked the rear and side mirrors. Nothing but night. "I'd have to be bound, gagged, and drugged to go back to Renton."

"Where's that?"

"Washington. State, not D.C. Between Seattle's sprawl and the trackless Cascades. Lots of green because there's lots of rain."

"You sure got all the way out," she said.

"Meaning?"

"Green and rain are the last words I'd think of to describe 'Lost Wages,' Nevada."

"Love at first sight," he agreed. "How about you?"

"The same. All the distance. The space. The emptiness. It was alien as hell, and I loved it instantly. Watch the—!"

Shane swerved to avoid a skunk and cursed when something on the undercarriage scraped on a rock.

"Whew," Risa said, fanning the air in front of her face. "I'd forgotten what they smell like. Did you miss it?"

He checked the rearview mirror and saw a black-and-silver shape waddle toward the creek bed.

"Yeah." The bottom scraped again over a combination of a pothole and a rut. He swore. "Can you tell me what the hell point there is in putting four-wheel drive on a baby pickup truck that has the same clearance as the average minivan?"

"Gee, let me see," she said. "I'm guessing that minivans have a low dick quotient."

"Never thought of it that way."

"You're a man," she said, turning to look back over the road.

"You noticed."

"Oh, yeah. Yeah, I did."

Her smile made Shane wish they were on the dirt road for no other reason than to find a quiet place to steam up the windows and each other. But they weren't.

"See anything?" he asked.

"Stars, moon, black cliffs, sycamores like ghosts . . ."

"And the back of your neck itches," he finished.

"And the back of my neck itches," she agreed. "Yours?"

"Like fire."

"Well, hell. You were supposed to go all dick quotient on me and say how it's my hormones or something."

" 'Or something' has my vote."

"I sure don't see anything back there but a whole lot of nothing." She gave up and half turned in the seat to make checking over her shoulder easier. "But the moon is bright enough for someone to run without headlights."

"Is that a suggestion?"

"No. I gave up that kind of midnight tag when I was fifteen."

"What kind of tag?"

"The kind where you shut off your headlights and play bumper cars on country lanes until you're the last idiot on the road."

Shane whistled. "Sounds like fun. Why'd you give it up?"

Risa started to duck the question, then shrugged. "Because the guy driving pulled off the road and tried to rape me. He probably would have, if Cherelle hadn't come over the backseat and shoved his balls up his ass with her knee while she screamed that just because she did it for money didn't mean her friend did for free."

Shane's hands flexed on the wheel until his knuckles were pale as bone. "That's one I owe her."

"I think ten thousand dollars is adequate repayment," Risa said dryly. "A little later Cherelle left town with a traveling drug salesman. All kinds of drugs, apparently, but that's not why she left. The kid she'd kneed was the son of the county sheriff. Maybe if that hadn't happened, maybe she would have steadied down and . . ." Risa's voice died.

For a time there was only the thump and grate of tires over a rough dirt road.

"Do you really blame yourself for the choices Cherelle is making now?" Shane asked finally.

"My mind doesn't. My emotions . . ." Risa shrugged slightly and tried to explain what she rarely thought about. "She was my mother and my sister and my friend all in one."

"Is she the same girl now that you remember from fifteen years ago?" he asked.

Risa wanted to say yes. She couldn't. "Sometimes. Just sometimes."

"And those are the times that really hurt."

She closed her eyes for an instant. "How did you know?"

"I have my share of fifteen-year-old regrets. And they don't change a damn thing about the world today."

"Your father?"

"And my mother. I wanted them to love me as much as I loved them, but I gave up on my father before I was ten. It took me longer to see what my mother was and wasn't."

Even now the words stuck in Shane's throat, in his mind. Until a few years ago he had blamed his father for everything, a blanket condemnation born of a boy's helplessness and rage. "She never stood up for her own child against him, even when I was way too young to do it myself. Especially then. She'd just wring her hands and make cupcakes. Jesus. To this day I can't stand the sight of cupcakes."

Risa ached for the boy he had been. "Did your father beat you?"

"That would have been too crude. Bastard Merit isn't a crude man. He simply, systematically, stripped me of every thread of self-respect. Nothing personal. He does it to everyone who hangs around him long enough."

She let out a long breath. "And here I thought he just got bad press."

Shane smiled. "The man gives more than two billion dollars a year to various tear-jerking causes. It improved his press to no end. Mother's idea, by the way. It hurt her that her husband had a reputation as the biggest shit-heel since Nero."

"What a pair we are," Risa said. "I always wanted a real family, and you always wanted to get the hell away from yours."

"Like I said, I'm no good at the relationship thing."

"How would you know?"

"Mother tells me every time we talk and I refuse to 'get along with' my sweet old man."

"Well, that clinches it. You're hopeless. Your mother ought to know, seeing as she's such a howling expert on healthy relationships."

Silence, then a sound that wasn't quite a laugh. "I never looked at it that way," Shane admitted.

"As an adult?"

"Yeah."

"If it helps, I avoid looking at Cherelle that way every chance I get."

He hesitated. "That could be dangerous."

"I figured that out about the time I was playing hurdles in the casino. But . . ."

"But Cherelle still saved your ass when you were fifteen."

"Yes."

Shane could picture it all too well, including the part that Risa didn't talk about. "Did you ever think your ass wouldn't have needed saving if Cherelle hadn't been having sex in the backseat while the sheriff's son raced through the night drinking beer and listening to all the grunts and moans?"

Risa didn't answer, which told Shane that his assumption had been right.

"Someday," he said, "you might think about the fact

that you and Cherelle ended up in different places because you started out different in the same place."

"Then I have nothing left of my childhood but lies."

"No, you have a child's memory in an adult mind. Not the same thing at all. Your love for your friend was true."

"And yours for your mother, your father?" Risa challenged.

"Inevitable. Hell, part of me still loves them. I just don't like them worth a damn."

Risa was still wrestling with that when the road bent to the right and ended in the dusty front yard of a clapboard house.

Fifty

John Firenze sat in his gleaming private office and wanted to kill something. Not just anything. One thing in particular. His fucking stupid nephew Cesar, whose fucking stupid face was plastered on every TV screen in Vegas.

It was just a matter of time before someone phoned an ID to the cops. Then Firenze would be answering questions before the Nevada Gaming Control Board. He would have to up his contributions to every politician in sight before this mess went away.

The intercom buzzed, telling him that his executive assistant was still on duty. He approached the switch the way he would a coiled rattlesnake. "Yes?"

"Your nephew called from a pay phone." The voice was quiet, cultured, and female.

"Did you tell him to give himself up to the police?" Firenze said.

"As you requested, yes, I did."

"And?"

"He declined. Vigorously."

Firenze could imagine. At the best of times Socks had a vicious temper. This wasn't the best of times. He closed his eyes and tried to find a way out. There wasn't one.

"Connect me with the police," he said.

"Yes, sir. I'm sorry, sir."

"So am I. At least his mother isn't alive."

"Yes, sir."

Impatiently Firenze waited while he was put through to whichever badge was chasing tips on the "Hawaiian Shooter," as the local Vegas channel had dubbed him. It was very important that Firenze, as a casino owner, appear to be cooperating with the police.

Not that he thought the cops had much chance of finding Socks really soon. Even his fucking stupid nephew would have enough sense to take the money his uncle had sent him and hang out on the houseboat at Lake Mead until they could cook up a passport and ship him off to some distant cousins in Italy and wait for everyone to forget his name.

Much as Firenze wanted to throttle the miserable son of a bitch himself, blood was still blood.

Fifty-one

Risa knocked on Virgil O'Conner's door again, waited again, knocked again. No light came on inside or out. No sound came from the small house.

"Still no one stirring?" Shane asked as he came around from the rear of the house.

"No. Is there a car parked back there?"

"Just a bike."

"As in motorcycle?"

"As in pedal your ass off." While Shane spoke, he absently rubbed the back of his neck.

"Still itchy?" she asked.

"Yeah. You?"

She hesitated. "It reminds me of . . ."

"What?"

Silence. A sigh. Her hands gleamed in the moonlight as she made a fluid gesture that managed to evoke both giving in and refusing to give in. "Wales."

"Where you dreamed?"

She looked surprised that he had remembered. "Yes."

He turned toward the blank windows and closed door of Virgil's home. The wood was the color of sycamore bark, ghostly. "Is the house making you itchy?"

"Not quite. Or not only." Risa made a frustrated sound. "Damn it, I don't want this! I didn't want it in Wales, and I don't want it now." She hissed between her teeth. "But it's real, isn't it?"

"For some people."

"The odd ones, you mean." The line of her mouth was unhappy.

"Someone with musical ability is odd to people who are tone deaf."

"Are you?"

"Tone deaf?" he asked, deliberately misunderstanding. She simply waited.

"Yes," he said after a minute. "I'm one of the odd ones. I guess." He shrugged. "Hard to tell. All I know for sure is I live in a time and a place that financially rewards an understanding of numbers, of patterns, that damned few people have. The fact that many of my business choices—also known as hunches—have no basis in Western logic is politely ignored. Whenever I'm interviewed, I join in the chorus and sing about long-term trends and short-term gains and analyzing markets with fuzzy formulas and all the reassuring bullshit that explains why I'm rich and the next guy isn't."

"You work hard."

"So do other people."

"You're intelligent."

"So are—"

"—other people," she finished. "But you see things other people who are hardworking and intelligent don't see, is that it?"

"If seeing is another word for dreaming, and if dreaming is another word for knowing without logic, yes, I see."

"I missed that part of your biography," she muttered.

"I never told anyone except you. How many people have you told that you dream of things you have no way of logically knowing?"

For a few moments it was so quiet that he could hear the night wind sliding down from the top of the bluffs, stirring over the land like a breath out of time.

"You," she whispered. "That's it. I don't even like admitting it to myself."

"Why?"

She made a sound that could have been a laugh or a cry. "When I was a child, I thought that was the real reason my first mother abandoned me, because I was different. And that finding out about my difference killed my adopted mother."

"Did you dream that? Is that how you knew?"

She paused, then, "No. I don't dream about myself. Just . . . things. Antiquities. And not all the time or all antiquities. Just special ones. Very special."

"Like Wales."

"Yes," she said in a voice as soft as the wind. "Like Wales."

"Is it the place or the ritual use of the artifacts associated with them that calls to you?"

"I don't know. I'm not sure they can be separated." She rubbed her arms and turned away from him, toward the night. "I really don't want to go into this. Ever since I figured out that most people didn't react like me, I've done my best to ignore it."

"It hasn't gone away, has it?"

Angrily she spun back toward him. "What do you want from me?"

"The feeling that I'm not entirely alone in this. I've spent my life feeling like odd man out of the human race."

"Okay. Fine. I'm odd woman out. Feel better?"

"Two odds make an even." He grinned. "That makes us normal."

She stared at him, then laughed. "Fuzzy formulas, huh?"

"Works for me." He pulled her close, kissed her hard, and looked down into her moon-drenched face. "So do you. Wait here."

Risa was still tasting him and at the same time trying to follow his so-called thought processes when she realized that he was opening Virgil O'Conner's front door.

"You can't just—" she began.

But he already had.

"—walk in," she finished.

With his fingers still wrapped in his nylon wind shell, Shane felt around on the wall until he found a switch. Against the pouring white power of moonlight, the sixty-watt bulb in the overhead fixture looked like a round yellow candle flame. It was enough to show a couch with a pillow and a rumpled blanket, a scattering of thick books lying open on an old dining table, and an unlighted room beyond.

The only sound was that of something small and nocturnal that had been disturbed by the sudden light and was racing back toward darkness on tiny clawed feet. The air hinted of old food, more a suggestion than a smell. The feel of the place was indefinably empty. Not the ripe emptiness of recent death, but the thin sense of abandonment that comes without human life.

"Nobody home but the mice," Shane said, stepping into the light.

Risa's breath caught as she saw the gleam of something metallic in his hand. A gun.

Despite his comforting words, Shane checked out the dark room just off the main living area before he holstered his weapon at the small of his back once more.

The little room was like the rest of the house. Nobody home.

Shielding his hand with his jacket, he flipped on the light switch. The bedroom was no more than eight feet by eight feet, just enough space for a narrow bed, a chest of drawers, and a series of pegs on the wall that served as a closet. The area was messy, but not with the wild disorder of a place that has been searched. This was more the normal carelessness of a man who lived alone and didn't care if dirty clothes gathered dust bunnies in the corner until washday, whenever that might be.

Rubbing the back of his neck, Shane looked around again. He didn't know what was nibbling at him; he only knew that something was. Feeling like an idiot, he pulled out a penlight, knelt, and looked under the bed. All he saw were marks in the dust, as though something had been dragged out. Maybe a suitcase. It would explain the fact that no one was home and the only wheels around were on a bicycle.

He wished he could believe the nice, logical explanation. He couldn't. He found himself sweeping the area underneath the bed with his light again and again. He *knew* something was there.

He just couldn't see it.

"Shane?"

Something in Risa's voice brought him to his feet in a rush that didn't end until he was in the living room near her. "What is it?"

"The books."

"Did you touch them?" he asked more sharply than he meant to.

"I didn't have to. Look."

He glanced over the top of her head to a book that was open on a table a few feet away. Then he narrowed his eyes and walked closer. A beautiful photo of the Snettisham torc took up one page. The opposite page showed a series of gold brooches.

"I'm trying to believe it's a coincidence," Risa said.

"Having any luck?"

"No."

"Neither am I."

"The gold was kept in those boxes we found at Cherelle's place," Risa said bleakly. "I sensed it."

Shane didn't point out that she hadn't said anything about it. He didn't have to, because he had sensed the same thing.

And everything they found tied Risa's old friend more tightly to a theft that had ended in murder.

"Cherelle must have gotten the gold from Virgil O'Conner," Risa said unhappily. "That's what Socks meant when he said something about her getting it in Sedona. But where did Virgil get it? And how? This isn't the home of a man who has millions to spend on solid gold antiquities."

Shane pulled out his communications unit. "No cell coverage," he said. "Figures." He recorded a voice message that would go out to Rarities as soon as the unit got within range of a cell. "Let's see if we can find anything personal here that would speed up a Rarities search on him. If not, they'll have to make do with the addresses on the box. Do you have any gloves?"

"I always carry exam gloves in my purse. They won't fit you."

"Then I'll just have to watch over your shoulder."

"And tell me what to do," she muttered as she opened her purse.

"I was looking forward to that especially."

"Ha ha." She snapped on the gloves. "I don't suppose it would do any good to tell you I feel like slime going through someone's house this way."

"I'm not wild about it myself."

"But you're going to do it."

"If it would make my neck stop itching, I'd turn this place upside down."

"I'd help," she admitted.

Risa started her search right where she was. She flipped through the books with the efficiency of someone accustomed to sorting through pages filled with dense text and artifacts.

As promised, Shane looked over Risa's shoulder. The books covered everything possibly gold and probably related to Celtic style from 1000 B.C. to 1000 A.D. The pages that detailed figurines, brooches, torcs, bracelets, knives, and masks were often dog-eared. Other than that, and notes in the margins written with a kind of cramped desperation, the worn books held nothing of Virgil O'Conner's life before today.

There were no drawers, wastebaskets, boxes, or any other place in the main living area where papers might have collected.

Or gold hidden.

"Was there a desk in the other room?" she asked.

"No."

"Telephone?"

"No."

"Then I'll start in the kitchen."

It didn't take long. The kitchen was smaller than the

bedroom. The phone was a primitive wall model that didn't even have a speed-dial feature. The counter below the phone was stacked with bills and materials marked "Occupant." O'Conner didn't have an active social calendar.

"Electricity," Risa said, flipping through the messy stack of papers, working backward in time. "Telephone. No water bill, so he must have a well. No personal letters. Property tax bill, soon to be overdue. Bank account statement showing three hundred dollars and thirty-one cents. Savings account with one hundred and one and sixteen cents. Repair bill for a new tube on a bike tire. Random grocery receipts scattered through the rest. End of papers."

"No credit card bills," Shane said. "No vehicle payments. Wonder if he even had a driver's license."

"Maybe he kept business stuff somewhere else."

"Maybe," Shane said, "but I've got a feeling he kept everything that mattered to him right here."

"A feeling."

"Yeah."

She sighed and began going through kitchen drawers and cupboards. It didn't take long, because there wasn't much to see. None of it was useful, unless you cared that Virgil O'Conner liked pinto beans and rice, with occasional cans of grapefruit juice to spice things up. The electric stove had pots and pans and burned-on food. The refrigerator was small and empty but for a few pickles floating in cloudy liquid. A gel-filled knee brace and a tray of ice cubes waited in the freezer.

"I really don't want to paw through his closet," she said.

"He doesn't have one. Just a dresser."

"Oh, goody. I feel so much better."

Shane watched her walk into the bedroom, sensed her shiver of recognition more than saw it, and waited, wondering if she finally trusted him enough to share what she had spent a lifetime trying to hide.

"O'Conner kept the gold here," she said in a low voice.

"Thank you."

The smile she gave Shane was almost sad. "Two odds make an even, right?"

Fifty-two

SEDONA
NOVEMBER 4
NIGHT

Shane waited for Risa to say something more. He couldn't see her face, but the tension in her body told him how tightly strung she was. His voice whispered through the darkness like another shade of night. "Is the gold here now?"

"No. But . . ." Risa rubbed the gooseflesh on her arms. "Can't you feel it? It was here. And something still is."

"Yes, I feel it. I just didn't identify it as fast as you did."

"Practice," she said bleakly, looking around Virgil O'Conner's empty cabin. "Christ, I hate feeling like this, knowing I'm different. Maybe I should have been a nurse instead of a curator."

"Maybe I should have been a proctologist."

She gave him a disbelieving look and then laughed out loud. "Sorry. Was I whining?"

He touched her cheek gently. "You're entitled. If there was a way to keep you out of this, I would."

"If you tried, I'd fight you tooth and nail."

The corners of his mouth turned up. "Could be fun."

Shaking her head, she started pulling out dresser drawers. There weren't many clothes to look at. All were of the kind that gave thrift stores their reputations as centers of low couture.

No papers. Certainly no gold.

She glanced at the unmade bed.

"No need," Shane said quickly. "Nothing on top or underneath except skid marks in the dust left by suitcases or ammo boxes."

"Short of pulling up floorboards and poking holes in the wall, we're out of luck."

"Dead end," he agreed. "But I know there's more."

"Here?"

"Or close by."

"I wish I didn't agree with you." She put her hands on her hips, did a slow circle, and shook her head. "Not this room. The only thing in here . . . isn't in here anymore."

"The gold?"

She nodded.

"Like Wales?" he asked.

"Exactly. Damn it." She rubbed her arms briskly. "I've had tingles from artifacts before, but nothing like Wales until Smith-White's gold. And now this."

Just like, she thought, glancing sideways at Shane, she had had tingles from men before, but nothing like him. What she felt with him was so different it should have terrified her.

Sometimes it did.

"Same here," he said.

At first she thought she had spoken aloud about how he made her feel. Then she realized that he was simply agreeing with her about the gold.

"And the gold, too," he said.

"Stop that!"

He laughed and stroked her bare wrist above the exam gloves. "You have very speaking eyes, darling."

"I'll get mirrored lenses."

"Would it help if I said I felt the same way?"

"About mirrored lenses? Not particularly."

He lifted her hand and nipped the skin he'd just stroked. "You know what I mean."

The goose bumps that went up her arm owed nothing to ancient Druid gold. "What if it burns out in a few weeks or months?"

"What if it doesn't?"

She blew out a breath that was almost a laugh. "One day at a time, huh?"

"That's how life comes. One day at a time."

Her smile was shaky but real. "Okay. A day I can do. But I want to get out of this house right now."

Silently Shane took her hand and walked through the house into the night. "Better?"

"Yes." She peeled off the gloves and put them in her purse. "Much better."

"Feel up to a walk?"

She looked down at her shoes. Since her barefoot sprint through the casino, she had made a point of wearing footgear she could run in. That didn't mean she was eager to take on rough country in tennis shoes.

"How far?" she asked.

He glanced up to the long mesa that loomed behind the house. "Maybe half a mile."

She followed his look, tossed her purse inside the truck, and said, "Do you know where we're going?"

"No."

"Oh, well, that makes it so much better." She waved a hand toward the cliff looming out of the darkness. "After you, boss."

The moon's radiance was strong enough that Shane didn't have to use his penlight. The trail was well defined by previous hikers. Even if it hadn't been, he wouldn't have hesitated. Every step farther up the rise to the base of the bluff made him certain he was heading the right way.

"Feel it?" he asked quietly.

"Yes." Risa's voice was clipped, saying more than words about how much she disliked sensing something she knew she couldn't touch.

Shane paused and looked over his shoulder at her. "Does it bother you that I can feel it, too?"

"No. Should it?"

"I just thought it might be part of what had you running in the other direction for such a long time."

"That was pure common sense. I didn't want another job."

"That's not what you said when you brought those offers to me and I had to match them."

"I didn't say I was stupid. I just said I didn't want another job."

He smiled despite the tightening of his skin with every step up the trail. It wasn't uneasiness exactly. It was more an awareness of *difference,* a sigh breathed across primitive nerve endings, the faint burned scent in the air after a nearby lightning strike.

He rather liked it.

"How are your goose bumps?" he asked after a bit.

"A lot happier than I am. Why?"

Something rustled in the brush about twenty feet off

the trail. He looked, listened, saw only what might have been four-legged shadows sliding away into deeper shadows.

"It can't be much farther," he said, turning back to the trail.

"How do you know?"

"Because O'Conner was an old man, and old men don't climb cliffs." Shane stopped walking. "Certainly not this one."

The pencil beam of the flashlight couldn't begin to penetrate the darkness that concealed the top of the cliff.

"It's to the right," Risa said.

"What is?"

"Whatever is whispering to a part of me I don't even want to know about."

Despite her words, she stepped around him and walked along the lighter thread of darkness that was the trail at the face of the bluff. Shane was right. Ignoring what she was hadn't made it go away. Besides, it was easier knowing that she wasn't the only one who had odd wiring.

Two odds make an even.

She was smiling at the memory of Shane's words when she stumbled over a rock in the dark, put out both her hands to catch herself, and came smack up against one of three leaning stones.

Sensation poured through her, a rush of gold-masked faces, ritual blades of death and renewal, voices chanting sacred words, and all of it swirling through time and moonlight, through her, until her head spun and she would have cried out if she could have breathed at all.

Then it was night again, just herself and Shane's muscular warmth along her back, his hands over hers against the cold rock, his breath tangling softly, rapidly, in her hair, echoes of the chant retreating, common reality returning.

"You okay?" Shane asked, his voice rough and low.

"I think so." She blew air out in a shaky sigh. "You?"

"I'm working on it."

"You get the name of the train that ran over us?"

The sound he made wasn't quite a laugh. "No. And I don't want it."

He pulled her hands away from the rock. Then, deliberately, he put his own hands back.

She watched, waited. "Anything?"

"Cold rock. And . . ."

She didn't want to ask. Couldn't help it. "What?"

"Time. Distance. Night. The kind of night that has no dawn."

"That's why they marked the summer and winter solstice," Risa said in a low voice, knowing what she couldn't touch. "That's why they cast their dreams and prayers in gold, gold that never corroded, never corrupted, never changed. Gold and ritual and blood sacrifice to all the gods named and unnamed who controlled life. The darkness that had no dawn, the cold that wasn't followed by warmth, the death that had no afterlife, the end of all life, including the life of the gods. The Druids feared that."

"So does anyone with the intelligence to imagine it. Entropy by any other name is still, ultimately, extinction."

Risa hesitated, then put her hand back on the rock. All she sensed was a stirring of air, a fading murmur, trembling silence. Frowning, she lifted her hand and stepped through the opening until she stood in the center of the three stones.

"Anything?" Shane asked.

"Not anymore. It was here, though. The gold."

"And now it's gone."

She nodded as she touched the cool, rough surface of each sandstone slab in turn and sensed the silent stirrings. "I can't say I like what I sense, yet I'm not worried by it now." She looked at him and admitted, "But I'm not volunteering to fall asleep here either."

"Yeah. C'mon." He took her hand and urged her out of the shadows of the three rocks. "Let's get to a place where there's cell coverage. I want to know if Rarities has anything new to tell us."

Risa walked behind Shane down the trail toward the empty cabin. Too empty. "Can we put out an anonymous tip so that the police start looking for Virgil O'Conner?"

"Right after I call the local hospitals. If possible, I'd like to talk to him before the cops do."

Not far down from the cliff, Shane heard things sneaking through the brush in the same place he'd noticed them before. This time there wasn't any itching on his neck to distract him. He switched on the penlight and raked its beam through the brush.

Three sets of gleaming eyes flashed and then vanished in a scrabble of claws over rocks and sun-hardened dirt.

"Wait here," he said to Risa.

"With those eyes watching me? No thanks."

"Then stay close enough to share the light." He reached around behind his back and pulled the gun. "I'll need it to find a way through the brush."

Holding the penlight and the gun so that both swept over the brush simultaneously, Shane started off the trail. Risa followed close enough to touch his back.

The wind shifted.

The smell of death clogged the air, telling Shane that the resident wildlife had been enjoying a not-so-fresh kill. Grimly he moved the penlight in ever-widening arcs. The edge of the beam picked up a worn boot, shredded clothes, and remains only a coroner could look at without gagging.

Swiftly Shane turned around and blocked Risa's view of Mother Nature at work.

"Time to go back," he said.

She swallowed hard. "O'Conner?"

"Let's just say I won't be calling any hospitals. As soon as we're well away from here, I'll call the cops like a good little anonymous citizen."

"I'm glad I know you don't want that gold enough to murder for it."

"Why?" Shane asked.

"Every time someone has died lately, they've taken with them one more link in the chain leading back to the true owner of the Druid gold."

"Leave it to a curator to worry about provenance."

"Somebody has to worry."

"Oh, I am. I'm worried about the fact that too many people who touched this gold ended up dead."

"Cherelle hasn't." *I hope.*

"I wouldn't announce that to the cops," Shane said.

"Why?"

"It could tag her as the murderer."

"I'm voting for Bozo," Risa said instantly. "Or Tim."

"You don't think Cherelle can kill?"

Risa didn't answer.

Shane didn't ask again. He just followed her down the rise, away from the smell of death.

Fifty-three

Rich Morrison and Gail Silverado looked at the six gold artifacts from every angle. Both of them wore exam gloves. So did John Firenze, even though he'd done nothing more than set the gold out on pages of casino letterhead on his desk.

"What do you think?" Firenze asked when he got tired of listening to silence punctuated by the soft beep of his computers when new e-mail arrived. "Is it real?"

Rich looked at Gail.

She didn't notice. She was holding a heavy gold ring whose exterior and interior were incised with letters or symbols from a language she couldn't read.

But she knew someone who could.

"Shane has a ring like this," she said, savoring the weight of gold in her palm. "At least the outside is like it. He never takes it off, so I don't know about the inside."

"Where did you get this stuff?" Rich asked.

Firenze shifted uncomfortably. "It just came to me."

"Try again," Rich suggested.

"A guy—"

"Try harder."

Firenze looked at Rich's eyes. They were as cold as his voice. He wanted answers, and he was going to keep pushing until he got them. Firenze was just irritated enough at the world in general and his stupid nephew in particular to push back. Besides, no matter how worthless Cesar was, he was still blood. Firenze's mother would make life living hell for him if he implicated her grandson in a lousy pawnbroker's murder.

"Why do you care?" Firenze said. "I'm not asking you to buy the fucking stuff. I'm just giving you a chance to set up Tannahill. That's what you wanted, isn't it?"

There was a tight silence, a muffled curse. Rich looked back at the gold. He wanted Tannahill, sure.

But that wasn't all he wanted.

"I want to be sure the goods are hot," Rich said.

"Be sure."

Gail's lips quirked at Firenze's retort, but she didn't let Rich see it. He was in a pisser of a mood. Even the thought of nailing Golden Boy's ass to the courthouse wall hadn't brought a smile to Rich's grim face.

"And I want to cover my ass when the cops start asking me questions," Rich said.

Firenze shrugged. "What's to ask? I won't mention your name. I'm just letting you preview the gold so I can be sure it's the sort of thing that will snag Tannahill."

"I don't like it." It was a snarl as much as a statement. "Tell me how you got the gold or there's no deal. I'm not buying a pig in a poke."

The spike in Firenze's blood pressure showed in the darkening of his face. He really hated being reminded that he wasn't top cock of this walk. "My nephew got it from a friend of a friend."

"Which nephew?"

"Cesar."

"The one who shot up the Golden Fleece?" Gail asked, drawing Firenze's angry attention from Rich.

Firenze grimaced. "Yeah."

"Where is he now?" she asked.

"Cooling off at the lake until we can get him out of the country. He hates the family houseboat, but tough shit. Do him good."

Gail hid a smile. The Firenze women's love of the huge Lake Mead houseboat was the despair of the men, who would rather be staked out on anthills than spend a weekend at the lake. But they did it anyway, at least once a year, along with everyone who was anyone in Las Vegas. Firenze's Fourth of July bash was as famous as Gail's own Halloween party.

Firenze glared at Rich. "You in or out?"

"I'm thinking."

"You got until tomorrow. After that, you ask me about gold and I don't know shit about nothing." Firenze shot Rich a slicing glance. "You disappoint me. You asked to have Tannahill on a platter, and I'm giving him to you and you're backing up."

"What do you want out of this?" Rich asked.

"A bigger slice of the laundry pie."

"How much?"

"Twice as much."

Rich looked back at the gold. "Then who gets cut?"

"Whoever isn't here."

After a moment Rich turned back to Firenze. "Good work, John. When I've set things up, I'll call and someone will pick up the gold. A few hours, no more."

"You're going for it?" Gail asked Rich.

"I'd be stupid not to. I'll even get a gold star in my files from the feds on this one. It sure as hell will keep their nose out of my business for a while. They'll be too busy sticking their nose up Tannahill's."

Gail looked uncertain.

"What?" Firenze asked her.

"I think he's too cagey to get caught by a blind call."

"It won't be blind," Rich said. He gave Firenze a look that told the other man he had better answer with something more to the point than *a friend of a friend*. "Who did Cesar get the gold from?"

Firenze wasn't stupid. "A bitch named Cherelle Faulkner."

"The one who's tight with Tannahill's curator?" Rich asked, as though he didn't already know the players.

"That's what my tip said."

"Then the message will come from Cherelle." Rich looked at Gail. "You in?"

She shrugged. "Yeah, it's the smart call. But Vegas sure won't be the same without him."

"Who?" Firenze asked.

"Shane Tannahill."

Fifty-four

Slowly Risa awoke from a dream of lying naked on her stomach at a tropical beach with the taste of the sea on her tongue and surf beating close by. Smiling, she burrowed deeper into the dream . . . and tasted Shane.

Her eyes flew open.

"Do you always wake up all at once?" he asked.

His voice was deep, amused, and he was as naked as she was. What had been sand in the dream was in reality a mat of dark chest hair and warm muscle. What she had thought was surf was the slow, strong beating of his heart beneath her cheek.

The part about tasting mildly salty was real. Licking her lips, she decided that she enjoyed the taste of him in the morning. Surprise and heat streaked through her; Shane was even sexier to her now than he had been when they fell asleep locked together like a flesh-and-blood puzzle that had just been solved.

"Never had an alarm clock like you," she said, nibbling. Tasting. Licking. Enjoying the feel of his erection nudging between her legs. "Or I would have spent a lot of time waking up."

His fingers slid down her hips, probed, found liquid silk and woman. With a sound that was both anticipation and pleasure, he lifted her over him and filled her in a slow, thick stroke that made her moan. He kept moving that way, slowly, deeply, and she answered with a subtle, repeated roll of her hips that redoubled their pleasure. Though both of them trembled with leashed ecstasy, they kept the rhythm easy, dreamlike.

Then she could bear no more and arched back, stretched and shivering on a rack of exquisite pleasure. His smile was as elemental as the release he felt washing through her. When she lay spent and boneless on top of him, he rolled her over and began moving again. Slowly. Thickly. Her eyes opened, dazed with a pleasure that was both old and burningly new. She shifted, rising up, taking more. Giving more.

This time they went blind together in a hot darkness that smelled and tasted of intimacy.

When she could take a breath without echoes of ecstasy shivering through her, she lifted her head and nuzzled his jaw. Tiny touches of her tongue filled her need to taste him, just as slow strokes of his hands over her back answered his need to feel her close and warm against him. She was just drifting off to sleep again when his bedside telephone rang.

"Sugah?" she drawled.

"Hmmm?"

"Kill it."

"I'd rather kill the idiot who put in the override code in spite of my instructions."

When she started to slide off him, his arms tightened. Taking her with him, he rolled closer to the phone and hit the conference button. "What?" he demanded.

The man at the desk talked fast, saying one of the three magic names that would allow him to keep his job. "Ms. Cherelle Faulkner left an urgent message for Ms. Sheridan. As you are the only one who knows Ms. Sheridan's whereabouts, I thought it prudent to tell you right away."

Risa stiffened and reached for the phone. With casual strength, Shane caught her hand and held her in place.

"Not yet," he said very softly. Then, loud enough for the phone to pick up, "What number did she call from?"

"It was blocked, sir."

"Why am I not surprised. One moment." He let go of Risa's hand, hit the hold button at the base of the phone, and said, "Would you rather have the message in private?"

She closed her eyes and shook her head.

He brushed a kiss across her eyes and whispered, "Thank you."

"For what?" she said unhappily.

"Trusting me."

With a wry turn to her mouth, she looked at their bodies tangled together. "All things considered, it would be stupid not to."

"There are many kinds of intimacy. Of trust."

She met his level green eyes. "I trust you not to hurt Cherelle."

"If I can avoid it, I won't, because it would only hurt you. But if she puts you in the line of fire again . . ." Shane didn't finish. He didn't have to. The subtle flattening of his features said it all. "I fight for what matters to me. You matter, Risa."

"So do you. Jesus, it scares the hell out of me." She let out a shaky breath. "How did this happen?"

He smiled crookedly. "I guess we both stopped running at the same time."

"Yeah." She brushed a kiss over his whisker-rough jaw and released the hold button. "Sheridan here," she said. If her voice was husky instead of crisp, she couldn't help it any more than she could help noticing the easy strength and living warmth of the man underneath her. "What's the message?"

"Good morning, Ms. Sheridan. The message was taken by our VoiceWriter service and has an 'urgent' flag stamped on the exterior. Would you like me to open the envelope?"

"No." She hesitated, then told the front desk what everyone at the Golden Fleece had already figured out for themselves—Shane and his curator were an item. "Send it up to Mr. Tannahill's private quarters."

"Right away, Ms. Sheridan."

Risa disconnected from the call and, more reluctantly, from Shane. She began pulling on clothes that would look like they'd been worn yesterday, stripped off in haste last night, and dumped on the floor next to the bed until morning.

"There's a robe in the bathroom," he said, watching her with lazy male lust.

"Stop smiling," she muttered. She felt as though every extra ounce on her breasts and hips was jiggling a neon message of excess.

"I don't think so, darling. Looking at you makes a man pleased. So much woman to enjoy."

She looked up, saw the smoky concentration in his eyes, and knew that he meant it. "And here I thought you liked swizzle-stick models."

She snapped on her bra and settled it in place with a casual shimmy that made his breath thicken. "Why the devil did you think that?"

The rasp in his voice made her pause in the act of pulling up her underwear. He was watching the glide of dark lace. And his arousal was as naked as he was.

She stared. He was worth staring at.

"Close your eyes," she said finally.

"Why?"

"I'm shy."

The corner of his mouth curled up. He hooked an arm around her hips, pulled her against the bed, and nuzzled the hot curls between her thighs. "Okay, I can't see you now."

The slick probe of his tongue loosened her knees. Underwear forgotten, she buried her fingers in the short, midnight pelt of his hair. She told herself she was going to push him away.

She pulled him closer.

A melodic chiming came from the front room of his apartment.

"What did he do—teleport?" Shane muttered.

"I imagine he took your direct elevator." Her voice was husky, as raspy as the beard stubble caressing her thighs, as hot as his tongue.

"Sometimes staff efficiency is a pain in the butt," he said, and burrowed deeper.

Her knees buckled.

The door chimed.

"*Damn.*" With a lingering love bite he eased her panties up until his mouth was against lace rather than woman. Then he rolled aside, flipped an intercom switch, and said, "Thanks for the speedy delivery. Just shove it under the door."

Risa drew a shaky breath and ran for the bathroom before she changed her mind and fell all over him like hot rain. She grabbed a robe that was brushed silk, black, and too big for her by half.

As fast as she moved, the delivery service was faster. When she got to the hall door, a smooth, creamy envelope with the Golden Fleece's raised gilded logo had already been pushed under the door. "VERY URGENT" was stamped on the envelope in red.

She ripped open the message and read quickly: *If Shane Tannahill wants six pieces of Celtic gold for his show, tell him to bring two hundred thousand dollars in hundred-dollar bills to the parking lot of the Water Stop by seven o'clock this morning. If he comes with anybody but you, he'll never see these six pieces of gold again. There are other buyers in Vegas.*

"Damn," Risa said. "I was sure there were more than six pieces."

"You talking to me?" Shane asked from the bedroom.

"Only if you have clothes on."

"Waste of time. You'll just tear them off."

"I wish." She looked at the clock—6:37. "Next time, I promise. What's the Water Stop?"

Barefoot, Shane walked into the living room, buttoning up a pair of jeans. "A downtown sex club with slots."

She took one look and glanced away. The man was a walking invitation to sin, and she didn't even have time to drool. She shoved the message into his hand and ran past him to collect her clothes. "Okay. Parking lot should be pretty empty at this hour, so we won't have any trouble spotting them."

He read the message in one lightning scan and felt something really unhappy settle in his gut. "I'll let you know how it goes."

She appeared in the doorway, her hands fisted on her hips. "What do you mean, you'll let me know?"

"Guess." He walked past her and pulled a fresh shirt from his closet.

Risa hurriedly pulled on slacks and shook out a rumpled blouse. "Wait! How do you know it isn't a stickup?"

"I don't." He grabbed shoes and kicked them on. "That's why you're staying."

"But—"

"Sometimes it's better alone." He tied his running shoes with sharp, quick motions. "This is one of those times. You're staying here."

"Shove your orders! I don't work for you anymore!"

"Call Niall. He'll tell you the same thing."

Without a word she went over and punched in Niall's very private number. It went through before Shane got to the wall safe and put his hand over the scanner.

"What's up, Shane?"

"It's Risa."

In another room down the hall, Niall smiled because she was calling from one of Shane's private numbers. Maybe the atmosphere around those two would stop crackling now that they had spent the night destroying a bed together.

"Good morning, luv. What's up?"

"Cherelle has six pieces of gold she wants to sell Shane for two hundred thousand dollars cash in the parking lot of a downtown dive called the Water Stop. Twenty-one minutes and counting."

"I'm on my way."

Before Niall finished talking, the sound of the connection changed as it went on the speaker.

"Don't bother," Shane said. "This party is by invitation only. You weren't invited."

"No worries. I've crashed a lot of parties in my day."

"You crash this one and six pieces of fine Celtic gold disappear forever. Dana wouldn't be happy. 'Buy, Sell, Appraise, Protect,'" Shane said, quoting Rarities Unlimited's motto. "Remember?"

"All right. I'll hang back so nobody gets nervous. Risa, you still there?"

"Yes."

"Good. Stay there."

"But—"

"That's an order," Niall said over her objection. "You don't have security training, so you'd just be a liability if it all goes from sugar to shit. Lapstrake will take over guard duty on you."

"This is crap! I know Cherelle. You don't. I can—"

"Stay put or find another employer," Niall cut in. "Shane, I'll send Ian over to your room and meet you downstairs in two minutes. Do you have enough cash on hand?"

"I own a casino. What do you think?"

"I think I'm in the wrong business."

Fifty-five

Shane drove to the Water Stop with one eye on the traffic, one eye on the mirrors, and the memory of Risa's anger ringing in his ears. He didn't envy Ian the next hour or two. The lady was passionate in more than the sexual sense of the word.

By the time Shane was two blocks from the Water Stop, he still hadn't discovered any tails. Nobody seemed interested in him at all. Niall had taken an alternate route and was already in place. After a final check of mirrors, Shane picked up the cell phone and punched in the redial while he waited at a stoplight.

Niall answered instantly. "There are maybe thirty cars in the parking lot. Several have people in them, but only one has a female alone. She's already sent off three separate men who approached her."

"What kind of car?"

"An old Bronco. Can't see the plates."

"Sounds good." Even as he spoke, Shane wished his

instincts *felt* good. But they didn't. They were sitting up and howling alarms. "She has a Bronco."

"From here the woman sure doesn't look like a blonde with good tits."

"Cherelle likes disguises."

Niall grunted. "I'm not happy with this, boyo. I'm across the street. You'll be in the open with two hundred big ones in cash. There are panel vans and RVs scattered around the lot. Someone could pop out and dump you before I could take two steps."

Shane didn't like it either, but he didn't see any way around it except to walk away from the gold. He wasn't willing to do that. If the pieces were anything like what he'd bought from Smith-White, they literally defined "priceless." They were golden icons from a time that was long since gone and a culture that would never live again.

It was worth some risk to save them.

"I've taken bigger chances," Shane said. "And I'm wearing the body armor you gave me."

"Body armor ain't worth shit if you're shot in the head."

"You're such a comfort."

"Dana points it out to me daily."

"I'm a block away," Shane said. "Let me know when you see me."

There was silence for ten seconds.

"Gotcha," Niall said. "You see the Bronco?"

"Yes. I don't see you."

"That's the whole idea. Remember, if it goes to shit, take care of yourself first. I'll take care of the rest."

"I don't think it's a rip-off."

"I hope you're right. How's the hair on the back of your neck?"

"Restless," Shane admitted. "But not on the subject of robbery."

"Then what?"

"I don't know."

"Bloody hell," Niall said, disgusted. "You and Erik North are a real pair. Not an ounce of useful precognition between the two of you."

Shane was still smiling when he drove into the Water Stop's parking area. It didn't take him long to locate the Bronco, but he drove past it anyway, doing a slow lap around the lot. Other than an itchy neck, nothing happened. If anything, he felt better. Between the hookers and semipros cutting deals in the backs of campers, and the steady trickle of randy johns walking out of the club looking for some parking-lot action, there were too many witnesses for a crook to feel comfortable about armed robbery.

Unless the crook was as stupid as Socks. But the call hadn't come from Socks. It had come from Cherelle Faulkner.

When Shane pulled up next to the Bronco, he couldn't help wondering if Socks was with Cherelle. Even as the thought came, he shrugged it off. From what Risa had heard Socks say about Cherelle, they weren't what anyone would describe as close.

As soon as Shane got out of his car carrying a small suitcase, the door of the Bronco popped open and a woman climbed out.

She wasn't Cherelle Faulkner.

Fifty-six

Gnawing on the inside of her mouth, Cherelle sat in the middle of the unmade bed and stared at the television. She had gone through a whole cycle of news promos and ads for breath mints, "sexergizers," and gambling tips. Other than running the tape of Socks busting through the Golden Fleece and saying that the police had identified him as Cesar Firenze Marquez, nephew of the CEO and part-owner of Roman Circus, John Firenze, who was cooperating with police in the search for his nephew, the news had nothing to say about the apprehension and lockup of Socks.

"Well, shit," Cherelle said.

She dragged her fingers through her hair so she wouldn't have to look at their fine trembling. She wanted some crack. She wanted it bad. Not that she was hooked. She could take it or leave it.

Right now she wanted to take it.

Problem was, she wouldn't have any money to get crack unless she hit another jackpot, sold her ass on a street corner, or Socks got nailed so she could sell the gold without falling on her face from looking over her shoulder the whole time.

"How many cops does it take to find one stupid ass-hole?" she asked.

The TV cut back to the judges of the Santa Claus bikini contest. They had big hair and tits like rocket ships, probably used to find out if a man had any working equipment under his big belly.

"You dumb bitches! Give me some news! Tell me the cops took him down!"

Somebody in the room next door pounded on the wall and yelled at her to *shut-the-fuck-up*.

Cherelle came off the bed like a tiger and started to heave the lamp at the wall. All that stopped her was that the lamp was nailed to the bedside table. Cursing, she yanked until her nails were bloody. Then she caught a glimpse of herself in the dresser mirror. At first she didn't recognize the woman with the pale, sweating face and dull hair standing out in all directions. Then she did.

Christ Jesus. I look like some whacked-out crackhead. That isn't me!

She stopped pulling at the lamp. Carefully she smoothed her hair down and forced her breathing to level.

"It's okay, mama-chick. You'll do fine. You always do. Take a big ol' shower. Get some coffee. Some food. Maybe a beer or two. If they haven't caught the dumb fuck by then, he's left town, and you don't need to worry no more."

Nothing answered her words but an earnest middle-aged man on the TV, telling her that her sexual troubles were over. No prescriptions. No harsh chemicals, just Mother Nature's own—

The shower came on, drowning out everything else for Cherelle but the gnawing need to sell the gold and get a little crack.

Not much. Just a little.

Just enough to take the edge off.

Fifty-seven

Hands empty, Shane leaned against his car. As soon as he'd seen that the woman wasn't Cherelle, he put the briefcase full of money into the trunk and locked it. He would have turned around and driven off, but the closer he got to the Bronco, the more his instincts were reminded of how it had felt at Virgil's house.

Only stronger.

Almost as strong as when he'd picked up the first of Smith-White's offerings and felt time peeling away like smoke in a hard wind and he was standing in an oak grove with the moon in his face and a solid gold knife in his hands.

"No gold until I see the money," the woman said for maybe the sixth time.

Though she was dressed like a tart in crotch-length black skirt and half-unbuttoned see-through blouse, Shane knew she wasn't in the business of selling herself. He couldn't have said why he was so certain, but he was. Right clothes, wrong everything else.

"Lady, you can huff and puff all you like," Shane said. "You aren't Cherelle. Your Bronco has Nevada rental plates. That's two big strikes against you. Until I see the gold, you don't see the money." He looked at his watch. "Fifty seconds more and I'm gone."

"There are other markets for—"

"Forty-five," he cut in calmly. He'd heard it all from her before. It hadn't impressed him the first time. It was downright tiresome the fifth time.

Body armor itched in awkward places.

The woman looked at his stone green eyes and discovered what many another player had—Shane Tannahill didn't give away anything he didn't want to. She could pick up the cards he dealt or she could get out of the game.

With a hissing curse, she turned on her four-inch platform shoes and swung her hips hard all the way to the back of the Bronco. She yanked open the cargo door, reached inside, and unzipped the lid of a small suitcase.

"Okay, big man," she said. "Drag ass over here and take a look."

None of Shane's relief showed as he slowly straightened and reached into his pocket for exam gloves. He hadn't expected the woman to be so stubborn about not showing the artifacts; it had made him wonder if this might be some kind of scam after all. If it hadn't been for the prickling along his nerves that reminded him of a dead man's gold, he would have been long gone from the parking lot.

He wondered if the cops had found Virgil's body yet. If so, it hadn't made the Vegas news. But then, there was no reason it should. Lots of old folks died every day. Some of them were murdered. There probably hadn't been enough left of the corpse to determine yet if Virgil had died on his own or had a big shove off into the night.

"You coming?" she asked.

Casually Shane snapped the gloves into place, walked the few steps to the back of the Bronco, and glanced into the open cargo door.

Gold glowed against red velvet as though lit from within.

The woman started to move closer.

Shane stepped away. "Give me room. Or do you really think I'm going to grab and run?"

The woman hesitated before she backed up a few steps. Her glance moved restlessly over the parking lot before darting back to him.

He shifted position so he could keep an eye on her as well as the gold. He was vulnerable to attack while he examined the gold, but his greatest danger was when she saw the money. If she had any confederates parked around the lot, that was when they would act.

Though everything in Shane yearned to savor the artifacts like a fine, rare wine, he held each piece for only a few moments. The torc was magnificent, heavy, shimmering with power. Two brooches, each as extraordinary as the one he'd purchased from Smith-White. Each with a current of power. The figurines were obviously part of a fertility ritual. A golden phallus and an impressively potent bull.

And a ring like the one he wore.

He knew it would fit on Risa's hand. Perfectly. It was all he could do to put the ring down.

Fingers tingling, Shane zipped up the suitcase and moved back. "Where did you get these?"

She laughed derisively. "Where do you think?"

"I don't know. That's why I'm asking."

"Cherelle had them. She sold them to me. I'm selling

them to you. You want paperwork, you don't buy shit in parking lots."

Without a word Shane went to his own car, unlocked the trunk, and opened his own suitcase. Bundles of used hundred-dollar bills filled it. He gestured to the woman and backed up to give her room.

She bent over and riffled through five bundles at random in the manner of someone who is used to judging stacks of money. Then she closed the suitcase, picked it up, and turned to him.

"Looks good to me," she said, and headed for her vehicle.

Shane took her suitcase out of the Bronco and laid it in his open trunk.

As he closed the lid, the woman grabbed a gun from the side pocket of the Bronco's door. When she spun toward him, the sun flashed on a very modern kind of gold.

"FBI, Tannahill," she said, showing him her shield. "You're under arrest for receiving stolen property."

Fifty-eight

Cherelle had gnawed at her mouth until beer stung like iodine whenever she took a drink. Crumpled cans lay in front of the TV, losers in a drinker's demolition derby. No matter how many empties she threw at the screen, the newsreaders still kept silent on the subject of the apprehension of Cesar "Socks" Firenze Marquez.

She hesitated, scowled at Gail Silverado's number, and decided Socks must have headed out of town. Even if he hadn't, he was too dumb to find a smart one like her. All she had to do was swap the gold for money, shake the dust of this losing city forever, and find a new place where mirrors didn't show her something out of a freak show.

It took ten minutes and five levels of assistants, but she finally got through to the big lady herself.

"Ms. Silverado, I'm told you like buying gold before Shane Tannahill can."

"Depends on the gold."

"You can see for yourself tonight. Seventeen pieces."

"Will Shane be there?"

"His curator will be." Cherelle smiled and rolled the word on her tongue again. "This meeting is just for chicks."

"Who else?"

"Just the two of you. And me."

"Who are you?" Gail said, her tone irritated and interested at the same time.

"Someone who has a suitcase full of fancy Celtic gold. Minimum bid is one million cash, used bills."

Gail laughed. "Well, you don't lack balls. Give me a number. I'll call you after I check with my bank."

"I'll call you in an hour. Be there or Tannahill gets it all."

Fifty-nine

Rich Morrison opened the office door himself and gave Gail a kiss on her softly powdered cheek.

"Lovely of you to come by with a surprise for my wife," he said for the benefit of his executive assistant, who was fading back into the wallpaper in the adjoining office.

"You only celebrate this kind of occasion once," Gail said easily, kissing his cheek in turn.

The door shut with an expensive-sounding click behind her.

"Bet half of Vegas thinks we're having an affair," she said, tossing the gold-foiled box of candy onto the nearest chair.

"Half of Vegas would be right. The other half."

Laughing, she stepped back. "A woman called about twenty minutes ago. She has seventeen pieces of Celtic gold to sell to me or Shane Tannahill. Wants one million. Cash. Used bills."

Rich's eyebrows lifted. "Interesting. She give a name?"

"What do you think?"

"No."

"I can go five hundred thousand without setting off alarms from my investors," Gail said, "but no more. Shane can go the whole way twice and give me change. You want him bad enough to spend half a million of your own money?"

"Yes."

"That fast, huh? Don't even have to call your money men?"

"They're waiting to wash eight hundred million a year through here. We skim ten percent for the service. You're good at numbers. You do the math."

"Okay, half a million is chump change for them. But not for me. I'll need the money by tonight."

"Early or late?"

"She didn't say. She'll call back with the particulars."

"I'll send someone as soon as the money is packed. Used bills, I trust?"

"It's all I'd be comfortable with."

He smiled. "You'll have the money in two hours, maximum. Anything else?"

She gave him a sideways glance from under her thick lashes. "What do you have?"

"More than you have time to enjoy." Then he smiled wryly. "Hell, Silver. It's too late for us now."

"Haven't you heard? Take a pill and turn into a teenager."

"New wives aren't that easy to find."

"Especially ones with the kind of political connections you need."

"Especially not them," he agreed.

"You going to be our next governor?"

"I'd prefer a position with more power."

"Senator?"

He shook his head.

"C'mon, Rich. You're not going for president, are you?"

"I like Nevada too well. I think I'd make a very good head of the Gaming Control Board, don't you?"

She whistled. "Can you take the background check?"

"Of course."

"Talk about the fox guarding the henhouse . . ." Gail snickered, then laughed aloud.

She was still chuckling when she shut the office door behind her.

Sixty

Down the center of the table, resting on what looked like unused Halloween napkins, six gold artifacts lay, gleaming condensations of time and human dreams. Shane felt their presence like a sigh just below the level of hearing, a breath moving softly over his skin.

Minus handcuffs, he and the artifacts waited in an anonymous room in an anonymous government building two miles and worlds away from the Golden Fleece. The furniture was turn-of-the-century waiting room—steel frames, worn battleship-gray seat cushions, metal conference table, a water dispenser in the corner, a plastic wastebasket half full of paper coffee cups. No rug, no telephone, no computer, and no windows.

Two people who had declined to give him a name or a badge number had taken turns trying to get him to agree to handing over the four pieces of gold already in his possession on the grounds that they, too, clearly had been stolen from the same source as the six he'd been arrested for buying this morning.

Other than noting to himself that the Rarities search for the source of the gold artifacts was attracting all kinds of sharks, Shane ignored the questions—and the questioners—until they gave up and left. They were only place-holders until the real power arrived. He knew it even if they didn't.

Finally, too late, a pattern had become very clear to Shane. Now all that remained was to figure out what his losses were and then cut them without having to give up the gold.

His lawyers were somewhere in the building raising hell with everyone who might have the power to get Shane released. Other lawyers were on the phone raising hell with lawyers in Washington, D.C., who would in turn raise hell with whatever government officials might get the job done.

Because no charges had been filed, it was hard for Shane's lawyers to get any action. According to the only paperwork available, he had come to the building "voluntarily." If that meant he'd agreed to come to the building and talk to government-issue employees instead of being formally booked, locked in a cell, and communicating with his lawyers through a speaker in a glass wall, then Shane had indeed volunteered to be a temporary guest of Uncle Sam.

The door opened. A petite woman with black hair, measuring black eyes, and the absolute confidence of a tiger walked into the room. And like a tiger, she was as deadly as she was beautiful. She shut the door behind her. Though she wasn't wearing a name tag, he knew who she was.

"Hello, April Joy," Shane said. "I was wondering if you would show up personally."

April gave him a tiger-measuring-prey look that said

he would wish she had stayed on the West Coast. Crossing her arms over her chest, she leaned against the door and simply stared at him for the space of a slow ten count.

"It would have been much easier on all of us if you'd agreed to work with me the first time you were contacted," she said.

"About the gold?" He knew what her answer would be, but he needed to hear the words. He had overlooked too much in his obsession with the upcoming Druid Gold show.

And with Risa.

April dismissed the gold with a wave of her elegant hand. "The Red Phoenix laundry is all I care about."

Bingo.

With his fingertip Shane touched the gold ring in the center of the table. The outer runes called upon gods more Nordic than Welsh to protect the wearer. The inner symbols were purely Celtic, speaking silently of gods who bent to listen to the Druid king. His own ring had ogham symbols on the outside, Celtic on the inside. He would have bet his life that both rings had once belonged to people who had the power of earthly gods.

"The two agents who took turns on me cared about the gold," Shane pointed out.

"Their problem. I don't care except inasmuch as the Brits are leaning on D.C. to repatriate it. If Uncle decides to pass the bad cess down the line to my department, you'll hear about it from me until hell won't have it."

He half smiled. "I don't doubt it."

"Then why are you being such a prick?"

He gave her the other half of the smile in a flash of white that did nothing to soften the stone green of his eyes. "I learned it at my daddy's knee."

"If you think being Bastard Merit's kid will get you out of this, think again. You're swimming alone in the shit. When we made a courtesy call, he said you were fair game and he didn't even want to hear about it."

"That's my daddy."

April tilted her head to the side. In her years working for various departments of the floating alphabet soup that was Uncle's way of sliding under Congress's radar, she had taken apart some dudes who thought they were the toughest men ever to swing their balls when they walked. Before she finished with them, they were boys looking for Mama. She liked to think it would be that easy with Shane Tannahill.

Experience told her it wouldn't.

She looked at her watch, muttered a few carefully selected phrases in Cantonese, and decided to save everybody some time. She looked at the gold, then at Shane. "Are you working for Rarities on this one?"

"I'm self-employed."

Black eyes narrowed. "Okay, tough guy. Is Rarities working for *you* on the gold?"

"Why do you care?"

"If you were a tenth as dirty as your reputation, Dana Gaynor wouldn't touch you with fire tongs. When it comes to her core customers, she is one very picky bitch."

This time Shane's smile went all the way to his eyes. "That she is. She has even been known to sidestep Uncle Sam on occasion."

April waited.

He got his pen out of the pocket of the green wind shell and began walking the slim gold cylinder over his fingers.

She leaned harder against the wall and kept waiting.

Click as gold met gold. Silence. *Click*. Silence.

"Basically," he said after a time, "you don't have enough on me to stick up a fly's ass." *Click*. "In order to prove that I was receiving stolen goods, you have to prove that the goods were stolen in the first place. You can't."

"You seem real sure of that."

Click. "I am."

"You don't think they were stolen?"

"When? Last year? A hundred years ago? A thousand? Two thousand?"

"I'll let the lawyers dance on that pinhead. Meanwhile, you can help me out or you can spend time in jail while everyone does the dance."

"I'd be out on OR before you were back on the West Coast."

"On the gold, yes. On money laundering? Uh-uh, slick. You'd do some time. I'm the head of the interdepartmental task force that's been working to bring the triads down."

"So that's where the FBI came in."

She showed him a curve of hard white teeth.

"I don't launder money, and you know it," Shane said.

"I thought I did. Then a little birdy did the tweet-tweet thing in my ear, and I went and got a piece of paper from a judge that says I can vet your casino computers right down to the last byte."

"Be my guest."

April smiled. It made her looks even more striking, more intense. "That's what Dana said you would say. So suppose you and I will make a little bet, slick. You show me your computers without benefit of the search warrant. If you're clean, I'll bow out and let the lawyers dance, and you'll be home in an hour. If you're not clean, I'll bury the evidence—if you'll help me set up a sting that will shut down the Red Phoenix casino laundry before it really gets going in Vegas."

It didn't take Shane two seconds to get to the bottom line. "I'm out of here now. The gold goes with me. Not negotiable."

April didn't like it, but she had expected it. She straightened from the door and reached for the handle. "All right. Let's go."

"Not quite yet."

She turned so quickly that her cranberry-colored jacket flared out. "What."

It wasn't a question.

"Since I'm being such a generous and helpful citizen," he said, "one who isn't even yelling about false arrest on top of entrapment, I think Uncle should give me something in return."

"A gold medal? Lunch in the Rose Garden with the Secret Service passing the salt?"

"Nothing that fancy. I just want Uncle on my side when it comes time to explain to the Brits that unless and until they prove the gold was stolen from them *at a time when ownership of the antiquities was covered by international law,* they shouldn't expect me to hand over millions of dollars' worth of Celtic artifacts just because I'm such a sweet guy."

"And if they can prove ownership?"

"It's theirs."

"I'll do what I can. No guarantees, Tannahill. Antiquities are a hot-button topic in international diplomacy."

He gave her an amused smile. "You think?"

"Yeah, I think." Smiling in spite of herself, she shook her head. "If I didn't know better, I'd think Dana chose her core male customers by their shoulders and their smiles."

Shane laughed. "You'd probably arrest me if I told you why I think Uncle sends you after men."

She lowered her dense black eyelashes and gave him a very female kind of smile. "If I had thought that approach would work with you . . ."

"It wouldn't. I can appreciate without touching."

"Yeah. That's what the three women we ran past you said."

His eyebrows shot up. "Three? When?"

"Jesus, you didn't even notice. They'll be heartbroken." Shaking her head, April opened the door. "After you, slick."

Sixty-one

"You're sure you didn't see any of the gold at all?"
Dana Gaynor demanded, glaring from Risa to Niall.
"Not even a glimpse?"

Rather warily, Niall watched the dark-haired dynamo
who had showed up with no warning at the Golden
Fleece's front desk and demanded to be taken to S.K.
Niall. Dana almost never lost her temper, but she was
looking more than halfway there right now. Her small
and very female body fairly vibrated with pent energy.
He had already told her the story of Shane, the gold, and
the FBI more than once, but he knew her too well to
point that out.

She really hated losing priceless artifacts. If someone
gave her a target right now, she would start shooting and
apologize later.

"No," Niall said. "The angle was wrong. All I saw
was Shane sticking his head into the Bronco."

"Well, bloody, *bloody* hell," Dana snarled. "Then
how do we know they're good? It could have been a

sting from the start, complete with manufactured gold, and we're all running around like ants in scalding water for nothing."

Risa didn't say anything. She just kept pacing from her living room to her bedroom and back. With every step she remembered all the angry words she had slung at Shane before he left. She would have eaten every one of them just for the chance to hold him.

Assuming he would even let her after she had chewed him up one side and down the other.

Big assumption.

"If he bought the gold," Risa said, "it's good."

Dana cocked her head. "You sound certain."

"I am."

"If he's that good, why does he have you?"

"He doesn't. You do," Risa shot back. "That's why I'm here and Shane is waiting in a cell somewhere." Abruptly she held up her hand. "Sorry. It's not your fault." She shrugged jerkily. "Shane gets hunches about certain kinds of artifacts. I can fault him on provenance, but not on what he decides to buy."

"Things that go bump in the night?" Dana asked, glancing sideways at Niall.

Risa rubbed her arms. "That's as good a way to describe it as any." She spun around and began pacing again. "*Damn it.* What are all those expensive lawyers doing, taking the FBI out for a ten-course meal while they discuss what does and does not constitute entrapment?"

Niall put an arm around her shoulders as she paced on by. The mouth that had made more than one man look twice was pale, thin, and as hard-looking as anything that lush could be.

"Easy, luv," he said. "Shane's all right. They won't be hauling out the rubber hoses for Bastard Merit's only son. The FBI is jumping salty and hard, which means they want something from Shane. The lawyers are doing everything they can to get him loose."

"It isn't enough!" She bit back the tears that wanted to flow—tears of rage. She hated feeling helpless. "Oh, God, don't you see? I'm the one who brought Cherelle into the Golden Fleece. It's my—"

"Shane's a big boy," Ian interrupted. He was leaning against the kitchen doorframe, drinking coffee. "He knew the rules of the game before he took cards in it."

Risa rounded on Ian. The fact that he was right didn't stop her from opening her mouth to tell him what she thought of useless bodyguards who let the guy who really needed guarding go to jail.

Before she could get the first word of her tirade out, the phone rang. She made a dive for it.

"Whew. Saved by the bell," Ian said, grinning and sipping coffee.

Risa gave him a slicing glance as she spoke into the phone. "Sheridan here."

"Hi, baby-chick. I've got some gold pieces for you that will knock your eyes out."

"Cherelle! Where are you?"

Ian swiftly crossed the room and turned on the recorder he had installed on her apartment phone.

"Yeah, it's mama-chick," Cherelle said. "Glad that Socks didn't hurt you. That boy has a big ol' streak of mean in him."

"You could have told me you were passing around the apartment key."

"I didn't give it to him. I must have lost it somewhere. Have the cops picked him up yet?"

"Not that I know of."

"Shit."

At the other end of the line, Cherelle bit the inside of her mouth and winced. She was already raw from gnawing on herself. The beers she had drunk took a little of the edge off her cocaine hunger, but not nearly enough. She kept hoping to see a handcuffed Socks on the news channel so she could sell the gold and get the hell out of Vegas.

No such luck.

So she would just have to keep on making her own luck. "Here's the deal. I've got seventeen pieces of gold."

Risa's breath hitched. "Even after the six you sold today?"

"I never sold any. Socks must have unloaded Tim's gold. What an asshole. Bet he didn't get gas money for them. He sure didn't get dick for the first four pieces."

Risa forced herself to unclench the fist she'd made. "You didn't sell six pieces of gold today?"

"I just told you. Socks did. Or maybe even Tim. I don't know. His mother isn't answering her phone, so I don't know what happened to him. But don't worry. I kept the best gold for my very own baby-chick."

"Considering what happens to everyone who touches that gold, I'm not sure you're doing me any favors."

"Don't you want it?" Cherelle asked.

The raw edge to her voice said a lot more than her quick question. Risa heard worry and something darker, a kind of general desperation that was racing on a short track toward a train wreck. Part of Risa wanted to help. The rest of her wanted to scream at her childhood friend for coming back into her life and carelessly ripping it apart.

"I haven't seen the gold," Risa said. "How can I tell if I want it?"

"It's better than anything you have now. Guarandamn-teed. Your mama-chick wouldn't lead you wrong, now, would she?"

The wheedling voice reminded Risa of the times Cherelle had coaxed and nudged and dragged her into boosting candy bars from the convenience store. As a child she had bought in to the idea that good friends always helped each other, no matter what. As an adult, the *no matter what* part began to grate.

She didn't want to be part of Cherelle's wreckage.

"How much for the gold?" Risa asked.

Cherelle had spent a lot of time thinking about it. Dreaming about it. Hooking Silverado had been almost as good a high as cocaine. Though nobody else knew it, there was going to be a nice little auction going down. And Cherelle was going to walk away $3 million richer.

"Two million," Cherelle said. "Cash. Unmarked, used bills. Not too small, not too big. Fifties and hundreds are good. A few twenties are okay. After that, keep the change."

Risa looked at Dana. "Two million in unmarked twenties, fifties, and hundreds? That's a lot of cash."

Dana nodded.

"You're getting it cheap, baby-chick. From what you told me yourself, it's worth twice that, easy. Like I said, this is your mama-chick. I wouldn't do you wrong."

If the gold was better than what Shane had purchased from Smith-White, $2 million was indeed a good price.

If.

"One million," Risa said coolly.

"One!" Cherelle's voice was shrill, jagged. "What the hell are you talking about? It's worth—"

"It's worth whatever someone will pay for it," Risa cut in. "I'll pay one million cash, in unmarked bills."

"Gail Silverado will go two," Cherelle said instantly.

"Guess we'll just have to see who brings the most cash and—"

"Gail Silverado?" Risa said over Cherelle. "What does she have to do with this?"

Dana looked grim.

So did Niall.

"She's in it for the same thing your boss is," Cherelle said. "She has money, and she wants the gold."

Bitterly Risa wondered if Cherelle called Silverado her baby-chick. "Who else?"

"Just you two."

"Just the two of us, huh?" Risa repeated for the benefit of the people who couldn't hear Cherelle.

Dana nodded again, accepting the fact that there was competition, but it wasn't a free-for-all. Yet. She wanted to avoid that almost as much as she wanted to avoid another sting.

"Okay," Risa said. "But I have to see the gold before I bring any money."

Niall grinned and blew her a kiss.

"Silverado didn't put any conditions on it," Cherelle said.

"She probably plans to screw you out of the cash no matter what the gold is like. I don't."

Leaning against the wall, Cherelle laughed, hiccuped, and laughed again. Risa was so easy, it almost wasn't any fun scamming her. Silverado would have told her to go piss up a $2 million rope, but Risa wouldn't. She would just believe whatever she was told and show up with buckets of money.

Laughter clawed out of Cherelle's throat, along with so many tears that she choked.

"That's my baby-chick," Cherelle said when she could talk again. "So honest you squeak. You shoulda been a fuckin' nun, but I guess even God was too much man for you."

Risa's face tightened. Cherelle sounded drunk or high or both. Certainly her emotions were all over the compass—desperation, anger, wheedling, and now contempt for what her friend was and had been. Risa wanted to point out that the squeaky honest one was living better than the cheesy scammer, but didn't. The Cherelle she was talking to had little of the childhood friend left in her.

And the adult wasn't someone Risa wanted to know.

"Where and when?" Risa said.

"Tonight. You look at the gold, and then you hand over the money. That's the deal. I'm tired of being fucked."

"Tonight?" Risa looked at Dana. "I don't know if I can get the money together that quickly."

Dana looked at Niall.

He nodded. Part of his job was to be sure that Rarities maintained a multimillion-dollar cash pool for just such offbeat buying opportunities. Like Shane's casino, Rarities had more cash on hand than ninety-nine out of a hundred banks.

"All right. Tonight," Risa said.

"I'll call in a couple hours and tell you where. Bring lots of money. We're gonna have a big ol' auction, piece by piece." She laughed high and wild. "Whoever has the most money wins the most prizes."

"Cherelle—" Risa began, wondering what was going on.

Cherelle kept talking, her voice husky and yet hard as gravel. "Come alone, baby-chick. You bring anyone with you and I go out the back door, and you never see that gold again. Your boss wouldn't like that."

"I can't just drive off into the night alone carrying a trunkful of—"

Risa was talking to herself. With a disgusted sound she slammed the receiver back down.

"You're not going alone," Niall and Ian said together.

Risa gave them the kind of look that said she would do whatever she wanted, whenever she wanted, and they could take it or shove it.

"Rarities is fronting the money," Niall said, "I say you're not going in alone."

"The Golden Fleece will front the money," Shane said from the doorway. "And Risa won't go in alone."

Risa spun toward the door just as Shane stepped aside to let a beautiful Eurasian woman inside.

"I think you know everyone here but Risa," Shane said. "Risa Sheridan, April Joy."

Risa took one look and knew trouble had arrived. Even if she hadn't figured it out all by herself, there were the flat lines around Ian's eyes and mouth to give the game away.

Shane looked even grimmer.

"Hello, April Joy," Risa said. "Am I pleased to meet you?"

The agent's lips quirked in a rare, genuine smile. "Probably not, but you might get lucky."

Ian's dark laughter told Risa she probably wouldn't.

Sixty-two

Risa took a few steps toward Shane, then stopped. From his expression, she could have been a stranger. Or invisible. She didn't know if he was mad at her or mad at the world. Considering April Joy's presence, probably both.

Even so, Risa's hands itched to feel the heat and textures of her lover, to reassure herself that he was all right.

"I'm sorry I yelled at you," she said. "Are you okay?"

He gave her a hooded glance, then held out his hand. When she took it, he pulled her close and buried his face in her hair. She wrapped her arms around him and hung on, just hung on.

"I was so worried about you," she said softly against his neck. "Why wouldn't you let me come with you?"

He pulled back and looked at her brilliant, earnest eyes. "You're going to drive me crazy."

She blinked. "Because I lose my temper?"

"Because you don't seem to realize that someone could put a bullet in you and I'd spend the rest of my life wishing it had been me."

"I don't want you hurt either."

"I'm not talking hurt. I'm talking dead." Shane looked at Dana. "The gold artifacts I ransomed are locked in the casino safe."

"Hallelujah," Dana said with a delighted smile. "Ten down and seventeen to go."

"Seventeen?" Shane said quickly, wondering how much of the one-sided conversation he'd missed while he stood in the doorway. "Who? When? Where?"

"Cherelle," Risa said. "As for the when and where, we're waiting to be told."

"In the meantime," Niall said to Ian, "get over to the Wildest Dream."

"There's only one exit from the private garage," Shane said. "Gail Silverado drives either a white Mercedes or is driven in a white limo. License plates are on file with my security."

Niall grinned and said to Ian, "If Silverado gets the call before we do, follow her and guide us in."

Ian nodded, grabbed a dark jacket from the back of a chair, and brushed past April without even a glance.

She gave him the kind of once-over that suggested he was skid marks on underwear.

"What's the ante for this game?" Shane asked Niall.

"Two million cash," Niall said. "Nothing bigger or smaller than a hundred, as far as I'm concerned. Otherwise we'll have a bugger of a time packing it in something a woman can handle."

"No problem," Shane said. "I can take care of it."

April's sleek black eyebrows went up. "No wonder the Red Phoenix is slavering to get their hands on Vegas. You run more cash through one casino in one day than a central bank does in a week."

Niall gave April a narrow look but kept his mouth

shut. He fully respected her abilities, which meant that he wanted to have as little to do with her as possible on a professional basis. Riding that tiger was a good way to get eaten.

"I keep a minimum of five million in cash on hand," Shane said. "Some of the whales don't like wire transfers, and no one likes checks. The whales who pay cash on the way in get paid in cash on the way out. How they get the money into or out of various countries is their problem. Mine is making sure I have enough cash on the premises to cover whatever action a whale offers."

"Better and better." April's smile wasn't the kind that comforted small children. "I wonder how Red Phoenix tastes battered and fried."

"First you have to catch your dinner," Dana said.

"Tannahill will do it for me."

Dana gave Shane a speculative glance. "What changed your mind?"

"Nothing. Ms. Joy is counting her fowl dinner before it's hatched, much less caught, killed, gutted, plucked, and fried."

"Bleh," Risa said. "I'll stick with room service."

April snickered.

"How did you do it?" Dana asked April.

"Oh, Tannahill is as reasonable as he is handsome," April said. "But first you have to rub his face in reality to get his attention. After all, he's a man."

Risa gave Shane a troubled look.

He kissed her lightly. "She has a search warrant that might let her—"

"Might, hell," April cut in. "I don't bluff a professional gambler. The warrant is solid."

Shane kept talking. "—search Tannahill Inc.'s computers. Being a generous, patriotic soul, I struck a bargain with Uncle."

"Uh-oh," Niall said. "I don't like the sound of that."

Dana wasn't smiling either. "What?" she asked Shane.

"If Ms. Joy finds evidence that I'm laundering money, I'll help her set up a sting against the Red Phoenix."

Dana looked at April. "You're sure you're going to find something."

April just smiled.

"Why?" Dana asked.

"You don't think he's doing Red Phoenix laundry?" April said blandly.

"No."

"Neither do I. But I do think someone is setting him up for a long, hard fall." She smiled, displaying her white teeth. "When you look at it that way, I'm really doing Tannahill a favor."

"Who's setting him up?" Niall asked.

Risa looked at her friend and felt something cold sliding through her gut. She had heard from others that Niall could be a ruthless bastard, but she'd never really believed it.

She did now.

"Do you really want a list of people who would love to hang Golden Boy's ass higher than Peking duck?" April asked Niall.

"No. I want your best estimate of who it is."

"Best estimate, the Red Phoenix." She glanced at Shane with bottomless black eyes. "They have some really fine hackers, trained by none less than Sebastian Merit in his hands-across-the-water mode. How are your firewalls, Golden Boy? They up to the old man's best efforts?"

Sixty-three

April Joy watched Shane massage his computer. Seven separate screens displayed different parts of the comparisons they were making. An eighth screen kept running score in a complex spreadsheet represented as a three-dimensional graph that kept turning and changing in a hypnotic fashion.

"What program is that?" April pointed to the colorful graph.

Shane didn't look up from instructing his computers. "Mine."

"You created it?"

"Yes."

"Good thing I trust you." She stretched with the grace and balance of someone who spent at least one hour a day practicing various forms of unarmed combat. "You could wipe evidence and I'd never know it."

"I could, yes. But I won't."

"Why? Doing your patriotic duty?"

His laugh was as hard as his eyes scanning the complex graph. He didn't like what he was seeing. It was telling him that he really should have spent more hours with his casino data.

"If someone has penetrated the casino accounts, I want to know it," he said. "Then I'll find out how they did it. And then . . ."

"You going to kick some ass?"

"I'll leave that to your deadly feet."

She smiled. She hadn't found many men who were comfortable with her intelligence and her lethal skills. "You sure you're happy with the sexy curator?"

"I'm working on it."

"If it bounces, let me know."

He gave her a quick, sideways glance. "If I have anything to say about it, it won't bounce."

"Yeah, I figured that out for myself. Story of my life," she said, yawning. "The good ones are gone, and the bad ones aren't good. You have a coffeepot around here?"

"It's called the telephone. Room service is 01. Have them send enough coffee for two and some food."

"What kind?"

Shane's fingers sped over the keyboard, programming in new demands. He pushed back and slid to another computer station. "They know what I like. Get whatever you want for yourself."

"Sushi," she said.

"Ask for Norataki. He's our best Sushi chef."

April started to answer, then saw she had lost him. He was eyebrow deep in yet another computer program. The graphing screen was undergoing constant transformations that appealed to her as an art form but utterly baffled her as to meaning. For all she knew, he could have been running a connect-the-dots, 3-D sculpture program.

Frowning, she punched in 01 and ordered coffee, food for Shane, and a selection from the sushi chef for herself.

After she replaced the phone, she simply stood and watched Shane work. She'd been told by government computer specialists that Tannahill had been among the top programmer/hackers of his generation, but that he lacked the desire to dedicate himself to it full-time, so he'd likely lost his edge. She wondered if that was true or if Shane just didn't feel the need to strut his stuff for an admiring audience.

"Shit."

The soft, hissing word was all Shane said. Then he bent over and keyed in instructions for the special program he'd created to fry hackers if and when he found their tracks in his mainframe.

April wanted to ask what had happened. A look at his face told her to put it on hold. The man was angry, the kind of angry that burned like dry ice.

A minute later Shane hit the enter key and pushed back from the computer terminal. The screen showing the 3-D graph kept changing. He gave it a disgusted look and turned away. He had seen enough.

"What?" April said.

Shane glanced at the screen that was executing his most recent program and decided it was safe to let her in on the good news. Good for her, at any rate. It sure as hell wasn't good news for him.

"I'm the owner of an unusually profitable casino," he said evenly.

"Meaning?"

"My slots have been steadily earning more than they should, despite the losses from a techno-team last week. Instead of the usual autumn slump at the tables, things have been humming along. Nothing outrageous enough to send up an alarm. A few percent here. A few more there. It adds up fast. Because my watchdog programs are designed to chase consistent, unexpected *losses* rather than gains, no alarms got tripped."

April watched Shane with dark eyes and total concentration. She didn't say a word.

"I made it easier on them—whoever they are—by not shifting my firewall program every few weeks," Shane added. "I've been too busy chasing Celtic gold." And Risa, a fact he didn't figure April had any need to know.

"Keep going," April said.

"Somebody got into my computer. Instead of hosing me the usual way, they *added* money to my accounts, millions of dollars that I have no way of explaining but have already declared to the Gaming Control Board and paid all appropriate taxes on."

"Bottom line?"

"Looks like you have yourself a laundry boy."

The leashed emotion in Shane made her pause. He was agreeing to help her, but he was a long way from beaten. Angry, yes. He was furious. Yet there was a feral kind of triumph in his eyes that she didn't understand.

And what she didn't understand made her nervous.

"Drop the other shoe," she said.

"Did one of Uncle's computer experts set me up?"

"Not that I know of."

"You better hope it was the bad guys." Shane glanced at the program that was running and smiled when PROGRAM COMPLETED flashed on the screen. "Because I just destroyed somebody's very expensive toy."

Sixty-four

Gail Silverado, Rich Morrison, and Carl Firenze no longer sat around the table that had been rolled into Gail's office for dinner. The remains of duck, steak, and shrimp congealed on the abandoned plates. Only Carl had been hungry enough to eat everything he'd ordered. Gail never ate much anyway. Rich had eaten half of his duck, finished his wine, and watched the phone.

Now all three were drinking coffee in the "conversation" area of Gail's office. In Rich's case the coffee came with an extra kick. Gail and Carl were taking their caffeine straight up, no alcohol chaser. Neither of them wanted to be slow or stupid while carrying a million dollars in cash.

Nobody had much to say. The money had been counted and packed into two suitcases that could have fit in the overhead storage bin of any major airline.

Everyone was waiting for the call to come through the main desk and get switched to Gail's private number.

"Ms. Silverado," Carl said, setting aside his coffee, "sure I can't talk you out of this?"

She jerked, startled out of her own thoughts. Then she sighed and admitted, "I'm thinking about it."

"Think harder," Rich said. "I have been. I don't like what I'm thinking."

"What are you talking about?" Gail said. "You were the one who was so eager to—"

"I changed my mind. Yes, it would be nice to have you testify against Tannahill as an on-the-spot witness to an illegal act. Icing on the cake, as it were." Rich shrugged. "So who needs icing? We've got his cock in a wringer. No point pushing our luck."

Before Gail could answer, the phone rang. She reached for it with a hand that trembled.

"Yes?" she said.

"Now, that's a word I love to hear," Cherelle said. "You ready to buy some gold toys?"

Gail looked at the two men. Carl was already on his feet, settling his shoulder holster with an automatic motion of his body.

"Yes," Gail said.

"The Midas Motel. You know where it is?"

Gail hesitated, swallowed. "Yes."

"Room 121. Twenty minutes."

The line went dead.

Gail hung up the receiver and thought about walking out into the night with a million in anonymous bills.

"Well?" Rich said.

"Midas Motel, Room 121," Gail said. She looked at her hands. "I think I'll have that drink after all."

Sixty-five

Nobody looked at the telephone.

Everybody waited for it to ring.

No one talked about the fact that it was late, getting later, and Cherelle still hadn't called with instructions.

The only good news was that Ian, who was watching Gail Silverado with the help of some extra bodies from the Golden Fleece's security staff, hadn't called in either. Gail was still at her casino, waiting as they were waiting.

Niall put the half-glasses on Risa, adjusted them, and judged his handiwork. "You're going to make a cute little old lady someday."

Dana snickered.

Risa ignored both of them. She was trying not to look at Shane. He hadn't had a civil word to say to her since he'd walked back into her apartment, found her being fitted for special electronics, and was informed by Dana that Risa was going after the gold.

Alone.

It's the only way we can be sure that a spectacular, and spectacularly meaningful, piece of human culture won't vanish into an underground black market and never reappear.

Niall, usually Shane's ally, had weighed in on Dana's side. *Look, boyo, you've already fired Risa, Rarities can front the money if you refuse, and there's sweet bugger all you can do about it. She's going alone. Get used to it.*

End of discussion.

End of conversation, too.

Risa glanced uneasily in Shane's direction, wondering just how angry he was beneath his silence. Plenty, if the tightness around his eyes was any sign. And he was walking his gold pen again, jade eyes unfocused, thinking, thinking, thinking.

That alone made her more nervous than waiting for the phone on the table next to him to ring.

At the kitchen table Dana was polishing off the last of a meal of lobster, filet mignon, sinfully rich mashed potatoes, bread, buttered vegetables, salad drenched with dressing, and dessert. If Risa hadn't liked Dana so well, she would have hated her for the turbo-metabolism that allowed the petite woman to eat whatever she wanted, whenever she wanted it, and never put on an ounce. The thought of what all that food would do to her own hips made Risa cringe.

"Okay," Niall said, stepping back from her. "She's ready. Remember, to trigger the stereo camera you bite down on the gold cap we put on your left back molar. A short bite for one low-resolution frame. Continued pressure for higher resolution. You can store two hundred frames at low resolution. Twenty at highest. How does it feel?"

She plucked at the loose dark shirt and black jeans she was wearing. Beneath them her black "underwear" nibbled and pinched. "Fits better than the body armor you found for me. Whoever wore this last was at least two sizes smaller in the butt."

"Beggars can't be choosers. Is the trigger loose on your tooth?"

Risa delicately tongued the cap. She hadn't been able to stop fiddling with it since he had tapped it into place a few minutes ago. Like a sore tooth, it was irresistible. "No. It just feels strange."

"How about the earpieces on the glasses? Do they pinch or give you a headache?"

"No pinching yet. Headache? Every time I look down, why?"

"Don't look down," Dana and Niall said together. Then Niall continued alone, "Think of them as reading glasses. The focal length is approximately your reading distance. When an object is in focus for you through the glasses, it's in focus for the camera."

"Keep that in mind," Dana said, licking her dessert fork. "If things go to shit tonight, whatever bytes are stored in the earpieces will be our only record of some internationally important artifacts."

Before Risa could answer, the phone rang. She reached for it.

Shane was quicker. He didn't lift the receiver. He didn't let her lift it.

"If I was the one going in alone with two million dollars in cash, how would you feel about it?" he asked.

Ring.

Her eyelids flickered. "At least as mad as you are right now."

Ring.

"Even though you know I can take care of myself with or without a gun?"

Ring.

"That's being reasonable," she said in a low voice. "Fear isn't reasonable."

He lifted the receiver and held it out to her.

"Hello?" Risa said, grabbing the phone.

"What the hell took you so long, baby-chick?"

"I was counting money."

Cherelle laughed. "Two million?"

"Yes. Where and when?"

"Fifteen minutes. The Midas Motel."

Shane started for the door.

"The Midas Motel?" Risa looked at Dana and followed orders: stall. "Never heard of it. Where is it?"

Niall barely made it to the front door before it slammed in his face.

Dana didn't waste time yelling about what she couldn't change. She just flipped over the shopping list and started writing down the instructions as Risa unhurriedly repeated them aloud.

"Okay," Risa said. "I'm going to read the instructions back to you just to be sure." Slowly she read off the sheet that Dana handed over. "I'll be there as fast as I can."

"Alone," Cherelle said.

Risa thought of Shane and wondered if Niall would be able to keep him from kicking down Cherelle's door. "I don't like that part of it."

"Tough shit. Don't fuck with me on this one. I've been

waiting all my life for this break. Ain't nothing gonna get in my way. Are you hearing me, baby-chick?"

"Yes."

She should have saved her breath. Cherelle had already hung up.

Sixty-six

Socks flipped through the motel's piped-in channels twice before he switched back over to the commercial offerings. He was tired of waiting for the call, but he wasn't nearly as head-banging fed up with life as he had been on his uncle's boring houseboat tied to one of Lake Mead's boring docks under the boring winter sun. After the first few hours even the collection of porn tapes he'd discovered made him yawn.

When the call had come telling Socks to get back to Vegas and check in to the Lucky Sun motel under the name of Ed Hutch, he hadn't asked any questions. He just climbed into a rental car, wished it was his screaming purple baby, and headed for Vegas. Now he was waiting again, bored again. If it hadn't been for the promise of money—and a dead bitch—on the other end of the waiting, he would have hauled his ass out of the motel and gone for some long-overdue raving around town.

But the chance to make a bundle of money while getting even with Cherelle was just too good to pass up. The cocaine would wait. The pussy would wait. He had a date with a million dollars. The gun that had been put in the motel room before he got there was a sweet, hard weight against his belly. Fully loaded, semiautomatic, ready to party. All he needed was an address.

The phone rang.

He picked it up, listened, smiled.

Party time.

Sixty-seven

As Shane drove swiftly down the Strip, rivers of colored lights flowed in silent glory over the windshield. He didn't notice. To him the lights were like the night—just one more thing to get through before Risa was safe.

Niall glanced sideways with eyes as dark as the bottom of a well. "What if we lose the gold?"

"As long as we don't lose Risa, I can live with whatever happens."

"Yeah, I got that impression. So did Dana." Niall smiled. "She told me you wouldn't stay behind. Then she told me to stick to you like fresh shit on a hiking shoe."

Shane didn't say anything.

"I won't get in your way, boyo."

"Do what you have to do."

Niall grimaced. He had worked with enough commando groups to recognize Shane's state of mind. It was beyond anger, beyond rage. *Take no prisoners* didn't even begin to describe it.

Men were never more dangerous than when they were cold and calm.

"If you tell me what you're planning, I can help," Niall said.

More silence.

Lights, buildings, and other cars flowed past in a rainbow river. Shane pushed the yellow on two stoplights and took the third red. He wasn't careless about it, but he was quick.

Just when Niall thought he'd lost whatever trust the other man had had for him, Shane shifted his grip on the wheel and braked for a light that would have been too dangerous to run.

"I'm going to take Cherelle down before Risa gets there," Shane said. "You want to help, fine. You want to get in my way, fine. Either way Cherelle goes down."

"What are you going to do—kick in the door?"

"If I have to."

"What if she's armed?"

"So am I."

"You think she killed that pawnbroker?" Niall asked.

"Possible, but not my first vote."

"Socks?"

"Probably. Socks's police profile shows someone with a ninety-one IQ and a short fuse."

Shane switched off his headlights before he turned at the Midas Motel entrance. A glance at his watch told him he had perhaps six minutes to spare. He reached into his wallet, pulled out some twenties, and handed them to Niall.

"I might be recognized by the night clerk," Shane said. "Damn all news photographers anyway."

"Serves you right for having such a pretty face."

Shane ignored him. "Can you find out if the room on either side of 121 is available?"

"Will you be here when I get back?"

"If I'm not, you know where to find me."

Niall strode quickly into the office.

Shane didn't wait to see about rooms, empty or otherwise. He left the car and walked along the bottom wing of the motel. If the parking lot and the amount of lights showing through room windows were any indication, the Midas Motel was on a steep downward slide toward bankruptcy or flophouse status.

The room to the right of 121 showed lights. The room to the left didn't. The door lock on the left-hand room was the old-fashioned, nonelectronic kind. Easy, in a word. Shane pulled a credit card from his wallet, worked it between the door and the jamb, and finessed the lock in less time than it took for Niall to check in.

By the time Niall got to the room, the curtains were drawn, the lights were on, and the television was chattering loudly about the latest fashion trend—neon mesh underwear worn outside a black bodysuit. The door leading to the parking lot was slightly ajar. He didn't knock and he didn't lock the door behind him. They might want to get out in a hurry.

Shane was working on the inner door that opened into Room 121. The lock was proving much more difficult than the front-door lock had.

"Step aside, boyo."

Shane looked over his shoulder. Niall had a tire iron in one hand and an assortment of lock picks in the other. Shane got out of his way.

"I didn't see a good hiding place outside," Shane said. "How about you?"

"That's why I'm in here. We don't have a lot of time. Dana and Risa are about two minutes away."

"How do you know?"

"Cellular connection."

For the first time Shane noticed the nearly transparent earpiece and cord that connected Niall to a cell phone in his rear pocket. "Is Dana giving you a running commentary?"

"Nothing so obvious. She just turned her phone up to max sensitivity and put it in her jacket pocket." *Along with a gun, please God,* Niall added silently. Dana hated them, but he had made sure she knew how to use one. "Bugger!"

He switched lock picks and went back to work.

Shane stood to one side of the front window and watched for the flash of headlights entering the parking lot.

Sixty-eight

"Right at the intersection after the next light," Dana said.

Risa glanced in various mirrors as she braked for the yellow light.

"See anyone?" Dana asked.

"No."

Dana could have told her she wouldn't—not if the follower was Niall, at any rate.

Her cell phone beeped softly, warning her that a call was trying to come through the open line. With rapid motions Dana closed the connection to Niall and picked up the incoming call.

"Dana here. Make it fast."

"This is Ian. Silverado hasn't moved."

"All right. Obviously we're going to be first in. Risa will have my phone, so don't call back."

"Gotcha. Want me to come in?"

"Stay with Silverado."

Dana broke the connection.

Risa glanced sideways. "What's this about your cell phone?"

"It's going in your pocket with an open connection to Niall," Dana said, punching in numbers as she spoke. "That way he'll at least know what you're up against. Have you had any weapons training?"

"No."

"Unarmed combat?"

"No."

"As soon as this mess is cleared up, report to Niall for both. I won't have my staff ignorant of self-defense when their jobs put them in situations like the one you're in tonight."

Risa blew out a breath and didn't argue. Right now the few nasty little tricks she had left over from a rough childhood didn't seem like much of a shield against Socks or whoever had killed O'Conner and Cline.

Glancing at her watch, Risa silently willed the light to turn green. Eventually it did.

"How are we for time?" Dana asked.

"Five minutes."

Dana looked at the map she had printed off a Net site. "We're fine even if we hit a few more red lights. Go left at the next corner. After one mile the motel should be on the right about two-thirds of the way down the block."

Risa turned left.

No one else did.

The closer Risa and Dana came to the motel address, the less traffic there was. The distant, glittering Strip was a magnet sucking all the money away from this part of Las Vegas. The businesses that could move to the Strip did. The rest began a steep and dusty decline.

"When you make the turn at the motel, find the room and then back into a nearby slot," Dana said. "Turn out the lights and leave the engine running. When you come out to get the money, you won't see me, but I'll be behind the wheel. If you don't like what you see when you walk in the room, turn around and get out *now*. Clear?"

"What about the gold?"

Dana was counting on Niall to take care of any gold artifacts that were lying about, but she didn't think Risa was ready to hear that. Nor had Dana mentioned that there was a quicker way to the motel. They had been given fifteen minutes; Niall would need every second of it for whatever scheme his devious and yet breathtakingly pragmatic mind had hatched.

"We know who Cherelle is," Dana said. "We'll find her again."

Risa's fingers flexed and released on the steering wheel. The quality of Dana's voice said more than words about what she thought of Cherelle Faulkner's chances of getting away from a full Rarities search.

"Okay," Risa said. "You worry about the gold, and I'll turn and run if I don't like the setup." *And if I can.* "I have to admit that I'm beginning to see the appeal of self-defense training."

"From what I saw on the casino tape, you have the first requirement for coming out on top."

"Speed?" Risa asked dryly.

"Brains. You never stopped thinking."

"Cold sweat must lubricate the mind."

Dana laughed. "Niall will enjoy that one."

"Good for him. I sure didn't."

The gold neon crown that marked the Midas Motel rose along the right side of the road like a dusty, gap-toothed smile. When she saw it, Risa's heart slammed, then settled into a different, more rapid beat. She could feel adrenaline lighting up her blood, making colors clearer, more vivid, and each sound as crisp as glass breaking.

"Remember," Dana said as she slid down below the dashboard. "If it's a setup, forget the gold and *get out*."

Sixty-nine

Shane didn't bother to ask how it was going. The steady, whispering stream of curses told him that Niall was making progress, but not nearly as much as he wanted. One of the interconnecting doors was open. The other wasn't.

Stone green eyes glanced from the hinges on the offending door to the tire iron at Niall's feet and then back out the slit in the curtains to the parking lot. If they had to, they could wrench the door off its hinges in a few seconds flat. But that would make a lot of noise. Better to unlock the damned thing and take Cherelle by surprise.

The car that had just come in reversed, backed into a nearby slot, and shut off the lights.

"They're here," Shane said.

Niall grunted.

"What's the deal?" Shane asked.

"Risa goes in, looks, and if she doesn't like it—*bugger all lazy maintenance men, this sodding lock needs oil!*—

she leaves to get the money from the car and doesn't fucking come back."

Shane's only answer was the blue-steel gun that appeared in his fist. He put his hand on the front door, ready to yank it open. "Tell me when."

Seventy

Cherelle jumped every time lights flashed in the parking lot. Since the motel apparently was letting out rooms by the half hour, there were more vehicles coming and going than there were cars staying in place for an all-night rental.

"Come on, come *on*! It's been twenty minutes, for Chrissake. Where you at, Silverado? Where's all that sweet cash?"

Cherelle wanted the money so bad she could taste it. As she paced past the dresser, she reached for another warm beer—warm because the room didn't have anything as fancy as a small refrigerator. Against her clammy fingers the can felt almost hot, almost fragile, like life.

The thought made her pause. She decided she should wait before she had any more beer. She was drinking too fast, even though she couldn't feel a damn thing.

After chewing on her raw mouth, she put the can down without opening it.

On the next circuit of the room she picked up the can and ripped open the tab so fast that foam shot over her knuckles. As she licked it off her hand, the beer tasted like sweat and piss, but alcohol would help dull the raw edge of her nerves.

Lights swept over the closed curtains. Breath held, she waited. From next door the sound of some kind of sports show poured out in a wave of cheers and boos that peaked quickly and faded. The neighbor on the other side of her room was trying to hammer some working girl through the headboard, urged on by throaty groans scripted with an eye toward a big tip.

The car turned toward the opposite side of the lot.

A fresh round of cheers drowned out the fake passion. The *whumpa-whumpa-whumpa* of headboard slamming into wall continued. For an instant Cherelle pitied the poor whore who had taken on a jackhammer for a client. Of all the johns, they were the worst. Give her a sixty-second man anytime.

At first Cherelle thought the knocking sound she was hearing was a continuation of the sex next door. Then she realized it was her own front door.

"Who is it?"

"Risa."

"Wait."

Cherelle went to the door, peered out the cloudy peephole, and saw nothing useful. Leaving the chain on, she opened the door just enough to see that Risa was standing there alone. Quickly Cherelle shut the door, released the chain, and opened the door again. As soon as Risa was inside, she put the chain back on.

A fast look told Risa the room was empty of all but Cherelle and the gold artifacts laid out carelessly across one bed. She walked close enough to focus on first one and then the other, taking pictures as fast as she could. The lighting was awful. Even if it hadn't been, Dana had made it clear that she was supposed to find a way to check out the bathroom.

"I need better light," Risa said.

"Shit. Try the toilet. Light over the can's pretty good."

Risa scooped up gold at random, walked past the bed, and into a short, offset passageway that boasted a few hangers on one side and a sink on the other. The bathroom was just beyond. A brief look around didn't show anything unexpected. Toilet. Tub/shower.

She dropped the toilet lid with her elbow, spread out the pieces of gold . . .

And forgot to breathe. Dagger and sheath gleaming with ancient ritual. A torc made of braided gold chains that radiated power like heat off a fire. A golden god-mask looking through time into man's shadowed soul. The sight of the gold was so mesmerizing that Risa had to force herself not to fall into the deep past, where Druid gold was the burning center of death and renewal.

Forcing herself to move, Risa turned toward Cherelle, who had followed her partway out of the main room. From her position at the head of the passageway, Cherelle could see both the front door and Risa.

Risa could see only Cherelle. She was watching Risa with a stranger's eyes, brittle and calculating. Strung out. There was no point in trying to reach whatever was left of her friend beneath the hard surface. The Cherelle that Risa remembered wasn't there.

All that was left was the money and the gold.

"I'm amazed," Risa said. "All that gold and you don't even have a gun."

"Brains are better than guns any day."

"So where's Gail? You're all alone here."

"You snooze, you lose. She just lost. Where's the money?"

The front door crashed inward, gunshots exploded, glass shattered.

Cherelle staggered toward Risa and went to her knees in a bright burst of blood. "Baby-chick? What happened?" She shook her head and tried to brace herself against her palms. "No. Not like this. I'm too smart."

Seventy-one

Shane was out in the parking lot before the intruder's semiautomatic spit out the second and third shots. When he saw the blocky figure in the doorway to Cherelle's room, Shane snapped his gun into position and squeezed on the trigger.

In the split second before he could fire, a shotgun blasted from across the lot. The attacker's arms jerked up, and he staggered into Cherelle's room. Another blast spun him around. A third one knocked him down. He stayed there.

Both Niall and Shane had tracked the last muzzle flashes. They fired twice each in a staccato hail. A hoarse cry came, followed by the sound of something hitting the ground. Gun at the ready, Niall ran across the lot in a zigzag pattern.

Shane made a long, diving roll that took him inside Cherelle's room. *"Risa."*

"Back here. Hurry!"

He kicked the gun out of the intruder's lax fingers and

ran toward Risa's voice. As soon as he reached the little passageway leading to the bathroom, his heart jerked and his guts turned to ice.

There was blood everywhere.

Risa and Cherelle were in the middle of it.

He went to his knees beside Risa. "Where are you hit?"

"Help Cherelle!"

"Where are you hit?"

"It's not me. It's Cherelle. Oh, Jesus, it's Cherelle!"

If Shane hadn't already been on his knees, relief would have put him there. "Let me see her."

"I can't let go. She's bleeding too much." Tears left trails down Risa's blood-spattered face. "Cherelle! Cherelle, can you hear me?"

Shane saw what Risa couldn't accept: Cherelle's blood no longer pulsed between Risa's fingers. He measured the utter slackness of Cherelle's body. With gentle fingertips he closed the pale, staring eyes.

Risa made a raw sound.

In the front room Niall peeled off the attacker's ski mask. "It's our old buddy Socks. Deader than dirt. Risa?"

"She's all right," Shane answered.

"Cherelle?"

"Dead."

Shane eased Risa away from Cherelle's body. "What about the one in the parking lot?" he asked.

"White male, somewhere between fifty and sixty. Looks more like an executive than a shooter."

"Dead?"

"He should make it."

"I'll be right back," Shane said to Risa.

Wearily she nodded.

Both men headed out of the room at a trot. There wouldn't be much time before the cops arrived.

Dana was already at the second man's side. A gun gleamed in her hand. She pointed a flashlight at his face and hit the switch.

"Recognize him?" she asked Shane.

"Rich Morrison."

From all directions sirens wailed, still distant. But not for long.

"Get the money," Shane said to Dana. "Our story is that the gold changed hands before Cherelle died."

"Back to the room," Dana said. "We need to get the rest of our stories straight. It's going to be a bloody long bitch of a night."

Seventy-two

April Joy walked in and looked at the five people who sat around Shane's office in varying states of exhaustion. She knew how they felt. It had been a long night and longer morning for her, too.

Caffeine was no substitute for sleep.

"I think this pretty well defines the concept of cluster fuck," she said.

Niall and Dana watched April, wondering when she was going to drop the last shoe. They didn't know what it would be. They only knew that the brilliant, ruthless Ms. Joy always had at least one more weapon in her arsenal than people expected.

"What did Gail say?" Shane asked.

Not that he thought Gail would change her public story, but he had to be sure before he tried to cut a deal with the very sharp April Joy. His earlier talk with Gail had been private and to the point: either she helped him or he buried her. She knew he could do it.

More important, she knew he *would*.

"Same thing she said the first time," April said. "She got the call. She chickened out."

"I can vouch for that. She never left the building," Ian said. "Spent the night on the casino floor talking to the customers. It's all on video."

Shane began walking his gold pen across his fingers, end over end, the *click* of gold meeting gold, silence, silence, *click*. "Who did Gail talk to right after she decided to back out?" he asked April.

"Morrison and Firenze."

"Carl or John?"

"Carl. He took Gail's money back to the vault. Morrison left, supposedly to take his money back to his own vault."

Click. "Who did Carl talk to about the meeting?" Shane asked April.

"Gail."

"No one else?"

"Just those two," April said.

Click.

April looked at Risa. "You're sure Cherelle wouldn't have called Socks in for backup?"

"Yes. She didn't trust him. With good reason. He never gave her a chance. Just walked in and started shooting."

Click.

Shane's free hand smoothed over Risa's dark hair. She let out a long breath and looked at her hands as though expecting to see them covered in bright arterial blood.

"What about Tim Seton?" Risa asked in a low voice. "Has he turned up?"

"No," April said.

"If the amount of blood he left on his mother's doorstep is any indication," Ian said, "he wouldn't have been in any shape to hold a pump shotgun long enough to send several rounds through his buddy Socks. Morrison's lawyers can scream all they want. He's good for murder one. When he figures it out, he'll start talking."

Click.

"Don't hold your breath, slick," April said to Ian. "Morrison's lawyers are talking about their client the civic hero, who killed a felon that had just killed a defenseless woman and was about to kill another one."

"Even if I swallow that without choking to death," Dana said, "what was Morrison doing there in the first place?"

Click.

April smiled coldly. "He said he was worried that Gail would change her mind about going after the gold artifacts. He was there to protect her if she showed up. Then Socks came on the scene and started shooting. Morrison nailed him three times, only to be shot by two trigger-happy yahoos who should have known better."

Click.

The pen flashed and disappeared into Shane's pocket. "We have two separate problems," he said. "Druid gold and a fake laundry. They intersect with me. They intersect with Gail. They also intersect with Morrison. There's a pattern."

"What pattern?" April asked acidly. Her tone said *cluster fuck.*

"None of what I'll say can be proved legally, because all the parties are either dead or missing," Shane said.

Motionless, April waited.

"At some time in the past week, Virgil O'Conner was murdered in Sedona," Shane said. "Either before, during, or afterward, his Druid gold was stolen by Cherelle, Socks, and/or Tim Seton."

"Connection?" April said sharply.

"O'Conner believed in channeling," Risa said. "Cherelle and Tim represented themselves as channels. Also . . . we found three wooden boxes with O'Conner's name and address in Cherelle's rented room near Sedona. We believe, but can't prove, that they came from his home."

April filed away the name of Virgil O'Conner.

Risa threaded her fingers more deeply through Shane's. Every time she closed her eyes, she saw Cherelle and too much blood.

"The DNA on file for Tim matched the DNA in the blood left on Joey Cline's floor," Shane continued.

"How do you know that?" April asked.

He ignored her. His talent for picking apart various official firewalls and looking through computer files wasn't going to be part of the discussion. In any case, it was Factoid, Rarities Unlimited's very own computer guru, who had done the hacking. That wasn't something April needed to know either.

"Take it as a given," Niall suggested.

April never looked away from Shane. "I'm listening."

"There were two sets of footprints going through the blood," Shane said. "Tim Seton left one set. When the police get around to it, I'm betting that Socks will be a match for the other footprints."

"So?"

"So we have the two of them fencing stolen gold artifacts," Risa said, "and then killing the fence."

"Before he died, Cline turned the artifacts to Shapiro," Shane said.

"Can you prove that?" April asked.

"Cline didn't keep records, and Shapiro claims his computer ate his homework," Shane said.

Her black eyes narrowed. "Keep talking."

"The only real question left is why Morrison waited in a parking lot to blow Socks apart."

"You're not buying the white knight bit?" April asked.

"Are you?" Shane asked.

"Not unless I have to."

"The other question is why a limo hauled Miranda and her shot-to-pieces son off into the night to a place where he could be treated without being reported to the cops." Shane looked at Ian. "Did you get into her house?"

Ian nodded. "My hat's off to you, Tannahill. You hit it right the first time."

"What?" April said, turning on Ian like a tiger. "Spit it out, slick."

Ian's smile was all edges and silence.

"I have something you want," Shane said to April. "You have something I want. That's the traditional basis for making a deal."

Without missing a beat she switched gears, turned her back on Ian, and asked, "What do I have that you want?"

"Druid gold."

"And you have for me . . . ?"

"A pipeline to the Red Phoenix triad that's better than I ever could be. Interested?"

"Keep talking, you'll get there."

Shane looked at Dana.

"Ms. Joy has made deals with many people," Dana said. "She keeps her end of any bargain she makes."

"Do we have a deal?" he asked April.

"How did you find out that Uncle had already claimed

the gold from Faulkner's motel room?" April asked idly, but she was thinking at the speed of light.

Shane didn't answer.

She hadn't really expected him to. "I'll see that you get custody of the gold. What's the pipeline?"

"Gail Silverado will deny it to the last breath, but she finally told me that Rich Morrison is behind the attempt to make me look like a laundry. Morrison is in bed with the Red Phoenix. If you take apart his computers, I'll bet you find their fingerprints all over the laundry arrangements. I *know* Red Phoenix is the group that hacked into my computer and left damning trails leading to money I never took from offshore accounts I never created."

There was silence for the space of one breath, two, three.

"Interesting," April murmured. "If true."

"Talk to Miranda Seton. She called the Shamrock when her son showed up bleeding on her doorstep."

"How long have you known that?" April demanded.

"Since I told Ian to go to the Seton house and hit redial," Shane said. "Seton's last call was to the Shamrock. Very quickly a black limousine pulled up and hauled her and her son away."

"Keep talking."

"Even a cursory background check showed that Miranda is no more a widow than I am," Shane said. "She hasn't worked since her son was born and receives regular fat deposits into her account, deposits I'm still trying to trace. I would put money on Morrison being the father of Tim Seton and the source of Miranda's money. Now, you can blow a perfectly useful pipeline apart trying to prove all the linkages I've outlined, or you can use what you don't need to prove as a twist to turn the ever-heroic Morrison into a patriotic mole snitching off the Red Phoenix to Uncle. And if you need any help in the twist department, you might try Miranda Seton. I've got a cast-iron hunch that the lady has something on her former lover."

For a moment there was only silence and waiting.

Then April's smile flashed at Shane. "I like the way you think."

"I'm frightened."

"In my dreams," she retorted. "It's a deal, Tannahill."

Seventy-three

The golden dagger's blade was as long as Shane's hand. Ancient symbols that began with the wheel of the sun and ended with the Christian cross marched down the blade. Balanced on her palms, Risa held the gold sheath with its mesmerizing red inlay defining a three-part design. Originally the design had been picked out in pearls, but the soft gold indentations that had once held the gems were all that remained. The dagger was the most modern of the artifacts, for gems came into favor only after the Romans occupied Britain.

"What a pity that pearls are too fragile to survive being buried for centuries," Risa said.

"Tears of the moon," Shane said softly. "Whether the ground is wet or dry, they don't survive the centuries."

"The good news is that the residue of soil we found embedded in the deeper etched lines of every artifact is the same. All twenty-seven pieces were part of the same hoard."

"The really good news is that there wasn't enough soil

to place the artifacts exactly, even in the ground around O'Conner's house."

Risa's mouth thinned with reflexive pain. Thinking of O'Conner made her think of his killer—Cherelle Faulkner. Risa didn't want to believe it even now, but she did. Miranda Seton didn't have any reason to lie to the feds in order to protect her son. Tim was as dead as Cherelle. As dead as Socks.

If Miranda felt any guilt about blackmailing her former lover into killing Socks, she didn't show it.

"There were some similarities with a cross-section of British soils," Shane continued, "but nothing identical by any stretch."

"And the Brits," Risa said dryly, "were willing to stretch whatever they could get their hands on. Too bad that silica is such a common part of dirt. It would have been remarkable only if it had been absent from the artifacts."

"Do you blame them for trying?" Shane asked with a rakish smile. "I sure don't."

"Nope. And I'm glad you agreed to loan the artifacts to the British Museum for study."

"*After* New Year's Eve."

Blade slid into sheath with barely a whisper of sound.

As he lifted the sheath from her palm, Risa's breath caught at the glide of skin over skin. She wondered if she would ever get used to being Shane's lover. It was as astonishing to her as the fact that she would be married on New Year's Eve, wearing a Celtic ring as old as Shane's.

"Do you think Niall will find any close relatives of Virgil O'Conner?" Risa asked huskily.

"I doubt it. He never married. He had no siblings. Not even any half siblings." Shane placed the dagger and sheath in a display case that had more locks and alarms than met the eye. "Besides, there's nothing beyond circumstantial proof that he even had the gold in the first place."

"But we *know* the gold was there, at his house."

"That's proof from the gut. Doesn't work in a court of law."

"We know Virgil was sent to an air base in Britain during World War Two," she said. "Niall has his service record."

Shane nodded and picked up the bent, totemic artifact that Risa said was the equivalent of a bishop's crosier— the solid gold head of a ceremonial staff. The wood inside the gold was oak. Carbon dating placed it in the fourth century, plus or minus some years.

"And we assume," Shane said, "that O'Conner dug up the hoard during the chaos after the Allied victory in Europe."

"He dug it up in Wales. Gut knowledge," she conceded quickly, "not court of law."

Smiling, Shane brushed his lips over hers. "Then he shipped it home along with his other stuff in empty ammunition boxes. Nobody was checking incoming soldiers very closely. We were too damn glad to have them back."

She thought of Cherelle, who was never coming back.

"Don't, darling," he said, kissing her again. "You did everything you could for her. You can't save people from their own mistakes."

Risa breathed in the warmth of him. "Do you really read minds?"

"Just yours. It's those telltale eyes. And that mouth. Ought to be a law against it."

Her smile turned upside down. "Speaking of laws, there ought to be a law against getting away with murder."

His lips waited a breath from hers. "Morrison?"

"Yes."

"He didn't get away with it."

"Like hell he didn't," she retorted. "First he sics good old Socks on Cherelle, and then he kills Socks. Now he's a bloody hero. Just read the Vegas papers!"

"Morrison's lawyers would have gotten him off with probation and community service. This way he's a federal snitch who goes to bed every night sweating at the thought of waking up and seeing April Joy the next day. And someday, not too far down the road, he'll come face-to-face with the Red Phoenix triad he's betraying as fast as he can talk. Then he'll wake up dead."

Shane's smile made Risa glad she was his lover rather than his enemy. "In the meantime . . ."

"In the meantime?" she asked.

"We have a wedding to plan."

She tried not to smile. She didn't succeed. "I don't remember officially saying yes."

"I'm a mind reader, remember?"

She thought of her earlier vision of him as a Celtic warrior wearing blue paint and not much else. "I'll say yes officially right now, but only if you wear Druid gold down the aisle."

He looked both amused and wary. "Are we talking blue paint?"

"Blue paint is optional. Clothes aren't."

"In that case we'll invite witnesses."